WEDDING NIGHTMARE . . .

The woman seized her again. "You must resist," someone whispered in Turkish in her ear. "No bride should go to her husband willingly. You must resist."

Catherine wriggled and tried to catch hold of them. Gently they pushed her away, thrust her back on the bed. Then suddenly she found herself alone. But not alone. She sat up and stared at her husband, and with him another man; they had been concealed behind a curtain.

"You must fight me," Ricimer said. "You cannot come to me willingly. There is ill fortune."

She attempted to get up, and was seized by the shoulders and thrown down again. Her wrists were held, her legs bent up from the knees . . . a moment later she felt the cords that would bind her. . . .

THE
SAVAGE
SANDS

Christina Nicholson

FAWCETT CREST • NEW YORK

THE SAVAGE SANDS

THIS BOOK CONTAINS THE COMPLETE TEXT OF
THE ORIGINAL HARDCOVER EDITION.

Published by Fawcett Crest Books, a unit of CBS Publications,
the Consumer Publishing Division of CBS Inc.,
by arrangement with Coward, McCann & Geoghegan, Inc.

ISBN: 0-449-23762-1

Printed in the United States of America

10   9   8   7   6   5   4   3   2   1

Chapter 1

〽〽〽〽〽〽〽〽 THE ripple of laughter woke David Mulawer, had him rubbing his hands together and slapping them against his trouser legs; to doze off in the snow was a dangerous oversight.

He turned on his knees, peered through the bushes, and felt his heartbeat quicken. Because the girls were there, and as on the previous day, they were going to toboggan. He fumbled in the pockets of his threadbare greatcoat, found the small telescope, checked the position of the sun; it would not do for them to see the gleam of light. But on a March afternoon the sun was already low in the western sky, and behind him.

He focused first of all on the distant building, could even make out the name, "Madame St. Amant's Academy for Young Ladies of Quality," brought the glass lower, discovered a group of smaller girls engaged in throwing snowballs at one another, was disturbed by the shrieks of laughter from closer at hand as the first young woman came down the snow-covered slope towards his copse, legs and skirts flying as the toboggan got out of control. She made an attractive picture, because her woolen cap had come off and her hair was flowing in the slight breeze, but David spared her not a glance. She was not *her,* and was thus unimportant.

Yet the toboggan run ended immediately before the fence that marked the end of Madame St. Amant's property,. and behind which he knelt, and he must put away his glass and remain absolutely still until the girl had arrived at the bottom, gasping and laughing and red cheeked, and commenced her climb again, the rope of the toboggan held over her shoulder.

Would *she* be next? Yesterday she had not made the run at all. Perhaps she did not indulge in tobogganing. Yes, he thought with a delicious surge of disappointment, she was too dignified, too restrained, too perfect in every way, to allow herself such a display.

The glass was back to his eye, and now he found her, standing in the midst of her friends and making them seem as nothing, at least to his eyes. She was below average height, the shortest of the six girls, and appeared slender; it was difficult to decide as she wore a warm cloak over her blue woollen gown. But it would not have mattered, he thought, had she been fat—not with her face to look at. In keeping with the rest of her, it was small, shaped in a perfect oval. The forehead was high, the nose straight, the chin pointed. The mouth was surprisingly wide, a touch of imperfection that made the whole perfect. It was the face of an angel in repose, he thought, confidently and peacefully beautiful, but when she laughed, as she was doing now, the beauty became magnificently mischievous, seeming to double and include all those around her in a private world of secret delight.

He could not see her hair, lost as it was under her blue woollen cap and behind the upturned collar of her cloak, nor could he make out the color of her eyes, but her complexion told him she must be very fair; save for the cold-induced spots of red in her cheeks and on the tip of her nose, her skin was an almost translucent white.

And she *was* about to toboggan. He could not believe his fortune, kept his glass fixed on her as the sleigh was set in position by her friends, and she took her seat, pulling her skirts up to her ankles to reveal her boots and her

6

white stockings, and to suggest even a hint of the dark wonderland that must lie beyond . . . he lowered the glass to give himself a chance to breathe, and so missed the commencement of her run. But down she came, legs leaving the ground, snow flying from the edges of the sleigh, hair starting to flutter from above the cloak collar. And what hair, so pale it was almost white, like strands of purest silk floating in the air.

The toboggan came at the fence with a rush, and he nearly stood up for fear she would hurt herself. But at the foot of the slope there was a flat area some yards wide, and she was able to dig her heels into the earth and bring herself to a halt, inches from the fence itself, not more than two yards from where he crouched. And if her beauty had redoubled when she had laughed, what was he to make of this flushed and panting treasure, slowly rising to her feet, pulling her skirts straight and taking off her cap, to reveal that her hair was indeed white blonde, and long, for she swept her gloved hand round the back of her head to free herself from the cloak; the silver strands settled almost in the small of her back.

"Catherine, Catherine," the girls on the hill were shouting. "Bring it back, Catherine."

"Catherine," he said, without meaning to. Her name would have to be Catherine.

She turned, holding the toboggan rope, peering at the bushes, a slight frown creasing her forehead. Her eyes were a pale blue, large and almost disturbingly steady. As she had ceased smiling, she made him think of the Ice Maiden.

"Forgive me, mademoiselle," he said. "I did not mean to speak."

She took a step back. For a moment her tongue showed as she sucked her upper lip beneath her teeth.

"Do not be afraid, I beg of you, mademoiselle," he said. "David Mulawer, at your service."

"You are not French," she accused, arriving at her decision both because of his accent as well as his name; her voice was quiet, but clear and just high enough to be delicious. He thought of tinkling bells.

"By adoption, mademoiselle," he protested. "By adoption. But neither are you French."

"I was born in Boston," she said, with some pride. "My father is Colonel Scott, of the Embassy. Do you know him, monsieur?"

"Alas, no, Mademoiselle Scott. But I have heard of him. He recently took a new wife, I understand. Oh, my dear girl, does that mean . . . ?"

"That I am at least partly an orphan, monsieur? Indeed it does. Although I do assure you that my stepmother is quite the opposite to any creature from a fairy tale." Her frown was deepening. "But, if you do not know Papa, what are you doing here? Why are you speaking to me?"

Mulawer allowed himself a sigh. "I am an artist, mademoiselle. I search the world for beauty, and when I find it, why, I attempt to capture it for posterity."

"An artist? In Chantilly?" The frown gave way to that unforgettable smile. "I don't believe you. What is there to paint, in Chantilly?"

"Why, nothing, mademoiselle, in Chantilly. I but seek a livelihood. I paint, mademoiselle, I swear it. But when I cannot sell my canvases, why, I am prepared to turn my brush to the walls of a house, if need be."

"Ah," she said.

"A temporary arrangement, I do assure you. And then, but the day before yesterday, I walked in this wood, and heard laughter, your laughter, mademoiselle, and came to this fence to look, and saw the most beautiful creature in all the world. I have marked yesterday, the sixth of March, 1828, as the most important of my life."

Her frown was back, but now it was forced. "You are too bold, monsieur. I must rejoin my friends."

Who had stopped shouting, and were merely looking down the hill.

"Wait but a moment." His hand came through the fence. "Sit for me, mademoiselle. Let me paint you. I will make yours the most famous face in Europe. In all the world. Even in your native America. I swear it. And you, you will make my fortune. Just sit for me."

Once again she sucked her upper lip beneath her teeth in that curiously thoughtful manner. Then her smile returned. "You would have to ask Papa, Monsieur Mulawer. I shall look forward to hearing his decision. Now I must go."

"Mademoiselle." She had allowed herself to come against the fence, and he was able to catch her hand. "Will you play again tomorrow?"

"Why, sir . . . oh, Lord," she muttered, turning at the sound of a new voice.

"Catherine." This was no girl, but a tall and heavily built woman, standing at the top of the slope like an avenging angel. "Catherine. Come here this instant."

Mulawer released her hand, and she turned to the slope, and hesitated there for a moment.

"Am I really the most beautiful creature you have ever seen, monsieur?"

"Quite without question, mademoiselle. I shall dream of you, every night of my life, from now on."

Again the quick smile. "Then you *must* ask Papa. I look forward to seeing you again, monsieur."

"A man," said Madame Laurens. "Definitely a man. Why, they were holding hands. I could scarce believe my eyes."

Madame St. Amant pursed her lips, and endeavoured to look severe. As she was plump and good natured she found it difficult, especially when confronted with one of her favourite pupils. "Is this true?"

Catherine clasped her hands in front of her, took great care with her breathing. "I never saw him before in my life, madame."

"And now, lies," Madame Laurens said. "Why, she is the most shameless hussy. Do you normally hold hands with someone you have only just encountered, eh? Tell me that, mademoiselle."

Catherine continued to look at Madame St. Amant. "He . . . he took my hand, madame."

"And you did not scream?" Madame St. Amant inquired, gently.

9

"Well, I . . . I was so surprised. And he . . . well . . ."

"Ha," said Madame Laurens. "Lies. All lies, madame. She should be whipped. She must be whipped."

Catherine felt her knees touch each other. A whipping was Madame Laurens' remedy for everything.

Madame St. Amant sighed. "It would help if you told us the truth, Catherine."

"It is the truth, madame. I swear it. I rode the toboggan, and he was there, beyond the fence. He had been watching us."

"He must be imprisoned," Madame Laurens said, altering her strategy as she saw her victim escaping her grasp. "Watching our girls, indeed."

"I think it would be best if I spoke to Catherine alone," Madame St. Amant decided. "If you will excuse us, Madame Laurens."

Madame Laurens glared at her employer; her entire body seemed to seethe, and as she was both tall and broad she seemed to fill the room. Then she turned and left.

"Sit down, Catherine," Madame St. Amant said.

Catherine allowed her knees to give way, and sank into the chair before the desk. She shivered. She was still chilled from the park; Madame Laurens had brought her straight up here. And she had not had time to think about what had happened. But she knew she did not want the young man to go to prison. Not after he had called her the most beautiful thing he had ever seen.

"Now tell me the truth, Catherine," Madame St. Amant said.

"I have told you the truth, madame. When I reached the bottom of the slope, he spoke to me."

"What did he say?"

"He . . ." Catherine licked her lips. "He asked if he could paint me. He is an artist, madame."

"And what did you say?"

"I said he should ask Papa."

Madame St. Amant leaned back in her chair and smiled. "I do not think even Madame Laurens could criticise that reply," she said. "But of course you should not have spoken to him at all. As for holding his hand . . ."

"He held *my* hand, madame."

"Apparently you did not exactly attempt to resist him," Madame St. Amant pointed out. "Your friends were within a few yards of you. Yet you did not call for help."

"Well . . ." Catherine found her fingers were curled into fists. "He said I was beautiful. I . . . I was . . . well . . ."

"Flattered? Oh, you are beautiful, Catherine. But I would not let it go to your head, if I were you. Describe him to me." She picked up a pencil.

"Well . . . he was young. I think. Dark haired. Thin. He had . . . sort of narrow features. He looked terribly poor."

"Was he handsome, Catherine?"

"Oh, no. Well, perhaps, madame. Perhaps if he were given a good meal, and something decent to wear . . ."

"No doubt they will provide him with those luxuries in prison."

"Oh, madame, I don't want . . . well, he did no harm."

"Because Madame Laurens came along. Now, Catherine, I am not going to punish you. Partly because I believe your story, although you were very wrong even to exchange a word with him, and partly because you are about to leave us, and I would not have your last memory of the Academy an unhappy one. But, my child, I would beseech you, when you go out into the world, try to be more discreet, less responsive to those who will praise your beauty, and there will be sufficient of them. Oh, it is a marvellous thing, to be beautiful." Madame St. Amant uttered a sigh. "I was beautiful, once, myself. But it passes, my dear. And then you are left with just your character. And if that character has been based entirely upon your body and your face, and the effect they have upon the world, then will you be lonely indeed."

Catherine goggled at her. "Leaving, Madame?"

Madame St. Amant smiled. "So soon, you were going to say? Why, yes. I had meant to tell you before. Your new mother has decided that she would rather see to your upbringing herself. She is coming for you at the end of next week."

"Oh." Catherine could think of nothing to say. She wasn't at all sure she wanted to go home. Of course it would be lovely to be with Papa again, and Stepmama had seemed the kindest of women at the wedding. But home was too full of memories, of Mama.

"You have been happy here?"

"Oh, yes, madame. Well . . ."

Madame St. Amant's smile faded. "I will have no gossip. No taletattling. No, no. Well, that will be all, my child. You may go."

"Yes, madame." Catherine hastily got up, did a brief curtsey. "Thank you, madame." It was necessary to say thank you, madame, after an interview with madame, even if one had just been flogged. That was the first lesson learned at the academy.

Madame St. Amant nodded, and Catherine was able to step outside and close the door behind her, lean against the wall and utter a great sigh of relief. She really had supposed she had been for it then. She had never been flogged, but Seraphine had, and the tale was grisly in the extreme. Especially Laurens' part in it.

Seraphine. She would be waiting to hear what had happened. Catherine gathered her skirts, ran down the corridor and round the corner, and into Madame Laurens.

"Oh, madame . . ." Catherine stepped backwards. "I'm sorry. I didn't see you."

"In there," Laurens said. The door to her study was open.

Catherine hesitated. The girls had only ever said, *Stay away from Laurens,* and giggled as they had said it. But Laurens had no authority to whip on her own.

"I . . . it is nearly suppertime."

"In there," Laurens said again.

Catherine stepped through the door, listened to it closing behind her.

12

"Now, then," Laurens said. "What lies did you tell madame?"

"I told her no lies, madame, truly." What was she *doing*? Why did she not come round in front? But Catherine was afraid to turn her head.

"Talking to strange men," Laurens said, at her shoulder. Surprisingly, her voice was almost soft. "Holding hands with them. You deserve to be beaten until there is no skin on your behind."

Oh, Lord, Catherine thought. *Oh, Lord. But she wouldn't dare.*

"I suppose he turned your head," Laurens said, more softly yet. "I suppose he praised your beauty."

"Well . . ." Catherine licked her lips. "He said he would like to paint me. Oh."

Because Laurens' hands were suddenly on her waist, and slipping round to glide across her bodice, and suddenly close on her breasts. She felt quite weak.

"Oh, he would, he would," Laurens said, and her lips were against Catherine's hair. "He would wish you to undress, so that he could paint your body. Your so beautiful body. Because your body is beautiful, Catherine, my Catherine. Your breasts are those of a woman, not a sixteen-year-old girl."

The hands were gone.

"Madame . . ." She realised to her utter horror that Laurens' fingers were undoing the buttons at the back of her gown. "Madame . . ."

"You are a most fortunate girl," Laurens whispered. "To be so beautiful. But fortunate in more than that, my sweet child, in that it will be your lot to make others happy. So very happy."

Catherine found her mouth was open, and hastily closed it. Laurens' hands were inside her gown, and creeping under her arms, thrusting the petticoats aside to touch the flesh of her breasts. She felt paralysed. She adored having her breasts touched. It made her tingle from head to foot. She would stroke them herself, at the slightest opportunity, and feel delightfully wicked as well as delightfully

13

excited, and she could still remember that very cold night in December, just before they had gone home for the Christmas holidays, when Seraphine had crawled into her bed and they had hugged each other and held each other's breasts until she had felt she would burst with excitement.

But Laurens . . . the fingers were hard, and callused, however they tried to be soft. And she did not stroke the nipples, but rather pulled them. And yet the nipples were hard enough, and there was a delicious weakness spreading down from her chest and flooding her belly before reaching for her groin.

"Madame," she whispered.

"I would like to see your body, Catherine," Laurens whispered. "All of it. Take off your gown, Catherine. Undress for me, Catherine. Let me look at you." Her breath rushed against Catherine's ear as she smiled. "You may pretend I am your young man."

"No." Catherine jumped away from her, so violently Laurens' fingers slipped and she almost stepped out of her gown. She turned, against the wall, reaching behind her to fasten the buttons. "No."

"You'd defy me?" The softness was gone.

"I . . . I'll tell madame."

"And I will say you are lying again. And this time she will believe me. And you will be flogged. Oh, yes, my sweet child. Then I will see your body. Then I will turn those sweet thighs red. Then I will make them bleed."

Catherine gasped for breath. "I'll tell my stepmother. I'll tell all Paris."

Laurens smiled. "Paris is a long way away, my dear." She came closer. "Undress." Her cheeks were pink, and her breath rasped.

"Not for me," Catherine said. "Not for me. I am leaving here, next week. I am going home. I'll tell all Paris."

Laurens hesitated, frowning. "Leaving? I don't believe you."

"Well, I am," Catherine insisted. "You may ask madame. My new mother is coming for me." She listened. "There is the supper bell. I must go." She took a cautious step forward, but Laurens never moved, and continued

14

to frown. Catherine sidled past her, reached the door, and the corridor, and found she could breathe again.

"I bet you *were* whipped," Aimée insisted. "Laurens would have *made* her whip you."

"I was not whipped," Catherine insisted. She settled her nightgown over her shoulders, fluffed out her hair.

"Of course she wasn't whipped," Seraphine said. "Her bottom isn't red. And she sat down for supper. When last I was whipped I had to eat standing up."

"So there," Catherine said, and crawled into bed. She lay on her back, the blankets pulled to her chin while the other girls finished undressing, and Seraphine blew out the candle.

"Cathy," she whispered. "Cathy, are you awake?"

"Yes," Catherine said.

Seraphine sat on her bed. "Was it really a man?"

"Oh, yes."

"A young man? A handsome man?"

"Oh, yes."

"Did he wish to be your lover?" Seraphine claimed to have had a lover during the previous summer holidays.

"He wanted to paint me."

"To paint you?"

"Sssh."

Seraphine stifled a giggle. "That was just his way of making an advance. Oh, he wanted to be your lover. Is he a Chantilly man?"

"Oh, no," Catherine said. "He isn't even French."

"A *German*?" Seraphine was horrified.

"I don't think so. I have no idea," Catherine confessed.

"And you weren't whipped? I can't see how you escaped."

"I think because Stepmama is coming to take me home, next week."

"Take you home? Oh, you darling." Seraphine threw herself on top of Catherine, hugged her through the bedclothes. "Oh, you are lucky. To be going home. Why, that must have made old Laurens curdle. She has her eye on you, you know."

"Her eye?" Catherine's heart began to pound.

"Oh, well, she has her eye on us all, especially when we first come. But she never does anything until you've been here a year. I'll bet she was just getting ready to have you."

"Have me?"

"You wait," Seraphine said. "Well, you won't, actually, as you won't be here. But if she ever asks you into her room, you have to pretend you're on a mission from madame to the other side of the school. It's the only thing."

Her body was wriggling at the thought. And Catherine was herself finding it difficult to lie still. "Have you ever been into her room?"

"Oh, yes. Twice. She made me undress. Wanted to inspect my complexion, she said. My God, before I knew it she had her hand on my . . . well, you know."

"Your . . . oh, Lord," Catherine whispered. "Whatever did you do?"

Seraphine giggled again. "I screamed. Would you believe it? So she slapped my face. And the funny thing was, I screamed because I liked it. Oh, it was heavenly. I didn't want her to stop. Far better than doing it yourself."

"Doing it yourself?"

"Oh, for heaven's sake. You know."

"I have no idea what you are talking about," Catherine said. But she did. Her heart was pounding harder than ever.

"You mean you never . . . well, touch yourself?" Seraphine sat up. "Oh, Cathy, you are *innocent*. I do it every night in bed. Makes me sleep. I feel so good. Anyway, you may as well get used to it. It's what a man will want to do to you, you know. Only he'll want to do it with his cock as well as his hand. It's what your painter friend is dreaming of doing to you right this minute. You can be sure of that."

"I don't believe a word of it," Catherine said, heaving her friend off the bed as she rolled over. "Not a word."

"Are you going to get a surprise one of these days," Seraphine said. "Anyway, what does it matter who does

16

it to you, or if you do it yourself, so long as you enjoy it. You know my philosophy? I think you should enjoy everything, every single little thing that happens to you in this life. It's the only way to live. Do you know, I even enjoy having a tooth pulled? So it hurts like the devil. But even pain can be enjoyable, if you make up your mind to it. I'm going to enjoy dying. Believe me. It'll just be one other experience."

"Oh, go to bed, do," Catherine said. "I want some sleep."

But sleep was clearly out of the question. She supposed that this had been the most exciting day of her life. First of all the man, David Mulawer—*what* a strange name— then the news that she was going home to Paris, why, she had supposed that she would never see Paris again.

And then, Laurens. Seraphine had screamed, with pleasure. Perhaps she should have done what Laurens wanted, and then she too might have screamed with pleasure. Enjoy everything, Seraphine said. Everything, even pain. Even death.

And that was not all Seraphine had said. Was she lying there now, touching herself? Catherine rolled on her back, found her hands under the blanket, and hastily put them on top again. No doubt it was because Seraphine had had a lover. She really was a very wicked girl.

But David Mulawer. Would he be dreaming of her? Would he be wanting to touch her? Did Papa touch Stepmama Madeleine? He must. According to Seraphine. And she could believe that Madeleine wanted to be touched; she had a gleam in her eye just like Seraphine.

But had Papa ever touched Mama? There was an unthinkable thought. Mama had been so quiet, and dignified, and so ill, always. Her sole dream had been for Papa to complete his term of duty, so that she could return to Boston. Catherine could hardly remember Boston at all. She had been only a child when they had left. And now . . . now she was a woman. Madame St. Amant had said so. Laurens had said so. And David Mulawer had said so.

But she could not imagine Mama allowing Papa to touch her.

"Madame is ready for you now." Laurens' voice was stiff, as her whole body was stiff.

Catherine stood up, smoothed her skirt. For today she had been allowed to discard the blue uniform of the academy, and indeed to put on her very best outfit. She wore a woollen gown in dark green with a black trim, and a black silk spencer with lace frills at her neck and wrists. Her reticule was also black but her gloves were pale green, as her bonnet was pale green edged with black. Seraphine had said she had never looked so lovely, the dark colours perfectly setting off her pale cheeks and white-blonde hair. And Laurens clearly thought the same; her eyes were positively devouring.

Catherine stepped round her and hurried along the corridor, knocked, and entered.

"The culprit herself," Madame St. Amant said, but she was smiling.

"Catherine." Madeleine Scott held out both hands. She was a slim, dark, vivacious woman, dressed in the height of fashion, her gown a glowing crimson wool. Her face was a trifle aquiline, and she had a mole on the left cheek, but any suggestion of severity was relieved by the sparkle in her eyes, the glow of health and vitality. It was her age which always gave Catherine a shock; she was just thirty-two, and some twenty years younger than her second husband. "My dear, how pretty you look. Really, Madame St. Amant, had a young man *not* made advances, I would have been more critical."

"It was Catherine's response that was wrong, madame," Madame St. Amant said. "If I may say so."

Madeleine gave her a scornful glance, kissed Catherine upon both cheeks. "Are your things all packed?"

"Yes, madame. My box is outside."

"Have it taken down, will you, madame?" Madeleine said. "The roads are bad, and it is a long way back to Paris."

"But, will you not stay for luncheon?" Madame St. Amant asked.

"Thank you, but no. I must return to my husband.

And I am sure Catherine will wish to see her home again." She squeezed Catherine's hand. "To see what changes I have made, and to criticise." Once again the quick smile, then she released her to kiss Madame St. Amant in turn. "You have been so kind to my little daughter, and I am sure she has learned a great deal. Say goodbye to madame, Catherine."

Catherine curtsied, and kissed madame's hand. She supposed herself to be dreaming. Was this the slightly aloof young woman who had paraded on Papa's arm, last summer? But then they had only been betrothed. Now there was nothing but confidence, and humour. And even, dared she believe it, affection.

She followed her downstairs, where the yardboys were already loading her box onto the roof of the berline. A liveried coachman held the door for her, but she hesitated at the sight of the man within.

"Don't tell me you've forgotten Jean-Pierre?" Madeleine asked.

Because it was not, after all, a man. It was a boy of twelve, dark haired and slender, Madeleine's son by her first marriage; her husband had been killed on the field of Waterloo, leaving her a pregnant widow of nineteen. Fortunately he had also left her a sizeable estate, and she had been able to enjoy a decade of profitable widowhood before deciding to marry again.

"Hello, Jean-Pierre," Catherine said. They had, in fact, met at the wedding, when they had shared Madeleine's train, but they had hardly spoken.

"Hello," he said, and resumed staring out of the window.

"He would not come in," Madeleine explained. "All girls, he said. He would rather be cold." She seated herself beside Catherine, arranged the rugs over their laps. There was snow all about, and the breeze was chill. "Now," she said. "Tell me about this young man of yours. Everything."

Catherine related the incident. "So you see, madame, he is not my young man. I will never see him again. And he only wanted to paint me."

Madeleine tapped her on the chin with her fan. "I wish you to stop calling me madame. I wish you to call me Madeleine. Understood?"

"Madeleine? But you're my stepmother."

"I am your father's wife, my dear. But you are sixteen years old, and were I to be your mother I would have had to marry very young. No, no, I would prefer to be your older sister. I intend to be your friend. I never had a sister, you know. I always wished one, but it was not to be. Oh, I am a selfish person. I rescued you from that dragon of a St. Amant not for your sake, but for mine. Your papa is a very busy man, with this upheaval in Spain, and frankly I wish your company." She leaned forward to kiss Catherine on the nose. "Does that disturb you?"

"Of course not, madame. I mean Madeleine. I am flattered." Oh, Lord, she thought, her mind still bubbling with Laurens and Seraphine.

"And you may be sure I will have your young artist investigated," Madeleine said. "Who knows, he may have talent. Mulawer. Mulawer. Do you know, that sounds Austrian, or Polish. It would be Polish, I think. Paris is full of Poles who dislike being ruled by Russians. I sometimes think there are more Poles than Parisians. But, oh dear . . ." Again the quick tap of the fan. "David. Oh, dear, dear, dear."

"Don't you like the name David?"

"Only Jews are given that name. Your admirer must be a Jew."

"Oh," Catherine said. "Is that bad?"

"My dear Catherine, you could not possibly be friends with a Jew. I'm afraid, however much we have to do business with them, they really are not socially acceptable. No, no," she said. "I will find the right sort of young man for you to have as an admirer. Oh, yes, indeed." She reached across to squeeze Catherine's hand. "We shall be able to enjoy him together, my dear. You may safely leave the matter to me. I do adore nice young men."

Catherine supposed she was right. She had never

thought very deeply on the subject of comparative religion before. She had been the only Protestant girl at the academy, but that had not seemed to make any difference to Madame St. Amant, who had insisted she attend all services, even Communion Mass, although of course she had not been allowed to approach the altar.

But the difference between Catholic and Protestant was one of dogma, she reminded herself, not of fundamental belief. Although surely it should be possible for two people, given that they liked each other and were therefore prepared to respect each other's opinions, to be friends no matter what their religions?

And at this moment it no longer seemed relevant, because already they were through Le Bourget and Aubervilliers, and finding their way down the Rue LaFayette with the bulk of the Opéra looming in the distance. Catherine leaned back in her seat, to inhale, to enjoy. She loved Paris, the smell of it as much as the sight of it. She supposed, if there was anywhere in the world she should be forced to live, outside of Boston itself, she would prefer it to be this city, the very capital of Europe. Perhaps the very capital of the world. No one could possibly suppose that France was still recovering from having finally been defeated after the most terrible twenty years' war the world had ever known. But for the occasional maimed moustachio, a veteran of the Peninsular or the Russian campaign, one would not have supposed France had ever fought a war in her life. And the physical monuments erected by Napoleon—they turned the corner and joined the parade of carriages on the Boulevard Haussmann, with the Arc de Triomphe looming against the sky—remained in all their glory to make this the Queen of cities, as he had intended.

Madeleine squeezed her hand. "It is good to be home, isn't it, my darling?"

"So good," Catherine whispered. "So good."

Even Jean-Pierre was smiling, and a few moments later they had turned to the left, in the direction of the Madeleine, for the Scott town house was almost within sight of the church. And there were the wrought iron gates, and Henri the groom waiting for them, with Angelique the housekeeper, and at the top of the steps, Jackson Scott himself.

"Papa." Catherine scrambled down and hurried towards him, skirts gathered in her right hand.

"Cathy." Jackson Scott hugged her close. He was very clearly her father, only a little over medium height, and with the same delicacy of feature—although he did his best to conceal it behind a large moustache—and the same almost frighteningly steady gaze. "Oh, my dearest Cathy." In deference to his new wife he spoke French. "It is so good to have you back."

"It is so good to be back."

"A family reunited," Madeleine said. "You have no idea how your father has missed you, my darling. I suspect he has lacked an amanuensis rather than a daughter. He has told me how you edited his manuscripts. I think *Revolutionary Tactics in Warfare* should have been published under joint authorship."

It was Papa's most famous work. Catherine kissed him on the cheek. "I shall be happy to resume my labours, sir."

He smiled, and gave her another squeeze. "I suspect Madeleine has some rather more social activities in mind for you." He put an arm round each of their waists to escort them into the house. "But we'll find *some* time for work. You'll like what I'm doing now, Cathy. A study of Napoleon's marshals."

"Every military writer is studying Napoleon's marshals," Madeleine pointed out. "They wish to find out how, with so much talent, a war could possibly be lost." But she squeezed her husband's arm affectionately. "Yours will be the best, my sweet. Jean-Pierre. Jean-Pierre. Hurry along. We are going to have our very first family luncheon."

"It's awfully tight," Catherine protested.

"Mmmm," said Madame Dufour, her mouth full of pins.

"Well, it has got to be tight, my darling," Madeleine explained. "I really do not like to see a young girl's waist measuring more than twenty inches, and you cannot expect the corset to do *all* the work."

Catherine sighed, and received a slap from Madame Dufour on her bottom, and held her breath once again. And hoped that Madeleine was right. She wore only her shift, and stood on a low table, while Madame Dufour and her assistant fussed about her. Madeleine sat in a comfortable chair and kept an eye on the proceedings. But Catherine could not possibly be angry with her. The week since her return to Paris had turned into an unimaginable wonderland of presents and delights. Anyone less like the wicked stepmother of nightmare could hardly be imagined. Madeleine bubbled with gaiety and genuine good humour. And it was all devoted to her stepdaughter. They walked together and they sewed together and they played the piano together and they rode together; Catherine had hardly had a moment to devote to Papa since her return, and she really looked forward to helping him with his new book; military history had always been her favourite subject, which was not surprising as she had been entirely surrounded by it since she could remember. Papa's profession was at once a hobby and a pastime.

But Madeleine was such a delightful companion. Even Catherine's suddenly awakened suspicions that every woman had to be either a Seraphine or a Laurens had been allayed within twenty-four hours. In that time they had, in fact, become sisters, but Catherine had been restored to her own bedroom, and Madeleine never entered that doorway, preferring to summon her stepdaughter by means of one of the upstairs maids whenever she wished her company.

And meanwhile, her every waking moment seemed to be devoted to making Catherine into a prominent member of Parisian society. At least, it was going to happen very soon, the moment she was properly outfitted. To achieve which she must visit Madame Dufour every day, and stand on this pedestal shivering, for the dressmaker's shop was very inadequately heated, while she was measured and prodded and pulled and fitted and criticised and generally overhauled.

But at last Madame Dufour was standing back, and smoothing her moustache, because she did have a distinct growth on her upper lip. "There we are, mademoiselle," she said. "That will do for today. Things are coming along very nicely."

"I am glad to hear it," Madeleine said, getting up. "When will the gowns be ready?"

"Well . . ." Madame Dufour pulled her lip. "With fortune, the first in about a fortnight."

"Nonsense," Madeleine declared. "The ball gown must be finished by Friday."

"Three days?" cried Madame Dufour. "Why, madame, that is quite impossible."

"It must be done," Madeleine insisted. "I am having a soirée on Saturday, and I wish my stepdaughter properly dressed for the occasion."

"A soirée?" Catherine cried, her voice muffled as the assistant was at the moment dropping her gown over her head.

"Indeed. I have one every Saturday as a rule, but last week's was postponed in order that you might be suitably dressed. So, madame. Friday night."

"Oh, but madame . . ."

"Or we shall take our business elsewhere," Madeleine said, revealing a trace of iron Catherine had not suspected her to possess. "And I shall pay you not a sou." She looked around the room, at the designs and the already cut materials and the dozen half-finished gowns. "Not a sou."

"Oh, but madame . . ." Madame Dufour uttered a deep sigh. "The evening gown, by Friday night."

"Thank you, madame," Madeleine said, giving a charming smile. "I knew you could manage if you tried. Come along, Catherine."

Catherine hastily tied the ribbon of her bonnet beneath her chin, picked up her pelisse and allowed the maid to hold it for her. Then she hurried behind her stepmother, caught her up at the door.

"Is there really to be a soirée?"

"Of course. It will be your official arrival on the Parisian scene." Madeleine pulled on her gloves, peered at the street; there had been snow overnight and traces of white were still to be seen in the gutters and on the occasional branch. "Brrr. I should have ordered the carriage. Still, a brisk walk will do us good. Come along now."

Catherine hurried at her side. "I . . . I shan't know what to say. What to do."

"Oh, nonsense. You will look beautiful, both because you are beautiful and because you will be beautifully dressed, and therefore all the men will wish to speak with you. Flattery you may accept with a gentle smile and a flutter of your fan. But not all my guests are frivolous. No, no. I have a coterie of young men, and even a young woman, who possess great literary talent. It is my pleasure to encourage these poor creatures. Who knows, among them may be another Montaigne, even a Chateaubriand. But then, of course, I shall be having some real people, members of the aristocracy, you know. Oh, we shall very soon find you an admirer, my dear."

"But . . ." Catherine was going to say that she was not at all sure she wanted an admirer at this moment, and that in any event she had no idea how to cope with one, when she stopped in surprise. They were passing a café, and while the cold had driven most of the customers indoors, there was one young man seated at a table, sipping an aperitif, and she had recognised him as her strange acquaintance of the toboggan slope.

As he had recognised her. He was on his feet in an instant, raising his sadly tarnished beaver, and giving a slight bow from the waist. "Mademoiselle Scott."

Madeleine had also halted, and was giving him, or at least his shabby clothes, a severe inspection. "Are you addressing us, monsieur?"

"I am, madame," he said. "I have the honor to be acquainted with your charming companion."

"David . . . David Mulawer," Catherine said. "May I present my stepmother."

"Madame Scott." David reached for Madeleine's hand, but she hastily tucked it into her muff.

"So you are the scoundrel who assaulted my stepdaughter."

"Assaulted, madame?" Mulawer looked genuinely surprised. And he *was* handsome, Catherine realised. Why, given a few square meals to fill out those hollow cheeks and restore to them some colour, and presented with a suit of decent clothing and a warm coat to keep out the cold, he could be a dashing figure, with his lank black hair and his powerful dark eyes.

"Assaulted," Madeleine said grimly. "It is possible to assault the sensibilities just as it is to assault the person. Now, sir, if you will permit us to pass . . ."

"My apologies, madame," Mulawer said. "For imposing myself upon you. I shall not do so again. May I kiss your hand in farewell, mademoiselle?"

"Well, I . . ." Catherine glanced at Madeleine.

"Of course you may not," Madeleine said.

But Mulawer had already seized Catherine's glove, and was brushing it with his lips, while his fingers searched her palm in a most unusual fashion, and she realised he was pressing a folded piece of paper into it.

Hastily she closed her fist and withdrew her hand. "I shall wish you good day, monsieur."

"And it is, on a sudden, a good day, mademoiselle," he agreed. He raised his hat once more. "Adieu, madame. May the coming warmth of spring melt even a heart as hard as yours."

"Well, really," Madeleine declared, making her way down the street. "What a ridiculous young man. An artist, did you say?"

"A painter," Catherine explained. "You did say that you wished to encourage talent. Could you not invite him to a soirée?"

"My dear Catherine," Madeleine said, leading her through the gate to the house. "I am able to discern the possibilities of talent at a glance, and believe me, that boy has none at all. In any event, where would he find the clothes to attend a soirée? No, no, I think you should set your sights a little higher."

Catherine preferred not to argue. She wanted only to get inside and find the first opportunity to escape to her room, where she could at last unclench her fist and read the note.

"I saw you pass, earlier," Mulawer had written, "and thus waited for your return. Dearest Catherine, you are as the sun and the moon and the stars to me. Without your love I must inevitably perish. And sometimes I feel there can be no other fate for me, when I think of your eyes, so cool and steady. My Ice Maiden, is there a heart there at all? But I shall hope to survive until I know for certain, and I shall be at this table in this café every day from now on, from ten until twelve, in the hopes that you may be able to escape your guardian and meet me here. Until that joyous moment, adieu, my own dear love."

"My darling," Madeleine said. "You look divine. But now we really must go down. I am sure our guests have already assembled. Give me your hand."

Catherine obeyed, sneaking a last glance in the mirror. She supposed she did look divine, in her pale blue taffeta gown, absolutely plain in the full skirt, pulled right in to that breathtaking eighteen-inch waistline, and then allowed to billow again, with white lace ruffles on her sleeves and surrounding her bodice. Her shoulders were bare, and her neck felt terribly exposed, because for the first time in her life her hair had been put up, coiled on her head and held in place by tortoiseshell combs decorated with flowers. The result was to leave her face quite exposed, and almost frightening in its serene beauty. *My Ice Maiden,* he had written. It suggested a flattering quality of self-possession.

"Well," Madeleine had said, "it is sensible to make the most of one's assets," and she smoothed the bodice to make it sit tighter against the constricted breasts, pulled together to redouble the size of the swelling tops which were also exposed to view. *No doubt my second-best feature,* Catherine thought. And began to wonder if for all her apparent delight at having her back in Paris, her stepmother was not really intent upon marrying her off as rapidly as possible. Her only jewellery was a thin gold chain, which had belonged to Mama but which Papa had given her to celebrate her return, and which disappeared into that so fascinating bodice to lie against her stomach.

But how she wished, she thought, as she accompanied Madeleine on to the gallery above the stairs, that she could be sitting for David to paint. Or indeed, that he could be here. Which was total cowardice, because she had not even had the courage to go for a walk by herself and pass the café where he was, no doubt, still waiting. She had no idea how to escape Madeleine, even for that brief period. And she had no idea what to say or do should she find herself alone with him. It really was too forward a proposal. But a most romantic one.

Madeleine paused, at the head of the stairs, to allow Catherine to compose herself, and to allow the guests to glimpse their hostess, for the hall below was already well filled, and there was a babble of conversation and a clink of glasses, the whole only gently overlaid by the hum of music emanating from the withdrawing room, where two musicians scraped away at their violins.

"Oh, Lord," Catherine muttered, as the noise ceased and most heads turned in their direction.

"Smile," Madeleine commanded. "And keep smiling. You may frown at an improper suggestion, and you may look serious when a gentleman is putting a serious point to you, whether or not you understand it, but for the rest, smile."

They began the descent. Catherine's knees almost buckled on the first step, then she thought of Laurens, and how absolutely green that old dragon would be could she see her now, and tossed her head and smiled, with the sheer pleasure of it.

"Oh, splendid," Madeleine murmured. "Quite splendid. Jackson, my dear."

Colonel Scott waited at the foot of the stairs for his wife and daughter. He gave them each an arm, and paraded forward through the guests, while Madeleine smiled and greeted each one, and Catherine endeavoured to keep her own smile fixed.

"Why, Count. And madame. How very good to see you. May I present my stepdaughter, Catherine. Such a charming child. Why, Sir Harry. And Clarissa, my dear, dear girl. May I present my stepdaughter, Catherine. Such a sweet child. Why, monsieur. And where is your pretty wife? Ah, the croup. At this time of year it is everywhere. May I present my stepdaughter, Catherine. Such a pretty child, don't you think?"

The names, and the introductions, swirled about her head until they reached the very end of the room.

"Why, Honoré, my dear boy, you look quite upset."

The young man was at once short and stout, saved from being ugly by the twinkle in his eyes. "I am abashed, madame, at watching so much beauty approaching me."

"You are a flatterer, sir." Madeleine tapped him on the shoulder with her fan. "Allow me to present my stepdaughter, Catherine. Such a charming child. Honoré Balzac. Monsieur Balzac writes, my darling. Catherine is very interested in the arts."

"Indeed, mademoiselle?" Balzac kissed her hand. "Then I am doubly enchanted."

"Tell her about your latest novel, Honoré," Madeleine recommended. "I must see to my guests."

Catherine licked her lips. "I am afraid, Monsieur Balzac, that I have not read any of your books," she said.

"Perhaps you have, sweet mademoiselle," he said. "Without realising it. I use a pseudonym. Several, in fact."

"Oh. Why?" She felt her cheeks burn. "If I am not being impertinent?"

"Of course you are not, mademoiselle. Well, it is a necessary subterfuge. I write a novel, and it is described as rubbish by the critics, and is a failure with the public, so my publishers say, we wish no more of that, and yet, I must write if I am going to live at all, so I write another novel, and submit it under another name, and the whole charade starts again."

"Oh, dear," Catherine said. "You paint a grim picture, monsieur."

"I would have you call me Honoré, mademoiselle, if *I* am not being impertinent. Why, life is a grim business, at least in the beginning. Perhaps one day . . . well, why not? Dreams are at least free." His voice changed and so did his face, losing its animation and becoming almost hard. "Monsieur. A pleasure."

"And mine, Balzac," said the tall young man, very well dressed, as was the lady on his arm. "And this is our charming guest of honour. May I introduce myself, mademoiselle? Victor Hugo, at your service, and this is my wife, Adele."

The young woman did a brief curtsey. But Catherine was quite unable to respond; her knees had lost their strength.

"Monsieur Hugo?" she asked. "Not . . ."

"I write," he said.

"But I have just finished *Cromwell*."

"Indeed, mademoiselle?" Hugo smiled. "I am amazed your stepmother allows you to read such scurrilous nonsense. What did you think of it?"

"Oh, I . . . I thought it was very good. I could hardly put it down."

"You flatter me, mademoiselle. I am working on a volume of poems. Perhaps you will like them also. Ah, Balzac. What is it today? Horace de St. Aubin?"

"Why, no, monsieur. Today, for good or evil, I use my own."

"How quaint," Hugo remarked. "I am surprised you can always remember it. You'll excuse us, mademoiselle." He swept his wife on, to engage the next couple in fascination.

"Opinionated prig," Balzac remarked.

"Monsieur Hugo? Oh, but . . ."

"Oh, indeed, mademoiselle. He is the toast of the literary world. Of all Paris indeed. He has been, ever since he published those poems of his four years ago.

Now, whatever he writes, however banal, the critics shriek with joy and say here is genius."

"I suspect, monsieur, that you are jealous," Catherine remarked.

Balzac smiled. "Oh, indeed I am, mademoiselle. I am curdled with jealousy. But tell me truly, did you enjoy his play?"

Her turn to smile. "I did not really understand it. But I shall read one of yours, if I may. Was he calling you by your pen name?"

"One of them. Mademoiselle, I shall present you with a copy of my latest work, if you will but give me permission to call."

"*I* do, certainly. We shall also have to obtain the sanction of my stepmother. But if you are in any event her protégé that should not be difficult. Why, Madeleine, may I . . ."

"Catherine, my darling." Madeleine's cheeks were pink, and she was clearly agitated. "There is someone I wish you to meet. You'll excuse us, Honoré."

"Of course." The writer bowed.

"But Madeleine," Catherine protested. "I was going to ask you . . ."

"Later." Madeleine had seized her arm, and was half dragging her across the room to meet a man who had just come in. Catherine regained her balance in time to stop and look at him, and felt her own breathing begin to quicken. He was at once tall and big. Yet the size was beautifully proportioned, the heavy shoulders tapering to the slim hips, the obvious strength in the muscular torso continuing downwards into the powerful legs, and he was dressed in a dark blue cloth coat with a velvet collar over white corduroy trousers which displayed him to the very best advantage.

But it was his face which held Catherine's attention. It was long, and a trifle thin, with a straight nose and a prominent chin between which a flat, wide mouth suggested an angry gash. His hair was black, and lank, his eyes seemed to impale her. They were green, and glittered, and seemed to be stripping away flesh and bone

31

from her own face to see right into her brain. She realised that she was in the presence of perhaps the most powerful personality she had ever met, and Madeleine's voice seemed to come from a very long way away.

"My stepdaughter, Catherine. Catherine, I would have you meet Baron Ricimer."

Chapter 2

BARON Ricimer bent low over Catherine's hand. His grip was gentle, yet she had not a doubt that with a single twist of his powerful fingers he could break her wrist. "I am enchanted, mademoiselle. Why, when they told me Paris had just received her most beautiful visitor in years, I was almost sceptical."

"Monsieur is too kind." Catherine gave a desperate glance to her right, but Madeleine merely smiled at her.

"Another guest," she explained, and hurried off.

And Ricimer continued to stare at her.

"A . . . a glass of wine, monsieur?"

"Thank you, mademoiselle, but no. Perhaps I can obtain one for you?"

"I have one already, thank you. I suspect that will be sufficient for the time being."

"Very wise. Then let us escape some of this noise and heat." He offered her his arm.

"But monsieur . . ." She gave the room a quick glance. Was everyone looking at them? It was difficult to be sure. "I cannot leave my guests."

"For no more than a moment, mademoiselle. I cannot stay long, and my evening would be counted an utter waste did I not enjoy your company for at least a few minutes." He had taken her elbow as he spoke, and was guiding her along the edge of the room to the door into the library. Her knees felt weak and she had no idea what to say, or do. Save allow herself to be dominated, for these few moments.

She was in the privacy of the library, but the Baron did not attempt to close the door. She sank into the chair by Papa's desk, discovered he was once again staring at her.

"Will you not sit down?"

"I would prefer to stand," he said. "May I be impertinent, mademoiselle?"

"Why, I . . ." She suspected he was in any event old enough to be her father. "I assure you, monsieur, I shall not be offended."

"I must surrender to an unpardonable curiosity, mademoiselle," he confessed, "as to how a beauty like yourself has gone unnoticed for all these years. You have been secreted in a convent?"

"No, monsieur." She found herself smiling. "I have been secreted in Madame St. Amant's Academy for Young Ladies, in Chantilly."

"Chantilly," he murmured. "Will you not smile again?"

"Why, monsieur . . ." But she was, smiling again.

"Because, when you smile," he said, "you are more beautiful than ever, and yet, not more beautiful."

"Monsieur?"

"You seem to change personalities," he explained. "In your company a man is doubly fortunate, as he is in the presence of two young ladies, each an utter delight of charm and beauty."

"Monsieur," she said uneasily, and stood up.

"You promised me you would not be offended."

"Oh . . ." She sat down again. "Why, so I did."

"And now you have completed your schooling," he said. "And will be returning to your native America?"

"I hope to, certainly, monsieur. But Papa has another three years in this post, at the least."

"Three years," he murmured. "And supposing you

were invited to spend the rest of your life in Paris, mademoiselle?"

She forced a frown. "I would very much like to return home, again, if only for a visit, monsieur." She smiled at him. "But it would depend entirely upon who extended the invitation."

"Ah." Once again the long stare, which reduced her knees to jelly. He was being terribly forward, more forward even than poor David Mulawer, and in the case of a man like Baron Ricimer it could be no idle flirtation. She should end it now, she supposed. She had been alone with him for at least ten minutes, when she should not have been alone with him at all. But she felt curiously unable to move, certainly to oppose his will.

She looked past him, saw Madeleine in the doorway, and almost cried out in relief.

"Why, Baron," Madeleine said. "I trust my stepdaughter is not boring you."

"My dear Madame Scott," Ricimer said. "I would be enchanted were I able to do nothing more than sit and stare at her."

Which in the main is what he has been doing, Catherine thought. She stood up.

"Well, I think it is time we rejoined our other guests," Madeleine decided.

"Alas, madame, I must take my leave. I did tell you how short I was of time. But . . ." He hesitated, clearly a deliberate action in such a man.

"Yes, Baron?"

"I have only a few days more in Paris," Ricimer explained. "And it would really grieve me to depart upon a journey which will end I know not when, without repaying at least a fraction of your generous hospitality. I am staying with my sister, Madame Despards."

"Oh, indeed?" Madeleine asked.

"And I know she would be most happy if you and your stepdaughter could come to call on her. Perhaps tomorrow?"

"Well," Madeleine smiled at Catherine. *Oh, no,* Catherine thought. *I don't wish to call upon his sister. I don't wish to be thrust into his company again.* But why? Because she was afraid of him? Why should she be afraid of anyone? Or because she knew that sometime, perhaps very soon, he was going to extend an invitation she would find it very difficult to elude?

An invitation to do what, she wondered.

Or was it merely because he made someone like David Mulawer appear so very insignificant?

"Well," Madeleine said again. "I am sure we shall be very pleased to accept your sister's kind invitation, Baron. Shall we say, tomorrow afternoon, at four?"

"I can't help it," Catherine confessed. "I just do not like the way he looks at me. He makes me feel . . . oh, naked." She flushed, and adjusted her turban. Madeleine had decreed that she should look her very best, and thus she was wearing her pink silk turban, and a mulberry velvet spencer over a white gown, with lace ruffles at her wrists and at her hem. Her hair was once again tucked out of sight, and she looked much older than she was. Which presumably was what Madeleine was aiming at.

"My dear," she remarked, escorting Catherine to the stairs. "What a thing to say." But she gave a secret smile. "Yet you are quite right. He is a very strange fellow. But for that reason, entirely fascinating."

Catherine said nothing, although she could not help wondering just which of them the Baron really wished to entertain, at least in Madeleine's eyes. So, was she preparing to be jealous of her own stepmother?

There was a light covering of snow on the ground, and Madeleine tucked them beneath a rug in the back seat of the barouche. "For example," she said, "do you know that he never touches wine? Not a drop has ever been seen to pass his lips. Now is that not strange?"

"Perhaps he does not like wine," Catherine suggested.

"A gentleman, not liking wine?"

"Well . . . is he French?"

"No. At least, I don't think so. The rumour is that he is Austrian. But his nationality really does not matter, as he is fabulously wealthy, by all accounts. He spends a

36

deal of his time travelling, and only comes to Paris once or twice a year. Mind you, wealthy or not, one must be careful with a man like the Baron. Do you recall Thérèse Cavaigny?"

Catherine shook her head. She was peering through the window at the street; they were close to the café where David Mulawer had promised to wait for her. Of course, it was well past noon, but still she was disappointed to see the tables were all empty.

"Well, she was a most charming, and lovely young woman. Daughter of old Colonel Cavaigny. Not a great deal of money, of course, but then, that would hardly matter to the Baron. They were seen everywhere together, oh, it would have been four years ago, and then, she just disappeared."

Catherine turned her head. "Disappeared?"

"Just like that," Madeleine said, rolling her eyes most expressively. "Her maid went to her bedroom one morning, and she was gone. The bed had not even been slept in. And do you know, she had received a note the previous evening, her butler remembered it distinctly. So everyone assumed she had made an assignation with her lover."

"The Baron?"

"Well, that is what was supposed. But that night the Baron spent the entire evening, and until five in the morning, gambling with some friends. He swore he had no assignation, and that, indeed, the young lady had been no more than an acquaintance."

"So what do you think happened?" Catherine asked.

"Well, I think he was telling the truth. But I also think he had, perhaps, inadvertently, one can never be sure about these things, given poor Cavaigny cause to hope he might be going to marry her. After all, he is a man of the world, in every sense, and no doubt her pretty little head was turned. So I think that, when she realised he was *not* going to make her his wife, she took her life."

Catherine stared at her, mouth open. "She committed suicide?"

"What else could have happened to her, my darling? Women do not just disappear. Not ladies."

"But . . . even if she had committed suicide, would her body not have been found?"

"Not supposing she had thrown herself into the Seine. As a matter of fact, only a few weeks after she disappeared the body of a woman was fished out of the river. Naked, would you believe. Can you imagine that poor girl, standing on the banks of the river, removing all of her clothing, and then throwing herself in? It makes one shiver all over. Removing her clothing. She must have been in a very strange frame of mind."

"And it was Mademoiselle Cavaigny?"

Madeleine shrugged. "Who knows. She had been in the water for some weeks, and was quite unrecognisable. Horrible." She smiled, and pointed through the window. "Here is Madame Despards' Hotel."

The barouche was drawing to a halt.

"But Madeleine," Catherine protested. "How can you even wish to know a man who could do such a thing, much less visit his house?"

"Now, do not be a goose, Catherine. How could he have had anything to do with it? I told you, on the night it happened, Baron Ricimer was gambling with some friends. And his friends were all very reputable people. Why, do you know, I have a feeling your father was among them?"

"But . . ." Catherine gazed at the house. It was certainly splendid, in an almost medieval fashion, for it was surrounded if not by a moat, at least by a water-filled ditch, across which there led a most ornately carved and curved bridge. "Does Papa know we are coming here today?"

"Ah," Madeleine said, smiling at Henri the groom as he opened the door and lowered the step. "No, I have not actually told your father where we are visiting today. After all, he is such a busy man, don't you think? He really does not wish to know what we are doing every hour of the day. It would only bore him, I have no doubt at all. Ah, Madame Despards."

They had descended onto a cobbled driveway, immediately before the bridge, placing their feet very carefully as the stones were dusted with slippery snow. But on the far side of the bridge the iron-studded oaken door had swung inwards, and a tall, stout woman, handsome and undoubtedly Ricimer's sister, stood there, flanked by her butler, smiling at them.

"Madame Scott," she said. "And Mademoiselle Scott. What a pleasure. Kurt has told me so much about you. Alas, he has not yet returned from his daily ride. But he will soon be here. Come in, my dear mademoiselle, and let me look at you."

Catherine glanced at Madeleine, received a quick nod, and went forward. Her boots slipped on the first step of the curved bridge, and she had to hold the banister, while Madame Despards called, "Oh, do be careful, my dear child. Alphonse, you'll give Mademoiselle Scott your arm."

The butler bowed, and stepped forward.

"No, no," Catherine insisted, making her way up the slope. "I shall be quite all right." She reached the top. "It is all downhill from here on."

She took a step, onto the flattened apex of the bridge, and the wood gave way beneath her feet.

Catherine was too surprised even to scream. One moment she had seemed to be walking on solid wood, the next she was plunging feet first into the near freezing water of the ditch, which was considerably deeper than she had supposed. She had all the breath driven from her lungs at once by the cold and by the shock. Then her feet struck the mud at the bottom, and gave way, and her head ducked under the water as she knelt. She moved her arms, desperately, and her head broke the surface. She was aware of people shouting, of the butler and Madeleine's grooms reaching down for her, of Madame Despards wringing her hands, of Madeleine herself standing on the edge of the ditch with a most comical expression of distressed amazement on her face.

Then the cold struck at her. She was soaked, right through all of her petticoats and even her shift; her corset had turned into a clammy outer skin. Her hat had come off and her hair had come down, trailing damply, although her shoulders were so frozen she could not feel it. Her teeth chattered and she was too cold to utter a word.

"Oh, the poor child. Oh, the poor child," Madame Despards was shouting. "Oh, the poor child."

"Catherine," Madeleine cried. "Catherine. Are you all right?"

Catherine could only gasp. The butler had her shoulders now, and Henri, having made his way across the bridge, despite the gaping hole in the centre, was also reaching down. He seized her wrists and she was pulled out, to be overtaken by another paroxysm of shivering.

"She must be dried, and warmed," Madame Despards cried. "Quickly, now. A blanket."

The second Scott groom had also crossed the bridge, this time thoughtfully armed with Madeleine's travelling rug, which was wrapped around her shoulders.

"Now, quickly, child," Madame Despards said. "We must get those wet things off, or you will catch your death of cold. Come along now."

Catherine was hurried into the hallway.

"What about me?" Madeleine shouted. "What about me? Henri, help me across."

Catherine found herself dripping on to the parquet. "Madame," she gasped, her teeth still chattering. "I am ruining your floor."

"Tush," said Madame Despards. "After I have all but ruined you? Come along now. Ah, Cora. Come with us."

The maidservant relieved the butler on Catherine's right arm, and between them she and Madame Despards hurried Catherine up a shallow flight of stairs, along a brief corridor, and into a bedchamber, exquisitely furnished, but possessing best of all a roaring fire.

"Now," Madame Despards said. "Take your clothes off. Every last thing."

Catherine stared at her.

"You must, my dear, or you will surely become ill," Madame Despards said. And gave a coquettish giggle. "Ah, mademoiselle is modest. Then we shall leave you. Unless you will need assistance."

40

Catherine shook her head.

"Then ring the bell when you are ready, and Cora here will take your things to have them dried. There is a towel in the alcove. I must see to your stepmother. And also to a hot drink for you, eh? Oh, my dear child, I am so sorry. So very sorry. Every last thing, now."

She bustled her maid out of the room, and Catherine discovered she was still shivering. Water was gathering in a puddle between her feet. She stood by the fire, and immediately felt better, but undoubtedly madame was right. And yet . . . there was something *managed* about the whole affair. Still, she thought, they cannot harm me, with Madeleine here. Especially if she locked the door. She hurried across the room, turned the key in the lock, reached up for her turban and discovered it must have floated away. Oh, my Lord, she thought; that beautiful hat. But surely Henri would have regained it.

She unfastened her gown, let it lie on the floor, added her petticoats. The strings for her corset were soaked and knotted, and she had to tug and strain, walking up and down before the fire, being warmed at once by its heat and by her own exertions. But finally the garment came free, and she added it and her shift to the pile, paused for a moment, in front of the fire, wearing only her stockings and boots, and her gold necklace, while she towelled her hair.

But her feet also felt like lumps of ice. She sat on the hearth rug, unlaced her boots, took them off, rolled down her stockings, threw them over her shoulder, and then knelt before the blaze, almost as if she were praying, arms above her head, allowing the magnificent heat to reach for her, to warm her frozen breasts and to dry the icy water between her toes, to restore some sanity to her stomach, which had been feeling quite sick . . . and then suddenly being unable to move, as she was overtaken by quite another feeling, in strong contrast to the wellbeing rippling through her system. A feeling she was not alone.

Hastily she wrapped the towel round her waist and stood up. She turned, slowly, to look first of all at the bed, then at the armchair, then at the curtained alcove which contained the washstand with its china ewer and basin. But the curtain was drawn back against the wall, and the alcove was empty, as was the bed. And yet the hair on the nape of her neck still seemed to prickle.

She pulled the bell rope, then sat on the bed, and hastily stood up again, wrapping the towel tighter, staring at the fire. Above the fireplace there was a mirror, and she found herself gazing at herself, at the slightly anxious face, the still wet hair drooping onto her shoulders. Even wearing the towel, she was exposing all of her legs and most of her breasts.

But she was alone. There could be no question of that.

Fingers rapped on the door, and she hastily unlocked it. "I have a robe for you, mademoiselle," Cora said. "Until your own things are dry. And madame invites you downstairs for a glass of wine. The Baron has just this moment come in."

The robe, in crimson wool, was delightfully warm, and there was a pair of matching woolen slippers to go with it. Catherine wrapped herself up, and then was given a brush to restore some order to her hair, following which she allowed Cora to escort her downstairs. She felt delightfully wanton, to be entering the company of a man wearing only a single garment, and what a man. But of course, Madeleine would be there, and in fact, Madeleine was waiting in the doorway of the winter parlour.

"Catherine, my darling," she cried. "Are you all right?"

"I think so," she said. "I don't know about my clothes."

"They are ruined," Ricimer said, getting up and coming towards her.

"Oh." Immediately she felt breathless. "But . . ."

"It shall be my responsibility to replace them for you, mademoiselle." He took her hand, kissed her knuckles.

"Oh. But . . ." She looked at Madeleine.

Who smiled. "I think in this case, my darling, we could accept the Baron's generosity. After all . . ."

"It was entirely our fault that the accident happened," Ricimer said, still holding her hand as he led her towards a chaise longue. "That bridge is a death trap. I would never have been able to forgive myself had you suffered an injury." He released her, and she sat down; her knees had lost all their strength.

"I shall have it torn down and rebuilt," Madame Despards declared. "Immediately. But of course you must allow us to replace your clothes."

"Although," Ricimer said, holding out a glass of mulled wine. "Dare I say it, mademoiselle, you look more beautiful than ever. It is a fact, is it not, my dear Madame Scott, that any reasonably attractive woman, and indeed, some positively unattractive ones of my acquaintance, can look delightful when expensively dressed and suitably painted and coiffured. But it takes real beauty to survive in déshabille."

"Oh, indeed, it does," Madeleine agreed, not looking quite so pleased. "Do drink your wine, my darling. I really think, as soon as your clothes are dry, that we should be going home."

Catherine discovered she was still holding the full glass, and hastily drank some. She could feel the warm liquid tracing its way down her chest, accelerating the pounding of her heart.

"I will see about the clothes," Madame Despards said, pulling on the bell rope. Strangely, Catherine thought, she was looking at her brother.

"Oh, indeed," Ricimer said, seating himself beside Catherine. "Although it grieves me to be deprived of your company so soon. Ah, but I have a suggestion. I own a château, in Brittany. I would be so charmed to have you visit me there, Madame Scott." He continued to look at Catherine. "I will confess, there is an ulterior motive. The place belonged to my dear lamented Papa, and all the old servants are still in residence. Including, I may say, my mother's dressmaker. Believe me, mademoiselle, there is none finer in all France. And I have your clothes to replace, have I not?"

"Oh, but . . ." Catherine glanced at Madeleine, who was once again looking pleased.

"Why, that sounds a most pleasant suggestion, Baron.

I will have to ask the colonel, of course, but I am sure he will give his permission."

"My intention was that Colonel Scott should accompany you," Ricimer said, securing the wine jug to refill Catherine's glass. She accepted without quite knowing why; his presence, so close, seemed to rob her of the power of intelligent thought. And yet, her nerves were as taut as they had been in the bedroom.

"Oh, good heavens," Madeleine cried. "He would never agree to leaving Paris right now. Oh, no, no, he has a great deal too much work to do. Sometimes I worry about the poor dear man's health, he is so devoted to his studies. No, no. If I accept I must do so on behalf of my stepdaughter and myself. Although . . ." She paused, tapping her chin with her fan.

"Yes?" Ricimer inquired.

"It would be very pleasant if I could bring my son, Jean-Pierre." She smiled archly. "He will be a companion for Catherine."

"For Catherine, of course. How old is the boy, madame, if I may be so bold?"

"He is twelve, Baron."

"Ah." Ricimer smiled. "And no doubt as handsome as his mother is beautiful. He shall be most welcome. Although I would have supposed him a trifle young for a lady like mademoiselle."

"You know what children are," Madeleine said happily. "Well, that sounds delightful. Paris in March is always worth escaping. The winter seems to have gone on just too long. And then, my darling, when we return, it shall be spring, and the world will take on an entirely different cast. Ah, madame."

"Mademoiselle Scott's clothes are dried, madame," said Madame Despards.

"How splendid." Madeleine stood up. "If you will excuse us, Baron . . ."

"Alas, madame, it is you who must excuse me," Ricimer said, bowing over her hand. "As I have an important engagement, and am already late. A thousand apologies." He turned, lifted Catherine's hand to his lips.

His eyes seemed to have a physical force, and once again she felt the hair on her neck prickling as if it was rising away from her flesh. "Keep yourself safe, mademoiselle. Until we meet again."

"I do not like him," Catherine said, staring out of the window of the barouche. *No,* she thought, *I do not like him; but, oh Lord, I could so easily love him. How magnificent it could be if his personality, his obvious knowledge of the world, of women, indeed, could be grafted on a character like, just for example, David Mulawer's.*

"What nonsense," Madeleine said. "How can you possibly know whether or not you like him, when you do not even know him properly yet. But a visit to his château will remedy that." She smiled, and squeezed Catherine's hand. "Besides, he does owe you a new outfit, you know. That gown will never be the same again, and your hat is quite ruined."

"I wonder if that interests him at all," Catherine mused.

"Oh, really, my darling. Whatever can you have against the man? Tell me, now."

"Well, the way he looks at me." She felt her cheeks begin to burn. "He seems able to strip me naked, with his eyes."

"So you said before, and of course he can do that, my darling. And does. Why, he does the same thing to me. He is a man of the world. You may be sure he has seen dozens of naked women, of all shapes and sizes. So when he looks at you, or me, he tries to put our faces on a body he has known."

"But . . ."

"But, you see, he has never seen *our* bodies, so it must remain only supposition. That is our great attraction. He will never know, until he manages to make love to us."

"Good Lord," Catherine said. "What . . ." She had been going to say, what a terrible thought. But suddenly she found herself thinking how utterly delightful it might be. The only person ever to attempt to make love to her had been Laurens, supposing that was really what Laurens had had in mind. She had hated it, but surely only because it had been Laurens. Had it been a man like Baron Ricimer, now, and his fingers would have been soft, she had no doubt about that.

"Not, of course," Madeleine said primly, "that he will find that easy to do, with us." She shot her stepdaughter a quick glance. "Or possible at all, in fact."

"But he has *seen* me naked," Catherine muttered, half to herself, her heart commencing to pound all over again while her entire flesh broke out in a sweat. "Madeleine." She clutched her stepmother's arm. "I can't go to his château. He has seen me naked, already."

"Oh, really child, what utter stuff and nonsense. You are making me suppose that your ducking has brought on a fever."

"Listen, please," Catherine begged. "That bridge. Did you inspect it?"

"Good Lord, no," Madeleine said. "I am not a carpenter."

"It collapsed, did it not?"

"Of course it did."

"Yet, I have just remembered, no timbers fell into the moat beside me. They remained, hanging down from the bridge itself. Almost as if they had been hinged."

"Hinged? Whatever can you be talking about?"

"I think I was meant to fall into that ditch, Madeleine. I think I fell through a trapdoor."

"You *have* got a fever," Madeleine said. "Why on earth should Madame Despards wish you to fall into her moat?"

"Just so I would have to take off all of my clothes," Catherine said. "Don't you see? I was upstairs, in a bedroom selected by her, frozen stiff, and naked. So naturally I would kneel in front of the fire."

"So? You were alone in the room."

"In the room. But I was being watched. I know I was being watched. There must have been a peephole, somewhere about the fireplace."

"Oh, really, Catherine, my darling. I shall have to speak with Monsieur Hugo. You have been reading too many romances. Who on earth would wish to do such a thing?"

"The Baron. Who else?"

Madeleine stared at her for some seconds, the colour for a moment threatening to leave her face. Then it returned again in a rush, and she smiled. "You poor deluded child. Why, the Baron was not even at home. He arrived after you had been taken upstairs."

"How do you know?" Catherine insisted. "Merely because his sister said he was out?"

"Merely because he entered the parlour, in his outdoor clothes, while you were still upstairs."

"And that means he was out? Did you see him arrive? How did his horse cross the bridge?"

For a moment Madeleine frowned, then once again smiled, as her flush deepened. "No doubt there is another entrance. In any event, my darling girl, you are really living in a dream world if you could suppose a man like the Baron Ricimer would be at all interested in a child like you."

"Then how do you account for the way he looks at me?"

"The Baron looks at every woman like that, my darling."

"And our invitation of today? Our invitation to visit his château, which you so carelessly accepted?"

Madeleine sighed, and looked out of the window. "The invitation was extended to me, goose."

"You?" Catherine was aghast.

"Ricimer and I have, what shall I say, been aware of each other for some time." Madeleine turned her head to look at her stepdaughter. "Does that shock you?"

"Why, I . . ." She had no idea what to say.

"Will you rush up to your father's study when we get home, to tell him the dreadful news?"

"Of course not." She felt herself flushing. "If only I could understand."

Madeleine sighed again. "It is not so very difficult, my darling. I am twenty years younger than Jackson. I have been accustomed, over the past ten years since my first husband died, to living a very free life. I find that I continue to need the stimulus of male company. Varying male company. Exciting male company. Do not misunderstand me. I love your father. Dearly. I would never betray him. But if I am to remain the vivacious, charming, exciting creature he married, I require that stimulus. He is the ultimate beneficiary."

Catherine discovered she had sucked her upper lip between her teeth.

"I am sure he would agree with my reasoning," Madeleine said, gazing at her. "But I also feel it would be best for all were he never to know. So that is why I endeavoured to make a friend of you, my darling. Now, the choice is very simply yours. Should you tell him, I will of course deny it, and the odds are that he will believe me rather than you. On the other hand, should you agree to be my friend, my accomplice, my confidante, not only will you find me the very best of mothers, but I shall also be more than willing to reciprocate, should the occasion ever arise."

Catherine inhaled, slowly. *Poor Papa,* she thought. *Oh, poor, poor Papa.* And yet, Madeleine was stating no more than the truth. He was happy, and for the first time that Catherine could remember. When she thought of the permanent frown on his face, the permanent misery in his eyes, as he had listened to Mama coughing, and Catherine could not remember back to when she had not been coughing. He was happy, and it was Madeleine who was making him happy. And if it seemed that every woman in the world wanted more than conventional life was prepared to offer, why, Madeleine had at least just sworn her undying loyalty to her position as Madame Scott.

Every woman in the world? Was that not far too sweeping a condemnation? *She* did not want anything more than a husband and children and some contentment in time. Or was she deluding herself? Her eyes widened as she slowly realised that Madeleine's confession had placed her in a position of tremendous power.

"Well?" Madeleine inquired. "We shall be home in a

moment, and I really do feel we should have decided upon our true relationship before we arrive."

"I shall not betray you, Madeleine," she said, and was amazed at the evenness of her voice when compared with the thumping of her heart. "But it occurs to me that you can reciprocate now, rather than later."

"How?" Madeleine's tone was sharp.

"By permitting me to walk by myself, tomorrow morning. Oh, just for half an hour."

Madeleine frowned. "To meet that artist?"

"To stimulate myself as a woman," Catherine said, wickedly.

She walked slowly along the street, hands tucked into her muff, watching her breath clouding in front of her face, feeling the fur collar of her pelisse brushing her cheeks, and feeling, too, her heart pounding. Her decision to take advantage of her sudden position of power had been entirely an impulse, but having obtained Madeleine's consent she had determined to take her walk. Yet now she had no idea what to say, how to look, how to behave even.

Because there he was, seated at his table, as usual, a single glass of wine in front of him, hands in the pockets of his greatcoat. His shoulders were hunched and he looked tired, and hungry, and very, very cold.

"Why, monsieur," she said. "How pleasant to meet you again." And was once more amazed at the calmness of her voice. She seemed to be listening to a stranger speak.

Múlawer was on his feet in an instant, almost knocking over his wine.

"Mademoiselle? Catherine? I had supposed you would not come."

"You are too bold, monsieur," she said. "I happened to be passing, and there you were."

He glanced left and right; there were, as usual, few passersby on the street. But there were some people. "Will you sit down for a moment?"

"I should like to." She seated herself.

"A glass of wine?"

"Thank you, but no."

"Ah." He sat opposite her, picked up his own glass, looked at it, and set it down again. "You are more beautiful than ever."

"Monsieur," she said, uneasily.

"I cannot help but speak my mind, Catherine. It is very rarely given to a man to see a woman, and know there can be no other in the world for him."

"Really, monsieur, I have stayed too long. I must be returning home."

"Catherine." He held her hand as she would have risen. "Say you will pose for me."

"Well, I . . . I really cannot say. I will have to ask my stepmother. She does not approve of you, you know. I had to press very hard for permission to come out today." She bit her lip; she had not meant to say that.

"But you obtained your permission, eventually," he said. "Catherine, you can, if you wish. Do you wish to?"

"Well, I . . . I have never posed for anyone before."

"It is a simple matter, really. You merely sit very still, at least until I have made a sketch. Then I just need you there, for the inspiration of your smile, to be sure I catch your colour, your beauty."

Catherine discovered her heart was pounding. "Here?"

"Oh, no. That would arouse too much curiosity. It would have to be somewhere private."

"Oh. No, I could not . . ."

"Private, and yet public," he said. "I would not ask you to compromise yourself. The Bois de Boulogne. There is the perfect setting."

"The Bois de Boulogne," she whispered.

"Tomorrow, at one o'clock. You will ride?"

"Well, of course. If . . . if I went to the Bois, I would ride."

"Then I shall find you. Tomorrow, at one. Say you will be there."

Catherine stood up. "I shall ask Madeleine."

50

But Madeleine need never know. Catherine gazed at herself in her mirror, admired the calmness of her features, adjusted her beaver. Her habit was dark blue and between its collar and the black hat her hair lay like a scarf. Madeleine would never know, unless she told her. Unless she brought home the completed portrait.

She was excited. But then, she had suddenly become perpetually excited. Life had taken on a dimension she had not supposed possible at Madame St. Amant's. She had dominated the soirée. She had flirted with Baron Ricimer. Supposing the Baron ever indulged in anything as innocent as a flirtation. So she was not really what he wanted. He had given her a glimpse of that adult world into which she was moving.

And she possessed her own, secret admirer. Madeleine was aghast. But Madeleine valued a man by what he seemed, how he dressed, what he might have paid for his carriage, the size of his home. Was that because she regarded all men as intrinsically worthless, placed on earth for the benefit of women? No doubt that was uncharitable. Madeleine had been married, to a handsome and dashing cavalry officer. She had loved, then. It was best to suppose that she still loved, a memory. She and Jackson Scott had come together, he a widower looking for a beautiful housekeeper, she a widow, looking for a certain security. Neither could be blamed for no longer feeling the hot flush of passion for the other. Certainly *she* was not going to blame them.

But how odd that Madeleine could not remember that passion, as it might affect others. Why, David Mulawer, had he been born fifty years ago, might well have been a member of the Girondins. And was, indeed, a Polish revolutionary, at least in the eyes of the Tsars. What a disturbing thought. But what an exciting one, as well.

And a thought which meant what, to her? How could a man like David Mulawer possibly measure up to a man like Baron Ricimer? Save that David would wish to give, and give, and give, where Ricimer would seek only to take. Her instincts warned her of that.

51

Henri the groom saw her safely mounted, and she walked her horse through the streets, enjoying the spring sunshine, enjoying the expression on Madeleine's face, as she had peered from the window at her stepdaughter. Oh, she was being very wicked, taking such advantage of Madeleine's unexpected confidence. But how *exciting* it all was.

She left the street, walked beneath trees. Midday was not the most popular time for riding in the wood, and the bridle paths were empty. And sleepily damp. She emerged on to an open meadow, looking right and left, wondering if he would recognise her, wishing to raise her hat so that he might discover the sheen of her white hair, but afraid to disturb the careful arrangement. And watched a very old grey mare coming towards her, David on her back. She smiled. He must have hired the very last animal left in Paris. Her smile died. Because he could afford nothing better. That had not occurred to her before. But what was he sacrificing, in meeting her here?

"Catherine." He reached for her hands, but her horse sidestepped away from the mare.

"We'd best dismount." She dropped to the ground, and he followed her example. They tethered the horses to a clump of bushes, where there was grass for them to munch. His shoulder brushed against hers, and his haversack, no doubt containing his sketching materials, swung against her thigh. Her heart pounded. Because they were alone, to all intents and purposes. Madeleine would be furious. And Seraphine? Seraphine would be green with jealousy.

Then what of Catherine? She had no idea what was going to happen.

He held her gloved hands. "I wondered if you would come."

"I said I would try. What would you like me to do?"

He hesitated, and she realised she might have made a mistake, and flushed. Which caused him to smile.

"I would like you to look beautiful, Catherine, which is the simplest of all tasks, for you. But you must sit

52

. . ." He looked around, pointed. "There. Beneath that tree. Wait, I will spread my cloak for you."

He hurried in front of her, taking off his shabby greatcoat as he did so, spread it on the ground beneath two roots of the great elm.

"This is a perfect setting."

Catherine sat down, drawing her legs beneath her, allowing the skirt of her riding habit to settle about her.

"Enchanting," he said. "Could you take off your hat?"

"Of course." She removed her beaver, laid it on the ground.

"That is splendid," he said, and suddenly became very efficient, kneeling in front of her, sketch book open on his knee, while he made rapid strokes. "Just splendid," he said, half to himself, and raised his head. "Would you like to talk?"

"Would you like me to?"

"I should adore you to. And it will keep your face relaxed. This is important. I wish to catch that smile. Say something which will make you smile."

"I have no idea how to make myself smile," she protested, and found that she was, while she watched in fascination his pencil rippling across the paper. She was dying to see what he had done, how he had made her look, but she didn't want to appear too inquisitive, so she looked away at the great trees and the bridle paths, at the small meadow across which they had walked their horses, at the rippling stream, and at a group of men who had suddenly appeared on the edge of the trees, not fifty yards away.

She regarded them with only mild curiosity at first, for they were perfectly well dressed, better dressed than David, indeed, almost dandies, each with a cane and a carefully askew beaver, all talking, and somewhat red faced. Clearly they had dined far too well, and were attempting to aid their digestions by walking. But she frowned as she saw them pointing in their direction, and then begin to cross the meadow.

"No, no," David said. "You must not frown. Although

you are twice as lovely when you frown. But that is for a different portrait."

"We are to be interrupted," she said.

He turned his head, to glance at the young men, and then turned his entire body, on his knees. "*Jeunesse dorée*," he muttered.

Catherine rose to her knees. She had heard, often enough, of those young men who called themselves the Gilded Youth, sons and grandsons of those aristocrats murdered during the Revolution, who, even thirteen years after the Restoration, still roamed the streets of Paris seeking to execute their vengeance on anyone they suspected of republican sympathies. But she had never seen any of them.

"How do you know?"

"I know," David muttered. "Catherine, run for your horse."

She frowned at him. "Run from *them*? Why should I?" In any event they were far too close.

David got up, and she followed his example.

"The Pole," one of the men shouted. " 'Tis the Pole, lads."

"And his mistress," shouted another.

"We'll strip them," yelled a third.

"And tie them together. There'll be sport," shouted a fourth.

Catherine discovered she was panting, and her back was pressed against her tree. She was afraid. She had never been this afraid in her life before. The anxiety she had felt when alone with Madame Laurens had been nothing to this.

David looked over his shoulder. She was amazed to find that his eyes were dancing, although his expression was tight. Or perhaps hard would be a better word, she thought. She had never supposed he could look hard.

"Run," he said. "Please. I cannot fight them unless I know you are safe."

"You cannot fight four men in any event."

He smiled, a strange, almost demoniac widening of his mouth. "I shall certainly try. Please run."

The four men were very close, spreading now, as if able to hear what they were saying. Catherine inhaled, gathered her skirts in both hands, and left the safety of the tree, stumbling across the meadow in the direction of the woods, hoping to be able to double back and gain her horse. Behind her there came a whoop, followed by a startled exclamation. She checked, and looked over her shoulder. David had broken off a stout branch from the tree—she had never suspected he was so strong—and had laid about him so vigorously as to send his first attacker crashing to the ground. But the other two had closed with him, and as she watched he also fell over, taking his assailants with him.

The other two. Her heart seemed to constrict as she saw the fourth man, who had dodged round the tree, running towards her. She gasped for breath, ran for the trees again, and heard his breathing. She was not going to escape. She was going to have to fight for her own safety.

She stopped, and turned, releasing her skirts and trying to control her breathing, and saw David. He had rid himself of his other enemies and was coming towards them.

"David," she screamed.

The man had also checked, grinning at her. Now he turned in consternation, looked past David to where his friends were just sitting up, scratching their heads, and then took to his heels himself.

"Come on." David grasped her arm, hurried her into the trees. He had lost his hat, and had not had the time to pick up his cloak.

"Your things," she panted.

"They were worn out, anyway." He paused, to look over his shoulder; they were surrounded by trees and bushes, and the meadow was only just visible. There was no sign of pursuit. "I seem to have discouraged them."

"You were magnificent."

"I was a scoundrel to have endangered you in the first place. I've lost my sketch book as well."

"But . . . how did you escape three of them?"

He winked at her. "They are not as fearsome as they

appear. And I was a soldier in Poland, before we were defeated by the Russians and I had to flee. I think that is why they hate me."

"You know them?"

"I have encountered them before. And I shall again, I imagine."

"Oh, but . . ."

"I shall survive." He took her hands. "It is you I worry about. To think that he might have caught you, might have touched you . . ."

"He didn't, thanks to you."

"Then you forgive me?"

"Of course I do." She watched his face coming closer, and realised he was about to kiss her. She had never been kissed before. She did not know what to do, could only wait, for the touch of his lips on hers, a gentle touch, quickly withdrawn, leaving her with scorching cheeks. "Monsieur," she mumbled.

"You'll pose for me again, Catherine. Say that you will."

"Well . . ." She licked her lips, seeking for his taste and finding none. And looked over her shoulder. She had been the cause of his losing his sketchbook, and his cloak and hat. "We shall have to fetch our horses," she said.

They crossed the river and entered a maze of dingy little streets, with towering houses, three and four storeys high, leaning towards each other and almost seeming to touch above their heads. The air was heavy with garlic and the smell of new made bread, the streets were equally crowded, with old moustaches, who sat outside the cafés and drank their wine; with stout, vigorous women proceeding about their business; with children, playing interminable games; and from time to time, with young men like David, who called out a greeting and raised their hats to his beautiful companion.

"It is cheap, down here," he explained.

"It is fascinating," she said, uncertain whether or not she was lying.

He reined the mare outside a somewhat more decrepit building than the rest. The ground floor was a café, and a young man sat at the table outside, with a single glass of wine. Hastily he got to his feet. "David? You were . . ." He checked himself, flushed, and removed his hat. "Mademoiselle."

David assisted Catherine from her saddle. "Tether these for me, will you, Philippe."

"Of course. The wood was not suitable?"

Catherine smiled at him. "It became crowded, monsieur."

"And now you are here. Well . . ." He took her hand, kissed her glove. "How bright Paris has suddenly become."

"We have work to do," David said, very brisk. "You'll not interrupt us, Philippe."

"Of course not." Philippe collected the two reins. "I look forward to seeing the finished result." Once again he squeezed Catherine's gloved hand. "He is a fortunate fellow, mademoiselle. To have such a subject."

David urged her inside, where an elderly man leaned on the counter. "Monsieur."

"Monsieur." The black eyes lazily roamed over Catherine, and she felt herself flushing.

"I . . . I am to pose."

"Indeed, mademoiselle." He poured himself another glass of wine, and Catherine hurried behind David, and up a flight of stairs. There was dust or sheer dirt everywhere, and the place smelt stale. She felt a pang of horror at the thought of living all of one's life in such surroundings, and had the strangest thought, of what the Baron would make of it. But that was disloyal, when in the company of David.

As if she had any reason to feel loyal to him in any event. He had saved her from a most unpleasant experience, but it was he who had involved her in the risk in the first place. And having saved her, he had kissed her, the first man ever to do so, save Papa, on the lips. Had that not been taking advantage of the situation? She should not be here at all. It was very wrong of her. And what Madeleine would say . . .

David paused on the third landing, opened a door, allowed her into a surprisingly large room. Not that there was much space. There were two beds, close together in the top corner, and a washstand with basin and ewer, and near by a curtained alcove. But the entire rest of the room was taken up with canvases, scattered against the walls and on the floors, and dominated by the two easels near the single large window.

David closed the door. "I share it with Philippe. But he will not disturb us."

"Not . . ." She bit her lip, stood in the centre of the room, while David hastily stuffed some dirty shirts out of sight.

"I had not expected to bring you back here today, or I should have tidied."

"But you did expect to bring me back here one day," she said.

"Well . . . I can only complete the portrait here. Let me get you a chair."

There was one chair in the room, and this he hastily placed for her, where the light was best. "I'll get my pencils."

Catherine watched him burrowing into another pile of rubbish. He really did seem anxious to sketch her, and nothing more. She was being foolishly apprehensive. "Would you like me to take off my coat?"

"If you could. And your hat. I'm afraid there is no fire, but the sun will soon be on the glass, and it warms it up very quickly."

Catherine removed her hat, and then her cloak, hesitated, and as there was nowhere else, laid them on the floor by the door. And gazed at some more canvases. One in particular . . . she frowned, pulled it out, and gasped in horror. The young woman was naked, and sat in the same chair he had just offered to her, one knee delicately crossed above the other, elbow on the knee, chin on the elbow. She was not pretty, but she was certainly buxom. "Oh, Lord." She hastily straightened.

David stood at her elbow. "That is Martine. She poses for us whenever she needs money." He smiled. "And whenever we have sufficient money to pay her. Or at least a bottle of wine."

Catherine slowly backed across the room. "You mean . . . she undresses here, in front of you?"

"Well of course. One could not imagine Martine."

"Oh, Lord." Catherine realised that the concierge must have assumed she was coming here for the same purpose. She stooped to regain her coat. "I really must be going."

He held her shoulders, raised her to her feet. "I have not asked you to undress for me, Catherine. Nor would I, unless you were my wife. If such a happy dream could ever come about."

She turned her head, discovered his face only inches away, tried to wriggle, and was brought close. "I love you," he said. "But you know that. I wrote it in my letter. I love you, Catherine. And you must love me, or you would not be here at all."

"Monsieur," she whispered, tried to push against him, and felt herself pressed even closer, while his lips were coming closer too, and her own parting, and a moment later his tongue touched hers.

She didn't want to move. She thought she could stay there forever, in his arms. She was quite surprised when he released her. Her eyes opened, and she stared at him. His cheeks had gone very red, and he retreated even farther.

"I apologize. I . . ." He made a gesture with his hands, as of a man unable to control his emotions. "I did not mean to offend you."

"You did not offend me."

"But you will think I brought you up here for that purpose."

"I'd not think that of you, David. And *I* must apologise, for seeking to leave. I . . . I suppose I never realised that girls would pose like that."

He came forward again, took her hands. "Then you'll stay?"

She gazed at him. Oh, Lord, she thought. If I stay, I will never want to leave again. And I will . . . what were all those whispered tales Seraphine had told her, which had almost made her hair stand on end? She had supposed Seraphine was making them up, fantasies to accompany her own midnight passions. But David . . . to have him touch her, as Laurens had wished to do, as Seraphine had suggested she do to herself . . . "Oh, Lord," she said.

"Catherine?"

"Oh, David," she said, and found she was sitting, on the straight chair while he knelt at her side.

"You *are* offended."

"No. I am frightened."

"Of me?"

"Of myself."

He smiled, kissed her hands; without her noticing it he had drawn off her gloves. "I will take that as a compliment. Oh, Cathy, Cathy, we shall be so happy."

She frowned at him. "When?"

"When I ask your father for your hand."

Her frown deepened, and then cleared in a laugh. "Papa would never agree. Besides . . ." The moment of passion was past, and she was beginning to think again. He kissed beautifully. At least, she thought so. But was that not entirely because she had never been kissed like that before? And for the rest . . . she looked from left to right.

"Oh, but I shall not live in this garret for the rest of my life. Cathy, Cathy, I have talent. I know I have talent. I need just to meet the right people, show them my canvases . . . perhaps your stepmother could arrange it for me."

She withdrew her hand. "Is *that* your reason for bringing me here?" He really was no older than herself. As to talent, she could not tell. Besides, if he proposed to paint naked girls, how could he marry anybody? And when she compared him, his stuttering advances, his quick embarrassment, his poverty, with someone like the Baron Ricimer . . .

60

"Of course it isn't." He regained her hands, kissed them again. "I brought you here to paint you. Because it is your portrait which will make me famous. I love you, Cathy. And if I can paint my love for you into the portrait, why, it will be hung in the Louvre."

"Well," she said. "I'm not sure I wish to be stared at by every visitor to Paris."

She was being absurd, and she knew it. But the fact was she was more embarrassed than she would admit, even to herself. He was too forward, far too pushing, far too much in a hurry, and he was not even of her own social class, really. He was poor, and desperate, and he himself admitted he had been a revolutionary soldier . . . and he fought so gallantly and kissed so delightfully. But he simply could not take her so very much for granted.

"All right," he said. "Then we'll hang the painting over our bed. So no one can see it except us."

"*Monsieur,*" she said, and stood up. "This conversation is becoming improper."

"But I love you." He still held her hands.

"And anyway," she pointed out, "if you do that, then you will never become famous, and you will never be able to support me, and Papa will never give his consent."

"Damn his consent. It is *your* consent I wish, Cathy."

"Mine?" How simple, she thought, just to say yes, and know that I am his, for the rest of my life. What a warming feeling that would be. What a delicious feeling that would be. Because, if he kissed so splendidly, what else might he not do as splendidly. And what a disturbing thought, when alone with a man in his bedroom. "I really could not possibly think of it." She allowed her tone to soften. "At the moment." She escaped his grip, crossed the room and picked up her hat and coat. "I must be going, monsieur. I have stayed out far too long as it is."

"But you'll pose for me again, Catherine. Say that you will."

She couldn't make up her mind. Oh, how she wanted to. Just as she wanted him to kiss her again. But not now. At their next meeting, whenever that might be.

And then she remembered Ricimer. "I cannot, for a fortnight."

"A fortnight?" he cried.

"My stepmother and I are going on a visit to the country."

"Tell me where," he begged. "I will surely manage to follow."

"You are far too bold, monsieur," she protested, although she could not stop herself smiling. "Anyway, it is impossible, and thus it is better for you not to know. I am merely telling you at all because I would not have you sitting out in the cold to no purpose. We shall be back in Paris at the beginning of April."

"And I must wait until then," he said. "Catherine . . ." His grip tightened. "At least give me some token, to remember you by, and to convince me you do wish to come back to me."

"Come back to you, monsieur?" *Of course I do*, she thought. But if she admitted it, he would kiss her again. "Why, I mean to come back to Paris, certainly."

"Oh, Catherine, Catherine. You are the cruellest of women."

"The Ice Maiden, you called me," she pointed out. "But really, monsieur, I do not mean to be. You are forgetting that this is only the third occasion on which we have met. And anyway, I have no token."

"Your glove."

"My glove? Why, monsieur . . ."

"You may tell your stepmother that you lost it. And it is only a short ride back to your house. Your glove, my dearest Catherine, else I will surely throw myself in the Seine."

Like that woman, she thought, *Madeleine was telling about*. Perhaps she had been, after all, just disappointed in love. It could happen easily with a man like Kurt Ricimer. But she was already pulling at the fingers to the glove. It could happen equally easily with a man like David Mulawer. Who would have supposed him capable of defeating four ruffians? Or of kissing her so tenderly.

But she had never been kissed before; perhaps all men were as tender.

"I really do not know what to say." She placed the glove in his hand.

"You have said sufficient." He seized her hand, kissed it, pressed it between his own. "I shall be at my table from April first."

"The day of fools," she pointed out. "Are you sure you are not studying to become one, monsieur?"

"Only you can make me that, Catherine," he said. "Only you."

"Really, Catherine my darling," Madeleine remarked, for the seventh time. "I had not expected you to be so forward, or I should never have agreed. Those were very expensive gloves."

"But he will give it back to me," Catherine protested, as usual. "When next we meet."

She had not told her stepmother what had happened, of course, save for losing her glove; Madeleine would have been horrified. While what Papa might say did not bear consideration.

She was unsure of her own reactions, now that she was away from Paris. David had kissed her. She doubted she would ever forget that. And he had fought for her, one against four, and successfully. She would *never* forget that. And yet . . .

"Ha," Madeleine remarked. "Supposing you do meet again. Supposing you obtain my permission again. Jean-Pierre. Jean-Pierre. Stop biting your nails. Put your gloves back on."

Jean-Pierre made a face, and pulled his gloves over his fingers.

"I am sure you will give me your permission," Catherine said. "As you are such a good and kind stepmother."

Madeleine glared at her for a moment, then looked out the window of the berline at the snow-covered countryside. "I certainly study to be," she agreed. "But I hope you will not endeavour to take advantage of my good nature. Oh, dear, dear, me. We seem to have been driving forever. I do hope we reach the château before dark."

"It is because of the snow, Mama," Jean-Pierre pointed out. "The coach is travelling very slowly."

They did seem to have been travelling forever, Catherine thought; this was their second day on the road. But she really did not care. She was in no hurry to reach the château, after which, if Madeleine's plans came to fruition, she was apparently to spend the next fortnight in Jean-Pierre's company, which was not a very exciting prospect, even supposing he appeared to like her, and he did not.

While, if Madeleine's plans did *not* come to fruition, or if she was wrong in her estimate of the situation, she might well have to endure the attentions of the Baron.

Could she be wrong? She stole a glance at her step-mother, who was continuing to look out the window. Certainly she had a beautiful profile, and from this side the mole beside her mouth was not visible. And she was certainly voluptuous enough . . . but so was she, and she was young, and she was beautiful from any angle. She started, guiltily, and closed her eyes. Madame St. Amant's words came back to her. But surely she was entitled to be proud of her looks, even if of course she should constantly remind herself that it was her brain which mattered.

But what mattered with a man like Ricimer? Madeleine thought it was experience. Yet he had looked at her in the bedroom, she was sure of that.

Oh, Lord, she thought, and opened her eyes in alarm. She had forgotten about that. How on earth could she face a man who had watched her undress, had watched her parading a bedroom, naked. Why, she'd be unable to speak. And when he looked at her, in any event seeming to be undressing her with his eyes, oh Lord.

She closed her eyes again, braced herself against the bouncing of the carriage. They had entered a wood, and the road, already bad, had apparently become a mass of potholes. Well, she would just have to face it out. Perhaps she could repel him by hinting that she understood his little game. Supposing she *was* able to speak.

Supposing she was right. Because why look at her if he really wanted Madeleine? But perhaps it was all a mistake. Perhaps Madeleine had been the one intended to fall into the moat. He would have been waiting there all the time, hiding in his secret place, looking into the room. Then he might have received quite a shock. Quite a disappointment.

But then, supposing he had *not* been disappointed? Supposing Madeleine was right, and he had wanted a liaison with her, and planned for it, until the moment he had seen her stepdaughter, when all his plans would have changed.

She felt quite sick with excitement. And with fear as well. Not only of Ricimer. What would Madeleine say, what would Madeleine *do,* were she to discover that her own stepdaughter was preferred to her?

But what should she *do*, were Ricimer to make advances? For a moment she wished herself back in the safe confinement of Madame St. Amant's Academy, with Seraphine to confide in and only Laurens to fear.

And only David to think of. Dear, sweet David, who clearly was in love with her—madly, desperately, the way a man should be in love with a woman. And the woman? She really did not know what she felt about him, truly. She looked forward to seeing him again. She hoped they would be able to see a lot more of each other in the coming months. She had already formed the plan of using her influence over Madeleine to have him invited to a soirée no matter what.

But more than that? She really did not know.

"My God, this road," Madeleine complained; she rose a good six inches in the air as the coach entered a particularly deep rut and emerged again with a shudder. "I swear I shall be quite seasick, any moment. Whatever . . ." Her head twisted, for having performed its gyration, the coach was now dragging to a halt. "Roll down the window, Jean-Pierre. Find out what is the matter."

Jean-Pierre obeyed, pushed his head into the evening air, for it was getting quite dark. "Henri?" he called. "What is the matter, Henri?"

"A tree is down, Master Jean. Right across the road. Must be the frost. I'll see to it."

"I'll help you," Jean-Pierre volunteered, opening the door and jumping down.

"Be careful, do," Madeleine shouted. "Don't slip on the snow. Trees down," she grumbled. "Really. Oh, the careless boy has not latched the door. Pull it close, Catherine, there's a darling."

Catherine obediently leaned forward to secure the door, and to her utter amazement had her wrist seized so that she was jerked right out of the coach, to go flying through the air and land on her hands and knees in the snow, while ballooning through her ears there came the crack of a pistol shot.

Catherine sank into the snow, caught up in the cloying cold, until the freezing white powder actually threatened her nostrils. And as with her plunge into the icy waters of Ricimer's moat, she was too confounded to scream or to utter a sound.

But it was essential to get her head free of the snow, or she would likely suffocate, she thought. She pushed down, and discovered to her horror that she could find nothing solid; she had landed in the ditch bordering the road in which the snow had been accumulating all winter. *Oh, Lord,* she thought desperately. *What a place to die, and at what a time, when life was just promising to become exciting.*

Her shoulders were grasped, and she was pulled upwards. The snow fell away from her nose, and she was able to lick her lips clear and blink her eyes, and listen to Madeleine, screaming, "My God. Highwaymen."

And to Jean-Pierre, shouting. "Let me go. Let me go."

She supposed she should join in the attempts to save themselves from being robbed, and endeavoured to turn, at least to see who was holding her, when a sack was dropped over her head. As the evening disappeared into blackness, the fingers holding her shoulders released her, while others were against her breasts, pulling the sack tight and apparently securing it with a cord.

66

She remembered how David had coped with *his* four assailants. Oh, to have David here now.

Desperately she kicked and struggled as best she could and was rewarded with a grunt from behind her and a laughed comment from the men in front of her. But she did not understand what they were saying.

She attempted to scream, but instead sucked the bag against her mouth and nose until she was afraid she would choke. Desperately she blew it away again, and felt herself being lifted from the ground. One man held her shoulders, digging his fingers right through the sacking to grip her flesh, and the other was holding her ankles. *Oh, the wretch.* Because she could feel the night air on her legs, seeping through her stockings, and therefore her skirts must have fallen back to at least her knees. To wriggle might be to send the skirts higher yet. She became even more desperate to lie still to prevent that ultimate humiliation, and felt herself being lifted, and then placed with some care on wooden boards. Her hands were pulled behind her, and secured, while the man who had held her ankles tied them together with another length of cord.

Then they were gone, and she could think again, and listen. Madeleine had stopped screaming, although there was an ominous gurgling sound. And Jean-Pierre had stopped shouting as well. While poor Henri had not uttered a word. He must have been the target of the pistol.

But whatever could the men want? Highwaymen were certainly an occasional hazard in lonely country districts, but kidnapping . . . *They must be mad,* she thought. Papa was comfortably off, but he was not a wealthy man. There would be no ransom to be gained for her, or for Madeleine. Well, then . . . a body was placed beside her on the boards, and the entire structure moved. So she was in a cart of some sort. No, a wagon, because the bite of the night air was dulled.

She rolled to her left, against the body, and it moved responsively.

"Catherine?" Madeleine whispered. "Is that you? Oh, say it is you, my darling."

"It is, Madeleine. Are you all right?"

"One of the wretches struck me," Madeleine said. "On the face. I declare I am going to have a bruise. But what of you?"

"They have not harmed me," Catherine said. "Beyond tying me up."

"Yet," Madeleine said, and gave half a sob. "But Jean-Pierre. My baby. Jean-Pierre . . ."

Another body was placed beside Catherine.

"Jean-Pierre?" she whispered.

"Cathy? Where is Mama?"

"I am here, you silly boy. Jean-Pierre. Jean-Pierre. Are you all right? Jean-Pierre, speak to me."

"I am all right, Mama. But what is happening?"

"You're going on a journey," said a strange voice, and speaking with a foreign accent. "All of you. And we don't want any noise, so you must lie quiet, eh? Or there'll be a gag."

"Now, you listen to me," Madeleine said. "You will all be hanged for this. I am the wife of Colonel Jackson Scott of the United States Embassy, and these are my children. We are on our way to visit Baron Ricimer, and when he discovers what has happened . . ."

"Be quiet, old woman," said the voice. "I was told to cut your throat if you gave trouble. It is the young ones we want. Be quiet."

The wagon started to move, jolting them from right to left as its wheels rumbled in and out of the ruts. But at least the resulting creaking and groaning gave them a sort of privacy.

"Madeleine?" Catherine whispered. "Madeleine, are you all right?"

Madeleine moved against her, and gave another little gasp.

"What did he do to you, Madeleine?"

"He hit me," Madeleine said. "The wretch hit me, in the stomach. My God."

"Mama?" Jean-Pierre asked. "What did he mean, when he said they wanted just Cathy and me?"

"What did he mean? Oh, my God," Madeleine said. "Oh, my God."

Catherine's head was banging with every bounce of the wagon. But the resulting pain seemed as nothing beside the sudden rush of feeling careering through her chest and into her brain. *Just the young ones. Then they were not being kidnapped for ransom. They were being kidnapped for something to do with their youth, and that led into unimaginable realms of horror, which had her remembering Laurens, had her remembering the first night she slept at Madame St. Amant's, when the other girls had all got into her bed to pull and prod her in the most intimate places, had her remembering standing before the fire in Madame Despards' bedchamber, and sensing she was not alone.*

Experience would take her no further. Experience could only attempt to remember what Seraphine had told her in their midnight whispers, of her summer lover and what he had done to her. She had not believed half of it. Seraphine was a girl who every night stroked herself to sleep, and imagined the most ghastly adventures while doing it.

But suddenly every word Seraphine had said seemed to be frighteningly true.

She felt tears trickling down her cheeks even as the sack over her head grew more and more stuffy and intolerable, and the jolting of the wagon more and more uncomfortable. She wanted to cry her misery to the world. But she did not want that strange voice to come back into the wagon, and perhaps hit *her* in the stomach. She wanted to faint, and perhaps wake up and find this had all been a dreadful nightmare, from eating too much cheese, perhaps, and that Papa would be standing at her bedside in his uniform looking so smart and so military, and so reassuring.

And perhaps she did sleep, or at least doze, for when she recovered her senses the rumble had become continuous while the jolting had lessened; the wagon was crossing cobbles. A few minutes later it came to a halt, and the flap at the back was raised. The breeze swept in like an icy hand, rippling her skirts, getting underneath and freezing her legs, even chilling her body. The man was there again as well. She could smell him, and suddenly Madeleine gave a faint shriek.

"What was that, Madeleine?" she asked.

"Tell them, old woman," the man said. "Tell them what that was."

Madeleine gasped. "You . . . he stuck me with a knife point."

"Mama?" Jean-Pierre wailed, and was silenced with a slap.

"That's just to warn you," the man said. "We're going for a walk. But if one of you makes a sound, or does anything I don't like, I'm going to drive this knife right through your mother's ribs."

Catherine felt his hands on her legs. *Oh, the wretch. Was it going to happen now?* It? She still had no idea what *it* would be like, what *it* would entail, how *it* would leave her, afterwards. But he was only cutting the cord binding her ankles together. She was able to move her legs, at last. Blessed relief. Then she remembered he was still there, and hastily clamped her knees together.

But now he was holding her shoulders, dragging her into a sitting position.

"Out," he commanded. "Move."

She obeyed, terrified he would lose patience and hit her, and felt her legs go over the back of the wagon. Once again her skirts were riding up, and so she thrust herself forward, bracing her muscles for a fall, and instead landing on the ground only a couple of feet away, so heavily that she nearly fell, and the man had to catch her arm.

"Now walk," he said. "This way."

Cautiously she stepped forward, discovering that the ground was in fact stone. And now the breeze had increased, and was whistling around her head and tugging the sack against her face.

"This way," the man repeated, and she was pulled to the left to find her feet on slatted wood, sloping upwards. Now she knew where she was going—up the gangway of a vessel. And if they were in a harbour then they were about to put to sea. About to be taken to sea. *Oh, Lord,* she thought. *Oh, Lord. What would happen after that?*

"Careful now," said another voice, but also speaking in a foreign accent. Hands gripped her elbows, and she was brought to a halt, then lifted from the top of the gangway and placed on the deck. One of the hands remained holding her arm, leading her forward.

"Step over," a voice commanded, and she raised first one foot and then the other, and blessed relief, stepped out of the wind, and was instead surrounded by the scents and odours of a ship, tar and rope and timber and brine.

"There's a ladder," the man commanded. He apparently went before her, because her foot slipped on the second step and she fell forward, to be caught in his arms. "That'll do," he decided, and swung her from the ladder to set her on another deck. She listened to a knock, and then to a door opening, and was led into a cabin, she supposed. Fingers were now pulling at the cord securing the sacking, and a moment later it was lifted over her head to cause her first of all to blink in the sudden glare, as there were several lanterns in the cabin, and secondly to stare in horror at the man who was facing her. For it was Baron Ricimer.

Catherine could only stare at him amazed. He was very strangely dressed, for in place of the coat and trousers of a European he wore a white woolen cloak, beautifully embroidered with gold coloured silk thread, while over this was a loose cape with a cowl that encompassed even his head, to conceal his hair, and leave only his face and neck exposed. The garment was held in place by a gilt embroidered band around his forehead, and the cloak by a heavy leather belt around his waist. She could not doubt the belt was usually stuck with weapons.

And he was speaking to the man who had brought her in, but in the foreign tongue her captors had earlier used among themselves. Then he glanced at her, and smiled, at the same time flicking his fingers. The sailor left the cabin. And it was a most elegant cabin, the entire width of the ship and in the very stern, for behind Ricimer there were the after windows, clouded with mist. The furnishings were exquisite. Two beds, one against each side, were covered with a cloth of gold spread; cloth of gold also covered the three very comfortable chairs, while the desk before which she had been placed was richly carved cedar that gave off a most delightful odour to mingle with the other delightful perfumes filling the room.

Ricimer got up. "My people assure me you have not been harmed, Catherine," he said. "As indeed I had given strict instructions. Can you therefore have lost the use of your tongue?"

Catherine licked her lips. Her mind seemed separated from her body, hovering above it, waiting, as indeed her body was waiting, for whatever would happen next. "I do not understand," she said.

Ricimer came round the desk and stood beside her. "It is called a *burnous*," he explained, touching his cape. "And my robe is a *gandoura*, by far the most comfortable of garments. See, it leaves the arms free, and yet provides ample warmth."

The wool brushed her arm. She inhaled, and made to step away.

"You will soon wear similar garments," he said. "Although yours will undoubtedly be more elegant. Will you not sit down?"

She glanced at him, then away again. She had no wish to meet those eyes. "No," she said. "Why am I here? Why were we assaulted on the road? Why . . ."

Ricimer was looking past her, as there came another knock on the door. "Why, Madame Scott," he said. "I am so very pleased you managed to survive your ordeal."

"Madeleine." Catherine turned to take her stepmother in her arms. Jean-Pierre stood beside her, blinking in the light, guarded by three sailors who waited patiently against the bulkhead. And now Catherine saw to her amazement that they were swarthy, dark-eyed men, possibly Frenchmen from the far south but far more likely Arabs.

"Ricimer?" Madeleine's voice rose an octave. The left side of her chin was discoloured by the blow she had received. "Ricimer?"

The Baron moved behind the desk, sat down. "I did invite you to visit, madame."

"You . . . to be assaulted? To have my driver murdered? To be threatened with a knife? To be brutally kicked in the stomach? Why, you . . ."

Ricimer cocked his head, and Madeleine's voice died. The ship was moving, and from above them there came the creak of a windlass and a series of shouted orders.

"My God," Madeleine shouted. "Let us out! Put us ashore . . ." She turned, and faced the three sailors.

"You are well on the way to becoming a nuisance, madame," Ricimer said. "Oh, you are a beautiful woman, and I have no doubt a fascinating one. I look forward to amusing myself with you on the voyage . . ."

Madeleine turned back to him. "Amusing yourself?" she whispered.

"Voyage?" Jean-Pierre whispered.

"But should you become intolerable," Ricimer continued, "I will have not the slightest reluctance to tie you in a sack and throw you over the side."

Catherine sat down. Her knees suddenly would no longer support her. And apparently Madeleine felt the same, because she sank into the other chair, her mouth opening and shutting grotesquely. Jean-Pierre clung to the back of her chair.

"Whereas," Ricimer said, leaning forward and placing his elbows on the desk, "should you be able to come to terms with your present position, I think I may be able to secure your survival into a ripe old age. As Catherine's slave, I imagine. Would that not be nice?"

Madeleine seemed incapable of speech.

"As . . . as my *slave*?" Catherine whispered.

"Indeed, my lady," Ricimer said. "You are going to possess a great number of slaves in the course of time, but it will surely be an advantage to have near you someone you know so well. Believe me, while I have no doubt at all that your future life will be filled with incident, it will also contain many long and lonely hours. The company of your stepmother may prove an inestimable boon. Presuming you wish her, of course. If you do not, you have but to say, and I will have her disposed of."

I was right after all, she thought. *He wants me for him-*

self. Her heart seemed to swell until she thought it would explode. All that power, all that stength, all that tremendous, forceful masculinity, wanted her, for himself. He wanted to marry her. "You mean to marry me," she whispered, without meaning to.

Ricimer's smile was sad. "Alas, my lady, I would indeed wish to marry you, were I my own master. But were I that, I would surely not have needed to abduct you to plight my troth. No, no, my beautiful girl, I work for one much greater than myself, or than you, for that matter. I act now in the interests of my master, may his shadow never grow less. The bed for which you are destined is that of His Highness the Agha Hussein bin Hassan, Dey of Algiers."

Chapter 3

"PROVIDING of course," Ricimer said, still smiling at her, "that you are indeed as exquisite as you seem."

Madeleine made a slight sound which might have been described as a groan. Catherine dared not look at her. She dared not look anywhere, except at the smiling face in front of her. She could only think, *I am dreaming. This has got to be a dream.*

"But we need be in no hurry about that," Ricimer said. "As I am perfectly confident. And His Highness will be pleased. It was his privilege to spend some time in Paris when he was a young man. As he is now somewhat elderly, this was forty years ago, you understand, when indeed, His Late Majesty King Louis the Sixteenth was still on the throne. But His Highness was delighted with everything French, and especially, with French women. They are his especial joy. It is therefore my duty, as His Highness's European agent, to keep a look out for young women of suitable birth, suitable condition, and above all suitable beauty, to take their places in his *harem*."

"You . . . you monster," Madeleine whispered. "You pimp."

Ricimer continued to smile, though his eyes were cold. "Call it what you will, madame, though if I were you, I should not use that word to me again. The skin of a prospective *odalik* is inviolate, but the skin of a prospective slave is meant for mutilation."

Madeleine stared at him as if he were a snake.

"I am not French," Catherine whispered. "You have made a mistake. I am not French."

"Which is one reason why you are here, Mademoiselle. His Highness's last French acquisition, Mademoiselle Cavaigny . . . you remember Mademoiselle Cavaigny, madame? . . . did not turn out as successfully as we might have hoped. But you, my dear child, not only are you beautiful, and French-educated, but you are an American. We of Algiers have a long score to settle with the Americans. In the last twenty-five years they have not only bombarded our city, they have even had the temerity to land an expeditionary force to assault us. To possess you, my lady, will make His Highness the happiest man in the world. Now come, would you like a last look at France?" He stood up, and snapped his fingers. Instantly two of the seamen came forward to grip Madeleine's arms and set her on her feet; the third man was already holding Jean-Pierre.

"Where are you sending us?" Madeleine gasped.

"To your quarters, to be sure, madame. My invitation extends only to my lady, here. Cora."

Catherine turned, discovered another woman in the room, and that she was, in fact, Madame Despards' maid. If that was her true function. She had not taken any notice of the woman before, but now she realised that Cora was tall and slender, dark-skinned and dark-haired and extremely good-looking, and that she was wearing a garment similar to Ricimer's, and holding another in her hand.

"If my lady will put this on," she said. "It is cold on deck, and my lady should not be exposed longer to the gaze of the seamen."

Catherine opened her mouth and closed it again. Madeleine and Jean-Pierre were already being hustled through the door, and she was alone with Ricimer and the woman. And the garment being wrapped around her shoulders was exquisite silk, in dark blue with a gold design worked into the hem and around the cowl that was being settled over her hair.

"For the time being," Ricimer said, "you can hold the fold across your nose and mouth. We will outfit you properly tomorrow. Come."

He left the cabin for what appeared to be a passageway, and then mounted some steps. Catherine followed him, her mind still tumbling, aware only that Cora was at her elbow. Ricimer opened a door at the top, and they emerged on to the waist of the ship, which was already under sail, and heeling to the wind; as it was an easterly and thus offshore breeze, the vessel had needed no boats or anchors to pull her clear of the dock, and indeed the lights of the harbour were already fading.

"Where is it?" Catherine asked, interested despite herself.

"It is called St. Malo. A famous haunt of corsairs," Ricimer said. "Although French ones rather than Algerian. But it is a very dangerous passage to the open sea." He pointed, and Catherine caught her breath as she saw a jagged black rock go by, very close to the ship's side. "There is nothing to be afraid of. My sailing master is a Malouine himself, who prefers to work for the Dey, and knows these waters as you might know your own bedchamber."

"And the rest of your men are Arabs?"

"Arabs?" Ricimer seemed shocked. "No Arabs, my lady. Arabs are not permitted to sail the ships of His Highness's Navy. My men are Turks."

"Oh." She was not sure she knew the difference. She only knew that there was France, receding into the distance. But if they were putting out into the English Channel, there was a long way to go. Surely ships would be sent after them, or ships could be sent out to meet them, from Brest or from Rochefort.

Ricimer seemed able to read her thoughts. "For the time being, of course, we fly the French flag. When we are off the Coast of Portugal we will adopt our proper colours. Not that the Portuguese are our friends. But I have arranged to rendezvous with three other Algerines in Lagos Bay. The latest acquisition for the *harem* of the Dey must be adequately protected, do you not agree? And her complexion also. You have been up here long enough."

She turned, for the hatchway. *Why am I obeying him like a frightened sheep,* she wondered? *Because I am a frightened sheep. What is to become of me?* To be kidnapped by Ricimer for himself would be terrible enough. But it would be a terror compounded by excitement, and even, dared she allow herself thoughts of such a nature, anticipation. To be taken by Ricimer just to gratify the lust of some man old enough to be her grandfather, and not even a European was too horrible to contemplate. She wondered she did not scream and scream and scream.

They were back in the warmth and light of the great cabin, and Cora was removing her cloak.

"Now," Ricimer said. "Supper. I am sure you must be starving."

Catherine licked her lips. She doubted she could stomach a thing. "I am not hungry," she said. "If I could have a glass of wine . . ."

Ricimer snapped his fingers, and Cora handed Catherine a filled glass. She sipped, felt the warmth enter her chest. The ship had commenced to pitch, very slightly.

"Are you sure we cannot tempt you to eat, my lady?" Cora asked, softly.

"No," Catherine said.

"Ah, well," Ricimer said. "No doubt you will inform us when you are hungry. But if you will not eat, then let us complete the formalities of accepting you as a future *odalik*. Will you undress, please."

Oh, Lord, she thought. *So soon?*

But why should she undress, she thought? He called her "my lady." He already seemed to regard her as a superior. And he had said that he dared not harm her.

She tossed her head at him; she had been passive too

long. She had been frightened too long. "I will not," she said. "I am sure you already know what I look like."

Ricimer sat behind his desk; he did not seem perturbed by her refusal. "Indeed I do, my lady. It was necessary to make a brief preliminary examination, of course. A venture like this costs time as well as money, as well as, in this case, the life of a man. It cannot lightly be undertaken. But before I can offer you to His Highness I must be positive firstly that you have no blemishes whatsoever, and secondly, and far more important, that you are a virgin."

"Of course I am a virgin," she said angrily. "What do you take me for?"

"A well-bred young lady, and therefore, most probably a virgin," he agreed. "But one must be sure. In this lax modern age, who can tell? So if you would be good enough, my lady. Cora, will you assist the mademoiselle?"

"Don't touch me," Catherine said. "Just don't touch me. I absolutely refuse." Once again she raised her chin to stare at him. "And should you try to force me, you will undoubtedly create some of those very blemishes you fear to discover."

Ricimer gazed at her for a moment, then spoke to Cora in Turkish. The girl bowed, and left the cabin.

"Sit down," Ricimer suggested, and after a moment's hesitation Catherine obeyed. "You may not believe it," Ricimer said, "but it is my intention to help you in every possible way. To be sure it is in my interest to do so, as the more His Highness enjoys your company the more pleased will he be with me. But I also wish to help you because I like you. I think you are quite lovely. And I suspect your personality is similarly delightful. I like everything about you. I should hate to think of you tied in a sack and sunk to the bottom of the Mediterranean Sea, because that is what will happen should you fail to please the Dey."

Catherine clasped her throat in horror.

"So you see, my lady," Ricimer went on, "you will certainly benefit by cooperating with me in every way. I can teach you a great deal. Of the art of satisfying a man, and of the art of being satisfied, by a man, at least to *his* satisfaction."

Catherine's heart began to pound. She was almost grateful for the sound of the opening door.

It was Cora, accompanied by Madeleine and three sailors.

"You will cover your face, please, mademoiselle," Ricimer said, and without knowing exactly why, Catherine obeyed.

"Catherine? My darling, are you all right?"

"She is very well indeed, madame," Ricimer said. "But is in a somewhat recalcitrant mood. She refuses to undress for my inspection. Would you command her to do so, please?"

Madeleine stared at him. "You must have lost your senses," she said. "Of course she will refuse to undress for a . . . a monster like you."

Ricimer considered her for a moment, then said something in Turkish, still speaking very quietly. Madeleine gave a gasp of anger as her arms were gripped by two of the sailors, which became a shout of mingled fear and rage as she was turned against the bulkhead, her arms carried above her head, and secured there by the wrists to two lengths of rope which were in turn attached to the deck by eyebolts.

"What . . . you . . ."

Cora was looking at Ricimer, who nodded. Cora stepped behind Madeleine and commenced to undress her, unfastening buttons where she could, but tearing the cloth wherever it hampered her.

Madeleine twisted and kicked. "You let me go, you . . . you bastard. You . . ."

Catherine was on her feet, the veil dropped away from her face. "What are you going to do?"

Ricimer leaned back in his chair. "I am going to have her whipped, until you obey me."

"You . . . you can't."

Cora had uncovered Madeleine's corset, and was loosening the strings. Madeleine panted, and strained at her wrists, but she was clearly incapable of freeing herself,

80

and now one of the sailors took down a long thin cane from a bracket on the wall.

"I can," Ricimer said. "And I will. I will enjoy doing so. She is a pretty woman, is she not?"

The corset dropped against the wall, and Cora tore down the shift to expose Madeleine's back. Catherine stared in fascinated horror. Her stepmother's breasts were smaller than her own, she realised, but attractive enough, and bobbing as she tugged on the ropes. While her back was smooth as silk. But perhaps not for long. And even worse was to come. Cora glanced at Ricimer, received another nod, and commenced to tear at the skirts of the gown and the petticoat to uncover the rest of her victim.

The sailor handed Ricimer the cane, and he swished it to and fro. Madeleine screamed, in sheer terror as she understood what was going to happen to her, and Catherine realised she was defeated.

"Stop it," she shouted. "I will do as you wish."

Cora ceased tearing, looked at Ricimer.

"You are sure, now?" Ricimer said. "Should you change your mind, my lady, I will beat your stepmother until the blood runs, no matter what you may then say."

"I will not change my mind," Catherine gasped, her fingers already seeking the buttons of the gown. "I will not change my mind."

Ricimer nodded to the sailors, who promptly grasped Madeleine's arms while Cora released her wrists.

"Catherine," Madeleine cried. "Oh, my darling, darling Catherine. What is going to happen to you, Catherine? Catherine . . ." She was hustled through the door of the cabin, which Cora closed, before turning to face Catherine.

"We are waiting," Ricimer said.

Catherine undressed, as quickly as she could. She did not wish to think about it, to understand what she was doing, what was happening to her, what might be going to happen to her in a few minutes. She dropped garment after garment on the deck, stood straight when she was naked, wearing only her stockings and boots.

"Those also," Ricimer commanded, sitting on the desk.

Catherine hesitated, then sat down and unlaced her boots, rolled down her stockings and garters, added them to the pile.

"Exquisite," Ricimer remarked. "Everything about you, every movement, is quite exquisite."

Catherine stood up. She felt her cheeks burning. Indeed, her whole body seemed to be on fire, caused partly by the pounding of her heart, no doubt, but more by the tremendous heat that she seemed to be generating from her mind. As if in a dream she watched him come closer, watched his hand come out. She closed her eyes, felt his hand on her shoulder, gently slipping down the front of her chest to surround her left breast, to grip the flesh, still with the utmost softness, and raise it. Her nipples started into erection, and she was aware of a most peculiar feeling that began in her belly, reached down to her groin, and then seemed to divide to affect each thigh.

His hand had left, slid down her ribs to slip round her back and in turn cup and once again gently squeeze her left buttock before descending lower. She opened her eyes and discovered he was kneeling, stroking her thigh. She wanted to open her legs, spread them apart. She wanted to tell him to come between, to . . . to do whatever it was Seraphine had done to her, whatever she had learned to do to herself.

But he was straightening again. "Quite exquisite," he said. "His Highness will be pleased." He lifted her chain from between her breasts, and over her head, handed it to Cora. "But your beauty needs no adornment."

It did not seem to matter, and her eyes were still open, to her amazement. "And what of Baron Ricimer?" she whispered. "Is he also pleased?"

He smiled. "Baron Ricimer is enchanted, and not least with your character, my lady. Truly he regrets his devotion to duty. To bed you myself would be an experience even for me, I have no doubt at all."

She gazed at him, and allowed her tongue to come out and slowly circle her lips. *If she could make him do that, then all their troubles would be over. Surely.* And what an incredible thought, that Catherine Scott, late of Madame St. Amant's Academy for Young Ladies, should actually be wishing a man to rape her.

His smile died. "I see I shall have to teach you caution as well as seduction, my lady," he said. "Will you lie on that bed? It will be yours for the duration of the voyage."

Catherine lay down on the port bed.

"Raise your legs," Ricimer commanded. "Bend them at the knee, and hold them in the air."

Oh, Lord, she thought. She could imagine no more undignified position. But it was Ricimer's wish. She obeyed, but to her infinite disgust it was Cora who bent over her, parting the knees, and then touching her. No, she wanted to shout. I will not have it. I would not permit Laurens, why should I permit you? No one has ever touched me there, saving myself, and those occasions were always accidents of bathing.

But she had wanted Ricimer to touch her there, and if she closed her eyes, perhaps she could imagine it *was* Ricimer. He was close enough.

Catherine closed her eyes, and inhaled, and felt the fingers entering her body, gently, cautiously, and then withdrawing just as carefully. "She has never known a man, my lord," Cora said.

Catherine opened her eyes, and released her legs to let them thump on to the bed. Ricimer was smiling at her. "His Highness will be well pleased," he said. "Now sleep well, my lady. Tomorrow your schooling begins."

He drew the curtain in front of the bunk.

As if sleep could be contemplated. Her brain still seethed with the thought of everything that had happened, just as her body still seethed with the touch of his hand, and, dare she admit it, of Cora's hand as well. Nothing had happened to her, and yet something *should* have happened to her. Something was going to happen to her, very soon, which would leave her different, end her girlhood and make her a woman. And she did not know what it was. There was the most distressing fact of all.

She could only attempt to remember Seraphine's giggled hints, her suggestive fumblings. But where Seraphine had fumbled, Ricimer and Cora had *known* . . . and had left her in a limbo of half-awakened desire.

But surrounding and overshadowing that core of physical stimulation there was a great cloud of unthinkable misery. She had been kidnapped, wrenched from the secure existence she had grown to expect would be hers throughout life. And destined for a quite ghastly fate. To be the plaything of an aged Turk who was also the leader of the most desperate band of pirates the world had ever seen, whose cruelty was a byword and who had amply displayed his ruthlessness in the manner in which his servants had carelessly killed Henri the coachman. Disappoint the Dey, and she would be put in a sack, no doubt still alive, and thrown into the Mediterranean Sea.

But disappoint him or not, she would never be allowed to escape. She would never see Papa again. Or David, she realised with a pang almost of curiosity. Why should she wish to see David again? He was nothing more than an itinerant artist, and a foreigner to boot. But he had fought for her, and won. And his kiss had been so gentle. He loved her. Surely he loved her. Surely he would pine for her.

But poor Papa, robbed of wife and daughter and stepson. The entire family he had so carefully reconstructed gone at a stroke. And the worst thing of all was that he would never know what had happened to them. The coach would be found, together with the dead body of poor Henri. So he would know they had been taken, by someone. What horrible fates he would imagine for them, what torments he would undergo on their behalf. As if any fate he could imagine could possibly be as terrible as the one for which they were actually intended.

Tears streamed down her cheeks, and she wondered why she did not get up and rush on deck and throw herself over the side; all sound from beyond the curtain had ceased, and as far as she could tell the candles had also been doused, to suggest that Ricimer and Cora had either gone to bed or left the cabin. But that did not mean *she* would be able to leave the cabin. There would certainly be a seaman on guard outside her door.

But why not at least get up and look? The fact was, she did not feel that she could. The ship was now beyond the reefs and in the Gulf of St. Malo itself, and the easterly breeze was still strong, causing the vessel to pitch and roll at the same time, making all the timbers creak while the hum of the wind in the rigging drummed in her ears. Her stomach seemed to be turning over and over; it was ten years since the voyage from America, which was the last time she had been to sea, and she remembered that she had spent most of that occasion being seasick.

A memory which only added to her misery. She was quite surprised to find herself awake, and gazing at Cora, who had just drawn the curtain.

"You will feel better for the rest, my lady. Last night you were clearly very tired. Will you rise?"

Catherine propped herself on her elbow, discovered it was daylight. The day Ricimer had said her education would begin. But it could not begin if she stayed in bed. And suddenly she did feel like staying in bed; her stomach was still revolving. She shook her head, and lay back.

Cora nodded, without sympathy but without condemnation either. "Eat these biscuits," she said, placing a plate on the bunk beside Catherine. "It is not good to be sick on an empty stomach. And here is a bowl."

The curtains were drawn, and she was left to herself. To the mind-whirling considerations of the previous night, save that today they were overlaid by her physical discomfort, and soon were quite obliterated by the nausea that overwhelmed her. She vomited, and lay back, and chewed a biscuit, and vomited again, and could only pray for some swift death to release her from her misery.

For several days she was unable to leave her bunk. Sometimes Ricimer drew the curtains to look at her, but even his presence could have no effect upon her illness. Always she was surrounded by the creaking of the timbers and the thrashing of the waves against the hull, by the whining of the wind in the rigging, and the tramp of feet over her head as sails were changed and tacks altered.

Until she awoke to a feeling of well-being, overlaid by a most tremendous hunger, and equally by a disgusting awareness of filthiness.

Cora smiled at her. "My lady has recovered," she said. "Are you hungry?"

Catherine sat up, the blanket pulled to her chin. "I am ravenous."

"There will be food, soon enough. But first, you must be washed clean. Will you get up, please?"

Catherine peered past her at the rest of the cabin, but it was empty and the door was closed. She thrust her feet out of the bed and discovered that Cora had spread a thick towel on the carpet beside the bunk, on which she could stand.

"My lady will understand that this can be but a temporary measure," Cora explained. "Your proper bath will have to await our arrival in Algiers." She busied herself, securing Catherine's hair on the top of her head with a ribbon.

"Where are my stepmother and Jean-Pierre?"

"They are in their cabins. I understand they are still suffering. But they soon will be well again. Now, my lady." Two wooden buckets waited on the deck. Into one of these Cora dipped a loofah, which she thoroughly soaped, and then commenced washing Catherine's body. Catherine tensed herself for the cold, but the water was warm, and felt quite delightful. Cora worked with tremendous efficiency, renewing the soap at regular intervals, washing under armpits and between legs, even separating each toe, for which Catherine had to rest her hands on the girl's head as she stood on one foot. *Why,* she thought, *it is just like having a nurse all over again.*

"Now, my lady," Cora said at last. "If you will step outside."

She opened a hitherto unnoticed door in the after bulkhead, beyond Ricimer's desk, and Catherine glimpsed the still heaving sea, and shuddered as a draught of cold air entered the cabin.

"Out there?"

"There is a balcony, my lady. And I cannot rinse you in the cabin.

"But . . . why cannot I just sit in that bucket?"

"That would be unclean," Cora said, primly, and Catherine sighed, and stepped outside, to hold on to the ornate balustrade and stare at the sea, a brilliant blue as the sun was shining, and only occasionally spotted with whitecaps, but distinctly cold. Her entire body seemed to rise in a gigantic goose pimple, and she had to choke back a scream as Cora emptied the bucket over her, slowly, to allow all the soap to be washed away—and this water was cold.

"Oh, my," she gasped. "Oh . . ."

"Inside, my lady," Cora commanded, and she hurried back into the warmth of the cabin, to find herself facing Ricimer.

"Oh, my," she gasped, fluttering her hands in front of her breasts and then hastily lowering them to protect her groin. But Cora now wrapped her in an enormous, thick white towel, which encased her from neck to ankle, and immediately induced a feeling of warmth.

"Breakfast," Ricimer said, indicating the table on which there was a collection of strange-looking dishes. "And Cora, will you tell Ahmed to prepare himself."

Catherine sat down in the offered chair; her mouth ached as it filled with saliva. She had never been so hungry in her life.

"Prepare himself?" she asked. "What is to happen now?"

"Why, as soon as we have eaten, my lady, your tuition will begin, and we will commence with the male function, rather than the female."

Catherine had already begun to eat; to her surprise she found she had picked up a sweetmeat; but a glance round the table convinced her that they were all sweetmeats. Ricimer was pouring coffee into an exquisite china cup, which he now placed beside her.

"Function?" she asked, her heart beginning to pound.

"I said, when you first came on board, that I would do all I could to assist you, and to assist you not only to live, but to prosper, my lady," he said. "To accomplish that you must satisfy His Highness more than any other member of his *harem* is currently managing. And how can you even consider that unless you know what you are about?"

Catherine drank coffee, and was once again taken by surprise; it was the strongest she had ever tasted, and the hottest. She had to stifle a gasp. *What is going to happen?* she thought; *What should I do? What can I do?* Her flesh seemed to break out in a gigantic flush.

And once again Ricimer seemed able to read her thoughts. "There is nothing for you to be afraid of. I will tell you what to do. Are you ready?"

She gazed at him with her mouth open. No, she wanted to shout. No, I am not ready. I shall never be ready. I want to be left alone . . . but she said nothing at all, and Ricimer rang the little brass bell at his elbow.

Catherine watched the cabin door open as if hypnotised, unable to move a muscle, unable even to swallow, and her mouth was once again filled with sweetmeat. Cora came in first, guiding a member of the crew, a young man, and to her horror she saw he was stark naked, save for a blindfold around his eyes. Hastily she looked away, took refuge in her coffee cup, and yet could not prevent herself raising her head again, to watch the man. And he was splendidly built, with broad shoulders tapering to narrow thighs and long muscular legs, while between . . . once again she drank coffee. The man was placed against the wall, exactly where Madeleine had been positioned on her first night on board, save that he was standing with his back to the bulkhead, while Cora took his arms above his head and secured them to the looped ropes, not that he showed any inclination to resist.

"You must not speak," Ricimer said. "You should already consider youself as at least a *guizde*, and as your face should be seen by no man save your lord, so your voice should be heard by no man, save your lord."

She opened her mouth, but he shook his head, gently

88

smiling. "I am an exceptional case, my lady, as I am the agent of our lord, and also his closest associate. But even I may never speak with you or see your face once I have delivered you to the *Harem Agha*. Now come."

He rose, and she stared at him. Her muscles seemed paralysed; her entire body seemed paralysed. She was not even sure she was breathing.

"There is nothing to be afraid of," Ricimer said again, and took her hand, slowly to draw her to her feet. The towel slipped from her shoulders, and she attempted to regain it with her free hand, but once again he shook his head. "It is best done naked," he said, "as it will usually be done, naked. Not, of course, that His Highness will permit himself to be tied to a wall, or indeed, will wish you to sweeten him while standing. But on the other hand, my lady, it is more difficult to accomplish on a standing man, and this is important, because His Highness is a very old man, and therefore is difficult at the best of times. I fear he may prove slow even when confronted with a beauty such as yours. Thus you will have to use all your wiles."

Catherine discovered she had been led across the room. She gazed at the man's face, only half-hidden beneath the blindfold. His cheeks were pink, and he was breathing heavily. He might not understand French, but he understood what was about to happen to him.

"You have no brothers, I understand," Ricimer said. "And your education was completed at Madame St. Amant's Academy. There you will have heard tales, perhaps. From girls who had brothers? Even from girls not so chaste as yourself, perhaps."

Catherine remembered Seraphine's stories that had filled her at once with excitement and with disgust. She remained staring at the man's chest.

"On the other hand," Ricimer continued, "French men are not as a rule circumcised. That is a ritual preserved for Jews and for True Believers. His Highness is of course circumcised, as is this man. Touch it."

Oh, Lord, Catherine thought. *I cannot.*

"You must," Ricimer said. "Kneel."

Her knees gave way and sank into the carpet. She

gazed at the penis, already swelling, seeming half to point towards her. *Only Jews and True Believers,* she thought. *David will look like this. Would look like this, should he and I ever . . .*

"Touch it," Ricimer said. "It cannot harm you, in that position, at the least. Stroke it. Touch the balls beneath. Watch its reaction to your fingers."

As if she were in a dream, Catherine obeyed. The flesh was velvety. She had never touched anything so beautiful in her life. And the immediate hardening beneath her fingers made her want to shriek for joy, to . . .

"It has lips. Kiss it," Ricimer commanded. "He has been especially washed for this occasion. Kiss it."

Because that was what she wanted to do. *Oh,* she thought, *I am bewitched. I am damned forever. I am cursed. I am . . . kissing something utterly beautiful, something I wish to be mine, something I wish to possess forever.*

"Now," Ricimer said. "Now, in the case of His Highness, you must make him enter you. Remember always his age. He cannot sustain the blood pressure necessary for penetration for more than a few seconds. You must know when to act, and act, decisively. Even should he protest, he will be grateful, after."

Catherine raised her head, replaced her lips with her hands. She did not want ever to let go. But the penis was moving between her fingers, jerking against her, and suddenly her hands were wet.

"Congratulations," Ricimer said, offering her another towel. "Cora herself could not have done it better." He took Catherine's hand, raised her to her feet. "You should pray to Allah that His Highness is similarly responsive."

Catherine found herself leaning against him. She didn't want to move. Certainly she didn't want to look at him, or at Cora, or even at the blindfolded man. She was aware of the most amazing sensations, seeming to run from her still trembling fingers all the way up her arms and through her chest into her belly. Her nipples were flaming, her stomach heaved; but this was no sickness. Rather was it a feeling she wanted to grow, and grow, and grow, until something happened. Something for which, surely, she had waited all her life.

"Now," Ricimer said, his mouth against her hair. "You must start again."

Her head jerked, and her mouth opened. He laid his finger across her lips.

"Of course, I told you that His Highness is no longer a young man, while Ahmed, why, I am surprised he did not spurt at the first touch of your fingers." His grip on her shoulders tightened. "Don't you want to?"

Oh, how she wanted to. She wanted to touch that slowly drooping member more than anything in the world, unless it was to touch Ricimer's. *Oh, how she wanted to touch Ricimer's.* She wanted to make him shriek with agony and moan with ecstasy in the same moment.

She sank to her knees, took the member between her hands, was dismayed to discover no reaction.

"It is not so easy, this time," Ricimer said. "You must be patient, and above all, gentle. You must enjoy it, Catherine. You must want it as much as Ahmed."

Because Ahmed certainly wanted it. His belly heaved, and he was panting, and working his backside against the bulkhead. *Pretend,* she thought. *Pretend he is Ricimer.* He cannot be so very different. They are both big, strong men. Oh, pretend. She kissed, and sucked, and stroked, and felt at last the sudden strengthening between her hands. But it was more than that. The desire which reached out from her fingers, which filled her arms, consumed her breasts, had her belly and her groin soaring to hitherto unimaginable heights of pleasure, was growing all the time. She moaned her ecstasy, threw both arms around the sailor's body to lose her face in his hair, twisting her own body, pressing her thighs together and forcing sensation from between her legs, and collapsing around the man's ankles in the same moment that he once again ejaculated.

She wanted to lie there forever, panting, feeling the passion slowly ebbing, draining away from its focal point in her crotch, leaving her at once exhausted, and tremendously happy, and equally guilty. *What have I done?* she thought. *What has become of me?*

She felt Ricimer's hands on her shoulders, gently pulling her to her feet. "You are born for love, my Catherine," he whispered. "Oh, His Highness will be well pleased." He escorted her across the cabin, and on to the stern gallery. Now she noticed that astern of them, perhaps half a mile away, there were two other vessels, low, sleek, and heavily armed. Instinctively she made to step back through the doorway, but Ricimer merely smiled. "They cannot see you, without using telescopes," he said. "And no one on board either of those two ships would dare use a telescope to inspect the Dey's intended. Gather your hair."

She obeyed. She supposed she would always obey him without question now. She scooped her hair on top of her head and held it there with both hands, felt the cold water dribbling down her shoulders, flooding her breasts and her back.

"Aye," he said. "His Highness will be well pleased. One could have scoured the entire earth to find a girl like you. Perhaps in Circassia. But in Circassia the women are all ignorant savages."

She opened her eyes, still shivering. "Ricimer," she said. "Kurt . . ."

He was smiling again, and opening the door for her. "Destiny, my lady. *Kismet.* No man, and no woman, dare oppose *Kismet.*"

She stepped inside, gazed at Madeleine, who wore a robe similar to Cora's.

"Catherine," Madeleine screamed, running across the deck. "Oh, my darling Catherine. I have been so worried. I have been so terrified. What have they been doing to you?"

"Why . . ." She glanced at Ricimer, could feel the heat in her cheeks.

"I have been attending to her education, madame," he said. "An education which must now proceed a stage further. Cora, would you have my lady catch cold?"

Cora hurried forward with the huge, enveloping bathrobe. Madeleine stared at her in utter disbelief, then at Ricimer again, as she might have looked at a coiled snake.

"Education? What education?"

"Her education as a successful lady of the Dey's *harem,* madame. Will you undress?"

"Will I . . ." Madeleine took a step backwards, cheeks flaming. "Never. For you."

Ricimer sighed, sat on the edge of his desk. "Madame, you grow tiresome. Cora, will you fetch four of the crew. I wish Madame Scott stripped. Catherine, my lady, I wish you to cover your face. Here." He reached into a drawer of his desk and gave her a small rectangle of thin white linen, to which was secured two linen bands. "It is called a *yashmak,*" he said, "and you tie it over your nose, leaving only your eyes exposed. You will wear it, from this moment forth, whenever you are in the company of any man save the Dey and myself, at least as long as you are on my ship."

Catherine took the *yashmak* as if in a dream. Madeleine had backed against the far bed, and Cora was already at the door.

"Catherine," Madeleine gasped. "Catherine," she wailed. "What are they going to do to me?"

Cora reached the door and waited there.

Catherine licked her lips. "It is no use fighting them, Madeleine," she said. "The Baron will do as he says." *You may as well enjoy it, whatever it is,* she thought. Seraphine had said that. *Enjoy everything, even death.* Had she unconsciously been following Seraphine's advice when she had enjoyed handling the man? Oh, she had enjoyed it.

Madeleine's turn to lick her lips. Her shoulders rose and fell. "I will obey you," she whispered.

"Thank you, madame." Ricimer nodded, and Cora stepped away from the door.

"If you will tell me what you mean to do to me."

"Of course, madame." Ricimer left the desk, walked across the cabin. Madeleine watched him as if hypnotised. He reached her side, put one arm round her waist to bring her against him. His other hand thrust up into the rich brown hair, holding the head. "I am going to make love to you. Is that not what you have always desired? Is that not what you planned to use Catherine's beauty for? As a bait, for me? And for how many others, I wonder?" He lowered his head, kissed her on the lips.

Catherine discovered that Cora had returned to her side, was gently urging her across the room, until they were only a few inches away. She watched Ricimer in fascination; his mouth moved constantly, seeming to slide across Madeleine's lips, now kissing them, now parting them to thrust his tongue between. And for all her exhaustion, for all the crowded emotion of the past hour, she felt the passion once again beginning to build in her own belly.

Ricimer raised his head, and released Madeleine in the same instant. She sat on the bed; her eyes were still closed.

"Undress, madame," he said. "You will have observed, my lady, that a kiss is not a static gesture. It requires constant moving. One caresses with the lips as much as with the hands. One communicates, with the lips. Remember this."

Catherine also wanted to sit down, but when she attempted to move, she found Cora's hand on her elbow.

Madeleine's eyes opened. "You cannot mean to love me in front of the girl."

"Now, madame," Ricimer said. "Why else should I wish to love you at all? Catherine must learn."

She glanced at him, her cheeks flaming as much with anger as with embarrassment. But a moment later she had discarded the robe. She wore, or had been allowed to wear, nothing beneath.

"Now, my lady," Ricimer said. "Watch closely. I sit beside her, like this, and I take her in my arms. I will kiss her again, but watch my hands." He took Madeleine in his arms once more, kissed her on the mouth. His hands were on her back, sliding lightly across her shoulder-blades, tracing the serrated bones of the spine all the way down to the cleft of the buttocks. Madeleine's body seemed to undulate, like a snake. But, still kissing her, Ricimer's hands were now moving round to the front, fingertips sliding over the ribs, moving upwards to raise the breasts, from underneath, to stroke them outwards, gently to caress the nipples, and then to release the woman with mouth and hands at the same time.

"Oh." Madeleine gasped, and her eyes opened. She glanced at Catherine, and looked away, cheeks crimson. Ricimer was on his feet before her, and removing his gown. It was Catherine's turn to gasp, had she been capable of uttering a sound. All the promise of the man when wearing Western dress was more than fulfilled, the broad shoulders, the ripples of muscles in chest and back, the flat belly and slender thighs, the long, perfectly proportioned legs, the tight buttocks, and, as he half turned for her inspection, the huge, already erected penis, bigger even than Ahmed's, towering up to his navel, seeming almost to possess a life of its own in its blood-filled anxiety. And exactly like Ahmed's in every way. Did that mean *he* was a Moslem, or a Jew? Once again she endeavoured to move, and once again she was restrained by Cora's arm. But Cora was also breathing deeply, and Catherine could not doubt that she had already possessed that magnificent object, or been possessed by it.

"Watch closely," Ricimer repeated, sitting beside Madeleine. Her eyes were again closed, and she seemed to be scarcely breathing at all, although her skin had taken on a hectic pink glow, and there was a rash of sweat at her neck. Once again Ricimer's hands performed their magical inspection of her body, but this time he gently urged Madeleine on to her back, lying on his side beside her, while his hands stroked her thighs, cupped her breasts in order to kiss and to suck the nipples, slid down the fluttering depression of her belly to scratch her hair. To Catherine's surprise Madeleine parted her own legs at his touch, allowed his fingers between, moaned her ecstasy even as her own body became again convulsed with passion, moving to and fro, restrained only by the fingers of Cora on her arm.

Ricimer raised his head. "Your true lover, my lady, will always stimulate his partner to orgasm before making his entry. This is to insure that she is wet and able to receive him without discomfort, nor will it in any way detract from the eventual mutual pleasure, because almost all women are capable of reaching a climax several times during intercourse, whereas your humble male must perforce rest for at least a few minutes before being able to renew his passion."

Catherine leaned against Cora, and felt the maid's arms go round her body. She no longer felt able to stand unaided.

Ricimer had raised himself on his knees, looming above Madeleine like a huge animal dominating his prey.

"Of course," he explained, "it is not necessary to use the fingers. It can be done by stroking with the penis itself. The end result is the same. She is ready now, would you not say?"

Madeleine was moaning and moving her body to and fro, raising and lowering her thighs, mouth opened and eyes shut, sweat-damp hair clinging to her temples. Ricimer knelt between her legs, and slowly lowered his body. Madeleine gave a gasp of pleasure, and her eyes opened, then Ricimer suddenly thrust his body downwards with tremendous force, so that Catherine supposed Madeleine would be crushed beneath his weight. But his own hands stopped his fall, although his belly was now flat on the woman's, and from Madeleine's throat there uttered a wail of the most perfect pleasure. But Ricimer was not yet done. Up and down he went, up and down, gasping himself now, his own face and chest flushed, sweat standing out on his own shoulders, his breath finally escaping in a long sigh which swept across the room, while in the same moment he finally allowed his entire body to descend on Madeleine's, to lie there, in absolute unison, their breaths mingling.

And Catherine, turning in Cora's arms in an excess of unfulfilled passion, felt the morning grow dim as she fainted.

"Was it then so distasteful to you?" Ricimer sat on the side of her bed, his eyes glooming at her. "If so, then the

96

best thing I can do for you is strangle you now, to save you the agonies you will certainly undergo soon enough."

Catherine inhaled, and bit her lip. She was aware of a tremendous feeling of well-being, quite at odds with his stern expression. Her head moved, to and fro. "No," she said. "I did not find it distasteful, Kurt. I wished it could have been me."

He continued to gaze at her for some seconds. "You *are* a treasure, after all, my Catherine," he said.

"Kurt . . ." She raised herself on her elbow, careless of the coverlet which fell away from her chest. "Kurt . . . if you wished me, I would be yours. I swear it. I will be yours, and I promise you I can persuade Madeleine and Jean-Pierre to return to Father without a word, and I would persuade Father himself to take no action. I swear it. I could make you happy, Kurt. I can see that in your eyes."

"Make me happy," he muttered. "Aye, you would make me happy. But there is more to life than the happiness of a woman's arms, my Catherine. I told you yesterday, your destiny is written. So is mine. I can never return to France now. My work is finished there, which is why I did not trouble to seek an alibi for your kidnapping, as I have done in the past. From this minute forth, *Kismet* decrees that we should find our fate in North Africa. It would be foolish to attempt to stem that flood."

She tossed her head at him. "Are you then a Moslem, sir?"

"No. No, I have never become a Believer, although I hold a great many of their tenets. I am a godless man, Catherine. But I will tell you this. If I were to believe in any god, it would be Allah rather than Jehovah."

She lay back, her fingers still on his arm. "Oh, Kurt. What a fool you are. What fools all men are."

At last he smiled. "A fool, perhaps, my lady. But not that much of a fool. Your education is not yet complete. You have still to learn to feel."

His fingers slid across her shoulders, and she rose once more, and into his arms. Her mouth found his, and as she had watched him do to Madeleine, she worked her lips on his, pressed her tongue on his, thrust it into his mouth and then withdrew it to make him chase her down her own throat. And all the while his fingers were tracing delicious patterns on her back, sliding down to find the cleft of her buttocks and slip between, moving back up again to cup her breasts, to take the nipple and gently elongate it, to stroke their way around the aureole, suddenly hard and demanding.

She discovered her mouth had lost his, and was against his ear. "Do I please you, sir?" she whispered. "Are not my breasts too large, my legs too long, my shoulders too square?"

He smiled against her hair. "Your breasts are too large, my dear, sweet lady," he said. "Your legs are the longest I have seen, in regard to your height, your shoulders the squarest. But you please me, my lady, as you would please any man."

She was lying down again, on her side, her thighs closed on his hand, while delicious ripples of the sheerest passion stroked away from her groin, filled her belly, reached up to paralyse her brain. But not to stop her thinking. He was preoccupied, one hand between her legs, the other still caressing her breast. And he wore no more than a robe. She parted the wool, found her way inside, touched his thigh and was rewarded with an almost feminine wriggle of pleasure, then located the penis, felt it swelling into her hand, stroked it and squeezed it, parted the lips and closed them again, and knew the tremendous power of his exploding ejaculation even as she herself reached an orgasm which made her as dizzy as the day before.

His breath rushed against her face. "You learn well," he said. "Far too well. Remember, for God's sake, Catherine, that once you enter the *harem,* to look upon another man, much less to touch him, means death. And not a pleasant one."

She gazed at him; the passion flush was just beginning to leave his face, although no doubt it still consumed her own, judging by the pounding of her heart. "And will you still expose me to that fate, Ricimer? Can you so deprive yourself?"

He pushed himself away from her, got up, secured his robe. "I will do my duty. Your destiny is the bed of the Dey, and it is there you will know your next happiness, or you will know the execution sack."

Chapter 4

〰〰〰〰〰〰〰〰〰 "IT is time for you to dress, my lady."
Cora stood by the bunk.

Catherine raised herself on her elbow, swept hair from
her eyes. She sometimes thought that this cabin must be
imprinted on her heart. Over the past week she had loved
and been loved and watched Ricimer loving Madeleine,
in seemingly endless procession. She had lived in a sex-
oriented world, to which even the extravagant sweetmeats
and the occasional glass of wine belonged no less than the
daily baths on the stern gallery. She had been prepared,
mentally and physically, for her coming duties. And now
the moment was at hand. The night before last they had
drifted past the rock of Gibraltar during the hours of
darkness, not wishing to encourage any Royal Navy frigate
to rush out upon the hated Barbary corsairs.

And was she ready? She had no idea, mainly because
she had no idea what to expect. She no longer even considered resisting Ricimer or Cora; she was too completely
at the mercy of the Baron's fingers. Her moments of
solitude were spent remembering, and anticipating. She
supposed she was as if drunk, with sex, and kept in a state
of constant inebriation.

She had spared few thoughts for Madeleine and Jean-Pierre. They were alive, and that was sufficient. But she spared even less for Papa, and people like Seraphine and David Mulawer. Because they no longer existed? Or perhaps it would be more true to say that the girl they had known no longer existed. She knew that now. After three weeks on Ricimer's ship she could never return to Paris, even less Boston. She was no longer an American young lady; she was a *guizde,* and she could do no more than play the part.

She swung her legs over the side of the bed. "No bath?"

"It is not necessary, my lady. You will be bathed in the *harem.* Please."

Catherine frowned. For the past week she had either been naked or worn a robe. But today Cora was holding up what suggested a man's shirt, although not opened down the front, and without sleeves; there were slits for her arms as well as for her head. She stood up, and the garment was dropped on to her shoulders and settled into place; she realised it was made from finest linen, and reached only to her thighs.

But now there was another garment, also shirtlike, although considerably longer, and this time with sleeves, and once again of linen, exquisitely decorated on the cuff and hem with gold thread. She stepped away from the maid and gave a little twirl in the centre of the cabin, delighted at once with the texture of her new clothes and the tremendous freedom they afforded her body.

Cora waited with felt slippers, in maroon but also decorated with cloth of gold designs.

"And now, my lady, the *haik.*"

Catherine waited. This was made of white wool, and when wrapped round her it covered both her and the shirts. There was no hood or cowl, but the *haik* was quite voluminous enough to allow a fold to be thrown over her head, and another fold to be drawn across her mouth and chin if need be, although as Cora was already tying the *yashmak* into place this double protection seemed unnecessary.

But she still was not finished, for Cora now enveloped

her in yet another cloak, the *tcharchaf* made of black wool, which had a cowl, and which left her totally concealed save for her eyes.

"Now, my lady, you may go on deck, and look at your new home."

Catherine gathered the garment around her as she had been taught, folding it over her left arm and holding it with her hand so as to leave her right hand free. Cora had already opened the door for her, and she climbed the ladder, slowly and carefully, emerged into the waist, and gazed in surprised delight at the distant shore. Her first impression was entirely of mountains, for the morning air was clear and the serrated ranges seemed to lie only a mile or so behind the coast they were approaching; some of the peaks seemed almost to touch the sky.

"The Atlas Mountains," Ricimer said at her elbow. "The ancients supposed the entire universe rested upon those peaks."

She drew her *tcharchaf* closer, leaned against the bulwark. He had reduced her to gasping ecstasy with his questing fingers, every day for the past week. She could no more have resisted that soft, so experienced, so knowledgeable touch than she could have stopped herself eating when hungry. And yet, she now knew where she stood with him. *He was not a man,* she told herself angrily, as she had told herself endlessly during the voyage. He was a creature, a thing who but possessed the attributes of a man. He gave her pleasure, because it was his task to prepare her to receive pleasure, but not from him. From the Dey. He would abase himself, he would subject his own desires, to the will of the Dey.

Oh, Lord, she thought, *that I could feel nothing for him but contempt.*

She felt his shoulder against hers. He was pointing. "There, my lady."

She looked as directed. The coast itself was fringed by high cliffs against which the surf pounded with foaming intensity, but now she saw the land dipping to the right, and fronted by a gigantic mole, topped at its elbow by a light tower, and behind which there rose a quite startling town, because of the whiteness of the buildings which gleamed in the morning sunlight and made her eyes water.

"Algiers," Ricimer said. "The name is a corruption of *El-Djezair,* which means the islands."

"I see no islands."

"That is because they have been linked by the mole. In the beginning the Barbary fleets sheltered merely behind the islands, but over the centuries, as the fleets have grown, it became necessary to provide a more secure harbour, and so the mole was built."

"Over the centuries?" she asked, interested despite herself.

"It is a matter of three hundred years," he said, "since the Deys first defied the Sultans and set up the Regency. The first, and greatest of the Deys, Khair-ed-din Barbarossa, of whom even you must have heard, was actually encouraged to be as independent as possible by the Porte so long as he waged perpetual war against the Genoese and the Spaniards. But the Porte never managed to regain true control." Again he pointed. "The *Kasbah,* with the citadel behind."

She peered into the morning. Even from this distance she could tell that the streets were incredibly narrow, and that the houses were huddled together. But the brilliant sunshine and the waving palm trees prevented any impression of sordidness.

"Where I shall become enslaved to a monster," she muttered. "I wonder I do not throw myself over the side this instant."

"Where you shall become a *guizde,*" Ricimer corrected gently, "and as I would wager that is but a stepping stone to higher things, it is where you shall live the rest of your days in the lap of luxury."

"You have used that word before," she said. "Will you not tell me its meaning?"

"Literally, it means in the eye, and it is the lowest rank of the *harem.* You will, of course, be taken to His Highness's bed soon after your arrival. Tonight, I have no doubt. He will have seen you, and he will sleep with you. And if you do not please him sufficiently, he will not wish to sleep with you again. You will be, in the eye, waiting in the wings for the summons that may never come. But should you please him more than the average, you will be an *ikbal,* that is the second rank, and means, the lord has favoured you, in that he has sent for you on more than one occasion. But at the very top, and it is to this that you must aspire, Catherine, is the *odalik,* which means, of the room. An *odalik* is a girl for whom the lord has conceived such a liking that he sends for her regularly. Only a wife ranks higher than an *odalik,* and from a sexual point of view, indeed, a wife often ranks much lower."

She turned away from the gunwale. "And I am supposed to aspire to be prostituted more than the average," she said.

Ricimer smiled at her. "If you possess the character I perceive in you, my lady, you will do just that. Fate has given you this role to play. Will you not make sure you at least play it from the highest edifice, rather than from the lowest pit?"

Or will I not enjoy it, she wondered? *Enjoy everything, even death? Even a living death?*

Surprisingly, she was not as desperately unhappy as she had supposed would be the case. The voyage had been a limbo, but it had been a limbo dominated by Ricimer, who excited her even as he terrified her. She had supposed the landing in Algiers would be a climactic catastrophe which would crush her beneath its weight. And now she felt only excitement. Even her apprehension was an excited apprehension.

The ship was brought into the harbour and alongside a wooden wharf with immense skill, and before the last sail had been furled the gangplank had been run ashore and they were disembarking.

Catherine cast a last look at the vessel which had changed her life, at the seamen standing patiently to attention. It was impossible to tell which one was Ahmed. They were nearly all tall, and well built. But he was *there,* even if he would not meet her eye. And he would remember the touch of her hand, of her lips, forever.

As she would remember him?

"Oh, Catherine, my darling," Madeleine whispered. She also was hidden beneath a *tcharchaf*. "What is to become of us?"

"We must wait and see," she decided. "But for God's sake, Madeleine, do nothing rash. Jean-Pierre?"

For he too was enveloped in an enormous woollen robe, which almost entirely concealed his face. She had not seen him throughout the voyage, had no idea what had been happening to him. But he stood erect and moved freely enough; he had not been ill-treated. On the other hand, he would not meet her gaze, looked away, and did not reply.

"No matter what you see or hear on this journey," Ricimer said, joining them, "you will utter not a sound. Understand me, my lady. If you do, your stepmother will immediately be killed and others may die as well."

"But *I* will survive," she said, getting as much chill into her tone as she could

He bowed. "That is your destiny, my lady. Come."

He walked ahead of them, while Cora walked at her side, with Madeleine and Jean-Pierre behind; they were completely surrounded by armed guards. Her first reaction was to the heat, which seemed to rise from the stones beneath their feet to join that battering on their heads; the morning was now well advanced, and within seconds of leaving the ship they were sheltered from the gentle northerly breeze. Inside their woolen *tcharchafs* they might have been concealed in movable ovens.

Then there were the people. On the dock they had been to some extent secluded, but as soon as they began the ascent to the *Kasbah* they were surrounded by men, all wearing long robes like themselves, headgear divided between the fez and the turban. But these were either Turks or Arabs, and thus free men. She observed a great number of men who were obviously slaves, both from the way they were treated, or hastily removed themselves from the path of any Moslem, and from the heavy loads they were often carrying; and these slaves were either Negroes or, she realised to her distress, Europeans, with skins as white as her own. She was assailed by a variety

105

of smells and scents she had never known before, and by an even greater variety of voices and, she supposed, languages, as she could understand none of them.

The streets of the *Kasbah* proved even more narrow than they had appeared from the ship, barely wide enough for three people to walk abreast, or for one man and his donkey to proceed, and donkeys appeared to be the principal beasts of burden, patient and silent. Unlike their masters, and their mistresses, for now she was aware of the presence of women, although there were none on the street. But above her head, where bay windows all but touched those from the houses opposite, and where from the flat roofs she occasionally caught a flutter of white or blue, there could be no doubt that all the women of Algiers were inspecting these latest additions to the Dey's *harem*.

She supposed she should be ashamed. But they could not see her face, and besides, she could not control her growing excitement, just as she found it difficult to concentrate because of her growing heat, the sweat which clung to her back and shoulders, dribbled down her legs. *A draught of cool air, or better yet, a dip into a cool bath would be heaven,* she thought.

They climbed, slowly, over the uneven streets. The crowds began to thin, and they emerged into an open space. Before them were the walls of the citadel. She allowed her gaze to sweep over the immense embrasures, the heads of the guards looking down at her, and could not repress an exclamation of horror as she saw other heads, these sightless and in some cases even fleshless, impaled on steel spikes driven into the wall over the gate.

"My God," Madeleine said behind her. "What is to become of us?"

Ricimer had checked, and his entourage with them, for the gates of the citadel were opening, and not entirely to allow them entrance, as through the doorway there now hurried three men, and Catherine observed with a mixture of surprise and panic that they were white men, looking very hot and bothered, to be sure, but undoubtedly

Europeans, and of consequence, judging by their clothes; certainly they were not slaves.

She made to step forward, and was checked by Cora, who gripped her arm. "Remember my lord Ricimer's warning, my lady," she whispered. "Utter a sound and your stepmother dies."

Catherine looked over her shoulder. One of the guards had moved alongside Madeleine, and was holding her arm in turn. His right hand rested upon the knife at his belt.

Oh, Lord, she thought. *So near and yet so far.* But the men had already disappeared, sparing not a glance at the party or even at Ricimer, for he had drawn the flap of his *burnous* across his face and looked like any Arab from the desert. Now he nodded and snapped his fingers, and they proceeded inside, to find themselves in a large courtyard at the opposite end of which were the marble balustrades of the Dey's palace. Catherine could only stare in amazement, because it was indeed a palace, a vast area of gleaming white marble fronted with verandahs and ornate staircases and dominated by sudden pointed spires, above which a variety of flags fluttered.

She was still appreciating the beauty of the place when she was distracted by a high pitched chant, which came from one of the *minarets,* and at the sound of which the guards surrounding them dropped to their hands and knees, facing the east, and touched the ground with their foreheads.

"It is the hour of *dhohor,* the midday prayer," Cora whispered. "Remain still." Then she knelt herself.

Catherine waited, as did Ricimer and Madeleine and Jean-Pierre, for about ten minutes, then the guards stood up again, and Ricimer led them across the opened space, through ranks of Turkish soldiers, clad in no uniforms but every one armed with a most fearsome assortment of weapons—pistols, musket, knives and an enormous curved *tulwar*—until they arrived at the foot of the grand staircase. Here there waited three other men, who bowed low as Ricimer approached them. Or were they men, Catherine thought with another pang of horror. Their fezzes were decorated with gold, their black *jibbas,* robes which hung straight from the shoulders, were also decorated with gold thread, and they moved with a studied dignity, but they were clearly overweight, and had not a hair on their faces.

Ricimer had been speaking with them in Turkish. Now he turned to her, and held out his hand.

"I say farewell, my lady."

She hesitated, then allowed him to take hers. He lifted it to his lips, kissed it, and raised his eyes. "Be yourself, Catherine," he whispered. "Be yourself, and survive. All things are possible, should you remember those two essentials. Now, you are to go with the *Harem Agha.*"

He released her, turned, and mounted the staircase, not once hesitating or looking over his shoulder. Catherine's knees felt weak, and she might have fallen had Cora not once again caught her arm. But now Cora was leading her forward in turn, and Catherine found herself face to face with the eunuch.

His eyes gleamed at her. He seemed able to look through the layers of cloth in which she was enveloped, as Ricimer had been able to do. She realised that women were these people's business, rather as a European gentleman might be able to size up a thoroughbred horse at a glance.

The eunuch smiled. "His Highness will be pleased," he said in perfect French, his voice a little high and thin. "You will follow me, please."

He turned, and walked round the great staircase to a door set in the wall of the palace at ground level. His two subordinates duly fell into line behind him, and Cora led the remainder of Ricimer's procession, but Catherine, glancing over her shoulder, discovered that the guards had gone, and that Jean-Pierre had also disappeared.

As Madeleine now noticed. "Oh, my God," she cried. "Jean-Pierre. Jean-Pierre. Where is my boy?"

The *Harem Agha* checked, in the doorway, and turned. Now he was frowning. He said something to Cora in Turkish, and she nodded. He stepped past Catherine and slashed his hand across Madeleine's face. Madeleine gave

108

a shriek and fell to her hands and knees, from which position she was immediately dragged upright by the other two eunuchs.

"You . . . she is my mother," Catherine shouted, seizing the *Harem Agha's* shoulder.

He smiled at her. "She is your slave, mademoiselle. It is good for slaves to be reminded of their place." He went through the doorway, and Cora gripped Catherine's arm. She glanced at Madeleine, now weeping quietly to herself. *What is to become of us?* she thought.

Cora half-pushed her inside, and the door closed behind her. The *Harem Agha* was leading them along a wide but completely enclosed corridor, which ended at a flight of steps, up which they climbed, entering a silence more complete than Catherine could ever remember. It might have been a palace of the dead. Then from in front of them there came a tinkle of laughter. It was like a beam of light entering a darkened room. *They can laugh,* she thought. *They can still laugh.*

The steps ended at a door, before which there waited a guard, and this was no eunuch, she decided; his biceps alone indicated that. He was a Negro, tall and powerfully built, and armed with a *tulwar* which he raised ceremonially as the little party approached. The *Harem Agha* exchanged a word, and then pushed the doors inwards, and Catherine blinked in the sudden light, and at the sudden explosion of sound.

She found herself on a marble gallery, which ran away to left and right and then faced her again across a small courtyard to form a square. The length of gallery that she was in was fronted by a lattice wall, which extended into latticework doors to shut off the two immediately adjacent arms. But the latticework allowed her to see through, into the courtyard, which included a pool of water in the centre, and several palm trees, and a crowd of women, all young, all extraordinarily handsome, and every one dressed in wide, heavily embroidered trousers with a matching bolero jacket, and a small jewelled cap on her head. Both jacket and trousers were sheer save for the decorations, and the bolero was not in any way fastened, but in fact covered only the shoulders to leave the entire chest as well as the midriff bare. Catherine could only stare at them in amazement, aware that, however attractive, there was something unusual about every one of them, but she could not at the moment decide what it was; although certainly she observed that nearly all of them had a reddish tint in their hair. The women in turn left their various occupations, which had included embroidery and conversation and even some playful wrestling, to flood to the latticework to peer at her, and shout at her in a variety of tongues.

"They will be your companions," the *Harem Agha* said. "But you must always remember that the lattice wall is the limit of the *harem*. Come through either of these doors and you will be executed." He smiled at her. "Slowly."

She licked her lips; her throat was quite dry. But he was leading her towards the left-hand doorway, and a moment later she emerged into the courtyard itself, when she discovered to her alarm that Madeleine and Cora had now also disappeared, and she was alone, save for the *Harem Agha* and the crowd of excited girls who gathered round her, pulling the *tcharchaf* from her hair, letting it fall to the ground and trampling it as they removed her *haik* and her *yashmak,* holding her hands to extend her arms, kneading her flesh, but being most taken with her ash-blonde hair, which they threatened to tear altogether from her head in their interest.

"Oh," she gasped. "Ow."

The *Harem Agha* came to her rescue with a series of barked commands in Turkish that drove the girls back, and she was left panting, endeavouring to regain some of her clothing.

"They think your hair is false, lady," the eunuch said.

Catherine panted as she attempted to smooth it. "It is certainly attached to my scalp," she said. "Or it was." She glanced at him to see if he would take offence at her retort, and discovered that he was no longer looking at her. And that indeed the babble had entirely ceased. She turned, and saw another woman emerging from a door-

110

way at the end of the gallery. She wore the same bolero and trousers as the other girls, hers in deep green, but she was undoubtedly different, being light-skinned and fair-haired.

She approached slowly, almost reluctantly, stopped about twelve feet away. "Ricimer has excelled himself," she said in French.

"Thérèse Cavaigny," Catherine whispered.

The girl appeared to smile. Her face must have been remarkably pretty once, Catherine thought; but the pert looks had dissolved into downward curves of misery, relieved only by a simmering hatred. "That was my name, once," she said, and came closer. "I should pity you, child. But I hate you. I hope he makes you scream." She paused again, only inches away, stared into Catherine's eyes. Her own eyes were green, and molten. "He made me scream. He made me hate the day I had been born a woman." Her lips twisted. "But then, no doubt the same fate would have been mine had I been born a man."

* * *

Catherine could think of nothing to say. There was so much she wanted to ask Thérèse, so much she knew she could learn from her, but not while she was so filled with hatred. And in any event the *Harem Agha,* having bowed to the French woman, was now waiting to lead her on. And she was happy to escape the half-jealous, half-contemptuous looks of the other girls.

She followed the eunuchs through a door at the end of the gallery, the same door through which Thérèse Cavaigny had entered the courtyard, and found herself in another corridor, but this was wider and with a higher ceiling than the entrance to the *harem*; the walls were hung with magnificent drapes, though the ceiling was bare white, but the air was filled with a heady variety of delightful scents.

The *Harem Agha* opened another door, on his left, and waited for her to enter. Catherine stepped inside, and stopped in surprise and more than a little apprehension; it was clearly a bathing chamber. She stood on a slight dais, the walls of which were occupied by magnificently draped divans. A shallow flight of steps led down to another level, also with a marble floor, in the centre of which there was a large, raised marble slab, rather like pictures she had seen of a sacrificial altar. Then another three steps led down to a third floor, still in marble, although covered with wooden slats, off which there led several large drains. On each level there was a doorway, but the entire room was at this moment empty of anyone to greet her, but she was not to be left alone, she discovered to her dismay, for all three of the eunuchs had entered the room behind her, and the door was closed. Now she realised, to her surprise, that although the afternoon was warm, there was a fire burning in an open grate on the second level, almost as if they were intending to cook a meal, for above the glowing embers there waited a spit.

"The lady will disrobe," the *Harem Agha* said.

Catherine tossed her hair. He was a slave, and not even a whole man at that. "I am perfectly capable of performing my own toilette," she said.

The eunuch continued to smile. "To your own satisfaction, no doubt, lady. But not to the satisfaction of His Highness. I am empowered to use force, if need be, but I should warn you that should you, in the result, become injured or tarnished in any way, then you will have to be discarded."

She stared at him. Always force, in the end. That was her lot from this moment on. And, she realised with a growing sense of horror, *he* did not regard *her* as possessing any life of importance, either. She was a thing, an object to be presented for his master's gratification, but an object which, if broken or tarnished, could, as he had just said, be discarded.

And why should she fear to undress before three half-men, having spent the previous fortnight virtually naked in the company of Ricimer?

She shrugged, and removed her *haik*, then lifted her two shirts over her head, laid them on the nearest divan, and received another shock, for the eunuchs were also divesting themselves of their clothing. *They cannot be going to strip,* she thought. *I do not want to see. I cannot be allowed to see.*

She discovered she was shivering despite the heat, but the three had stopped at a cloth they wore wrapped around their waists and then passed between their legs, and she felt she could breathe again. At which the *Harem Agha* smiled, as he came closer. "Lady is even more beautiful than is at first supposed," he said. To her utter horror he touched her breast, rather as Ricimer had held it, from underneath, but with no tenderness; he might have been estimating the quality of a piece of beef. "Indeed," he remarked, perhaps to himself. "Lady will lie down." He pointed at the marble altar on the second level.

"Why?" she demanded.

"Lady's hair must be removed," he said.

Oh, Lord, she thought, remembering the girls outside. Because that had been the strange thing about them, she realised; not one had possessed any body hair.

The three eunuchs were waiting, standing in a row, and looking at her face, she realised, rather than her body. Somehow their impersonality was harder to bear than if they had been visibly aroused. She turned away from them, went down the three steps, lay on the slab; the marble was cold and her flesh came up in goose pimples. She heard a door open and close but refused to turn her head.

The *Harem Agha* stood beside her, raised her head, and gathered her hair, scooping it out so that it flowed over the edge of the altar. She discovered that another— he had to be a eunuch—stood beside her, and this man carried a tray.

The *Harem Agha* now lifted her right arm, extending that above her head in turn. "Lady must lie absolutely still," he said. "I am very skilful, but even I may not be able to cope with a sudden movement."

Catherine sucked air into her lungs, slowly, as he began to hone a curved knife, perhaps eight inches long, which he had taken from the tray. Meanwhile another of the eunuchs was powdering her armpit, coating it thickly and then pulling the hairs through it. *Well*, she thought, *he should not find these difficult, for she had been taught to shave under her arms by Madeleine, and only over the past fortnight had they been neglected.* It was what was coming after that concerned her.

And what of Madeleine? Poor Madeleine, whisked away into the recesses of this palace, to be treated as a slave. And if she, destined for the bed of the Dey, was so firmly enslaved, what could she possibly suppose might be the fate of one who had been brought here *as* a slave?

The blade had scraped with the utmost gentleness across her flesh, and her left arm was being equally treated. "Now, lady, spread your legs," commanded the *Harem Agha*.

How strange, she thought as she obeyed. *I give not a thought to defying him, where but three weeks ago such a suggestion from any man, much less a totally strange half-man, would have sent me into a swoon. How remarkable must be the ability of the human mind to adapt.* But to resist could only involve her in humiliation and possibly worse.

She closed her eyes as the fingers began to sort the powder into her flesh, to pull the hairs through it. There was nothing gentle or enticing about these fingers, and yet because at once of where they were touching her and of the state of continual half arousedness into which she had been sent by Ricimer, the passion immediately began to surge in her groin and in her belly, and it was all she could do to keep still. For once again the *Harem Agha* was scraping away; she recognised his touch, and opened her eyes to look at the top of his head as he bent low over her stomach. "Those ladies who prove recalcitrant," he said conversationally, "are depilated by having the hairs plucked from their flesh. It is very painful, and often leaves a considerable inflammation for some time. You are wise to submit to the requirements of the *harem*, lady."

Catherine closed her eyes again. *And I am but being prepared for his bed,* she thought. No wonder to disappoint him would be to involve myself in a fate too horrid to be imagined. Or was this not an aspect of that fate? For the knife was moving between her legs, guided and assisted by those so knowledgeable and yet so disinterested fingers. And how she wanted to close her legs, to feel the insides of her thighs touching, to enjoy that marvellous release she had first known when kneeling before the sailor Ahmed. It required all her willpower to lie still, and before he was finished she became distracted by a peculiar smell which began to seep through the bathing room, a sweet titillating odour which had her nostrils dilating.

"If the lady will stand," the *Harem Agha* said.

She opened her eyes, sat up, and looked down at herself. She realised that she had never known what a woman truly looked like, how her body was in fact so obviously designed for sexual intercourse. She felt the heat in her cheeks and looked up anxiously as she swung her legs to the floor, but the eunuchs were politely disinterested, busy with an enormous pot, which two of them were stirring with great endeavour, the pot itself being suspended on the spit over the fire.

Now one of them looked up and nodded.

"This may feel hot to the flesh, lady," the *Harem Agha* said, "but it will be only a temporary discomfort. Now kneel, and stretch your arms across the table."

Catherine obeyed, still quite without understanding why she was so subservient. In fact she was curious to discover what next would be done to her. She watched in amazement as the heavy pot was carried across the room and also placed on the table, between her arms, and then with a mixture of fear and disgust as a giant ladle was lowered and a molten brown mess lifted out. Some of this was dripped on to her left arm, causing an immediate gasp of pain, because it was extremely hot, which was overtaken by fresh pain as more was heaped on her right arm. But now one of the eunuchs was smearing the mess over her flesh, coating every inch from her wrist to her shoulder, while another was doing the same to her other arm.

"It is a mixture of sugar and lemon," the *Harem Agha*

said at her shoulder. "Brought to a molten state. Is it cooling?"

Her head jerked as she nodded.

"Well, now you must remain absolutely still, lady. What follows is an enormous test of skill. My skill, to be sure, but I will not be responsible if you move. The slightest mistake in applying pressure will result in your skin being removed."

Oh, Lord, she thought. The *Harem Agha* had gone round the table to face her, and now he half-knelt upon the marble surface while he held a length of silken thread between his hands. This thread he placed on her shoulder, where the flesh joined that of the upper arm. He pressed gently, until it cut into the toffeelike mixture covering her skin, and then slowly and carefully, watched with intense interest by his subordinates, he drew the thread down the length of Catherine's arm, removing the main part of the smothering mess as he did so, but also, she discovered to her fascination, removing every trace of hair. The golden down which normally covered her forearm was entirely gone, by the time he had reached her wrist, leaving her flesh absolutely white and clear.

She discovered her mouth had dropped open, as she watched him turn his attention to the other arm. All manner of thoughts were chasing themselves through her mind. She did not only have hair on her arms, thus the shaving process, so carelessly done, could have been no more than a preliminary. *Will I be able to stand it?* she thought.

She was about to find out. Her arms completed, he made her lie down again while her legs were attended to. Then she was made to kneel again while her back was coated and cleaned, and then she lay down while her armpits received yet another scouring.

Then he smiled at her. "Now is the truly difficult part, lady. I can only warn you again, lie still."

She closed her eyes. She could not bear to look at their faces, so close, so eager now, although still without the slightest suggestion of sexual interest. The mess was smeared over her chest and breast—she could not possibly have hair on her breasts, she thought desperately—coated her stomach and belly, and reached her groin and between her legs. How could they avoid skinning her down there, she thought in sudden desperation. Especially as the heat now induced another series of sexual urges, causing her body to quiver, which brought her an admonishing pat on the buttock from the *Harem Agha*.

"I am commencing now, lady," he said.

She attempted to hold her breath, then abandoned that in favour of slow and careful breathing. She felt the cord sliding over her skin, slipping between her breasts, and discovered that a subordinate had taken each nipple, gently but firmly holding the mounds of flesh apart to permit their master's thread to pass between. Then her breasts were released as the cord passed over her stomach. She tensed her muscles, made herself lie still, and felt it coursing across her groin. She felt fingers once again upon the insides of her thighs, stretching them so wide she thought she must be torn in two. She wanted to cry out in sheer anticipated pain, but there was none, and suddenly she was released, and received another gentle pat, and looked up to see the *Harem Agha* smiling at her.

"You are well disciplined, lady," he said. "Now come, it is time for your bath."

She sat up, slipped off the table. The eunuchs had already descended to the lower level, where two bowls were waiting, filled with water, the large one steaming and the small one still, beside two even larger buckets of water; she realised to her surprise that the bowls were actually made of silver. She was first of all made to kneel, while the *Harem Agha* carefully soaked and then washed her hair, using a soap the scent of which was strange to her, but unbelievably fragrant. Her hair was rinsed, also by the *Harem Agha,* and again with great care, then it was bound on the top of her head with a piece of ribbon, and she was made to stand on one of the slatted wooden boards, and the larger bowl was emptied over her, then refilled again and again until seven had been used. The water, she discovered, was already soapy. Then the smaller bowl was used to rinse her, obtaining water from the second tub, and this was fresh.

"Now if you will lie down, lady," the *Harem Agha* suggested.

Catherine lay down on the wet boards, and the eunuchs each armed himself with a loofah and commenced massaging her from her neck to her toes. The water was warmed, and the feeling of cleanliness and well-being was overwhelming. She discovered she had quite lost both her horror of them as creatures and her embarrassment at being so intimately manhandled by them. There seemed there was nothing more they could possibly do to her which compared with what they had already done.

The soaping process completed, she was made to stand again, and the rinsing began all over again, once more repeated seven times with soapy and then seven times with fresh water.

"Now, lady," said the *Harem Agha*, who was holding a large towelled robe, similar to that used by Cora on board the ship, in which he proceeded to wrap her, following which he released the ribbon holding her hair. He then escorted her back up the steps to the top level, where she was made to sit on a divan. She was amazed to discover just how exhausted she was, and wondered for the first time just how long she had been in the steamy confines of the bathchamber.

Several hours, apparently, for no sooner had she sat down than the sound of a gong echoed through the palace, and her attendants immediately prostrated themselves in the afternoon prayer, apparently knowing which direction was east even in the enclosed room.

She closed her eyes, and leaned against the wall, and waited for them to finish, and perhaps escort her to her bedchamber. She wanted only to sleep.

But her toilette was far from completed. While she sat on the divan, feeling her body slowly drying and cooling, the eunuchs continued to fuss about her, extending both arms and both legs first to trim and then to paint her fingernails and her toenails with henna, while the *Harem Agha* supervised. He himself was gently

118

rubbing her hair dry, seeming to work from strand to strand.

"In most cases," he explained, "we henna the hair as well, as no doubt you have already noticed. But in your case, lady, it could do nothing more than detract from your own beauty. His Highness has a great predelection for yellow hair; I doubt he has ever seen hair as light as this, save in an old woman."

She supposed he was paying her a compliment. Her nails were now completed, and a eunuch was offering her a tray on which were cups of steaming black coffee, so strong it made her gasp, to be followed with a mouth-watering sherbet which seemed to trace its way down her chest like a cascading waterfall. As she had eaten nothing since early morning, and then only a few sweetmeats, she was extremely grateful for the food, especially as she realised, by looking at the skylight, that it was now all but dark.

She accepted another cup of coffee, while the *Harem Agha* continued to busy himself with her hair, brushing it and combing it, smoothing it with his fingers, endeavouring to remove the very last suspicion of a curl, to have it lie absolutely straight on her shoulders and down her back. And discovered that one of the eunuchs was standing before her, holding another tray, on which was a fearful mess, all of the hair removed from her body, still sunk into the coagulated sugar and lemon mixture, together with all the parings from her nails.

"He wishes you to confirm firstly that there is none missing," the *Harem Agha* said, "and secondly to tell him your wishes as to their disposal."

"Should I be concerned with either?" She was coming to regard the *Harem Agha* as an old friend. Certainly he was the most intimate acquaintance she had ever possessed; she would not even rank Ricimer as his equal in personal knowledge of her, she supposed.

"Of course, lady. For if any is left about, to be secreted by some other *guizde,* you may be sure one of your rivals will secure it and use it to cast an evil spell upon you. A sickness perhaps, or a skin blemish."

"Then what do you suggest?" Not that she believed in such nonsense, but he most clearly did.

"That they are consumed in the flames, here and now."

"Very well," she agreed. "Will you instruct him?"

The *Harem Agha* gave the necessary instructions in Turkish, and the contents of the tray were immediately thrown into the still-smouldering fire, causing it at once to flare up and also to give off that titillating smell once again.

The *Harem Agha* then removed her robe and made her lie down on the divan, following which she was massaged by all four of them, legs, arms, front and back, with an unguent which gave off the same delicious fragrance as her hair, and left her smelling sweeter than she would have imagined possible, and also more sexually aware than even during the depilation.

"And now, lady," the *Harem Agha* decided, "you are ready. Will you dress?"

A eunuch waited with another tray, on which there lay a pair of the silk trousers, a bolero jacket, and a jewelled cap, together with the inevitable pair of felt slippers. The prevailing motif was crimson, with gold thread intertwined at the hems and on the shoulders. It felt extremely odd to be wearing clothes without a single undergarment, and she could not reconcile herself to the way the bolero failed to reach farther across than her nipples; despite the heat in the room, her chest felt quite cold. And then, to her surprise, the *Harem Agha* adorned her with a white *yashmak,* following which he clapped his hands, and one of the eunuchs hastily produced a large mirror, which he held up for her inspection.

She supposed she did look quite magnificent. The heat and the bath had induced a faintly pinkish tinge into her flesh, which in any event seem to glow after its massage. The crimson of the sheer trousers did no more than outline the shape of her legs—another shock, she had never exposed her legs in her entire life before—and provided a titillating shadow to the nakedness of her groin. Her nipples peeped round the hem of the bolero, and she was delighted with the way her breasts seemed to leave her chest in a straight line, without a trace of sag, although this was assisted by her carefully controlled breathing.

And then, to top it all, the concealed face, and the long white hair flowing out from beneath the crimson cap. *Why,* she thought, *I could almost fall in love with me. But whatever would Madame St. Amant think of such a thought? Madame St. Amant. Laurens. Seraphine. If they could see me now,* she thought. *If they could know me now.*

And David?

"Well, lady, are you satisfied?" inquired the *Harem Agha.*

"I am amazed," she said. "How often do I suffer such a metamorphosis?"

"That depends on how you please His Highness, lady. As a *guizde,* why not more than once a month. As an *ikbal,* why, perhaps once a week. But should you ever attain the dizzy heights of an *odalik,* why then you will spend much of every day in a chamber such as this. Although clearly on a future occasion you will not require so much work."

"I am glad to hear that," she said, "And now, if it is possible, could I be shown my bedchamber? I am extremely tired, and wish only to go to sleep."

The *Harem Agha* permitted himself a smile. "Sleep is not for you this night, lady. Come. It is time for you to visit the bedchamber of the Dey."

"Now?" She discovered her voice had risen an octave. So soon, her mind wanted to shout. *Not so soon. Not until I have had a rest.*

"It is His Highness's custom to retire early, lady," the *Harem Agha* explained. "And certainly when he is expecting his latest acquisition, and from Paris to boot. If you will accompany me . . ." He was already opening another door let into the wall.

Give me strength, Catherine prayed. *To do what?* Refuse him, and be dragged off screaming? Or worse yet, to be thrust straightaway into a sack and dumped in the

121

sea? *No, no.* The strength had to be to remember every-thing Ricimer had taught her. That should not be diffi-cult. Until the excesses of the bath had seized hold of her mind she had thought of nothing else.

The *Harem Agha* was waiting; he had taken a torch from its holder in the wall, and the light flared to make him seem twice his actual size. She hurried into the corridor, and one of the other eunuchs closed the door behind her. She thought of the Greek girls being taken to the Minotaur. She had no idea how she would react when faced with the monster, because that he was a monster she did not doubt for a moment.

The *Harem Agha* led the way, down some steps, along a corridor, and then up another flight of steps. Once or twice she thought she heard a sound beyond the wall, even a giggle of laughter to suggest that she was passing close to the apartments of the other ladies of the *harem*, and she also passed several doors let into the otherwise bare walls of the corridor. But these were firmly shut, and there were no guards. In any event, her brain was too preoccupied with her coming ordeal, fearing her heart might beat too loudly, her body might sweat, which would surely undo much of the work put in by the eunuchs.

The second staircase climbed for some time, and then just as she was running out of breath, they entered a small room furnished only with two divans.

"This is the *mabeyin*," said the *Harem Agha*, "the room connecting the *harem* with the *selamlik*, the part of the palace reserved for men. It leads directly to the chamber of the Dey." He opened a door on the far side of the room. But he did not go through. Instead he waited for her.

"Oh, Lord," she whispered.

He smiled. "You will have time to collect your thoughts, lady. His Highness is not yet in the room."

Still she hesitated. "Shall I undress?"

The *Harem Agha* shrugged. "You will do as you see fit, lady. Now go, I will remain here."

Remarkably, she found that a most reassuring thought.

But he seemed able to read her mind. "In case of a summons from my lord, lady. Not to assist you."

She sighed, and stepped through the door, felt it shut behind her. The chamber was large, and clearly high in the palace; the left-hand wall was nothing more than a series of arches leading on to a balcony, over which a gentle sea breeze wafted the sounds as well as the smells of the city, before ruffling the drapes on the bed, because here was no divan but a European four-poster. The only other furniture in the room was two divans; these, like the bed, were draped in heavy crimson brocade, decorated with gold thread, much as she was herself outfitted.

She was alerted by the sound of the gong. Evening prayer. He would come, immediately after the prayer. Ten minutes. *Oh, Lord,* she thought, *ten minutes.*

Was she allowed on the balcony? She was, after all, wearing her *yashmak.* She crossed the room, noiselessly in her slippers, enjoyed the comfort of standing in the open air, allowing the breeze to play over her hairless body, tickling and caressing as it wrapped the silk around her legs. And was suddenly too cool. She shivered, re-entered the room. Should she lie down? Should she undress? But her instincts told her she would have more impact by undressing before him. Before him. *I am about to lose my virginity,* she thought. *I am about to be . . .* she did not even know a verb for it.

The door on the far side of the room opened, and she turned, hands clasping her throat. A eunuch entered, scarcely glanced at her and bowed as the Dey followed him in. Catherine's knees gave way and she sank to the carpet, head bowed, still clasping her throat. She felt, rather than heard him approach her, as he also wore felt slippers, predictably in crimson. Above that was the white wool of his robe.

The door closed again; the eunuch had left. She was alone with Hussein bin Hassan, the Dey of Algiers, and she could not move a muscle.

"You are beautiful," he said, in French, his voice remarkably soft. "Ricimer does not lie to me. Rise."

She pushed her head back, rose in the same instant,

her hands falling to her side, gazed at him in total consternation. What had she expected? A man old enough to be her father. But that had involved thoughts of Papa. And his friends. Mostly military men, crisp and vigorous of speech and habit. This man appeared old enough to be her grandfather, or Papa's grandfather, even. She gazed at a somewhat small face, from which the white moustache and white beard seemed to cascade; the beard reached the centre of his chest. He was not a big man, hardly taller than herself, and his brown eyes were the mildest she had ever seen. His whole expression was totally benign. He reminded her of a very senior priest who had once visited Madame St. Amant's to hold Communion, and was even more simply dressed, for he wore a white *jibba* and a crimson *fez*, and no insignia or jewellery, though there were several rings on the fingers of each hand.

She realised her mouth was open, and hastily closed it again. But if her distress had shown, he did not seem to notice it. "Let me see your face," he said.

She pulled off her *yashmak,* so hastily she disarranged her cap. She put up her hands to straighten it, but he shook his head. "That too."

She removed it, inhaled, watched his face.

"Quite lovely," he said. "Such hair . . ." He stretched out his hand, allowed the silver threads to trickle through his fingers. "And you are not even French, but American."

She licked her lips. "Yes, my lord."

He smiled. She had not noticed his mouth before, hidden as it was between beard and moustache. "We were visited by some Americans, oh, twenty-five years ago. I still have their heads."

Her chin dropped again, and once again she clamped her mouth shut. Hussein turned away from her. "Undress," he said, and sat on the bed, drawing his legs beneath him to suggest that whatever was his age he did not suffer from rheumatism. Catherine tore at her clothes, her ideas of coquetry forgotten. *Where was the passion?* she thought. It had been there, in her belly, while the eunuchs had been bathing her. Now it was gone. She was aware only of exhaustion. Not even of fear. *Would he notice? How could he notice?* And she had been taught by Ricimer. She need do no more than she had been taught.

"Quite beautiful," the Dey murmured, and suddenly leaned forward, to catch her round the buttocks and bring her against him, so that he could kiss her recently shaved pubes.

She said, "Oh," before she could stop herself, and shivered, not so much at the touch of his lips but because his beard was tickling her thighs, although in fact she had anticipated nothing quite so direct.

He released her and raised his head. "Do you fear me?"

She licked her lips. "My lord, I . . ."

"Undress me," he commanded, standing.

She took the *fez* from his head, turned to find somewhere to set it, crossed the room and placed it on the divan, terribly aware that he was watching her every movement. Well, then, should she attempt to be more sinuous, more sexual? Or was the fact of her nakedness sufficient?

How could it be, when he had another hundred-odd waiting downstairs?

She returned to him, having trouble with her breathing, and eased his *jibba* from his shoulders. This too she laid on the divan, returned for his outer silk shirt, was placing this on the divan when she suddenly discovered he was behind her, once again holding her buttocks, parting them and sliding his hand between.

She jerked straight, this time choking back the exclamation.

"I have another shirt," he said.

She turned, slowly, heart pounding, raised this in turn. Now at last she could look down. And wanted to cry out in relief. He was hard. Not as hard as Ricimer or Ahmed, perhaps, but hard. And for all his age, and his somewhat large belly, he looked little different from them . . . except that she realised he was considerably smaller.

"You move like an animal," he said. "Like a cat. I like that."

She licked her lips, and he extended his hands. Slowly she removed his rings, even in her state of confusion estimating the value of the diamonds and sapphires and rubies at several thousand francs. She laid them in a row on the table, straightened, and attempted a smile. But he was waiting for her to do something. And he was hard. She stepped round him, went to the bed and lay down, on her back, spreading her legs. *Let it happen now*, she prayed to herself. *Now, now, now, and be done. Oh, let it happen now*.

Hussein followed more slowly, frowning. And to her horror she watched him begin to droop.

"Has Ricimer taught you nothing?"

"My lord . . ." She sat up, heart pounding. It was definitely lost now.

"Or is it that you do not like me?" His voice remained soft, but she discovered his eyes had changed. They glittered, like polished brown pebbles.

"My lord," she gasped. "Forgive me. I am so tired. I . . ."

"Tired?" he inquired. "Tired, in the bedchamber of your lord?" He snapped his fingers. The noise was not loud, but immediately both doors opened to admit his own eunuch and the *Harem Agha*, to suggest they had been watching through some concealed peephole. "The lady is tired," the Dey said, still looking at her. "Remove her to rest. I shall not see her again."

The *Harem Agha* bowed.

"And bring me the boy," Hussein said to the other eunuch, "that my evening may not be entirely wasted."

This eunuch bowed in turn, and left the room. The *Harem Agha* approached the bed, and Catherine realised that she had just been condemned to death. And for a moment welcomed it. Death would mean an end to fear, and humiliation, and misery. Death would mean . . . that she would never ever have the chance of seeing Papa again. *Or David Mulawer*. Why, David had not tamely submitted when faced with four men. He had used the skills he had been taught to defeat them, and save her from an even earlier humiliation, perhaps even from death.

Then she must use the skills she had been taught to keep alive, and if possible triumph. She rose to her knees. "My lord," she cried, her heart seeming to slow with desperate fear. "My lord, forgive me. I was but overwhelmed by your presence."

The Dey had turned his back on her, and the eunuch was reaching for her arm. She rolled away from him, reached her feet on the far side of the bed, ran across the room. Hussein turned to face her again, looking mildly alarmed. Behind her she heard the *Harem Agha* pant as he hurried round the bed.

"My lord," she said, lowering her voice and attempting to eliminate any suggestion of fear. "My lord." She threw her arms around Hussein's body, brought him against her. "Ricimer indeed taught me well, my lord, but I was unprepared for so much majesty." Disgust at her self abasement rose into her throat, and she forced it down. Now was a time to think only of sex, to create the passion in herself if the man could not do it, to will herself to orgasm, to carry him along with it.

She kissed him on the mouth, found it shut, and worked her lips and her tongue as Ricimer had taught her. She felt the eunuch behind her, felt his hands on her arms, and trickled her fingers up and down the Dey's spine. Now was no time for thinking. There was only time to do. She felt the penis move against her groin and rose on tiptoe to allow it between her legs and then closed her legs again, and in the same instant felt the eunuch's fingers leave her arms even as the Dey's mouth opened.

His breath was sweet, as was his taste. And his body was surprisingly firm, while there could be no gainsaying the rising power between her legs. She moved her face away from his, smiled at him, heart at last regaining its normal beat and then flooding past normalcy to race. "My lord will lack nothing from me," she whispered.

Hussein seemed to slide down her as he knelt, his lips once again searching for her groin. That was clearly his favourite occupation. She moved forward as she spread her legs, so that he was hugged against her flesh, holding his head while she almost stood above him, feeling his tongue, and feeling, too, the build of real passion. He was a man, and she was a woman. He fell over and she knelt above him, and then was seized with an idea, and turned, still on her knees, so that he had her groin as she had his. "It has lips," Ricimer had said. "Why not kiss them?"

She kissed and sucked and stroked and felt him doing the same and knew, instinctively, when he was ready, when to delay a moment longer might be to lose him in an ejaculation, and turned her body again, feeling his hands slide across her buttocks, twisting so that her mouth could reach his again, wrapping her legs around his, pushing her hands down to seize his own buttocks and bring him against her. His beard filled her face and she thought she would choke, but he was rocking with his pleasure, and now she felt him where only Ricimer's fingers had ever gone before. Instinctively her body began to tense, but she made herself relax, and rolled on her back, holding him tightly so that he rolled as well, and felt a surge of pain followed by a ballooning feeling in her belly, even as he jerked against her and his mouth became slack.

Slowly she allowed her muscles to unwind, felt for the first time the hardness of the floor beneath the carpet, wondered for the first time where the *Harem Agha* was, could breathe, it seemed, for the first time. Her passion had subsided, although it was quite unsatisfied; rather had it been overtaken by an exhaustion which was as much mental as physical.

And slowly Hussein rose to his knees. "On the floor," he said. "On the floor." He smiled. "I have not taken a woman on the floor since my youth. Allah has been good to me. And to think I nearly had thee smothered." He reached forward, ran his finger down the line of her jaw. "Ricimer will be rewarded."

Through clouds of exhaustion her brain still flickered. She had achieved a certain triumph. She was sure of that. "And what of me, my lord?" How quiet her voice. How calm. How perfectly confident. She should have been on the stage.

Hussein smiled again. "Thou will also be rewarded." He held out his hand, and she hastily got up, to turn in alarm as the door opened. It was the eunuch, and with him was Jean-Pierre.

He wore a robe, but it was opened down the front, and underneath he was naked. Instinctively she closed her hands over her belly, at the same time half bending as if thus she could conceal her breasts. He stared at her in total incomprehension.

"Ashamed of thy beauty?" inquired the Dey, softly.

"My lord . . ." She backed away, and sat on the bed.

Hussein waved his hand, and the eunuch left. Jean-Pierre continued to stare at them; he was very afraid—she could see his muscles trembling.

"You do not need him now, my lord, surely."

"Perhaps not," Hussein agreed. "Yet will it be sport. And he has already looked upon thee, lady. It would be a waste to send him away." He held out his hand. "Come here, boy."

Jean-Pierre licked his lips, then slowly crossed the floor. "Such a pretty child," Hussein remarked. "Ricimer has done doubly well."

"My lord." Catherine knelt on the edge of the bed, sheltering behind Hussein's body. "Send him away, my lord."

"Thou art jealous." Hussein himself took the robe from Jean-Pierre's shoulders; Catherine stared at the boy in horror. There could be no questioning his arousal. But he had never been circumcised. And suddenly she realised why he had not met her gaze as they had left the ship, why he flushed as he looked at her now; he also had spent the voyage being instructed in his duties. "I assure thee," the Dey continued, "there is no need to be. He will not, he cannot, rival thee. But he may amuse us both."

"My lord," she gasped. "He is my brother."

Hussein's head turned, and he frowned. "Thou wouldst

not lie to me, child. He bears no resemblance to thee at all."

"My stepbrother, my lord."

Hussein's frown cleared, and he even gave a short laugh. "But that is droll. It would have been better had he been thy brother. Come here, boy, I would handle you."

Jean-Pierre gazed at her in bemusement. But he had moved closer, and now his face changed, into a mixture of consternation and pleasure. Catherine turned away from them, threw herself on her face on the bed, hid her head in her arms. She wanted to stop listening, but she could not. Hussein seemed to coo, and Jean-Pierre gasped. *What has happened to me?* she thought. *What is to become of me?*

She felt a hand on her buttock, and then another. "She is beautiful, is she not?" Hussein inquired. "How are you called?"

She heard Jean-Pierre inhale. "Jean-Pierre."

"And she? Your sister?"

"Catherine."

"Catherine. There is a charming name. And yet, not charming enough. I shall call her *Ya Habibti*. Do you know what that means, Jean-Pierre?"

"No, my lord."

"It means my darling. Is she not a darling, Jean-Pierre?"

"Oh, yes, my lord."

"Then love her, Jean-Pierre. Be sure of only one thing, that you do not enter her. For should you do that, then I will have you boiled alive."

She felt fingers on her back again, and sliding up to grasp her shoulders, and thence under her armpits to stroke the sides of her breasts. She endeavoured to nestle further into the covers, and felt her legs being spread, and when she tensed her muscles and attempted to resist, received a light slap which convinced her that *those* fingers belonged to the Dey himself.

She was in more fear of being sodomised than of facing Jean-Pierre, and rolled on her back. His face was

130

pressed into her flesh and slid with her, over her shoulder and into her neck, and suddenly the passion which had seemed to dissipate itself without climax when she had lost her virginity swelled again, to take control of her limbs. If this was what the Dey wanted, well, then, who was she to gainsay the Dey? This no doubt was to be her life forever more. One of total immorality, or perhaps amorality would be a better word, of total lasciviousness, of total corruption. Well, then, as Seraphine would say, lie back and enjoy it. Oh, how Seraphine would love to be incarcerated in a *harem*.

She wrapped her arms round Jean-Pierre's neck, kissed him on the mouth, sucked his tongue into hers, attempted to find his penis with her groin and found fingers instead, the Dey's fingers, prying and exploring, and now she could feel his breath on her flesh, and he began to kiss her, but almost savagely, sucking mouthfuls of flesh before releasing them, and suddenly Jean-Pierre was thrust aside, to roll right out of the bed and on to the floor with a startled grunt, and the Dey was in his place, squirming on her belly, his beard as usual filling her mouth and nose, so that she gasped for breath, his penis once again stroking her clitoris before thrusting in, and this time there was no pain, only a surge of tremendous passion. *My time has come,* she thought with an almost triumphant feeling that she was about to explode. *I will have an orgasm, and then I will love him. Even the Dey of Algiers, I will love him, as I love Ricimer. Now, she thought, now.*

But the Dey was lying still. She had not even noticed his ejaculation so great had been the preoccupation of her own thoughts. She discovered her eyes were open, and his beard still lay across her mouth, his mouth was against her ear, and gently sighing. She watched the door open, and the eunuch enter, and tap Jean-Pierre, slowly rising to his knees, on the shoulder. The boy gave her a half-smile, rose to his feet, was escorted to the door. He had not climaxed, was harder than ever. But she supposed he would soon do so; the eunuch was also smiling. *But oh, Lord,* she thought, *that I can consider such an event without fainting. That I can lie here, beneath a Turkish pirate, without fainting. That I should so nearly have known complete happpiness, in his arms.*

"*Ya Habibti,*" he whispered into her ear. "*Ya Habibti.* Twice in one night, *Ya Habibti.* It is seventeen years since I have known twice in one night. I shall sleep sound. So sound." As he was clearly preparing to do, on her belly.

"Shall I withdraw, my lord?" she whispered.

"No," he said. "No. Thou shalt stay with me, *Ya Habibti.* For where twice is possible, why not three times?"

Catherine awoke, to a tremendous feeling of well-being, of utter languor, utter comfort. The sea breeze drifted through the open arches to ruffle the drapes around the bed, ruffle her hair, caress her body. She thought she could lie there forever. She did not wish to think. Thought involved memory, and she suspected memory would be distasteful. Nor did she wish to consider the future. The future was unthinkable, and not only on her account. Far better to live in the present, in the utter pleasure of the moment.

Yet now she was awake, memory refused to be ignored. She turned her head, discovered the bed to be empty, save for herself. She raised herself on her elbow, gazed at the *Harem Agha,* just rising from the floor; it had been the voice of the *muezzin* calling his people to morning prayer which had awakened her. He was smiling. "It is time for you to return to the *harem,* Lady Catherine."

Her head twisted, to and fro. Memory was in full command now.

The *Harem Agha* continued to smile. "You did well, Lady Catherine. There is naught to fear. His Highness was well pleased. More pleased than I can remember, and I have been here a long time."

Catherine sat up. "Jean-Pierre. Where is Jean-Pierre?"

The *Harem Agha*'s smile died. "The boy? He has been removed, Lady Catherine. He will be disposed of."

"Disposed of?" she shrieked, and got to her knees. "He cannot die."

"He has looked upon my lady's beauty," the *Harem Agha* said, severely. "He has *known* my lady's beauty. No man save the Dey may do that and live."

She caught his hands. "He is my brother. Please understand. My brother. He cannot die. Listen . . ." She gasped for breath. "His Highness promised me a reward, because I pleased him. I do not know what he had in mind, but I wish only the life of my brother. He can be banished. He can be made a slave. But I wish his life. If he is to be executed, then tell His Highness to execute me as well, because I will never please him again."

The *Harem Agha*'s face was a mixture of bewilderment and severity. "That is foolish talk, Lady Catherine. It may be that the world of Algiers is at your feet. What, would you cast it away? That boy is not your brother. He is your stepbrother. There is no blood relation."

The world at my feet, she thought. *Oh, God, give me strength. Or give me stubbornness, however foolish.*

"I will not have him die," she whispered. "I will not have him die."

"Then he shall not die," said the Dey.

Catherine turned, still on her knees, instinctively threw herself on her face across the bed. He had been there all the time, in the adjoining room, being dressed by two other eunuchs.

"My lord," she gasped. "My lord, if you could understand . . ."

"I do." The Dey took her hands, and assisted her back to her knees. "To discover a creature as lovely as thee, *Ya Habibti,* is a rare privilege. To discover that she also possesses emotions, feelings, compassion, is rarer yet. I give thy brother to thee, as a slave."

"My lord," she said. "I know not how to express my gratitude."

The Dey smiled. "By loving me. Selim will see to the matter of thy stepbrother. The Lady Catherine has my permission to be present at the castration, Selim."

The *Harem Agha* bowed.

While the words slowly sank into Catherine's brain. "Castration?" she gasped. "Castration, my lord?" she shouted. "Where is the generosity in that?"

"Hush, lady," Selim said, and reached for her arm.

She wriggled free and scrambled from the bed. "My lord, a man would rather die than suffer such a fate."

Hussein frowned at her. "Not all men, *Ya Habibti.* Selim and these others have survived quite happily, and contrive to live a pleasant and useful life. Nor are they as devoid of feeling as thou mayst suppose." He shrugged. "The choice is thine, *Ya Habibti.* The law is perfectly plain. No man may look upon another man's woman and live, save he is a member of the *harem* himself. That is point one. Point two is that no whole man may belong to the *harem,* save he is a son of the house. The choice is thine." He turned and left the room.

The eunuchs closed the door behind him. Catherine continued to stare at it for some seconds. *What have I done?* she thought. *What can I do?*

"Lady?" Selim draped her *haik* around her shoulders. "It is time to return to the *harem.*"

She turned, into his arms, rested her head on his shoulder. And but a few hours before she had regarded him with fear and with horror. "What am I to do, Selim? What am I to do?"

"As His Highness has said, the choice is yours, lady." Gently he escorted her across the floor to the inner door, left her there while he gathered her discarded clothes of the night before. "My advice would naturally be prejudiced."

"Will he be happy, Selim? Could he?"

"I am happy enough, lady. Consider a famous warrior who loses his right arm in battle. Can he not also be happy? But your stepbrother is more fortunate even than that. He is too young to have learned his own prowess. Last night will have been the only occasion he will ever have known the delights of the flesh, and you may be sure that this morning he is in a sorely confused state. It is always so. He may even be grateful to you, should he survive."

134

"Should he survive?" she cried.

"Well, lady, it is no simple matter. Oh, to wield the knife requires only skill, and provided the boy's heart is sound he will overcome the pain of it. But yet does it remain a hideous wound for some time, and in a part of the body which is required for natural functions. The bladder must empty, lady."

"Oh, my God. But . . ."

"A wooden tube is inserted immediately after the operation, lady, through which this function may be performed. If painfully. But in any event the intake of water is kept to a minimum for three days. There is the crucial period. For it is then that the assaulted area swells, and here is the risk, that the tube may become so embedded that it cannot be removed, and death invariably follows an attempt. But should he remain healthy, and not become infected, why, after three days the swelling goes down, the tube may be removed, and within a month he is able to go about his duties, which in his case will be constant attendance upon you, lady. Will that not be pleasing to you?"

"To me?" She pushed herself away from him, entered the corridor. "And you expect me to expose him to so much pain, so much risk of death, on top of so much humiliation?"

"I fail to perceive where is the risk of death, lady, when death is his only alternative."

What a blessing my hair is already white, she thought, *for it is surely turning at this moment*. Even her hunger had disappeared in misery.

Whereas Selim apparently considered her mind already made up. "It is your privilege to visit him, before the operation, if you wish. It is your privilege to grant him one last hour of pleasure. Provided you do not allow him entry, of course. But I will attend you, and restrain you."

"To . . ." She stopped to stare at him. "I have never heard of anything quite so horrible."

"The boy will survive, lady, if he is healthy. Is it not always better to live, however maimed, than to die?"

135

That I should have to make such a decision, she thought. *Should I not ask Madeleine?* But that was impossible. Madeleine's reactions were impossible to imagine. Certainly it was not a decision she should make.

"Lady?"

She sighed, and proceeded down the corridor. "You are right, of course. I would have him live."

"Then it shall be as you wish."

"And now is there somewhere I may lie down? I am quite exhausted."

"Your bedchamber awaits you." He seemed embarrassed, which was totally unlike her expectation of his character.

"Do I share it?"

"No, no, lady. It is yours. And your slaves also await you. I have but to say . . . lady, I consider your future to be bright as the stars, and I am glad of this, for during these past hours I have grown to admire your spirit as much as I may admire your beauty. But I must warn you that this future of which I speak is not yet arrived. I would beg you to be on your guard, and this day more than any other. I fear your ordeal is not yet complete."

Catherine had no idea what he was talking about, nor was she at this moment particularly interested. She was aware only of exhaustion, as much emotional as physical, while despite her revulsion at what was about to happen to Jean-Pierre, she was once again becoming very hungry. After all, she recalled, since her attenuated breakfast of the previous morning, on board Ricimer's ship, she had taken only a glass of sherbet and two cups of coffee.

Was it only this time yesterday that I was on board Ricimer's ship? she thought.

Selim continued to lead her down the passageway, considerably farther than they had travelled the previous night to gain the *selamlik,* so that she realised they had passed the bathing chamber and were proceeding even deeper into the depths of the *harem.* At last he opened another door to allow her into a broad and light corridor, beyond which there were again the sound of female

136

voices, and off which there opened several other doorways. At one of these he paused.

"I will say farewell, lady. May Allah go with you."

"And you?" She was suddenly terrified at being left alone.

"I shall attend to the matter of your stepbrother, before anything else." He hesitated. "You are sure you do not wish to be a witness?"

"I am quite sure," she said. "Will he be told the decision is mine?"

"Not unless you wish it."

"I would prefer to tell him myself, at some more suitable time. When his survival is assured."

Selim bowed. "I was told that you are extremely young in years, lady. I can but say that you are old indeed in mind. Allah will surely protect one as you." He continued on his way, and Catherine continued to hesitate before opening the door. *Young in years*, she thought. *Have I not been forced to change from a child to a woman in a single night?* She had a sudden desire to look at herself, to note the changes, for surely there would be visible change.

She pushed the door open, paused in surprise. The room was light and airy, with one wall open to the sky, as in the Dey's own bedchamber. But not to the outside of the palace, she realised; she could see other galleries opposite her, and the sounds of laughter from below told her that she was on one of the upper floors overlooking the central court where she had first entered the *harem*.

"Catherine. Oh, my darling girl." Madeleine threw herself across the room. She was dressed in a plain blue *haik*, which also covered her hair, but was not wearing a *yashmak*. "What have they done to you, Catherine?" Having embraced her, Madeleine stepped back in dismay, for the loose robe was swinging open and she could see that her body hair had been removed.

Catherine kissed her on the cheek. "I have been prepared to see my lord."

"And have you seen him?" The question came from

Cora, who was also in the room, and dressed very much as Madeleine herself.

"I have seen him," Catherine said.

"Oh, my darling," Madeleine wailed, again throwing her arms round her stepdaughter. "Was it so terrible?"

"No, Madeleine," she said. "It was not terrible at all." *Not for me*, she thought. *What will you say, dear step-mama, when you learn the truth?*

"But was he pleased?" Cora asked.

"I am here," Catherine pointed out, once again disengaging herself.

"Thus he was not *dis*pleased. But there is yet a world of difference between a *guizde* and an *odalik*."

Catherine shrugged. She was looking around the room. It was simply enough furnished, with the inevitable two divans and several rugs on the floor; the walls were not bare, as in the Dey's chamber, but were instead decorated with a variety of coloured plates, of a Dutch design, she decided, to her surprise. And in the corner there was a vast trunk, which suggested all manner of hidden treasures. But for the moment she wanted only to lie down. "Of that," she said, "I have no idea. Supposing he was pleased, will he send for me again?"

"Perhaps," Cora said. "Should the *Harem Agha* require you for your toilette before the week is out, we may assume that His Highness is pleased. It must be our responsibility to keep you safe against that moment."

"Safe?" Catherine threw herself across the bed. "Oh, *I* am safe enough. I am so tired. And so hungry." She propped her chin on her hands. "Is it possible to eat?"

"Of course. Woman," Cora snapped. "Food for your mistress."

Madeleine stared at her in amazement, and Catherine sat up. "I can fetch my own."

"What absurdity. This woman is your *halaik*, your woman slave. She must see to your requirements."

"And are you not a slave also?" Catherine demanded.

Cora bowed. "But I am a *khalfa*. I am a head slave. It is my business to see others carry out their duties, not

138

to undertake them myself. You heard your mistress, woman, food and drink."

"I will do it," Madeleine said, and actually smiled. "What a topsy-turvy world it is, to be sure, my darling. But at least we are alive, and cared for. Had I only my dear Jean-Pierre, or at least news of him, then I would be as content as possible in these circumstances." She hurried off, while Catherine bit her lip. News of him. Oh, God, news of him.

"It is not wise to be indulgent with slaves," Cora said severely.

"I will not have my stepmother ill-treated," Catherine said, equally severely. "Now, is there such a thing as a mirror in this place?"

"I have one here, lady." Cora hurried forward with an ornate hand glass. Catherine took it, almost reluctantly, looked at herself. No change at all. She could not believe it. The face regarding her was calm, unnaturally beautiful —for where was the harm in thinking that now, when her entire life depended upon that simple fact—the pale blue eyes almost disdainful in their coolness. *The Ice Maiden, David Mulawer had called her. Well, no longer a maiden, to be sure.*

She put down the glass as Madeleine hurried into the room with a tray laden with jugs of milk, pots of honey, bowls of yoghurt. "Breakfast?" she asked in dismay.

"They eat differently from us," Madeleine explained.

"This food is all healthy, lady," Cora admonished.

"No doubt. What I would really like is a glass of wine. Will you see to it, Cora?"

"Wine? That is impossible."

"Impossible? But I have commanded you."

"And the Prophet Mohammed has forbidden it, lady."

Catherine stared at her. She had forgotten that this place was not even Christian. Something to discuss with Madeleine, whenever they were left alone. "Are you a Moslem, Cora?"

"I am a Believer, lady. I was taught the way when I was first brought here. If you would prosper to the limits of your talent and beauty, you will follow the same course."

"Never," Madeleine declared. "Tell her so, my darling."

"*Ya Habibti*," Catherine muttered. "You will have to teach me Turkish, Cora." She ate, slowly, allowing the various liquids to slip down her throat. Would it matter, whether or not she remained a Christian? Cora supposed it did. But only from a point of view of convenience, surely. To change one's religion, without a total loss of faith in it, was surely the lowest of human acts. Besides, she suddenly realised, do that and you have lost your very last individuality. Then truly will you sink into the depths of the *harem*, to be forgotten.

She was so tired. She lay down, and closed her eyes, and a moment later was sound asleep. To awake with a start, some hours later, she knew immediately, for the day had grown very hot, to suggest it was about noon.

And there was noise. She opened her eyes, gazed at faces, listened to giggles and whispering voices. She sat up, hastily trying to close her robe, which had fallen open as she slept, looked from left to right. There were at least thirty women in the room, varying from young girls scarce older than herself to matrons older than Madeleine. But where was Madeleine? And where was Cora?

"Hello," she said. "I know no Turkish. Does no one here speak French? Or English?"

"Why, I speak French," said Thérèse Cavaigny.

"Well, then," Catherine said. "Perhaps you could convey to these ladies my pleasure that they have come to call, and my apologies for being asleep. I was very tired."

"After your night with the Dey," Thérèse said.

"Why, yes."

"Was he pleased with you?"

"I think so."

Thérèse spoke rapidly in Turkish to the other women, who burst into a chorus of mingled laughter and comment. Then one leaned forward and seized Catherine's hair, fingering it and pulling it at the same time.

"Ow," Catherine shouted, and attempted to free herself, only to find her wrist seized by another woman, while a third grasped her ankle.

"Oh," she cried. "Help me." She looked at Thérèse.

Who continued to smile. "Help *you*, my dear. We are going to show you your place." Once again she spoke rapidly in Turkish, while more and more women seized hold of Catherine, ripping the *haik* from her shoulders, and dragging her naked from the bed. *What is going to happen to me?* she thought.

"Cora," she shouted. "Stop them. What are they doing?"

Cora had appeared at the back of the mob, together with Madeleine, where no doubt they had been thrust by the avalanche of women, all of whom were their superiors. Now she attempted to remonstrate in Turkish, to be slapped on the face and pushed away again. Catherine listened to Madeleine screaming, more in anger than pain, but she was too preoccupied with what was happening to herself, for now she was thrown back on to the bed again, losing all of her breath in the process, and held by her ankles, which were lifted into the air, while a new ripple of excitement drifted through the crowd, and she gazed in horror at an instrument which was suddenly produced from the back of the room, two planks of wood, hinged together at one end, with matching semicircular cutouts in the centre.

Thérèse was very close, behind her head, pulling her hair and smiling at her. "The bastinado," she said. "It makes you think."

Catherine gasped, and attempted to wriggle, and had her ankles lifted higher yet, so that she was almost resting on her shoulders, a position as humiliating as it was uncomfortable.

"You cannot," Cora gasped at the French woman. "The Dey was pleased. He will send for her again. If she is marked . . ."

"Pleased?" Thérèse demanded. "With this child? Oh, he will send for her again, *khalfa,* but not for at least a week. By then no doubt she will be able to walk again, and she will have learned some humility. She will be even more pleasing to him."

Oh, my God, Catherine thought. She had heard too many tales of the bastinado. Once again she attempted to wriggle herself free, and one of the women stuck her long painted nails into her stomach, so hard that she lost all of her breath, and could only gasp as the two planks were parted, and one of her ankles placed in each of the cutout apertures, whereupon the two planks were brought back together and secured at the free end, to leave her legs in a sort of movable stocks. This was bad enough, but now the planks were lifted again, by two of the fattest and strongest of the women, and rested on their shoulders, while at the same time they moved away from the divan, so that Catherine found herself being dragged forward, and off the bed. She just had time to put her hands down to stop her head smashing into the marble floor, and then she found herself suspended from her ankles, while her hair trailed around her and the women laughed and screamed their enjoyment.

Which had not yet started. For now another of the older *guizdes,* also a big, strong woman, produced a thin bamboo cane. Catherine discovered Thérèse once again smiling at her. "You may scream if you wish," she recommended. "Everyone does."

Help me, Catherine thought. She pushed her hands down and attempted to hold herself from the floor, attempted to turn, realised her total helplessness while she was held at this angle, watched the big woman smiling as she raised the cane for the first blow, opened her mouth to scream, and felt her bottom hit the floor with a tremendous impact as the wooden frame was suddenly released by her tormentors.

For a moment she lost her breath again, and could only gasp, dimly aware that the women had all retreated against the wall, and were bowing their heads, while some were even prostrating themselves on the floor, as a whisper spread along the corridor outside and seeped into the room:

"The Dey comes. The Dey comes."

Still breathless, and too bemused even to attempt to move, she watched an expression of the most utter disbelief crossing Thérèse Cavaigny's face, as she too sank to her knees.

"It cannot be," she whispered. "The Dey does not visit the *harem*. He sends, when he is ready."

Selim entered the room. Catherine realised how undignified she must look, and sat up, for behind Selim there were three other eunuchs, and then, indeed, Hussein bin Hassan himself. The eunuchs stood aside, and their master occupied the centre of the floor, glancing from left to right. Then he pointed at the frame, and two of the eunuchs hastily knelt and released Catherine's legs. She drew them out, forgetful of the pain in her ankles as she pulled them beneath her and rose to her knees.

"My lord . . ."

"Ya Habibti," said Hussein, in the softest of tones. "I am unable to concentrate. I am unable to think, save of thee. I will spend this afternoon in my bedchamber. Come." He held out his hand, and she grasped it to be pulled to her feet. She could almost feel the quiver of suppressed emotion which ran round the room.

She licked her lips. "I . . . I must apologise for . . . for this game."

The Dey smiled. "Thou art too generous, *Ya Habibti.* I know their little games. They shall be whipped." He spoke in Turkish, and Selim bowed. Once again the quiver went round the room, but this time it was composed of fear.

"They will receive fifty lashes each," the Dey said in French. "If we listen, as we eat, we may hear their screams."

"My lord," she said. "They will hate me forever more."

"What is the hatred of cattle?" he inquired. "When one experiences the love of the sun." He offered her his arm.

Chapter 5

ഇഇഇഇഇഇഇഇഇ THE wailing cry of the *muezzin* drifted through the still air, penetrated the recesses of the palace. Catherine stirred, comfortably, and nestled herself deeper into the divan. It was the hour of *fedjeur,* the dawn prayer, and all around her the court would be stirring into life. But for her there were a few moments longer of comfortable relaxation; last night she had not been required to attend the Dey. Here was a rare occasion, and the more to be treasured. However much he valued her, however much, indeed, he loved her, for she did not think there was much doubt about that, she could not rid herself of the feeling of imminent disaster when in his company. She knew him too well, and if she no longer felt any personal insecurity, she could never be sure when his utter contempt for human life and dignity might not reach out and strike down someone else.

Troublesome thoughts, when she was enjoying her morning lie-in. And this was a special occasion. She rolled on her stomach, hugging the pillows close. It was the seventh of December, by European calculation, in the year of Our Lord 1829, or the third of *Zul Kadeh,* in the year of the Prophet 1207, by Algerian calculation, and she was eighteen years old.

She sat up in sudden alarm, rising to her hands and knees, and staying there for a moment, her hair trailing past her cheeks to brush the pillow. Eighteen years old. Slowly she lowered herself to sit on her own heels; she slept naked, save for the silver anklets which she and every other inmate of the *harem* had been given by their master, and the morning breeze was cooling to her flesh. She had been here nearly two years. A lifetime. Certainly a period which made that life she had once known seem a dream seen through the wrong end of a telescope. Nearly two years in which she had hardly read a book, had played not a note on the piano, had attended no soirées and ridden no horse.

Two years in which she had been allowed to fulfil only woman's most basic function, that of providing happiness for a man. So then, what did *she* feel for Hussein bin Hassan? Not love, certainly. She feared him, as she dreaded the nights when he was overtired, or had overeaten, or, if the truth could be whispered, had even overindulged in wine, for he was not that orthodox a Moslem. And if her surroundings, her life, the Dey himself, constantly awakened and reawakened her own desires, he was daily less able to satisfy them, daily left her more and more aware of the unthinkable desert, devoid of either emotional or physical fulfillment, that stretched in front of her.

Yet he was the fount of her power. From the moment he had entered the *harem* on that never to be forgotten April day last year, he had raised her to a pinnacle of success and omnipotence. No *odalik,* even, could aspire to such a height, of being summoned to the all important bed five nights out of seven. They had had to accept the title which he had bestowed upon her, and thus she was *Ya Habibti,* the darling, and her rivals could only watch, and wait, for him to grow tired of the long ash blonde hair, the long white legs, the flat belly, the high, full breasts. But those others all possessed beauty in no less

145

abundance. So then, was her secret her face, the composure which controlled her features, the steadiness of her gaze? An Ice Maiden, locked away in a pirate's *harem. Oh, David, David, so brave and so gentle, and so loving, do you ever still think of the girl you wished to paint?*

Her door opened and her solitude was over.

"My congratulations, my darling." Madeleine came into the room, waited by the bed. "Selim and Jean-Pierre are without."

"Madeleine." Catherine held out her hand, and her stepmother squeezed it. But this was not her stepmother. This was her faithful *halaik,* her personal slave, with whom she shared every hour of the day, every secret thought. And more than that.

But where, then, was the contemptuous, careless woman who had married Jackson Scott? Had she ever recovered from her experiences on the voyage from France, her humiliation by Ricimer? And when she might have recovered, she had been faced with the dreadful fact of Jean-Pierre's castration, the equally dreadful fact of Catherine's part in it. She had screamed, and thrown herself on the floor, and rolled about in her agony. She had seized a vase and rushed at Catherine, murder in her eyes, and been restrained by Selim. She had moaned, "Better that he be killed," over and over again.

Then for weeks she had not spoken, and gone about her duties in silent misery. And her duties had been considerable, as Cora had left to rejoin Ricimer on his travels, perhaps to look out for some other European beauty to grace the Dey's bed. Presumably he had been forced to abandon France, as surely, eventually, his departure at the same time as Jackson Scott's family had disappeared when on a visit to his château must have been linked. But no doubt he still travelled, to Italy, to Austria, to the German States, performing his master's requirements. Although if they *had* sought a replacement none had ever appeared. Hussein was satisfied with his *habibti.*

And in time had come acceptance. She could speak

Jean-Pierre's name, now, without twisting her lips. She had accepted her position as her own stepdaughter's slave, to live her life in a suitably humble station, although Catherine went out of her way to be kind to her. But had she forgiven? Even more, had she really come to terms with her situation, as a woman? Or did she find solace in the embrace of some dusky, despairing *halaik* like herself? Almost every female in the *harem,* from slave to *odalik,* had a lover; there was no other way to sanity.

Saving only *Ya Habibti.* But was that merely because *Ya Habibti* was granted no time for anything, save the pleasing of her master?

And this morning, at the least, Madeleine was smiling.

"Then I will be pleased to see them," Catherine said.

"Highness." Selim came first. He was her friend. *Her closest friend in all Algiers,* she thought. In all the world. He kissed her hand. "Felicitations. Dare I say that you grow more beautiful with every passing day, every passing hour?" He spoke in Turkish, as it had been his task to teach her the language.

She smiled at him, and replied in kind. "Dare I say that in you the world of women lost one of the great flatterers, Selim?"

"I am complimented, Highness." He straightened, allowed Jean-Pierre to stand beside him.

"A present, Highness." The boy was fourteen, his voice still high. It would never break. As his face was haunted by a perpetual frown, a memory perhaps of the agony he had suffered, perhaps of the unbearable humiliation he had known, when he had regained his senses. She had received him alone, in this room, when he had been able to walk. She had explained her situation, the choice with which she had been faced, the decision she had made. It had been the most courageous act of her life, she supposed, and it had needed a constant growth of courage, as she had searched for some reaction and discovered none. He treated her with perfect faithfulness, and his was the most difficult of tasks, for he was her personal attendant. He massaged her after her bath, as he poured the water over her shoulders. He saw to her clothes and he prepared her food himself, as it was he who gathered every scrap of discarded hair, every last paring from her nails, and burned them, to protect her against spells and incantations cast by jealous rivals, and there was not a girl in the *harem* who was not jealous of *Ya Habibti*.

So now he offered her a glass of sherbet, solemnly raising the spoon to his own lips first, and swallowing, for this was another of his duties. He held out the glass. "It tastes good, Highness."

She took the bowl, sipped herself. "I thank you."

He bowed, gravely. He did not smile. *He never smiled, and no doubt,* she thought, *he never would smile.* Then he straightened, and withdrew to the back of the room, watched by his mother. Madeleine's eyes smouldered. But with frustration as much as with angry pity. Because he accepted nothing from her, not her love, not her pity, and not her hate. She was a *halaik,* and he was a *harem agha.* They shared their duties. There was nothing else for them to share.

Selim remained standing by the bed. "It is a fine day, lady. Will you walk?"

Because the ladies of the *harem* were allowed to walk, perhaps two days a week. Wrapped in their *tcharchafs,* guarded by mounted horsemen of the palace guard, who kept their distance and kept passersby at even greater distances, accompanied by their *halaiks* and their eunuchs, they issued from the door under the great staircase in a long procession, for all the world like the young ladies of Madame St. Amant's academy being taken for *their* weekly meander through the meadows surrounding Chantilly.

They reminded Catherine of her schooldays in more than that. For they *were* children, even the oldest inmates. They had been kidnapped or purchased or presented for the *harem* in their early teens, and their lives, as citizens of the world, had come to a stop on the day they had taken their first bath. From that moment not one of them, herself included, she realised, had been allowed mentally to age a day. Even the mothers, for

148

there were several, and some still possessed their children; the girls remained in the *harem* for most of their lives, unless the Dey chose one of them to marry to a successful general or rival potentate; the boys were removed from their mothers at the age of seven, to be brought up as future commanders of the army.

Thus the entire group, which numbered over a hundred, exploded from the doorway in a rush of giggling gossip, proceeded through the palace courtyard, especially emptied for this occasion, through the great gates and beneath the rotting heads fixed to the lintel, and down the hillside towards the beach. The whole thing was intensely undignified, to Catherine's eyes. She preferred to walk at a slower pace than the others, Madeleine and Jean-Pierre at her elbow; none of the other concubines wasted their time in speaking to her, and she would not demean herself by addressing them. But in fact she enjoyed the biweekly outing more than she would admit, even to herself. It was a joy to escape the cloying sensuality of the *harem,* the constant scent of perfume, the oppressive silences, the long, boring hours when there was nothing to do but lie on her divan and stare at the ceiling. A walk was a reminder that there still remained a real world beyond those cloistered walls. Here was brilliant sunshine, beating down on their *tcharchafs*. And real dust, eddying from their feet, and from the hooves of the horses which guarded them. To their left were the brilliant white walls of the city, and before them the sparkling blue waters of the sea. And beyond the waters? An empty horizon. But could she see and see and see, that horizon would eventually end in the Balearic Islands belonging to Spain, and beyond even that, in the shores of France, the bustling docks of Marseilles. A world she would never see again. It was necessary to brush the cowl of her robe across her face to smother the tears. *Ya Habibti* did not weep.

The ladies of the *harem* reached the beach, with squeals of joy. Slippers were thrown off, *haiks* hoisted above the knees, and they entered the gentle surf to wade,

149

screaming and shrieking, throwing water at each other, while the guards prudently withdrew to a safe distance.

"Will my lady not wade?" Jean-Pierre asked.

Catherine hesitated, as she always hesitated. But she stepped out of her slippers, as she would always step out of her slippers. *Because I am still nothing more than a girl myself,* she thought. *However much I may know of man.* She walked down the beach, allowed the little wavelets to brush across her toes and across her ankles, smiled at two little girls who scampered by, pursued by two little boys throwing sand and water. It was amazing what a capacity for enjoyment these people had.

And found that she was surrounded, by staring women. While one of them, a girl not much older than herself, dark haired and dark eyed and intensely pretty, left the water and paraded by. "And how are *you* today, *Ya Habibti?*"

"Very well thank you, Leila. And you?" Here was a surprise; Leila had never spoken to her before.

"Oh, not well," Leila said. "Not well at all."

She paused, and glanced at the other girls, who immediately burst into shrieks of laughter.

"She has the sickness," someone shouted.

"The sickness in the morning," shouted another.

Catherine felt her cheeks burn, and was grateful for the *yashmak.* "Then you are to be congratulated," she said.

"He has never made *you* pregnant," Leila said. "But me, we have slept together only three times, and I am pregnant."

Catherine gazed at her for some seconds. *Am I jealous?* she wondered. *Am I afraid? Surely he will prefer her to me, should she truly be pregnant. And will that not be a blessed relief? Or will it mean that I will lose favour, that these girls will be able to avenge themselves upon me?*

"I hope you can prove the father," she said.

"What?" Leila cried. "You say His Highness is impotent? She says His Highness is impotent," she shouted.

"For that you will suffer the bastinado," Thérèse Cavaigny said. "Even you, *Ya Habibti.*"

Catherine gathered her *haik* around herself. "I made no reference to His Highness," she said. "It is you who have done that. My reference was to Leila's habits. Perhaps I should advise His Highness to investigate them."

She walked away from them, leaving them speechless with anger, and with fear. For no one could doubt her position with the Dey. She was to all intents and purposes his wife. Indeed he had proposed marriage on more than one occasion. But she had always refused the vital preliminary step, that of becoming a Moslem herself. Sometimes she wondered why. Marriage to the Dey could only provide her with additional security. She needed none while he lived, and loved. But he was a very old man, and she was well aware of the enmity with which she was surrounded, and not only by the ladies of the *harem.* The Dey's four wives also hated her and feared her, for they undoubtedly knew of their husband's ambition, and knew too that for it to be realised one of them would have to suffer the indignity of a divorce.

What action they might persuade the Dey's successor to take against her was a frightening thought. But the certainty of Hussein's death was the very fact that made her resist his offer. All things were possible then, and as they hated her, to be his wife might not after all mean any additional protection.

She reached her slippers and her *tcharchaf,* found that both Madeleine and Jean-Pierre had left, Madeleine to gossip with the other *halaiks,* Jean-Pierre for a wade. She smiled, and stooped to pick up the first slipper.

"Lady. Lady." Jean-Pierre panted up the beach, leaving damp footprints. "Allow me, lady."

She straightened again as he fell to his knees beside her, aware once again that the chattering around her had ceased, and that she was being watched. Jean-Pierre picked up the slippers by the toes, knocked the heels smartly together. From the right hand slipper a scorpion dropped to the ground, tail held high as it sought its enemy.

"Aaaaah." The sigh swept through the watching women. Catherine said nothing at all, watched Jean-Pierre as he seized a large stone and pounded the deadly insect into pulp. Then she turned to survey the women.

"She should be whipped." Madeleine hurried to her side.

"Who, do you suppose?"

"All of them. They all knew. You can tell they all knew."

Catherine balanced herself on one leg, holding Jean-Pierre by the shoulder as he fitted the slipper over her foot. This was not the first time there had been a scorpion in her shoe. "Oh, yes," she said. "They all knew."

"Pregnant? She?" Fatma allowed herself a massive guffaw, setting all her bangles to jangling in rhythm with her rolls of fat. She was the oldest of the concubines, and had been in the *harem* for forty-seven years. Her word was law, save to those few sufficiently senior to share her swing at the bottom of the garden. "Because she has missed a period?"

"Our lord has not conceived a child for ten years," Nejlah pointed out. She was only slightly younger than Fatma, but instead of growing progressively stouter had grown progressively thinner, until she now seemed nothing more than a bag of bones. "You have naught to fear from that direction, *Ya Habibti.*"

For the Dey's favourite was granted automatic rights of seniority—so long as she remained favourite. The senior women were too old for jealousy.

"Yet I have cause to fear," she remarked. Every time she saw a scorpion she had a nightmare, that one would somehow be inserted beneath her blanket while she slept.

"Of a scorpion? Of little girls who play the assassin?" Fatma gave another bellow of laughter. "They tried to knife *me,* once, when first I came here. Because I was beautiful, then. Not so beautiful as you, *Ya Habibti,*" she hastily added. It was necessary always to flatter the favourite. "But beautiful enough for our lord to favour

152

me. And so one night as I entered my room, a girl dashed out upon me with a knife."

"But what happened?" Catherine cried.

"I heard her coming, and avoided the blow, and summoned my eunuch."

"And the girl?"

"Was suspended by her ankles until she died, as a warning to all the others. Ah, those were the days, *Ya Habibti*. In those days our lord was truly a lion. His very word was law, and he was not the Dey, only commander of the army."

"In those days we marched, with the army," Nejlah said dreamily. "When Constantine would revolt, we took the city by assault. Across the great ravine, we stormed. For four days the city was put to the sack."

"And now," Fatma said sadly, "Constantine is independent. And Oran also. Our power is sadly fallen. Because our lord is too old. There is sadness. But we shall rise again."

Catherine watched the younger girls gossiping, the youngest girls playing at ball. The morning air was filled with chatter, with laughter, with whispers. They had had their walk and, she thought bitterly, they had had their sport, with *Ya Habibti,* and now they could enjoy themselves before their siesta, while they waited for one of their number to be summoned to the bedchamber of their lord. As if they did not already know which of their number that would be.

"And then there was Decatur," Fatma said, half to herself.

"Tell me about Decatur," Catherine begged, as if she had not heard the story so many times before.

"Ah, Decatur," Nejlah said. "He came with ten vessels, sailing up the coast. And without warning, without so much as a declaration of war, he suddenly altered course and sailed into the harbour, guns run out and double shotted. 'I do not declare war upon pirates,' he said. I thought our lord would suffer a seizure."

"Go on," Catherine said.

"He demanded the release of every American citizen

held captive here, and he threatened that if tribute was claimed from any future American vessel sailing in these waters, he would return and lay Algiers in ashes."

"And what did the Dey do?"

"The Dey surrendered. Our lord was beside himself with anger, and I do believe it was because of that surrender that soon after he deposed the Dey and became ruler himself."

"But he no longer levies tribute on American ships," Catherine said.

"That is true. There are not very many of them, in any case."

"But those were *men*," Nejlah whispered.

"Did you see them? Him? Decatur?"

"I watched through the hole in the wall."

"What was he like?"

Nejlah sighed. "It is hard to say. I remember his uniform. Blue. And there was gold braid. And his skin was so fair. Yet his voice was so quiet we could scarce hear what he said."

Stephen Decatur, Catherine thought, her eyes filling with tears. How splendid if he could still be alive, or if some successor of his could sail proudly into this harbour with double shotted guns run out and force an Algerine surrender. And free her, to return to France in triumph. How splendid.

But no American fleet would ever appear off these shores. There was no reason for it to do so. Algiers had learnt its lesson from Decatur, and the Stars and Stripes could sail the Mediterranean unmolested, while the flags of greater nations, at least in military reputation, were still assaulted.

So probably in all Algiers she was the only American captive, and no one knew she was here. Nor could anyone ever find out. She was trapped, to a lifetime of aimless gossip and boring afternoons, her greatest thrill a biweekly walk down to a lonely beach, surrounded all the while by the whisper of hating tongues. Would they ever forgive her, for being so well taught by Ricimer, and so beautiful, that she held the Dey in thrall? Or would she

154

have to wait until she was in her sixties, like Nejlah and Fatma, waiting only for death, living only on her memory?

And how strange that she should *wish* this herd of cattle, because they were no more than that, to forgive her. What interest had she in their forgiveness? It was essential to remember this, to be her own woman, never to surrender to the cloying insipidity of the *harem*, never to lose Catherine Scott entirely in *Ya Habibti*.

For while Catherine Scott lived there was hope. Her life was not so circumscribed. For there was Selim, entering the garden, ignoring the other girls as he waited for her to make her excuses to Fatma and Nejlah, and cross the sand towards him. As he was her friend, he shared her thoughts, her intrigues. It was his pleasure, as it provided him with undoubted power, made sure that *she* remained *his* friend, now and always.

"His Highness gives an audience this day, lady. 'Tis the Baron Ricimer."

* * *

Catherine seated herself on the low divan, pressed her shoulder against the wall. The room was dark, so that no chink of light should show through the peephole. At her shoulder Selim waited, ready to warn her should it be necessary for them to leave in a hurry. But Hussein was well aware that his wives and concubines overlooked his councils from time to time. So long as his councillors could not see *them*, he had no objection to their titillating themselves with the merits of another man.

Titillating herself. How her heart pounded at the thought of Ricimer. Even after eighteen months she could remember every tingle induced by his fingers, every surge of passion created by his caress. Indeed, she used him as her fantasy lover, thus constantly re-creating memory, for Hussein was far more interested in what she could do for him than in what he might do for her; he used his hands only when it gratified *him*, and as he grew older he could seldom maintain an erection long enough to give her an orgasm. In her feverish despair she would turn to Selim, thus even more sealing their intimacy, thus descending even farther into the sex-drugged existence of the *harem* from which there could be no escape. But it was certainly necessary to close her eyes and pretend the massaging fingers belonged to somebody else, and the only person it could be was Ricimer.

Yet today she was interested despite herself, in the council itself. For the hall was packed; she supposed the entire *mejlik* was assembled, for there were the retired *aghas,* or generals of the army, together with all the half-dozen *yehia bashaws,* the colonels, over a hundred men wearing the insignia of the *boulouchi bashaws,* the captains, and some fifty *oldak bashaws,* the lieutenants. Algiers was a military state, and the *mejlik* was thus composed entirely of officers, but for them to meet in the palace was unusual, and their faces were grim enough, as were those of Hussein, and his son-in-law, Ibrahim, who sat at his side; Ibrahim was the current *agha* of the armed forces.

The guards entered the chamber, thumped the floor with the base of their lances. Her heartbeat quickened yet again, and she licked her lips in anticipation. Ricimer wore his Arab robes, and his face was half-concealed; while it was several months since his last visit, and the last time she had seen him, but there was no mistaking that tall, powerful figure striding across the floor, to come to a halt before the throne of the Dey, and give his *salaam,* that utterly beautiful sweep of the hand, down, as far as was consistent with the rank of the person greeted, and then up from chest to forehead in a single movement.

As he was addressing the Dey, Ricimer's *salaam* was very deep indeed, but there were no other formalities. Hussein nodded and returned the salute, more perfunctorily, and then Ricimer began his peroration. Catherine could not hear what was being said, but there was no doubt his words were having a powerful effect upon his audience, even the first sentence. They leaned forward, lips parted, hanging on his words, while he strode up and down, gesticulating, cowl thrown back from his head to allow his strong features, his powerful black eyes, the fullest range of emotion.

The man who had murdered to obtain her, who had

kidnapped her, who had debauched her, who had sold her into slavery. The man who had made it impossible for her ever to be Catherine Scott again. The man she should hate. As perhaps she did, even as she loved him. The man she must dream about while a eunuch's fingers gave her satisfaction. *My God,* she thought, *that I should think such thoughts, should be able to recognise such events, such feelings. Should be able to look at myself in the mirror, and admire my beauty, and not see the steaming cesspit that is my soul.*

And that man did it, caused it to happen, made me what I am. And what I must remain, forever? Or was that the reason she rejected the safety of Mohammedanism, the increased power of being wife to the Dey, instead of merely chief concubine? Did she hope, and pray, that one day she might be delivered from this gilded hell in which she existed? And who else could accomplish so much, but Ricimer?

He had finished, and took his seat. But he sat with his back to her, and in any event, she was too excited to remain watching a moment longer. She rose to her knees, turned away from the peephole.

"Do you know of what he speaks?"

"There will be war." Selim's eyes gleamed at her. "Will my lady relieve her spirit?"

She glanced at him, her heart and her mind taking off in an entirely new direction. "War?"

Selim held her arm, sat her on his lap; he enjoyed feeling her pleasure, feeling her submission as a skilled craftsman might enjoy feeling a piece of wood taking shape beneath his ministrations. "With France, lady," he whispered, his hands sliding over the silk of her trousers. "The French would have it so."

War. And with the French. "Can it be true, my lord?" she asked Hussein that night.

The Dey sat on the edge of his bed, while she caressed his shoulders and back; that they arched was a sure sign of impending crisis. "It will be so."

"But why, my lord? I had supposed of all people, you

were on best terms with the French. Is it not true that your corsairs never attack French vessels?"

"Fool that I am," he grumbled, "for ever having issued such puerile instructions. Dost thou know their stated reason? Hast thou heard of that day, oh, more than two years ago now, that I tapped Deval on the cheek with my fly whisk?"

"Indeed, my lord," she said.

He turned, violently, catching her about the waist and throwing her on to her back, kneeling above her, stroking her face with his beard as he stroked her groin with his penis. "I had cause. We trade with France. Almost to the exclusion of any other. Our corn supply is largely of French origin. And in my trust I permitted the French to nominate two commissioners to attend to the financial side of the trade, here in Algiers. Thou knowest of them, Bacri and Busnach?" He lay on his back, exhausted.

"I do, my lord." She rose on her elbow to play with him. Clearly he was in an uncertain mood tonight, and her duties were going to be redoubled. There was no power beneath her fingers.

"And right royally did they betray me, embezzle my funds, embroil me in debt. I tell thee this, *Ya Habibti,* should I ever lay hands on either of those two scoundrels I will personally introduce the end of a sharp stake into their assholes."

She reversed herself, to use her lips instead of her fingers; clearly nothing less would suffice. Besides, when he talked like this, the fear of him overwhelmed the hate. She had never seen any of the ghastly punishments he claimed to inflict, and she believed he was quite capable of inflicting. Her life was lived within the walls of the *harem,* and save when Selim was instructed to apply his cane to some enchanting backside she had no acquaintance with pain. Her backside had never been in danger. But there was the evidence of Jean-Pierre, of Selim himself, constantly to remind her of the brutality with which she was surrounded.

"So I was angry, and incautious," Hussein grumbled. "And now they say, after nearly three years, mind, that by slapping their consul I have insulted France itself, and will demand satisfaction."

Catherine rested her head on his thigh. She had failed. Well, then, she must join his mood. She crawled up the bed once more, kissed him on the cheek. "It can be no more than an excuse."

"Of course it can be no more than an excuse," he snapped, throwing her away from him as he sat up. "Ricimer confirms that. The truth of the matter is, this Charles the Tenth finds his throne tottering. He has neither the wisdom to surrender to the wishes of his people, nor the courage to stamp out rebellion. By Allah I would know how to deal with those clubs, those societies which fill Paris. But he . . . he dreams of rallying the nation around him, by means of a foreign war. There was always the ultimate ruse of kings. And there is the true reason why he would tear up our treaties."

The French, she thought. *But the Dey is afraid.* She had not supposed it possible. But the Dey was afraid, of war with the French. He was afraid of being defeated. And if he is defeated, oh, *Lord,* she thought, *if he is defeated.*

"And we," he grumbled. "We are left to stand alone. I have proclaimed a *Jihad* against the infidels, but who has responded? A few Arabs, hoping for plunder. Morocco stands aloof, as does Oran and Constantine. They hate me, the scum, because I am Dey, and they are nothing more than beys."

She nuzzled his neck. "But what have you to fear, my lord?" she said. "From a few French warships? Have you not withstood bombardment, by the English, by the Americans? What have you to fear?"

"The French," he muttered. "The people of Napoleon."

"No longer, my lord," she whispered into his ear. "No longer. Napoleon was defeated. You have naught to fear, from the French."

She felt his arms go round her body, and he turned against her. "Aye," he whispered. "Thou art right, *Ya Habibti,* I have no cause to fear a French bombardment." He chuckled, against her cheek, and she felt the movement against her groin. "It will be sport. We will add French heads to those without. Thou art my strength, *Ya Habibti*. I will never know another like thee."

"Come quickly, lady. Lady, the French are here."

Selim quivered with excitement. But was she any less excited? Catherine put down her embroidery, leapt to her feet, suddenly aware of the vast stealthy murmur spreading through the *harem,* through the entire palace, through the *Kasbah* and down to the waterfront.

"What is it? What is it?"

Madeleine hurried in from the second room of the apartment.

"The French," Catherine shouted. "The French are here."

She tied her *bashurti*—a chiffon headscarf—over her head, then led the rush for the stairs, found them already filled with chattering women, all rivalries forgotten this day. They pushed and jostled with good-natured enthusiasm, the silver bangles with which most of them loaded their wrists and ankles tinkling. Here was spectacle. That it might possibly involve a change in their station did not seem to have occurred to them. *Or perhaps,* Catherine thought, *she was setting too much hope by the event.* As had been pointed out to her time and again, there had been bombardments before, and by the British, the foremost naval nation in the world. And Algiers still stood, and continued on its renegade course.

The crowd debouched onto the flat roof of the palace, where they were allowed to take their exercise and fresh air, and where, indeed, many of the women slept during the summer months, when their apartments were intolerably hot. She forced her way into the three-deep mass at the crenellated parapet facing north, being assisted by Selim, as ever eager to help his favourite.

And came to rest against the cool stone to stare in amazement at the scene which unfolded before her eyes. The June day was bright, and there was no more than a gentle breeze; the sea was a smooth carpet of blue with not a trace of white water to be seen. Not white water, but a great deal of white. Never had she seen so many ships, such a vast expanse of canvas, so many varnished prows pushing their way through the ocean.

Closest at hand, not more than five miles from the shore, she estimated, and forming a protective semicircle around the main fleet, were some sixty small sailing vessels, corvettes and brigs. Behind them were twenty-four frigates, and then eleven great ships of the line, tiered gunports already opened, moving with majestic power past the Algerian batteries. Behind these came an enormous number of merchantmen and troop transports, quite impossible to count, but she reckoned there were not less than three hundred.

"Look there. Look there," cried Thérèse Cavaigny, all enmity forgotten in her excitement.

There were puffs of smoke from amongst the merchantmen. For a moment Catherine supposed they were firing their cannon, although why *they* should do so when the battle fleet remained silent was a mystery.

"Steamships," Madeleine whispered. "Steamships."

For so they were. Seven steam-propelled vessels, ugly black funnels belching ugly black smoke, made their way in the midst of the fleet.

"Oh, it is magnificent, magnificent," Thérèse cried, in French.

Yes, Catherine thought. *It is magnificent. Hussein had been right to fear. And she had been right to hope. Supposing she survived.*

For now a great "aaaah" swept through the women, and she saw rippling smoke booming from the broadsides of the three-deckers and looked down at the pirate ships secured behind the great mole, at the scurrying figures on the mole itself. Plumes of water suddenly rose into the air, and the faint din of screaming men and shattered timbers seeped up the hill to rise above even the chattering of the women. And immediately to be lost in the crashing reply of the guns of the town, embanked behind the mole, clouding in black smoke to send new plumes of water rising among the warships.

She realised that she was witnessing a battle, that men

161

were dying down there, dying and being maimed. They seemed so far away as to be devoid of life. She was here, in safety, and they were there. But Ricimer might be among them. She did not know. In the six months they had awaited the coming of the French she had not seen him again. No doubt he had enough to do, guarding his master's interests.

Therefore she must guard her own interests. The French were here, and surely such a battle fleet, escorting such an army, must destroy the Barbary pirates forever. And free their slaves. She must be sure that she survived, that Madeleine and Jean-Pierre survived, for that rescue.

To be returned to Paris? To Papa? And perhaps to Boston? *But they will know what has happened to me,* she thought. *They will know I have lived in the Dey's harem for two years.*

They will not know what experiences I have undergone. They will never know what it is like to be stretched on a board by four eunuchs and have every hair removed from their bodies, every other day. They will never know what it is to be taught the arts of love by a man like Kurt Ricimer. They will never know what it is like to wear silk trousers and a bolero, and nothing else, day after day after day. They will never understand the boredom of being allowed to do nothing but prepare for love, they will never guess at the undercurrents of hate and resentment that course through this place, or at the strange love affairs that pulsate among the dissatisfied *guizdes* and *ikbals,* and, since the arrival of *Ya Habibti,* among even the *odaliks.*

But they will know, that I am not as they. They will allow their imaginations to run riot, every fantasy, every nightmare, they have ever known will be applied to me, in their imaginations, in their whispered comment.

Even Papa will be unable to resist that, and for him the pain will be the greater because of Madeleine.

And David Mulawer? Supposing, after two years, he even remembered the girl he had wished to paint. Did he ever come across that glove, and raise it to his lips? Or had he long thrown it on a rubbish heap?

How can I go back? How can I be rescued? She turned away from the wall, pushed through the crowd, found herself facing Jean-Pierre. The eunuch gazed at her with sombre eyes. *He hates me,* she thought, *and will always hate me, for having saved his life at the expense of his manhood. And he knows, just as I know, that we can never go back.*

She felt tears come to her eyes, and was distracted by the sound of the cannonade dying, by the chatter of the women rising again. The fleet had stopped firing, and was in fact receding, down the coast.

"What is happening?"

"They go," Selim said. "Algiers is too strong to be taken by a bombardment."

"Go?" cried Thérèse Cavaigny. "Oh, my God. They cannot go. They cannot." She clutched the stone of the parapet as if she would throw herself over.

"Lady, you should suffer the cane," Selim said. "For wishing to be rescued. Lady, you are a disgrace. Be grateful that I overlook your crime."

Catherine stared at the ships, already commencing to dwindle. "Do they really go, Selim?" she asked.

"For this moment, lady. As I said, Algiers will not fall to the sound of a few guns. But I have heard there are soldiers on board those ships. They seek a place to land. Then we will have sport." His eyes rolled. "Then we shall stick their heads upon spikes."

Catherine opened her eyes, instinctively pulled her *yourgan*—the quilted woollen bedcover sewn to the sheet to keep it in place—up to her throat.

But it was only Selim. "His Highness commands your presence."

"Now?" It was utterly dark, save for the glow of the eunuch's candle, and the occasional flashes of lightning that cut across the sky and turned her windows into flaming apertures of light. The storm had commenced three days before, and raged with varying intensity; she could hear the rain pounding on the marble of the courtyard.

"Now," Selim said.

Catherine extricated herself from the *yourgan,* felt for her slippers with her toes. "What time is it?"

"It is four hours past midnight."

"Four o'clock in the morning?" She stood up, and he handed her a robe. "I am not dressed. I have not been bathed." She fluffed out her hair. The bath was necessary, and not only to make her smell sweet; without it she doubted she could discover the necessary sexuality to excite the Dey. "Why did he not send for me at the proper time, last evening?"

"His Highness was concerned with affairs of state, last evening, lady," Selim said. "He sends for you now. Haste."

He had already moved to the door, waited there. Madeleine, disturbed by the conversation, rose on her elbow from the other divan.

"What is the matter?"

"I am to attend the Dey." Catherine went to the door. "Go back to sleep."

"Have the soldiers all gone?" Madeleine inquired.

The Algerian army, commanded by Prince Ibrahim, had commenced its march from the city the previous afternoon.

"They still go, *halaik,*" Selim said. "Can you not hear?"

For between the rolling thunderclaps and the steady pounding of the rain, the measured tramp of feet could be heard. Catherine felt her heart begin to pound; but it was the excitement of the coming hours, not of her coming session with the Dey. The French had commenced landing on the very day, not a week ago, that they had bombarded the city. They would all be ashore by now, or why should the Algerian army take to the field? Though she would have supposed, from her knowledge of military strategy and tactics, that the Algerian army should have taken the field a week ago, should have opposed the French on the beaches, should have hurled them back into the sea, and prevented them gaining any foothold at all.

But Ibrahim had chosen not to do that, in his wisdom, or his ignorance. And so a French victory must have come

164

closer. Algiers might be impregnable to assault from the sea, but surely no ill-armed rabble, for of Ibrahim's sixty thousand men she knew that only a third possessed firearms, could stand against French bayonets. Perhaps others, including the Dey, had felt this also, for since the bombardment neither she nor any other girl had been summoned to Hussein's bed. Until this so strange moment.

She hurried behind Selim, up the interminable staircases, along the interminable corridors.

"Is His Highness pleased with events?"

"His Highness is pleased," Selim said. "With the storm. He feels he has done all he can do, to insure victory. And thus wishes to enjoy you, lady."

"With the storm? What can the storm have to do with it?"

"Algiers has been invaded before. The first of all our invasions was by the Spaniards, commanded by the Emperor, Charles V. That was in the year 1541, by your reckoning. He landed a great army, and the then Dey feared to meet him in the open field. Women and children were fleeing, the entire Regency was in a state of alarm. And then the lightning began, and the thunder. And the rain fell and a great wind sprang up. Those of the Spaniards who were already ashore were smitten by the storm. Their ships were scattered, and many were wrecked. Those who survived were re-embarked, and sailed away, never to return. That was the mightiest force ever to assault Algiers, and it was destroyed by the weather."

It occurred to Catherine that the Spaniards were a trifle unfortunate in their campaigning weather, as she recalled the story of the Armada that had set out to conquer England and Holland only forty-odd years later. "So the Dey sees in this storm an omen of victory," she remarked.

"More than an omen, lady. He sees in this storm, and correctly, the very peal of victory. For if the heavens fight on our side, as they should against the infidels, how may we lose?"

He opened the door into the Dey's chambers and saved Catherine the problem of replying. *How strange*, she thought. *I hate and fear these people, look upon them as heathens, wait only for them to be destroyed. And yet, they see in me and my people, no less a spiritual as well as a physical enemy.*

And suppose Selim was right, and God fought on the side of the Moslems? But he could not possibly be right, she reminded herself. God fought on the side of right, the better side, always; the French might be technically wrong in declaring war over a financial fraud they had themselves encouraged, or to distract popular concern from their own internal problems, but they were entirely right in seeking to destroy a place such as Algiers, a regime such as the Regency. There were no *harems* in France, where hapless girls were forced to live an unnatural and dangerous life; there were no rows of heads on pikes outside Paris; French criminals were not impaled on sharpened stakes.

Hussein stood just inside the balcony, sheltering from the rain, but watching the last of his troops go forth. He did not turn his head, but he knew who it was had entered the room.

"Are they not magnificent?" he said. "I would I was at their head."

Catherine sank to her knees, and then lowered her body on to her elbows, kissed the hem of his gown. *Were she married to him she could kiss his hand,* she thought, irrelevantly. But the act of obeisance was necessary to her spirit; it maintained the hate and the fear she felt for him, reminded her constantly of who she was, and who he was. And now it was more important than ever to be reminded.

"They are magnificent, my lord," she said, regaining her feet.

"And they will need to be," he said, putting his arm round her waist to hold her against him, inhale the perfume of her hair. "These French will be no easy matter. They are commanded by de Bourmont. Dost thou know him?"

"No, my lord."

"Perhaps thy father knows him. Yes. I should have had him brought here as well, to advise me with his knowledge and his skill. This de Bourmont, now, I know *of* him, at the least. He is the premier marshal of France. An experienced soldier. But perhaps not a reliable man. They tell me he deserted the Emperor Napoleon, only days before Waterloo. Such a man must necessarily lack the constancy of spirit to make a good commander. Wouldst thou not say?"

"Indeed, my lord," she agreed. "But in any event, you have naught to fear," she added wickedly. "As this storm surely sounds the death knell of the French."

"Ah," he said. "Thou art a knowledgeable child, *Ya Habibti*." He walked towards the bed, still holding her round the waist. "Aye, the storm is an omen in our favour. All the omens are in our favour. All history is in our favour. There is a prophecy, that Algiers will only fall to soldiers in red. I feared the British, but they did not land. These French, they wear blue. My men will fight like demons. I have promised a reward of a hundred francs for every French head delivered before me. That will make them fight."

"They will fight, my lord," she said, feeling her belly roll with distaste. He had released her, and she shrugged herself free of her trousers, allowed them to lie on the floor. "Will my lord love me this day?"

Hussein lay down with a sigh. "I am too tired, *Ya Habibti*. Too tired even for thee. I but wish to lie here, with thee in my arms. There is happiness. And who knows, when we awaken, I will no longer be tired. Because when I awaken, the victory will have been won."

"Highness. Highness." It was Hussein's personal eunuch, standing by the bed and quivering.

"Eh?" The Dey raised himself on his elbow. "What is it? Speak man, or I will have your tongue torn from its roots."

"A victory, Highness. A messenger from the *Agha* Ibrahim. A victory."

Hussein sat up, while Catherine buried her head in the pillow. A Turkish victory. *No,* she thought. *It cannot be.*

"The man is without," the eunuch said.

"Well, send him in," Hussein cried. "Send him in."

"Here, Highness?" The eunuch was aghast.

"Here. I must know. Thou . . ." He slapped Catherine on the bottom. "Cover thyself up."

She pulled the *yourgan* over her, submerging even her head. Apparently she left some of her hair behind, because the Dey tucked this out of sight as well. *A Turkish victory,* she thought. The words seemed to batter at her brain.

"My robe," Hussein commanded, and the bed rose as he left it. "Well, man, come in. Come in. Tell me."

Catherine could imagine the *askar* performing a deep obeisance, at the same time attempting to peep surreptitiously at the bed, where the outline of her body would be clearly visible.

"The infidels placed themselves unfavourably, Highness," he said, "especially their left flank, and so the *Agha* commanded an assault there just before the hour of dawn."

"But . . . that was five hours ago," Hussein cried.

"Indeed, so, Highness. The mist was heavy, and the French were taken by surprise, and they broke, Highness. It was then that the *Agha* commanded me to ride with all haste, to inform Your Highness that the day is ours."

"By now, Highness, the French will have been driven into the sea," said the eunuch. "They will be destroyed."

"Destroyed," muttered Hussein. "Were there many killed?"

"Many, Highness," promised the soldier. "And I left before the slaughter had begun."

"Enough. Give this man a gold coin." Catherine heard the door close, and pushed her head clear of the covers. Hussein paced the floor. He did not look as pleased as he should.

"Highness? Can it be true?"

"Oh, it is true enough," Hussein said. "I never doubted the outcome. The omens were in our favour. I told thee that. And Ibrahim is a great general. Oh, it is true. But the dead. He said there were many killed. Thou heard him."

Catherine sat up in surprise; it was totally unlike Hussein ever to worry about people being killed; rather did he enjoy the thought as much as the spectacle.

"At a hundred francs a head," he muttered. "Great

Sultan, I will be bankrupted." He seized the striker and gave his gong a whack; the boom reverberated through the palace, and instantly the eunuch reappeared.

"Highness?"

"Announce the victory to my people," Hussein said. "Have the *muezzins* proclaim it from the *minarets*. But have them say, also, that as this is one of the greatest days in Algerian history, the day on which the French were finally taught their place, it would be unseemly that our glorious feat of arms should be commemorated by gifts of mere money. No, no, the names of those who have taken a French head must be exalted forever more. Have the *muezzins* tell the people that I rescind my guarantee of a hundred francs per French head, and that instead I offer something far greater, far more lasting. I will have a book prepared, of the best vellum, and inscribed in gold, in which will be entered the names of every man who this day brings me a French head. Have them say that."

The eunuch bowed, and withdrew. Catherine could only stare at her master in a mixture of contempt and admiration for his remarkable parsimony.

He turned to her. "A victory." He stripped off his robe. "I feel a young man again, *Ya Habibti*." He crawled on to the bed, and there could be no questioning this erection. "This day I will make thee pregnant, *Ya Habibti*. This day we will enjoy our own celebration."

And indeed she discovered that on this occasion, for the first time ever that she could recall, she was required to do nothing more than lie on her back with her legs apart. Even after his climax, he still worked his body on hers, caressed her breasts, kneaded her buttocks, with the enthusiasm of a young boy.

With the love of a young boy, perhaps. Because he did love her. There could be no gainsaying that fact. Bloodstained, vicious, mean, cowardly, and old enough to be her grandfather, he yet loved her, as, she suspected, he had never loved in his life. A love, she supposed, that she had better finally accept and attempt to reciprocate. The French had been defeated. All the legends had been supported by that sheer fact. There would be no regiment

169

of glittering curassiers riding in the *Kasbah* to effect the rescue of their countrymen and countrywomen kept in slavery. Algiers would grow even more powerful, more arrogant, more grasping.

And she would remain here growing old in the depths of the *harem*. *My God*, she thought, *that such a fate should be inflicted upon anyone. That* . . . she became aware that he had raised his head and was staring at her.

"There are tears in your eyes," he accused.

"I weep, my lord, for so many men who will have died."

"The most of them are French," he said. "And there will be prisoners. We will have sport with the prisoners. I will make a necklace of their genitals, and give it to thee as a present, *Ya Habibti*. Thou wilt like that, eh?"

She was rescued by the opening of the door.

"Are you mad?" demanded the Dey, without turning his head.

The eunuch was trembling. "There is another messenger, Highness. From the *Agha*."

Hussein turned on his side, still between her legs.

"Bringing news of the victory?"

The eunuch licked his lips. "Bringing news, Highness."

"My robe." Hussein heaved himself off the bed. "Cover thyself," he commanded, and Catherine did. Surely now he would dress himself and go about his duties, and leave her, to have something to eat, to allow the misery that was lurking at her consciousness to overwhelm her.

"Well?"

Once again the brief silence, while the *askar* performed his obeisance. But when he spoke his voice also trembled.

"The *Agha* sends me to you, Highness. He would have you know that his army has been defeated."

There was a brief silence, no doubt, she decided, while Hussein stared at him. But the words were too momentous for her to accept, at this moment. She just knew that she suddenly felt sick.

"The French left wing, Highness," the soldier said, slowly, "being but poorly positioned, and assuming that position slowly, the *Agha* launched an attack upon it, under cover of the morning mist, and drove it from the field in confusion."

Again the short pause, while the poor fellow, no doubt, looked at his master's face for some sign of sympathy, Catherine supposed.

The *askar* sighed. "So then, Highness, the *Agha* commanded the main part of our army to charge in pursuit, to complete the rout of the infidels, when, Highness, saddest of events, the sun rose and the mist cleared, and our people, having abandoned their ranks, were discovered by the rest of the French, streaming by to their left. Then the bugles rang out, Highness, and the infidels turned their weapons upon us. The slaughter was terrible, Highness. It is said four thousand Turks fell dead upon the field."

Once again the pause. Once again the sigh. Catherine could only imagine what Hussein's face must look like.

"Our people broke, Highness." His voice was lower. "They broke and fled. In vain did the *Agha* and his *boulouchi bashaws* attempt to rally them. The infidels advanced behind their bayonets, a wall of steel, Highness. There was no stopping them. The *Agha* commanded me to ride like the wind, Highness, to tell you of this, and to tell you also, Highness, that the infidels are marching upon Algiers, that there is nothing can stand in their way. I have ridden like the wind to bring you this news, Highness, that you place the city in a state of defence, that you may prepare your people for the coming siege."

This time the silence was longer. Catherine could hardly contain herself. It was impossible to suppose what Hussein might be doing.

Then the *askar* spoke again, and his voice was high and frightened. "Highness?"

He gave a shriek, and Catherine could wait no longer. She threw the *yourgan* back from her head, stared in horror at the scene before her. Hussein had apparently summoned a sword from his eunuch, for he still held the weapon, but the blade was dull with blood, which dripped from the point even as she looked. The *askar* lay at his feet, already dead; the sword had been thrust into his breast.

The whine of the shell made even Catherine sit up straight, and she had supposed herself immune to the noise by now; the bombardment had been continuous for the past three days. But this was nearer than usual; the explosion rumbled through the air and the entire palace shook.

"Oh, my God, my God," Madeleine screamed, wandering around the room with her hands over her ears. "We shall be killed. We shall be killed."

"Do sit down, Madeleine," Catherine begged. *Why should we not all be killed,* she thought, as she had thought little else over the previous three days? She could still see the staring eyes of the *askar,* lying on the marble floor with blood draining from his breast. It was the first dead man she had ever seen; Henri the groom's death had been submerged at once by the darkness and by her own misfortunes. *But,* she thought, *it will not be the last. Not if I am trapped here.*

"Why doesn't he surrender?" Madeleine demanded in French, standing in the middle of the room, her hands on her hips. "Why does he fight on? He knows he will be beaten. Does he mean to have us all immured in here?"

"Sssh," Catherine said. "Have you no faith in *Kismet*?" She often joked with her stepmother about the Arab belief in fate, but in fact she could think of nothing better to grasp, at this moment. God had given the victory to the French, as he should have done, but there was no saying He was going to take any notice of them. So, if they were willed to survive, they would. And if not, then eventually a shell would burst on the *harem,* and they would die.

They would die. Every last handpicked *houri*. The onslaught of the French had reduced them all, *odaliks,* and *ikbals,* and *guizdes,* and even the Dey's favourite, to a common level, waiting to be conquered, waiting to die.

She could hear the noise from all around her, the shrieks and the groans, the sobs of misery and the high-pitched laughter of hysteria. Of only one thing had they been sure, once the doors of the *harem* had closed behind them, that they were safe for the rest of their lives, from any outside influence, any outside danger. Only the temper of the Dey could in any way affect their lives.

Until now, when the rude infidels were battering on those very doors.

She sat up straight. For suddenly the noise had changed. The sobs and shrieks and moans were dying. Madeleine had heard it too, and was turning to face the door, and Jean-Pierre, stepping inside and flattening himself against the wall. "The Dey comes," he muttered. "The Dey comes."

For only the second time in her stay in the *harem*. And once again he was coming to see her. She knew that, instinctively, left the divan and rose to her feet, and then sank to her knees as Hussein bin Hassan strode through the doorway, accompanied by Selim and two other eunuchs.

"*Ya Habibti*," he said. "*Ya Habibti*. We are lost."

"Highness?" Catherine raised her head.

"We can withstand no more of this bombardment. My city is destroyed. My people are slaughtered. My army will no longer fight."

There is the true reason, she thought. "What will you do, my lord?"

"I have negotiated a surrender." The Dey crossed the room, allowed his legs to give way, slumped on to the divan. "I have no choice."

"A surrender, my lord?" How her heart pounded. "To the French?"

"They have offered terms." He lay down, rolled on his back. "They will occupy Algiers. They are determined on that. But I am to be treated as a noble prisoner. They have promised me honourable exile, in Italy, with my wives, and my concubines."

She turned, slowly, her cheeks burning.

He sighed. "Except for those of European birth or

173

descent. These they claim as prisoners of war, to be returned to their homes."

Oh, God, Catherine thought. *After all, she had been saved.* But Hussein was still speaking.

"Saving only any who should be a wife."

"There is no problem, my lord," she said, amazed at the evenness of her voice. "All of your wives are Turkish."

"Aye," he said, once again sitting up. "But I love none of them. I love thee, *Ya Habibti*. And if thou remainst nothing but a concubine, I will lose thee. I cannot consider this. I will not live without thee, *Ya Habibti*."

"My lord . . . "

"There is little time. I have sent a messenger to de Bourmont signifying my acceptance of his terms. We have no more than a few hours. There is no time for thy instruction. Thou wilt declare thyself to be a true believer, *Ya Habibti*, and I will declare thee my wife. There will be a *marabout* in my party who will instruct thee in the faith. Thy declaration will be sufficient."

Catherine gaped at him, her stomach rising to meet her descending heart. "You have four wives already, Highness."

"Three," he corrected. "I have divorced Khaila. There, it is done. Rise, now, and say the words."

Catherine licked her lips, looked from him to Madeleine, who was equally aghast, to Jean-Pierre, who had remained by the door, arms folded across his chest, face impassive, and thence to Selim; the *Harem Agha*'s arms were also folded, but his face was twisted; clearly he was trying to warn her. To condemn herself to a lifetime of this hell on earth? To lose her very last chance of escaping back to the world she had known and loved?

Hussein was frowning. "You do not love me," he said, very softly.

"My lord . . . "

"You do not love me," he said, his voice rising. "You do not love me," he screamed. "All of these years, you have not loved me. You have done no more than humour

174

me. You have not loved me." His finger pointed at the end of an outflung arm. "You have betrayed me."

Catherine found herself on the other side of the divan. "My lord . . . "

"She does not love me," Hussein shouted at the world. "After all the honours I have heaped upon her, the gifts I have given her. After I have given her my love. She does not love me. Selim . . . "

The *Harem Agha* hurried forward, bowed low. "Highness."

"Take her," Hussein whispered, his voice once again sinking. "Take her and bind her in a sack, and smother her. Smother her in mud, Selim. Let her know that she is dying. Let her know that she is dead." He left the room.

Catherine was too surprised to protest, for a moment, as she watched Selim coming towards her. Then she gasped, "No."

Selim gripped her arm. "You must obey the Dey, lady."

"To go to my death?" she demanded. "Selim, you are my friend. You know it is his anger, at being forced to surrender. He will recover his humour, and regret what he has done."

"My master has ordered me, lady," Selim said. "I must obey."

Jean-Pierre stood at his shoulder.

"Jean-Pierre," she begged. "You cannot harm your own sister." But he was going to obey Selim. "Madeleine," she shouted. "Stop him."

Jean-Pierre turned his head to look at his mother for a moment. But Madeleine said nothing. She had backed against the wall, a most peculiar expression on her face. *My God*, Catherine thought. *She hates me. After all, she hates me.*

But she was not going to walk tamely to her death. Survival was all that counted now, not dignity. Survival, until the French soldiers arrived. She wriggled her arm free of Selim's grip and jumped backwards, swinging her head from right to left as she sought a weapon. But the room was entirely devoid of solid objects, save she was strong enough to lift the entire divan and throw it at him.

She gasped for breath, turned and attempted to run for the door, and was brought up by an agonising jerk on her hair, which had been seized by Jean-Pierre. She fell backwards, and was caught round the waist by Selim, who swung her from the floor as if she had been a child.

She rolled in his hands, kicked at him and struck at him with her nails; he made no comment, but merely draped her over his shoulder. Her hair fell down to touch the floor and her face bumped into his back; he had both of her legs, just above the knees, gripping them tightly to hold her immobile. She attempted to hit him with her hands and had her wrists seized by Jean-Pierre, walking behind; his face had lost its impassivity, and he seemed almost pleased.

Now she was helpless. She attempted once more to wriggle, and Selim slid his hand up the inside of her thigh to squeeze where it met the groin. She had never suspected he was so strong. The pain forced a scream from her throat, and persisted for so long she thought he was actually breaking her pelvis. For a moment the corridor went dim, and she was only vaguely aware of being surrounded by people, the other girls, laughing and cheering as they saw their hated rival thus disgraced. Thus removed from their lives forever.

She could only lie across Selim's shoulder, and pant, and *feel*, she could not even think any more, her brain was a jumble of thoughts all trying to identify themselves.

She discovered they were in the open air. Jean-Pierre had released her wrists and Selim was sliding her down his chest to the ground. She realised they were in the centre courtyard, in the morning sunlight; the galleries to either side and on all three levels were filled with laughing women. She was to be drowned before them all.

She tried to turn, and was held tightly by Selim against his chest. His hand moved up and down her breast, and she wondered if he was stroking her, for a last time. They had shared so much together, beginning with the bath on

176

the very first day she had spent here. Now he was taking leave of her, in his own way.

"Selim," she gasped. "Selim," she begged.

"The Dey has commanded, lady," he said. "You have lived well, these two years. Do not be afraid to die."

"Afraid to die? Why should I die?" she shouted. "Because some old ratbag of a pirate commands it? Why should I die?"

She kicked him on the ankle, tried to get her hands free and was held again, while the laughter rose ever louder around her. And saw the sack, held by Jean-Pierre, and realised she was being lifted from the ground.

"Oh, God," she shouted. "Help me. Help me," she screamed, until she thought her voice would crack. But she was already being inserted into the sack, feet first, and suddenly released before she was braced, so that she collapsed into the cloying darkness. The memory of the night she had been kidnapped came flooding back to her. She had begun this life in a sack, and she was ending it in a sack. She attempted to push herself upwards, but the string was already being drawn, and she could do no more than wriggle, and now Selim and Jean-Pierre between them were swinging her from the ground, to the accompaniment of yet louder cackles of laughter from the watching women, before she was suddenly dropped again, with a jar which went right through her body, while the entire morning seemed to explode in a kaleidoscope of sound. The laughter of the women dissolved into high-pitched screams, there were a series of explosions from close at hand which she identified, even in her dazed state, as pistol shots, a yell from Selim and a groan from Jean-Pierre, and then her sack was seized again, and the top ripped open by a pair of powerful hands.

Catherine blinked, and stared at Kurt Ricimer.

Chapter 6

"RICIMER?" she gasped. "Ricimer?" She supposed herself to be dreaming.

He was holding her shoulder to pull her from the sack, while the morning continued to explode in violent sound. She discovered he was accompanied by a dozen armed men, and these were not French, nor even Turks, but men from the desert, as she could tell from their black *burnouses*, and ornate muskets.

"Quickly," he snapped. "We must make haste." He bent, and she discovered that Selim had fallen at her feet, shot through the head. Ricimer rolled him over, in the same instant pulling off his *jibba* to wrap around her nakedness. The eunuch's face had relaxed in death, into its normal impassivity. But then, it had not been particularly animated even when he had been carrying her to her death. She had supposed him her friend, because of the intimacy they had shared over the previous two years, but to him she had never been more than his master's favourite toy. *I should hate him*, she thought, but instead she felt only pity.

And for Jean-Pierre? She turned her head and discovered him, crouching by the edge of the pool.

"Aye," Ricimer said. "I'll drop him too." He pulled another pistol from his belt.

"No," Catherine said. "We must take him with us."

"He was going to drown you."

"He is Jean-Pierre. My stepbrother. Don't you recognise him?"

Ricimer hesitated, and one of the Arabs said something. Ricimer jerked his head. "On your feet," he snapped, "if you would leave. But haste, Catherine. There are guards coming."

"Madeleine," she said. "I could not leave without Madeleine. There is Thérèse Cavaigny too." She looked around her, but the galleries were empty, the women having fled inside at this unthinkable invasion of their privacy. Although they were still peering through the doorways of their chambers.

"For God's sake," Ricimer protested. "Why?"

"They are French," she said. "They must be rescued."

"And they will be rescued, no doubt, by the French," Ricimer said.

"But . . ." She gaped at him. Too much had happened too quickly. She could not understand.

"The French will hang *me*," he pointed out. "Are you coming with me?"

"Madeleine," she said again. "I could not abandon her, Kurt. I could not."

He snapped an order in Arabic, and two of his people ran into the *harem* itself. Ricimer himself waved the others to accompany him beyond the latticework wall and to the head of the corridor which led to the outer courtyard. Here she discovered the Negro guard, lying in his own blood.

"If I could understand," she gasped. "You told me once that the Dey was your master. That you owed him everything."

"So I did," he agreed. "The ship on which I was travelling was taken by an Algerine, when I was yet a boy, and I was brought here much as I brought you, two years ago. Save that my appointed fate was to lose my manhood, much as your stepbrother has suffered." They both looked back, to where a reluctant Jean-Pierre was being dragged across the courtyard by two of the Arabs. "But Hussein, who was not then Dey, but only *Agha* of the Army, saved my life by an impassioned plea to the then ruler, who was an even worse scroundrel than himself."

"But why?" she asked.

Ricimer cocked his head to listen to the sound of gongs. "If your stepmother is not here in an instant, I shall abandon her," he said. "Why? Oh, to share his bed. You may have noticed that he is an omnivorous rascal. Which I did, to be sure."

She gazed at him in astonishment. And decided that even after two years in the *harem* she had still a great deal to learn.

"But when he was elected Dey," Ricimer went on, "he discovered a new role for me. It was his money purchased my baronage, his money set me up in Paris and Vienna as a man of the world, to play the spy for him. I was willing enough. Those upstart European gentlemen had never taken note of my existence. Hussein had. I served him, Cathy, faithfully, for fifteen years. I swear it. And what is my reward? The French, having discovered my activities, have made me a part of their terms for surrender. And Hussein, coward that he is, has agreed."

"Oh, my God," she said. "What will you do?"

He smiled at her; his face was terrible in its anger. "Why, be avenged upon him, to be sure. And how may I be better revenged than to make off with his most valued treasure. Even if you at last seem to have lost his favour. But no doubt he will be even more angry to think of you alive, and prospering, when he has commanded your death." He waved his arm, and Catherine, looking round, saw the three Arabs hurrying acorss the courtyard towards them.

Ricimer asked them a question, in Arabic, and they replied.

"She will not come," he said. "She knows she will be rescued by the French."

"But . . ." She looked at Jean-Pierre, who was watching her. His eyes gloomed, although he would not speak. But how could he return to Paris, any more than she?

From the other end of the corridor there came a ripple of musketry. Ricimer spoke rapidly in Arabic, and his men began recharging their firearms. From his own belt he took his reserve pistol. "Can you shoot?"

"Papa taught me the use of a pistol," Catherine said. "Although I have never fired one in earnest."

He pressed the weapon into her hand. "Now is your opportunity to start." He glanced at Jean-Pierre, but apparently decided against giving him a weapon also. "Now, stay close to me, and remember, we either escape this place or we die. To surrender would be to expose ourselves to a far worse fate than a mere sword thrust in the belly. Are you with me, Catherine?"

"Escape or die," she said. She wanted to shout the words. She wanted to throw back her head and scream her joy, and then allow herself to laugh. Ricimer had come for her, after all. She was fighting at his side, and she would conquer, or she would die at his side.

"Then *en avant*," he shouted, drawing his *tulwar* as he did so. He ran down the corridor, Catherine at his heels, Jean-Pierre and his men following. The door into the courtyard was opened, and around it were another dozen Arabs, seeking what shelter they could as they exchanged shots with members of the palace guard. But the courtyard was almost deserted, and from the babble that arose beyond the opened gates it was obvious the news of the impending surrender had spread down to the *Kasbah*; the good people of Algiers were more intent on either escaping themselves or concealing their goods and their wives and daughters from the coming rapacity of the French soldiery than in defending anything of the Dey's.

"Form rank," Ricimer shouted, and his men drew up in a ragged line. "Now for the gate," he bawled, and they set off again. An Arab ran alongside Catherine, and suddenly gave a gasp and collapsed, ankles, knees, backbone and neck all apparently losing their strength in the same instant, so that he dropped straight down, and as his *burnous* clouded on top of him he suddenly appeared as a heap of discarded clothing, save for the ugly brown liquid that mingled with the dust. Catherine stopped in horror to look at him, and watched some of the dust itself seem to take life and spurt into the air. Then Ricimer seized her arm and jerked her forward again, and she was running through the hail of bullets to reach the gate.

Here they were opposed by a group of men, swinging swords and empty muskets. Ricimer brought up his *tulwar* and thrust and then cut. Blood flew. Catherine saw a bearded face in front of her, levelled the pistol, and fired. The cloud of black smoke blinded her and had her choking, but as it cleared she saw the face had disappeared; she had no idea whether she hit him or whether he had sought shelter. Then they were through, and in the square outside, where yet another party of Arabs waited with a group of horses, remarkably unmolested by the milling crowd; no doubt, up to this moment, they had not been connected with the firing inside the palace.

Ricimer leapt into the first saddle, reached down with his arm; Catherine was plucked from the ground and set behind him; she threw her arms around his waist and hung on for dear life as the horse reared. Shots continued to whang about them, and there was another clash of steel as more men rushed out from the palace yard, but the Dey's soldiers were too disorganised to resist the determination of the Arab horsemen, and a moment later they were galloping across the square and out the far side, turning away from the coast and towards the looming mountains.

"Free," she whispered, into Ricimer's shoulder. "Free," she shouted in his ear. "Free," she screamed at the wind.

"I had ever this in mind," he shouted back.

"But, no word? No hint, even? I might have died of misery and hopelessness."

"Not Catherine Scott," he replied. "Not the girl I came to know and love on board my ship. As for a hint, would that not have been cruel, to have so buoyed your hopes? I considered I would have to wait until the Dey died. That he might be dethroned had never crossed my mind."

"It is all like a dream," she said, hugging herself even

tighter against his back. "Following upon a nightmare. If I could understand it all. These men . . ."

"Are friends of mine. They have been friends of mine, for years. I have never shared the Turkish contempt for the Arabs."

"But . . ." She peered over his shoulder. The ground was rising, and already they seemed to be beneath the shadow of the Atlas peaks. "Why do we not fly to your ship?"

"It is in the harbour, and no doubt sunk by now. Certainly we should not be allowed to sail it out. Besides, where should we go? I am a fugitive from European justice." He drew rein, and his party did likewise, the horses blowing and prancing, the men themselves hardly better, and for the first time she could inspect them, although as they were all wrapped in their voluminous *gandouras,* with a *burnous* on each of their heads, it was impossible to decide what they looked like. Jean-Pierre, mounted behind one of them, seemed to have sunk into one of his brown studies, and scarcely seemed to know, or care, where he was. Now, in addition to his other miseries, he was separated from his mother, forever. So was she. But Madeleine hated her. Perhaps the fact had not yet really penetrated her consciousness. Yet she knew that after this morning they could never again share any intimacy. And Madeleine would be going home, to Papa. Then where was she going?

Ricimer pointed at the town, part of which was in flames from the bombardment, while all of it resembled a gigantic antheap in which people ran to and fro. His arm moved, and once again she followed the direction of his finger, to the road leading west, along which she saw what might have been a glittering, slow-moving snake, surrounded by other, smaller insects, also glittering in the midday sun.

"De Bourmont," he said. "Ah, he has accomplished a memorable triumph. No European before him has conquered Algiers, and a good number have tried."

Yet again his arm swung, and she could not resist an exclamation of alarm as she observed another group of horsemen, much closer at hand, and coming in their direction.

"They are more of my people," Ricimer explained. "They have been carrying out a mission for me. We will wait for them to catch up, and then we shall make for the desert."

"The desert?" Catherine was aghast. "But . . . is there nowhere we can find a ship for Europe?"

"I told you . . ."

"That you are outlawed in France. But what of Italy? What of Austria?"

"I am outlawed in those countries too. I am known as a renegade."

"My God," she whispered, because now surely he would be outlawed by the Turks as well. And all on account of her. "Well, then, what of America?"

He smiled. "To cross the ocean, to a half-barbarous country, and I know not what reception at the end of it? No, no, my sweet. We are far safer amongst the Arabs, at least among these Arabs, who know me and trust me, and whom I know I can trust."

She sighed, and rested her head on his shoulder. "And I had dreamed, of home, of Papa, of civilisation."

Ricimer turned his head to kiss her on the cheek. "You will have those things, my Catherine. I promise you. This furore will last but a few years, and then, who knows, it may be possible to return."

"A few years?" she cried.

"What are a few years, to an eighteen-year-old? And Catherine, when you return to Europe, you will do so in style. Those men who approach, their mission was to secure for me a man I know to be resident in Algiers these past ten years. A priest, who came here in an attempt to alleviate the lot of the Christian slaves in the city. But for us he has a very special task to perform. When I come to your bed, Catherine, when I take you back to Europe, it shall be as my wife. Come now, will that not suffice to alleviate your impatience, for a year or two? Will you not be content to be Baroness Ricimer?"

Baroness Ricimer. Had she not always dreamed of being Baroness Ricimer?

But she was already Baroness Ricimer. The Christian ceremony had been held that morning, with just an Arab and Jean-Pierre as witnesses. Father Rollo was on his way back to Algiers, suitably rewarded. What a tale he would have to tell. She had been afraid he would be able to guide the French soldiers into the desert, but Ricimer had merely laughed. "The French?" he had demanded. "Venturing into the desert? They have not the men, they have not the courage, and above all, they have not the knowledge, to risk this stony wilderness."

Which was no doubt perfectly true. She had herself been at once horrified and fascinated, as the party of Arabs with their European leader had travelled deeper and deeper into the mountains, traversing passes, crawling over escarpments, in the heat of the summer sun, although even the Arabs broke their journey for the four hours between eleven and three to shelter. Jean-Pierre had suffered in silence, as usual. And she had looked around her in delight tempered with fear. Here was surely a land where no man had been intended to enter, where the only inhabitants were the desert rats, remarkable creatures with furry tails, the puff adders which scuttled away to shelter amid the rocks, and the crows which circled overhead. She had been astonished, too, at the way Ricimer kept aloof from her, not in word, for he rode beside her most of the day, she having by now been furnished with a mount of her own, although it had been necessary for her to learn to sit astride, as the Arabs knew nothing of side-saddles. But more than talk, he would not do.

"You are still the Dey's woman," he would say. "When we are legally married, then, then may I come to you."

Ricimer, turning out to be the soul of honour, at least by his own lights? But in fact she had soon enough been grateful for his forbearance, as they had debouched from the mountains and entered the desert. For all that time she had not changed her clothing, had been also grateful to the *tcharchaf*, which kept off the worst heat of the sun, allowed her to sweat in private, concealed the filth that must be her body. No man should know her now.

And besides, she could wait, for Ricimer.

And then had been equally fascinated and awed by the desert itself. She had anticipated rolling dunes of sand, such as one might see on an endless beach. Instead there was no sand at all, but endless low hills and plains of scattered stones, some big, most hardly larger than pebbles, from among which odd patches of green thrust up to suggest that for all the aridity water might not be so far away. Ricimer explained that they were traversing a stone desert, a *hammada*. The sand desert, or *erg*, was far to the south, and not as widespread as legend would suppose.

As for water, it was relatively plentiful. Whenever they came across a *ouadi*, the bed of a river long since dried by the relentless sun, the Arabs had set to digging, and soon uncovered a trickle of water welling up through the suddenly darkening earth.

"The table is never more than six feet beneath the surface of an *ouadi*," Ricimer had explained, and if the liquid had been hot and filled with various salts, it had not the less tasted like nectar.

In all the ten days they had travelled they had never touched meat, as there was none to be had. They had eaten twice a day, dates, lentils, beans, and they had drunk mare's milk, for more than half their mounts, to her surprise, had turned out to be females. Yet every member of the party had remained healthy and sufficiently strong to continue the arduous marches.

Until one morning they had topped a rise, and been surprised at the sight of green trees and irrigated fields beneath them, and then by the dazzling white of the houses as the sun had risen behind them to send shafts of light into the *oasis* of Ain-Mahdi. They had drawn rein, to make sure that the inhabitants recognised them as friends, for indeed the *oasis* resembled nothing less than a fortress, with baked clay walls rising some twelve feet out of the desert rock, and itself apparently situated on a hummock within the valley through which the *ouadi* wound its way, here making one of its rare appearances on the surface as flowing water. Thus the houses rose beyond the walls, seemingly piled one on top of the other, and the whole was dominated, at the apex of the mound, by the *minaret*, also made from baked clay and possessing a somewhat lopsided appearance when compared with the stately spires of Algiers. The *minaret* was painted in pale blue, and stood out the more strikingly in the midst of the whites and browns with which it was surrounded.

They had descended the hill, to be greeted by the *kaid* of the tribe, Tedjini, who was also a famous *marabout*, or holy man. He was very old, with a white beard which reminded Catherine most disturbingly of Hussein bin Hassan. But he was not, apparently, interested in white women, even if they had ash-blonde hair. Certainly he could hardly have been interested in the rest of her, for apart from her unwashed body, and her pubic hair, which, freed from the attentions of Selim, was again starting to grow, her face had been attacked by the sun and was at once reddened and spotted with freckles; she supposed her complexion irretrievably ruined, and wondered if Ricimer, when he took a good look at her, would not change his mind.

But he had not changed his mind, and now she was again clean, and prepared for the Moslem part of the ceremony, which was to be after the Arab fashion.

For this great occasion in the life of his friend, Tedjini had offered the use of his own house, the largest in the *oasis*. It was situated well up the hill, separated from its neighbours by nothing more than a common earthen wall, and from those opposite by a street not six feet wide, and built, like all Arab houses, around a small central court-yard, off which the stairs wound up and up four storeys to the flat roof.

She, and the ladies of the *marabout's harem,* were now on the third floor, listening to the noise of feasting, of laughter and ribald jokes, which came from beneath them, the *selamlik* where the men were enjoying themselves. Not that there was less tumult up here. Apart from the ladies of the *harem* themselves, every relative and every female neighbour had also been invited, until the small room was absolutely crowded, and searingly hot. The women had discarded their *haiks* and lay around the place on mats or divans drinking coffee and eating enormous quantities of rice and sweetmeats, while for this special occasion there were also dishes of *couscous*, roasted lamb served on little cakes of unleavened bread. Despite the heat of the afternoon there was a brazier glowing, while the household slaves, to whom poor Jean-Pierre had been added, circulated among the women attempting to keep the air moving with fans.

The room bubbled with conversation, most of it in Arabic and therefore unintelligible to Catherine, but from the few words of Turkish that crept in she gathered they were discussing the finer points of both Ricimer and herself, praising his manliness and pointing out that breasts like hers were made for holding, while thighs like hers were intended, surely, by Allah to enclose a man. At least she did not have to look at their faces while she was thus dissected, for she sat by herself, rendered invisible to the rest of the room by a white sheet hung from the ceiling, and only occasionally offered a fresh cup of coffee or a morsel of food by a brown hand thrust under the screen. Occasionally one of the women looked round to peer at her, and shake her head when she smiled. She was not supposed to smile, although had it not been for the heat she would have been hard put not to burst out laughing. She had never been so happy in her life, and the slightly, to her, ridiculous ceremony only added to her pleasure. As did the garments in which she was encased, for she wore no fewer than seven silk robes, all in varying shades of crimson, one on top of the other, while her girdle had been knotted seven times as well, both, as the women had informed her with screams of laughter in which she had joined, to delay the ardour of her husband and to make sure that no evilly disposed *djinn* came into the house and beat him to it.

But now she had been sitting here for over an hour, and was feeling at once hot and uncomfortable, her bottom was sore and she felt that if she drank another cup of coffee she would burst; she could only be thankful that it was Ricimer she was marrying and not some total stranger, for to have that to worry about as well as her discomfort would be unbearable. But it *was* Ricimer, and he was coming closer. In only a little while, as the heat of the sun began to fade—for the Moslem day starts at sunset and a bride must be taken to her lord's house at the beginning of a day—she would be married, would finally become Baroness Ricimer, would finally enter upon that life which she now knew she had anticipated from the moment of their first meeting. Why, she thought, at this moment she could even forgive Hussein bin Hassan. For if he had never been much of a lover to her, he had at least made her into a complete woman, knowing what she wanted, knowing what a man wanted, and knowing how to provide that want.

Or should she thank Selim for that?

It was happening. The chatter suddenly died, and the sheet was lifted, to reveal someone bundled in a woman's *haik,* face concealed, crawling beneath to join her. But she had been warned of this essential visit, even if it was by no means essential in her case.

She opened her mouth, and the figure shook her head, and then threw back the cowl to reveal himself as a man, of perhaps the same age as Ricimer, but undoubtedly an Arab, who now rose to his feet, and opened the *haik* to prove himself naked. Catherine's chin snapped up again. He was certainly the same size as Ricimer, in every way, and mounted an enormous erection.

"You have seen before," the man said. "You are not a virgin."

She wondered if he was accusing her. Her chin bobbed up and down.

He grinned at her. "Then you will not fear your lord. Yet you must touch. You must know. You must not be afraid."

Catherine found her chin sagging again. The man stood immediately in front of her, not six inches away. And clearly he was not going until she had touched him. She raised her hand, gave him a gentle squeeze.

The man stooped, and kissed her on the forehead. "You will do well. Allah will smile on you."

He closed his *haik* and retreated beyond the sheet. The clapping and shouting resumed and Catherine felt her own excitement growing. After Hussein, that had been a man, and now she was about to be taken to another man, her man, her Ricimer. Because there it was. There was a sudden explosion of sound at the information that the groom was waiting, and she scrambled to her feet, as the sheet was torn from the ceiling and trampled under foot, and she was seized by half a dozen hands, to be followed immediately by others, throwing her into the air and catching her as she came down, all the breath gone from her lungs, sure only that she must be dropped, and that if she was dropped she would be trampled to death before she could make a protest.

She was settled, on her back, over several pairs of shoulders, her ankles across one, her thighs across another, her shoulders on another. Fingers dug into her legs and her ribs and her arms, and she discovered a new threat as they began their descent; the roof of the stairway was very low, and she momentarily expected to lose her nose on the undressed stone.

To her surprise the downstairs room was empty of men, although the wreckage of their meal remained. The noise outside had, however, redoubled; to the shouts and the claps had been added the clash of cymbals and the thud of a drum, while even this cacophony was punctuated by a fusillade of shots.

She was carried through the doorway and into the street, shaded now as the sun was beginning its droop towards the horizon, and behind the hills which surrounded the oasis. Here there waited a four-wheeled cart, somewhat like a miniature four-poster bed, she realised, in which she was dumped; there were cushions, but not sufficient to prevent her from again being winded, and she could only lie on her back and gasp as the crowd, consisting entirely of women and children in her vicinity, although from the constant rattle of firearms she knew

190

there were men as well, rolled her up the street to Ricimer's house.

Here the door was open, and the women seized her again, for all her laughed protests that she could very well walk, and carried her into the house and up another flight of stairs, into an empty room. Amazingly there were no men to be seen, but there was a divan waiting for her in the very centre of the chamber, and on to this she was once again dumped with bone-shaking force, scattering the several highly embroidered bolsters that acted as pillows.

"You must resist," someone whispered in Turkish in her ear. "No bride should go to her husband willingly. You must resist."

She wriggled and tried to catch hold of them, even as she could not stop herself laughing. Gently they pushed her away, thrust her back on to the bed as she tried to sit up, and then suddenly found herself alone. But not alone. She sat up, stared at Ricimer, and with him another man; they had been concealed behind a curtain.

"You must fight me," he said. "You cannot come to me, willingly. There is ill fortune."

"We can't have that," she agreed, having recognised his aide as her recent visitor. Perhaps they both meant to have at her in this strangest of ceremonies. She was too excited to care. She attempted to get up, and was seized by the shoulders and thrown down again. Laughing her excitement, she attempted to kick, and had her arms seized as well, and was then rolled on her face. My God, she thought, they cannot mean to sodomise me. But instead she felt her wrists being held as her legs were bent up from the knee, and a moment later she found cords securing each wrist to its matching ankle, leaving her as exposed and helpless as a trussed chicken.

Then she was rolled on her back, and her feet set in place, so that she was even more at the mercy of any assailant, but to her relief she saw that the best man was leaving, and a moment later the door was closed behind him.

191

"Kurt," she said, straining against the bonds. "Is this necessary?"

"But of course, my sweet," he said. "If I do not take you by force, it will not be well done. And we must make haste."

"Haste?" she demanded, wriggling her bottom. "I have waited two years for this moment. Haste?"

"These people respect a man by the speed with which he accomplishes his desire." He was sitting beside her fumbling at the knots of her girdle, undoing them with remarkable skill.

"Will you not at the least kiss me?" she begged.

He lowered his head, and his tongue came out. She touched it with her own, and wanted to seize his head and bring it closer, but he was away again, releasing the last of the knots, and then standing up to remove his *haik* and reveal himself as entirely naked underneath, and a positive monster of obvious desire.

"Ricimer," she whispered. "Ricimer. Let me touch you. Ricimer . . ."

But to her surprise he did not even trouble to undress her. Merely fumbled his way through her several veils to discover an aperture, and then found himself between her raised knees.

"Ricimer," she screamed. "Please. Ricimer . . ." Because in all the excitement she had had no time to discover passion, and she was dry, and there he was, his penis stroking across the inside of her thighs, forcing an involuntary contraction of her muscles. But that would be worse. She sucked air into her lungs, stared at his face, smiling now as it came closer, made herself relax, and was paralysed by the thrust, which crashed downwards so that his pelvis seemed to drum on hers, while his penis seemed to reach her very womb with the force of his entry. The pain was tremendous; perhaps, she thought vaguely, *I was always half a virgin.* She realised that she had cried out again, but now he was stroking up and down, holding himself from crushing her on his hands as he had done with Madeleine in the cabin of his ship, while now she was wet and she could begin to feel, and to enjoy, and to want, and to know the building passion, until his movements suddenly quickened and he gasped, and allowed his hands to give way, and lie on her chest. *If I was half a virgin before,* she thought, *I am surely not one now.*

*   *   *

"And now, sweetheart," she whispered, "as you have so speedily proved your manhood, will you not use your hands to grant me a pleasure equal to your own?"

He pushed himself up. "I must go."

"Go?" she cried.

"Aye. A man may spend no more than a few minutes with his bride on their wedding night."

"You cannot leave me like this," she said.

But he was already on his feet, and apparently misunderstanding her meaning. "The women will release you, and see to your wants."

"I do not want to be attended by women," she shouted. "I am married to you, not them."

He laid his finger on her lips. "*Kismet* has decided that we must live here, perhaps for more than a year. We would do well to follow the customs we find around us. That way will lie contentment. Any other will lead to conflict. Now lie still, and I will send the women to you."

"And you?" she whispered. "When will you come again?"

"Tomorrow night I shall be with you once more," he promised. "And then I may stay longer."

"But now," she begged. "Believe me, it will take you not five minutes to make me the happiest woman in the world."

"I must go." He pulled on his *haik*.

"At least kiss me," she begged. "At least tell me you love me."

He adjusted his *burnous*. "Why, yes, I think very probably I do love you."

She gaped at him. "You *think*? Why did you then risk your life to save mine? Why have you married me?"

He smiled at her. "I told you that, my sweet. I wished

193

to be avenged upon the Dey. Can you think how he is tossing in his bed, knowing his most treasured possession now belongs to me."

"You married me," she whispered, "to be avenged on the Dey?"

"Of course. And why look so vicious? You should be content enough. Are you not now Baroness Ricimer?"

Baroness Ricimer, she thought bitterly. *The apex of my ambitions. But not to be shut away in a primitive society in an oasis in the middle of the Sahara desert, with a husband who married me out of revenge. For more than a year? My God*, she thought. *I shall go mad.*

And then she remembered the Ricimer she had known on board the ship, the fount of all the real pleasure she had ever experienced. He was but playing the Arab. Soon he would be able to come to her as a husband, and then would she know that happiness again. She made herself accept this fact, made herself relax and await whatever was coming next, which was just as well because within minutes the horde of women once again descended upon her. Unable to ascertain that her maidenhead had been taken, they satisfied themselves with discovering traces of semen on her and within her, which was sufficiently humiliating. Then it was time for more feasting and more coffee and more female ribaldry before she was finally left alone in the hot and darkened bedchamber, with only her eunuch for company.

He stood just within the door, his arms folded. "Is my lady pleased?"

She tried to make herself comfortable. She had at last been allowed to empty her bladder, but her spirit was by no means contented, and the seething passion in her belly seemed only to be building. "Should I be, pleased?"

"My lady has a husband, who is in every way a man."

"Oh, aye," she agreed. "As he is so intent upon proving himself a man that he has no time to make me a woman. Will you stand there the night?"

"I am instructed to remain with you, my lady, as I am your slave," he said. "I will sleep here, on the floor."

Catherine sat up, stared at him as a wild, horrible, yet

consuming idea gripped her mind. Selim she had always thought of as a creature apart, and Selim lay dead in his blood in the courtyard of the Dey's palace. But Jean-Pierre had always been her brother. The presence of Madeleine had made him seem an actual blood relation; the mixture of pity and hatred with which Madeleine had looked on him had but reflected her own feelings, she thought.

But Madeleine was gone. By now, she realised with a start of surprise, Madeleine would have been returned to France, would once again be united with Papa, would be able to tell him the whole terrible story. What would happen then? Would he look upon her with horror, put her away? Or would he hold her in his arms and endeavour to forget, and make her forget?

Papa would always do the right thing. Yet would his misery be increased, as Madeleine could not help but tell him of her experiences, and by inference, of *her* experiences as well. She could not help but tell him of the agony undergone by Jean-Pierre, of the lamentable half-creature to which he was now reduced. And in all the world, now, she was his only friend. As perhaps he was hers.

Supposing he did not hate her still.

"Jean-Pierre?" she whispered.

"Yes, my lady?" He remained by the door.

"My spirit is sorely troubled, Jean-Pierre. Will you not offer me solace?"

"How may I, a poor eunuch, offer solace to a great lady, a baroness, my lady?"

"Come here," she commanded, and he left the doorway, slowly, reluctantly, and advanced across the floor. She caught his wrist. "You have hands, Jean-Pierre. Do you not also have feelings?"

He looked down at her. "Should I give way to my feelings, my lady, I would strangle you as you sit there."

Her head jerked, and she stared at him.

"But should you wish the use of my hands, my lady, you have but to command me, as I am your slave."

My God, she thought. *How You must be determined*

to punish me, for some crime of which I am unaware, some fault in my past known only to Yourself.

She released his hand and fell on her stomach across the bed. It would have been criminal. Incest cannot merely be a matter of sexual intercourse. Once it takes place in the mind, it has taken place, like any crime.

So then, at the end, she thought, *I am left with only myself to turn to. And Seraphine to remember. What blessing, to have Seraphine to remember.*

She did not see her husband at all during the day, but the next night he was able to come, and stay, at his leisure, or at least until an hour before dawn, when he was summoned away by one of the omnipresent women. His bride could not be exhausted.

In the hours they had together, however, he brought her to orgasm a dozen times, as he himself was able to climax on three occasions. It seemed she had waited all her life for this one precious night, when everything she had ever dreamed of, everything Seraphine had ever whispered in her ear, came true. When, she thought, every last memory of Hussein bin Hassan was swept from her brain.

"Oh, my sweetheart," she whispered in his ear, as he lay half across her, exhausted. Their sweat mingled, for it was very hot in the small, airless bedchamber. "How I love you, Kurt. How I love you."

He raised himself on his elbow. She could see his teeth as he smiled. "I had thought you once feared me."

"Oh, I did. I feared you at least partly because I knew I was falling in love with you."

"Now there is a strange confession."

"Not at all. You were represented to me as being a strange, sinister man." She smiled, and kissed him on the chin. "And those who gossiped about you did not know a fraction of the truth."

"Oh, I am, a strange and sinister man," he said.

"*My* strange and sinister man."

"That will be my pleasure, *Ya Habibti.* May I call you that?"

"*You* may call me that, Kurt. Only you."

"Well, then, I can tell you that the moment I saw you, I knew I would one day possess you. Do you remember what I said?"

"That I was two women."

"And now I have them both."

"Then why did you ever give me to Hussein?"

He sat up. "It was my duty to do so."

"But if you loved me . . ."

"I would like you to cease repeating that senseless word."

"Senseless?"

"I told you, I wished to possess you. Love has nothing to do with it. Love is a Christian concept, and like most Christian concepts has no foundation in fact."

He means it, she thought.

"I admire you," Ricimer said, "as much for your beauty as for your self-possession. I think it was your self-possession that most interested me, when I brought you to Algiers. I had never known such calmness, such acceptance of *Kismet*, such determination to survive, perhaps."

"The Ice Maiden," she said, without meaning to.

"Eh?"

"It is nothing. A name someone once bestowed on me."

He drove his fingers into her hair, taking her completely by surprise as she had not noticed the movement of his hand in the darkness. The sudden pain was intense, and her head was pushed flat on the bolster.

"Kurt," she gasped.

"A man?"

"Of course a man," she cried. "A man who wanted to paint me, nothing more."

Still the fingers were tight. "I knew nothing of this."

"Should you have? For God's sake, you knew I was a virgin when you abducted me. You took care to find out, remember?"

Slowly the fingers relaxed. "What is this man's name?"

197

"It does not matter. We never did a thing more than kiss, and that for five seconds at a time."

The fingers tightened again, and her head was once again driven into the bolster. "His name."

"David," she gasped. "David Mulawer. Kurt, you're hurting me."

The fingers left her hair, and he bent to kiss her on the forehead. "I am a jealous man."

"And a violent one," she grumbled, rubbing her forehead.

"But of course. I am a man of war. David Mulawer. I must remember that name."

"Oh, Kurt, really. I told you he was but an acquaintance."

"An acquaintance too many. But I shall not mention his name again, my sweet, providing you do not either." He bent low over her, kissed her lips, slowly, caressing her with his mouth as he had done at their first embrace. "And now, are you happy?"

Happy? To be married to a man who would not recognise the meaning of the word love? But who was yet jealous to the point of violence? *I should have stayed, and escaped back to France,* she thought, *whatever the humiliation.*

And yet, there would never be another Ricimer. Even if he hated her, it was his body she wanted to feel on hers. *And if I love him,* she thought, *enough, surely in time he must come to love me?*

"Yes," she whispered.

"And you are content to live with these people for a while?"

"For a while," she said.

"Only a while. But you will be alone, save for your eunuch."

"Alone?" She attempted to sit up, and was gently pushed back again.

"I must go away, for a few days. Perhaps longer."

"But why?"

"Because there are great moves afoot. The French are

marching on Oran. It seems they mean to conquer all of the Regency."

"Oh, my God."

"Aye. The Turks are few in numbers, and disorganised. But the Arabs see this as their opportunity to rid themselves of their old and hated masters. On the other hand, they are not eager to accumulate a new set of masters. There is going to be a long campaign, ending perhaps in the establishment of an Arab state here in Algiers."

"And you are interested in this?"

"Indeed I am. The Ain-Mahdi are not the only Arabs with whom I am familiar. I see great possibilities ahead of us. These people will need advice, European know-how."

"A long campaign," she muttered. "How can a few desert tribesmen oppose the might of France?"

"With difficulty, perhaps, supposing that might were concentrated. But there is also news from France itself. There is unrest there, with Bourbon reactionism."

"The Dey told me. He claims the invasion of Algiers was mounted only in order to distract the people from their internal politics."

"And he was right. But things have progressed even further. Benefitting by his success, Charles has attempted to be even more repressive, and has exacerbated the situation. They say the barricades are going up in Paris."

She pushed him aside as she sat up. "My God. Another revolution?"

"It appears likely."

"Then what of Papa? Madeleine? She will be returning to chaos."

"I suspect, as happened the last time, they will not overly interfere with foreigners, which includes even your stepmother, at least by marriage. But with the country divided it is unlikely they will prosecute the war here with any vigour."

"Then why can you not leave the Arabs to their own devices?"

He kissed her between the eyes. "You do not understand, my sweet. I am a man without a country. Which means that you are now a woman without a country."

"Your estates in Austria . . ."

"Are sequestrated. I am wanted for treason by the French government. I doubt the English would give me asylum. Italy is certainly a prospect, but scarce one which will bring me either wealth or fame."

"I had not supposed things were so bad," she said, and lay down again.

"Or you would not have been in such haste to marry me?"

"Now, you know that is not so," she protested, and he kissed her again.

"Of course I do. Yet must I, as your husband, do the best for us, for our children, for to be sure we shall have children. And if I am at present not welcome in Europe, why then, I shall carve myself an empire here in North Africa. It is my natural home, believe me."

"And if the French catch you they will hang you," she said.

"They are more likely to cut off my head." Another kiss, accompanied by a smile. "But they are not going to catch me. I would but ask that you play your part in this, stay here with these good people, try to become one of them, and welcome me when I return."

Try to become one of them. That, she soon decided, was impossible. The life of an Arab woman was totally unlike anything she had ever known, or suspected to exist. That they were secluded from all male company she had understood from her experiences in the *harem* of the Dey. But there she had been an aristocrat, had had slaves to wait on her hand and foot; her only problem had been boredom. Here the problem was a similar one, but on an entirely different scale. The house was a smaller version of Tedjini's, and Jean-Pierre was her only slave. It was necessary to do a great many things for herself, but she was grateful for this, however tedious

200

drawing water or her primitive attempts at cleanliness might be.

She could walk abroad, with her eunuch in attendance, once she was properly veiled and hidden from prying eyes. She could pay calls upon the other leading *harems* on the oasis, but these were hardly enjoyable occasions. Very few of the Arab women spoke French or even Turkish, their gossip was entirely of an amatory nature, and they spent their leisure hours stuffing themselves with coffee and sweets, usually of a horribly sticky variety. Their standards of hygiene were repulsive, as they thought nothing of placing their half-eaten delicacies on the floor, and later consuming them complete with a thick layer of dust and spiced by the presence of flies which were cheerfully swallowed.

It was invariably very hot down in the sunken *oasis*, and Catherine longed to be able to take a ride into the desert, but this was forbidden. The only time she could gain any coolness was at night, when she could climb onto the flat roof of the house—this was always available but was far too hot as long as the sun was up—undress down to her undershirt, and inhale the amazingly clean and crisp night air. Soon she took to sleeping on the roof, having Jean-Pierre bring up a mattress. But whatever her temptations, she never undressed completely. No Arab ever did, so far as she could learn and indeed she doubted many of them washed from one year's end to the other. Even in the *oasis* water was not exactly abundant, and in any event they were not conditioned to a great deal of bathing. Soon she had so far adopted the local custom that she reserved her baths for when Ricimer was expected, for these occasional visits were the only breaks in her otherwise monotonous existence. The luxuriousness of the Dey's bathing chamber receded into a dream.

She concentrated on learning Arabic, the better to converse with her neighbours, and then wished she had not, for all they wished to talk about was her life in the *harem* of the Dey. She endeavoured to invent some way of varying the unending diet of dates, lentils, flour, beans and mare's milk, for meat was eaten only on special occasions, and failed; she had never been much of a cook. She discovered she missed Madeleine's grumbling enormously, and endeavoured to discover for herself a pet, as the *oasis* was overrun with dogs. But they were universally vicious, and equally flea-laden.

She turned more and more to Jean-Pierre for amusement, although she never again risked an advance such as she had made on her wedding night. He listened to her, and he talked in reply, but really he was very little better company than the women. He had been snatched from his home and his surroundings at the age of twelve, at a time when he was interested in nothing except food, sleep, and his boyish games. His ghastly experience seemed to have stunted his mental growth as much as it had ended his manhood, and she was disgusted to watch him steadily growing more and more fat. Had he been an ordinary eunuch she would have taught him to be of more use, at least in a purely physical fashion, but he was Jean-Pierre, and he had expressed his smouldering hatred of her. She discovered that she hated him as much as he hated her, and would rail at him and shout at him.

"Why do you stand there?" she would demand. "Do you not know you are obnoxious to me?"

"I stand here because I am your slave, my lady."

"How can you be my slave? You are my brother. I give you your freedom. Go on. Go. You are free."

"How may I go, my lady? Where may I go? I would merely starve. I am nothing save your slave."

Which simple truth invariably reduced her to tears.

Worst of all, he was a constant reminder of who and what she was, what she had been, what she had become. She was Baroness Ricimer. Her place was in Paris or Vienna, attending balls and soirées, riding in the parks behind a magnificent team of horses, being titillated by innumerable flirtations, all of which she would end with a flick of her fan, for how could there be a man anywhere on earth to match Ricimer?

Instead of which she was hidden away in an unknown

Saharan *oasis,* waiting for she knew not what. *An Ice Maiden,* she thought with grim humour, *melting in the sun.*

But then Ricimer would ride in, with his escort of heavily armed Bedouins, and jump from his horse and sweep her into his arms, and her fears and desires and frustrations would be over for another season. He would carry her upstairs to the tiny bedroom and lay her on the divan, and make love to her while he told her what was happening in the world outside. Of how by the end of 1830, Charles X had been forced to flee the French throne, and replaced there by his cousin Louis-Philippe. In fact, his estimate of the possible effects a total change of government in France might have on the Algerian situation was rapidly proved wrong, for the French liberals seemed every bit as intent upon pursuing their course of African conquest as had the French conservatives. General de Bourmont was promptly retired, but his successor, Clauzel, was even more energetic, and Oran fell in January of 1831, while Tittery surrendered soon after. But now Clauzel made a serious error of judgement and appointed a Moor to the vacant beylik. The Arabs were incensed, and the spirit of revolt spread farther into the desert.

All of which made Ricimer's absences longer and more frequent, as he rode from tribe to tribe, exhorting them to go to war, exhorting the *marabouts* to preach a *jihad* against the infidel French, exhorting them to place him in command of an army which would sweep the invaders into the sea.

But these matters, and even his absences suddenly ceased to be of any great importance to Catherine; in the spring of 1831 she discovered herself to be pregnant.

Chapter 7

᪪᪪᪪᪪᪪᪪᪪᪪᪪᪪ HERE was happiness, at last. For while she had existed from visit to visit of her husband, from embrace to embrace, and in the joy of those passionate nights convinced herself that he was merely preoccupied with acting the Arab, with achieving his personal goal of power and fame as a renegade general, and that when this war was finished he would be the Ricimer she had known in her dreams, and a Ricimer who could be taught to love her as she loved him, in her long lonely hours she had often wondered if she had any right at all *to* consider herself really Baroness Ricimer. True, they had undergone both a Christian and a Moslem ceremony—she wore a gold wedding band he claimed had belonged to his mother—but Ricimer himself obviously believed only in the latter, and she was well aware what a simple matter divorce was in the Moslem world. She was still only nineteen, she had preserved her health through all of her misfortunes, and excepting her blemished complexion, for the freckles would not go away but rather seemed daily to increase in numbers, she was still as beautiful as ever—perhaps more beautiful than ever—she reasoned as she inspected herself in her spotted glass, for she had managed to fill out a little and lose some of the slender gawkiness of a girl.

But how long would she please a man like Ricimer, if his feelings for her were truly only those of possession? And although her friends in the neighbouring *harems* told her it would be the best thing in the world for him to take another wife, for only that way would she ever obtain any rest in a society where adultery was an unknown crime, she could not bring herself to accept the prospect of sharing her house with another, and then no doubt another, and then even a fourth, as the years would go by. Why, she was Baroness Ricimer. Would they also claim a share in the title?

But to be the mother of his child. Surely he remained sufficient of a European to set her above all others once that was accomplished. And when she told him the news she could see the delight in his eyes, soon to be replaced by a concern which for the first time since their marriage included herself. This dirt and heat was no place to have a child, surely, and yet there was no other place where the Baroness Ricimer might be safe. Save she surrendered herself to the French garrison in Algiers. But this would mean separation, perhaps permanently, from her husband. He even suggested this might be best for her, reasoning that he would soon enough be able to smuggle the child back to the *oasis*.

"And what of me?" she demanded.

"You as well, of course, *Ya Habibti.*"

She decided to take her chances in Ain-Mahdi.

Despite her happiness at the prospect of motherhood, her boredom grew even greater. Ricimer might be anxious for her, or at least for the child, but he could not spare any more time than usual to be with her; the information from the coast was that the French were at last losing interest in their colonial adventure. The garrisons were being reduced, said the Bedouin spies, and in fact they doubted there were more than two thousand soldiers left. Now more than ever was the time to raise that army of which he dreamed, and become the warrior ruler of his imagination. After all, as he never tired of telling her, Khair-ed-din Barbarossa himself had begun life as a Greek slave, and had risen by his own prowess and by taking advantage of circumstances. Surely Kurt Ricimer was as capable of carving an empire for himself.

He provided her with two additional woman slaves, neither of whom spoke either Turkish or French, as she was to undertake no work at all during her confinement, and left her largely to herself. She arranged seven sticks on the roof of her house, and every day cut a piece from one of them, watching them dwindle, slowly. And with the sticks her initial happiness also dwindled. She felt totally isolated, and not a little afraid. Although she refused to admit it, even to herself, the realization that all the while she had been friendless in Algiers, that her reliance on Madeleine and Selim and Jean-Pierre had been quite without foundation, lurked as a black pit at the back of her mind. If only Papa could know what was happening to her. Could know, even, if she was still alive. If only she could be sure he was still alive. If only . . . if only . . . if only. She could do nothing but dream, of when the child was born. It occurred to her that she was waiting, but not merely upon her swollen belly. She had been waiting all of her life. Perhaps every girl waits, she thought, to meet the man who will become her husband, who will love her and cherish her. So she had waited, and had at last met the man for her, surely the only man for her, and had been forced to wait some more. But now she had achieved her girlhood ambition, and she was waiting all over again. And this time she did not know on what. Certainly in her depressed moments, which were growing increasingly numerous, she could no longer believe that she would ever change him, that she would ever achieve true happiness with him.

And if that were so, then what *could* she be waiting for? She was his wife.

The year passed, and she grew ever larger and to her mind more grotesque. Ricimer's visits became even more infrequent, and on most nights she cried herself to sleep. She even thought of jumping up and down, in an effort either to deliver the child or force it into an abortion,

206

and was gently but firmly restrained by Jean-Pierre, who watched over her like the guard dog he was become, all without ever revealing the slightest sign of affection, the slightest glimmer of happiness or even contentment.

But at last even the purgatory of motherhood drew to an end, and shortly before Christmas, in fact two days after her own twentieth birthday, she knew her moment had arrived.

The ladies of Tedjini's *harem* knew it too, and Lalla, his number-one wife, was instantly efficient. Catherine was seized, rather as on her wedding night, and carried over to Tedjini's house, where she was installed on a divan in the *harem*. She was more than over frightened, a fear which had been growing during the final months of her pregnancy. Ricimer had not slept with her from the moment she had told him, but at least in the early days he had occasionally held her in his arms. These last four months he had literally done no more than touch her hand. Her loneliness had grown, as even Jean-Pierre had seemed more distant, in his case entirely because he had no idea what was happening.

And then, the thought of the birth, in such surroundings of dirt and squalor, without a qualified doctor or midwife . . . she could reassure herself only by thinking of the hordes of Arab children who thronged the oasis, and they all seemed to have a living mother tucked away somewhere in the recesses of the various *harems*. Certainly, the knowledgeable bustle of the women was to some extent encouraging, as were the smiles of the younger wives, who sat by her bedside and wiped the sweat from her face, and fanned her. They were all mothers already, although their ages varied from thirteen to sixteen. *In their eyes,* she thought, *she was an old hag who had grievously neglected her responsibilities.*

But now the cramps were more severe and closer together. The girls redoubled the intensity of their fanning and swabbing, and at the other end of the divan Lalla was marshalling her elder women.

It was amazingly quick. Catherine had no more time than to utter a few whimpers of discomfort, as she tried to control herself for fear the real agony would begin soon enough, and then the pain was gone, and Lalla was holding up the wizened scrap of reddened flesh for her to admire. In fact she was horrified, having never seen a newborn babe before, but Lalla seemed pleased enough.

"*Gerbek Ismeh*," she shouted. "*Gerbek Ismeh*."

Catherine allowed the exhaustion to creep over her. "*Gerbek Ismeh*?" she whispered. "What does it mean?"

Lalla cackled. "It is his name."

Which was the first intimation Catherine had received that he was a boy. "*Gerbek Ismeh*?" she cried, rising on her elbow. "I don't want to call him *Gerbek Ismeh*."

"It is his name," Lalla said, crossly. "All new born babes are called *Gerbek Ismeh*. Supposing the child were to die? Would you have him attempt to enter heaven without a name?" She patted Catherine on the arm. "When he is sure to live, then you can choose another name for him."

Catherine allowed herself to relax, watched another of the elder women hanging a charm around the baby's neck, consisting of a gold chain on which hung a flat triangular piece of gold inscribed in Arabic, and surrounded by blue beads. This was to ward off any *djinns* who might be in the vicinity, as was the piece of garlic that was also suspended about the boy's neck by a length of string. The garlic, she gathered, was even more important than the charm, and she could not help but remember the vampire legends she had heard, emanating from Transylvania.

But then the boy was removed to be cleaned of blood, and she was settled among her bolsters by the delighted young women, while bowls of dates were brought to her to eat.

"They are good," Lalla said wisely. "They open the bowels. They will make you healthy." To Catherine's amazement she leaned over the bed to kiss her on the cheek. "You have done well, *Ya Habibti*, your lord will be well pleased."

As indeed he was. The boy was five weeks old by the

time Ricimer next came to Ain-Mahdi, and Catherine had recovered both her figure and her health. She was, indeed, quite amazed at the speed with which her strength returned, thanks to the ministrations of Lalla and her fellows, and equally, she supposed, to the magnificent desert climate, at least in the winter months, for Ain-Mahdi was situated on the plateau behind the Atlas Mountains themselves, some eight hundred feet above the sea, and the air was delightfully crisp and clear, and even cool during the nights.

The christening ceremony was held immediately, with Tedjini acting as godfather. Ricimer wished the boy to be called Gebhard, as he had a passionate admiration for Prince von Blucher, and Catherine was happy to agree. So Tedjini, having performed the necessary prayers and ablutions, held the child aloft and whispered the name into his ear, and Gebhard Ricimer was officially born. The feasting lasted well into the night, but when it was done, and Ricimer crawled into their bed in the darkened room, he was as passionately eager as she had ever hoped he might be. *I was right*, she thought. *He is growing to love me for myself rather than as a symbol of his revenge, and Gebhard will, as I had hoped, bind us ever closer together*. That night for the first time she truly felt she could call herself Baroness Ricimer.

And yet he was away again within a week. "Because at last things are moving," he declared. "The Arabs have chosen themselves a leader."

She sat up in delight. "You?"

He sighed, and shook his head. "No. They will not be led by a European. They have chosen a worthy man, a *marabout* named Mahi ed Din. He has preached a *jihad*, and the tribes are rallying to his call. In fact the French have brought it upon themselves. This Savary, who now commands, was, as you no doubt know, once head of Napoleon's Police Force, and from all accounts is a perfect monster of cruelty. He has had his columns visiting various oases and demanding oaths of allegiance to France, and where this has not been forthcoming, he has been shooting whole families, women and children as well."

"My God," she whispered. "Will he not come here?"

Ricimer kissed her on the nose. "Two hundred miles into the desert is a bit farther than even Monsieur Savary will wish to penetrate. The odd thing is that all my efforts to draw Tedjini into the fight have proved unsuccessful. He will not give any allegiance to the French, but he will not ride with the Arabs either. He says he intends to pursue a policy of neutrality. Well, this is a well-fortified place as you can see, and I have no doubt that he will be able to protect himself. There are enough muskets, with bullets and powder, stored here to outfit an army. Why, do you know he even has four cannon? Not that he has much idea how to go about firing them. It's a pity he will not donate them to our cause. But here is certainly as safe a place as any for you and the boy to remain while the war continues."

"But you are riding again," she complained. "To fight?"

He put his arm around her shoulders to squeeze her against him. "Indeed I am. This Mahi ed Din is nothing more than a figurehead. I am his Chief of Staff. So I am the real commander. And do you know where I go to lead my hordes? Oran. That will surprise them, eh? And once Oran falls, let us see how long the French think they can hold on to Algiers."

So once again she was left alone, to the *harem* gossip and the heat as the summer approached. But at least her boredom was relieved by Gebhard, with whom she spent every hour, awake or asleep, for in Ricimer's absence she had him share her bed.

His company became more and more important, for in fact Oran did not fall, although the Arab army pressed the siege, on and off, until the autumn, when Mahi ed Din disbanded his troops for the winter. Then at last Ricimer returned to Ain-Mahdi, decidedly discontented.

"This fellow thinks more of uniting all the tribes into a nation, with him as their head, rather than prosecuting the war," he grumbled.

"But is that not the dream of all Arabs, to be united?"

"A dream," he snorted. "It can never be anything more than that. Most of these tribes hate one another more than they hate the French. The only call to which they will respond is the call to arms. Now, if he possessed but a tenth of the spirit of that boy of his . . ."

"Who?" she inquired.

"His name is Abd el Kader, and he is Mahi's son. Now there is a fighting man. Trouble is, he is too young. Can't be much over twenty. Anyway, we shall have to see, next year. At least they are pledged to renew the war."

"And for this season, at the least," she said, "I have you to myself."

But once again his lovemaking was perfunctory, however practised. She realised her dream was still a long way from fulfilment. He was far more interested in the empire he hoped to carve than in any domestic bliss.

She conceived herself becoming an entirely Arab woman, and fought against it, desperately. She sewed and she taught Gebhard both French and English, omitting Arabic altogether, although she had no doubt he would pick it up from the only friends he would know, as he grew older. Supposing things continued as they were going. For far from sitting on the defensive, the next year the French went back on the attack, and soon captured the city of Bougie, on the coast, while their intention of prosecuting the conquest as vigorously as possible was shown by the recruitment of a new regiment, composed entirely of foreigners and named the Foreign Legion, specifically for the conquest of Algiers, as recruitment at home was lagging.

Even Jean-Pierre at last gave way to discontent. "I consider it entirely possible that we are doomed to die here in the desert," he said.

"And what does it mean to you?" she demanded, angrily and cruelly, feeling her own despair bubbling in her chest. "Where else could you possibly live with any respect at all?"

He merely looked at her, and then bowed and walked

211

away. Poor Jean-Pierre. She was increasingly tempted once more to attempt to have him play the part of a properly educated eunuch, and more and more inclined to press until she won her point.

News trickled into the oasis throughout the summer, of how, following the death of Mahi ed Din, the Arabs had finally elected the youthful *marabout*, Abd el Kader, as their leader, giving him the title of *Emir el Miumenin*, Commander of the Faithful. Then the desert buzzed with excitement, as it was known that their new general had challenged the French to meet him in the open field. Perhaps at last the decisive moment was approaching, Catherine thought. The battle was fought outside Oran on 2nd December, 1833, without victory to either side. The Arabs suffered by far the heavier casualties, but the French retired within their encampments.

And yet, the battle had been decisive enough. As a result of it, both Abd el Kader and General Demischels, the new French commander in Oran, realised that winning a military victory was too difficult to contemplate, and a peace conference was arranged. Catherine could hardly believe her ears, especially when the messengers who brought the news to the oasis also brought instructions from Baron Ricimer. As the Arab Chief of Staff he could not leave the army, but now the war was coming to an end he hoped to negotiate a place for himself, and his family, and to this end his messengers were commanded to bring his wife and son to him, in the city of Mascara.

It took her only minutes to get ready. She had few possessions and only two changes of clothing; her silk trousers and embroidered boleros and felt slippers were things of the past, and she existed in woollen shirts and *haiks,* and leather sandals. She would take only Jean-Pierre and Gebhard with her, as the two slave women were really part of Ain-Mahdi society, and she returned them to Tedjini.

Who was apparently very sorry to see her go. "You

212

have been blessed here, my daughter," he said. "And you will return, I have no doubt of it."

"If Allah wills it," she agreed piously, at the same time making up her mind that she never would; the three and a half years she had spent in this mudwalled purgatory were the longest of her life. Only in the fact that it had been Gebhard's birthplace could she regard it with any pleasure at all. Wherever they were now bound, it had to be better than Ain-Mahdi.

Besides, to be travelling again, even if it was necessarily on a camel, a beast she had never mounted before. Not that she was required to mount one now, but as the wife of a great noble was installed inside an *aatatiche*, a silk-walled howdah suspended between two of the huge animals, in which she and Gebhard were concealed from the curious gaze of their guards. The motion was rather like being in a small boat in a confused sea, and by the end of the first day she was feeling distinctly seasick. At which she supposed she was better off than the unfortunate Jean-Pierre, who was forced to walk in front of her litter, leading the beasts, and suffering at once from footsoreness and the tendency of the camels to take nips out of his shoulder from time to time.

And yet she was happy. That night they camped on the open desert, beneath a sky full of stars which seemed close enough to touch. As it was January, the commander of her escort, Mustapha, warned her that the temperature would drop very rapidly during the night, and so she wrapped herself in her *tcharchaf*, Gebhard snuggled against her breast, and actually slept very soundly, although when she awoke there was a frost on the ground.

They proceeded across the desert for three days, as usual halting in the heat of the midday sun, to sit patiently, boiling and sweating, until it was cool enough to proceed. Water was doled out in very small quantities, twice a day, the camels receiving none at all, while again as she remembered from her earlier journey with these men, at the regulation five times a day the caravan was halted

213

while they knelt to face Mecca, and offer their prayers to their Lord.

On the third day they entered the foothills of the mountains, and the night air became even colder. She was certain she could see snow on the distant peaks. Here too they finally came across a *ouadi* for which Mustapha had no doubt been looking. Immediately his men were set to digging, and within a few minutes had water bubbling up through the sand, while at the same time they uncovered the opening of a cavern, which apparently issued away from the side of the long dry river.

"It will have been created centuries ago," Mustapha explained. "The desert by the *ouadis* is full of such things."

But he was more interested in water than in exploring caves, as was Catherine. Now at last the camels were allowed to drink, but to Catherine's surprise, after a few seconds they raised their heads and indicated that they were no longer interested.

"Bah, it is always so," Mustapha explained. "But wait. Within half an hour they will settle down to drink in earnest." Which indeed they did, each camel putting away several quarts of liquid, so far as Catherine could judge. By the time they had finished the narrow cave had all but disappeared again, covered with sliding earth and rock.

She settled herself back inside her litter, now placed on the ground, watched Gebhard playing his own version of marbles with rounded pebbles, and looked through the opened curtains at a man running down the slope over which they had just come. He was waving his arm and his *burnous* was flapping in the slight breeze.

Instantly the camp broke out in a pandemonium, with men rushing to and fro as they shouted. She scrambled to her feet and stepped outside, to see Mustapha hurrying towards her. "We must make haste, lady," he shouted. "There is a French force approaching us."

"French?" she gasped, her mind an absolute tumult of mixed emotions.

214

"They are devils. This is the *Légion étrangère*. Devils, lady, not humans, straight from the gateway of hell."

She turned to gaze at the slope, and he seized her arm. Already the Arabs were dragging the reluctant camels away from the water, putting saddles on them, and now several ran forward to lift the *aatatiche*.

"Be careful," Catherine screamed. "My son is in there." She pulled open the curtains, scooped out Gebhard as he slid across the floor with a delighted shout, supposing this to be no more than a new game, and stayed, head bowed, the little boy clutched against her breast as she heard a fusillade of shots. Mustapha, bending to help her to her feet, gave a gasp and crashed onto his face at her side, very like the man she had seen killed in the courtyard of the Dey's palace in Algiers. The other men dropped the litter, and turned to run for their weapons, but one of them too suddenly threw up his arms and fell forward.

Catherine discovered herself lying down, sheltering behind the half-collapsed *aatatiche*, next to Mustapha, with Gebhard still hugged in her arms.

"Mama?" he asked. "What happen, Mama?"

"Hush." She peered through the folds of her *tcharchaf*, watched a line of men topping the slope. They wore high blue shakoes, blue jackets, and white trousers; they carried muskets, but these were now empty, and each man had a bayonet fixed to the end of his weapon; she seemed to stare at a line of glittering pinpoints, advancing on her in the afternoon sunlight.

She rose to her knees, Gebhard still clutched in her arms, watched in horror as an Arab, lying between her and the slope, and at the very feet of the advancing men, wounded but not yet dead, rolled over and tried to get to his feet. Two of the soldiers thrust their left legs forward, and then their arms also came forward in perfect unison. The Arab gave a scream she thought she would remember to her dying day as the bayonets tore into his flesh, then he collapsed once more.

Now the line was very close. She looked past them, at a mounted officer, followed by another, and then another glittering line of bayonets. She cast a hasty glance over her shoulder at the several Arabs who lay on the ground, at the cloud of dust that marked those of the escort who had managed to mount and get away.

Then her shoulders were seized, and she was dragged to her feet.

"There's a spritely one," said a sergeant, in French. "She'll be ours, lads, but one at a time."

He attempted to pluck Gebhard from her arms. The little boy burst into tears and she jerked away, at the same time throwing the hood of the *tcharchaf* back from her head and ripping off her *yashmak*.

"Wait," she shouted, in French. "I am no Arab. I am Catherine, Baroness Ricimer."

The men stopped, and stared at her in amazement. But she kept her gaze fixed on the officer as he rode forward, and felt her belly roll, for never could she remember having seen quite such a grim face. It was long, and either sallow or very sunburned; the moustache was also thin, and like the corners of the mouth it drooped to make a frame for the pointed chin. The eyes were green, and glittered at her.

But to her indescribable relief, he was smiling and taking off his hat as he dismounted.

"Baroness Ricimer," he said. "By Our Lady. I have heard of you, madame. I have heard how you were carried off by these fiends. Major Yusuf, at your service." He glared at his men. "Well, have you no duties? Lieutenant, post sentries. Sergeant, I wish a tally made, and detail a burial squad. Baroness, the pleasure is mine. I will have a tent pitched for you and your son, and it shall be my pleasure to entertain you at dinner."

Catherine could only gaze at him in amazement, for while she had anticipated saving herself from rape by declaring her identity, she had expected at the least that Kurt Ricimer's wife would be placed under arrest. But before she could decide on an appropriate attitude, she was distracted by a shout. The second line of legionnaires had by this time come up to the camp, and were being given orders by their officers. But one of them now

216

broke ranks, and throwing away his rifle, ran towards her, shouting, "Catherine. Catherine. Oh, my darling Catherine."

She turned, her knees going weak as she recognised the voice. And she was not mistaken: It was David Mulawer.

He wore the blue and white uniform and the shako of the legionnaire, and, like his comrades, had clearly not shaved since the patrol had begun. But it was unmistakably David. In six years he had filled out, his shoulders had broadened, although his face was still thin and eager.

"David," she whispered, holding out her free hand. "David?"

For he had been checked by a sergeant, springing forward to grasp his arm.

"Catherine," he said again, his voice dropping to little more than a whisper, while colour flooded his cheeks as he realised the enormity of what he had done.

"It is the sun, major," the sergeant explained. "It drives them mad."

"Nonetheless, he must be punished," Yusuf commanded. "A touch of the *crapaud* will do him good. And it will set an example."

David stared at his commander in horror. "But, sir," he protested. "This girl . . . this lady . . . I only joined the legion to find her."

"Silence, dog," bawled the sergeant and struck him across the mouth. By this time two more non-commissioned officers had come across to assist.

"Six hours," Yusuf said. "No. Make it the entire night. He will have come to his senses by morning."

"You can't," Catherine begged, grasping his arm in turn.

"Madame?"

"He is speaking the truth." *Oh, Lord,* she thought, *suppose he is speaking the truth.* And why on earth should an artist wish to join an army to fight a colonial war if it were not the truth?

"You know him?"

"Yes. Yes, I knew him in Paris, before I was abducted."

"Ah." Yusuf allowed himself a smile. "How romantic. And you think he has followed you all the way to North Africa in the guise of a soldier?"

She felt her cheeks burning, and instinctively hugged Gebhard closer. "I . . . I can think of no other reason. He is an artist, not a soldier."

"He is a soldier now," Yusuf said. "And will be treated as one. These men I have the duty to command are the very scum of the earth. Criminals, all of them. Your artist as well, I have no doubt, madame. They must be kept in line. The slightest offence must be punished as rigorously as I know how. A night *en crapaudine* will settle his ardour."

"But . . . *en crapaudine*?" She gazed at David, who was being dragged away by the corporals. He still stared at her.

Yusuf smiled again. "We tie his hands and feet together in the small of his back, and fill his mouth with sand. It is a punishment I devised myself. Very appropriate to the desert."

"You . . . you can't," she shouted. "It will drive him mad."

"Ah," Yusuf agreed. "That depends upon the man. I do assure you, madame, that if it does not drive him mad it will make him into a very good soldier. Now come, my tent is pitched. I think we should take shelter from this sun, and I will pour you a glass of wine. Madame?" He offered her his arm.

"Wine?" she cried. "Shelter from the sun? What of that poor man? Go with you? I would sooner go with a snake."

Yusuf frowned at her. "Madame, I would like to remind you that your husband is an enemy of France. Now, we do not make war upon women, upon white women, in any event, unless they force us to do so. But should you make me treat you as a prisoner of war you will find life very uncomfortable." He glanced at Gebhard. "Your son will undoubtedly suffer. I am under instructions to take *no* prisoners."

Oh, my God, she thought. David was almost lost to sight in the circle of legionnaires who had surrounded him to witness his punishment. He had said not a word since he had heard his dreadful sentence. But Gebhard was burying his head in her arms.

Yusuf was smiling again. "So, may I repeat my invitation?"

She licked her lips, and her head jerked as they were again interrupted. The creature being dragged towards them by four soldiers was Jean-Pierre.

"Found this one skulking by the water," the lieutenant said. "His skin is very fair."

"These are fair-skinned Arabs," Yusuf said. "Shoot him, and add his ears to the tally. Let me have it."

"No," Catherine screamed. "Major Yusuf, that man is my personal slave."

Yusuf glanced at her, then at the lieutenant, then at Jean-Pierre, and gave a bellow of laughter.

"Man, did you say, madame?"

Catherine bit her lip. "He is my slave, my attendant," she said again in a lower voice. "It is necessary for me to have an attendant."

"Indeed it is, madame," Yusuf agreed. "Lieutenant, you will erect a tent for madame, and then show her attendant to it and have him prepare it for her. No doubt she has some belongings. And madame, why do you not allow your servant to look after your son for a while? I am sure you are exhausted."

She was exhausted. But suddenly she knew that her day was far from being finished. She gave Gebhard to Jean-Pierre. "I think he may be hungry," she said. "Will you see to him."

Jean-Pierre gazed at her, his eyes as usual smouldering hostility. Then he bowed, and took the child.

"Mama," Gebhard wailed.

"Go with Jean-Pierre," Catherine said. "I will join you as soon as I can."

"Will you enter?"

"There," Yusuf said, holding open the flap of the tent.

Catherine stepped inside, sat on the cushion provided for her. It was a blessing to be out of the sun. Yusuf also came in, allowed the flap to close. He sat beside her, cross-legged on a second cushion.

"It is warm, is it not? It will be another hour at the least before the sun starts to set. Will madame not remove her cloak?"

Catherine obediently took off her *tcharchaf*, wrapping her *haik* the closer around her shoulders. Sitting cross-legged, she was terribly aware that her shirts had ridden up above her knees and that her *haik* had a tendency to unfold itself and expose her legs.

A possibility not lost upon the major. "Will you not throw back that cowl, and reveal your hair, madame?" he begged. "I have heard that you possess the most beautiful hair in the world."

She would have to humour him. Ideas, plans, possibilities were already roaming around her brain, but none of them had any hope of success without the conquest of Yusuf. She pulled back the cowl. "I wonder how you know so much about me, major?"

He snapped his fingers, and a servant entered with a bottle of wine and two glasses. "It will be warm," Yusuf said sadly, "but one can only do what one can, in this pig of a country. Madame, you are the toast of Paris. When your stepmother returned . . ."

"She is well?" Catherine asked. "My father is well?"

"As well as can be expected," Yusuf said. "Knowing the fate that had befallen his only daughter. And then, to escape the *harem* of the Dey only to fall into the clutches of a man like Ricimer . . ." He handed her a glass of wine, and raised his own. "Your rescue will be a tonic to the bored citizens of Paris, I do assure you."

Catherine sipped. It was the first wine she had tasted in nearly six years. "Am I then rescued?" she asked. "I had heard, my escort supposed, that there was a truce between Arab and Frenchman, while peace is discussed."

"Peace? There will be no peace, madame. What, us

220

make peace with these desert scum? As for truces, why, they are a necessary subterfuge from time to time."

"Ah," she said. "But then I *am* your prisoner, as I am identified with the Arab cause. And as you pointed out to me just now."

Yusuf smiled, raised her hand and kissed the knuckles. "I am yours, madame, now and always. I but wished to prevent you interfering in army matters. Those men are villains, madame. There can be no mistake about that. It is my grave misfortune to be their commander. A temporary state of affairs, I do assure you. The *spahis*. There is where I belong, and where my ambition will certainly take me." He sighed, thoughtfully, and then smiled. "But you . . . it will be my pleasure, madame, to escort you to Algiers. Alas, it must also be my duty, should I be fortunate enough to encounter your husband, to make you into a widow. But no doubt you will thank me for that."

"No doubt," she said, and drank some more wine. How good it tasted. How splendid it felt to know the slight fuzziness of the senses which took away at once the heat and the trauma of the afternoon.

But she could not afford to get drunk. "I am indeed grateful, Major Yusuf, but I am also very tired. And now it is sunset. If you will excuse me . . ." She attempted to rise to her knees, and was gently restrained.

"You have not eaten, madame."

"I am not hungry."

"For European food? I have cheeses, madame. Camembert, none of this foul mare's milk nonsense. And you would not have me eat alone. But it will be served immediately." Another snap of his fingers, and the servant immediately appeared.

"Lieutenant Damas is here, major."

"Ah, lieutenant." Yusuf smiled at the young man who stood in the doorway, holding a canvas bag. "How many?"

"Nine pairs, sir."

"Ah. Madame, I wonder if I may ask you the size of your escort?"

"There were twenty-one of them," she said, staring at the bag and feeling her stomach roll. "What is in there?"

"Their ears, madame," the lieutenant said. "We are paid a bounty for Arab ears."

She gazed at him in total horror.

"Not that there will be much of a bounty for a mere nine pairs," Yusuf said disgustedly. "But for your rescue, madame, I would describe this as a botched affair. But your rescue has saved it from that. And now shall we eat?"

They dined on *couscous*, while Yusuf poured wine, although Catherine confined herself to sips. And he talked, endlessly.

"Like you," he explained, "I am not truly French. Indeed, madame, I see us very much as birds of a feather, eh?" His hand drooped, and brushed against her knee; with an effort she made herself keep still.

"I was born in Elba," Yusuf said dreamily, peering into his glass. "There is a famous place. I was but nine years old when the Emperor arrived to be our King. It is sad that he did not stay. Then . . . but what is the use, in thinking of what might have been." His hand was back again, the knuckles riding along her thighs. Catherine chewed, and took another sip of wine. She was so tired. But there was so much to be done.

There was such a decision to make, as well. This man would see that she was returned to France, to all she dreamed of, to Papa. But the dreams had been accompanied by Ricimer, or about David. To yield to Yusuf would mean that she would never see either of them again. And worse, that the one would be hunted down as a common criminal, and the other would be driven mad by mistreatment.

But how could she help David, when she was married to Ricimer? Because helping David would mean . . . what? A woman could help a man without becoming involved. Surely.

And in any event, as she had thought so often, how

could she ever return to France, without being the butt of every contemptuous gaze, every whispered rumor?

"But without the emperor," Yusuf said dreamily, "Elba has no power. These Algerines, they raid us constantly. They took me, madame, from my very house, having slain my mother and father. They sold me, to the Bey of Tunis."

Her head turned, despite herself. "You were a slave?"

"Indeed, madame."

"But . . ." She could not stop her gaze sliding down his body.

Yusuf gave a short laugh. "Oh, I am whole enough, madame. I will show you." He dried the fingers of his right hand, with which he had been eating.

"Oh . . . I am sure of it," she said. "I was but wondering how?"

"They wished me for his Janisseries," Yusuf explained. "Soldiering is my business. I rose to command. But I am also a man, madame. And the Bey had a beautiful daughter. Not so beautiful as you, to be sure, but charming enough."

"Good Lord," Catherine said.

"Indeed, madame. I am a wretched fellow. And you may be sure that having realised his mistake, the Bey would certainly have had my fortune removed. It was necessary to flee, which I did, to Algiers. I was there when the French arrived. Ah, madame, I have heard enough about you. *Ya Habibti*. Hussein bin Hassan was not generally a wise fellow, but in his choice of names for you, madame, he was being no more than accurate."

"You flatter me, major." Catherine sipped some more wine. "That was a delightful meal, but I *am* very tired. I wonder if now I may be allowed to retire?"

"Ah, madame, would you rob a lonely soldier of the pleasure of your company?" His hand turned over, and instead of his knuckles it was his fingers, sliding along her thigh. *What am I to do?* In the nearly four years since escaping Algiers she had not in fact given so much as a thought to any other man. Ricimer had filled her

223

dreams as much as he had filled her life; even so apparently disinterested in her, he had yet satisfied all her physical needs however empty he had left her emotions.

But now she was aware of a most peculiar sensation. Yusuf frightened her as much as his total callousness disgusted her. Yet his eager admiration was something she had not known since Hussein.

And if he was that desperate, could she not turn the event to her advantage? *Become a prostitute*, she thought. *My God, were you not a prostitute for two years, in the harem of the Dey?*

The fingers slid over her thigh and rested on her knee, and now he was seeking to find the end of the folded *haik*. But he was watching her face. "You are cold, madame," he said. "I fear you dislike me. What a fate, to be seated next to the most beautiful woman one has ever seen, and observe only distaste."

"I do assure you, sir," she protested, and gave a little start as she felt his fingers on her flesh; he had located the opening he sought, and now his hand slid down her calf. And she was sitting cross-legged.

"But if the Baroness Ricimer wishes to retire," Yusuf said sadly, "who is a mere major in the French army to say her nay?" He sighed. "I shall have to amuse myself in some other way. Ah, well, there is always that Mulawer. I could introduce a scorpion into his breeches. That would be sport, don't you think?"

Oh, my God, Catherine thought. His fingers were on her ankle, and the back of his hand was brushing her hair, as he would know well enough. She made herself keep still, made herself maintain the impassivity of her features. "Not for him, major," she said. "And supposing I stayed, might you at the least empty the sand from his mouth?"

The hand had turned over, and she felt her body stiffening. Yet the desire was there as well, even as he gently massaged her flesh. Ricimer had not visited Ain-Mahdi for seven months. In seven months, no man had touched her there, and then it had been a perfunctory

224

occasion. These fingers were at once gentle and eager, and now his face was close to hers.

"Why, madame," he said. "I suspect it would be my pleasure. Who knows, it could even be possible to offer the poor fellow a glass of wine."

His mouth was open, his breath smelt faintly of wine, but was otherwise surprisingly clean. And there could be no doubt that he was an accomplished lover. Even as his tongue reached out for hers, the fingers which had been gently sliding through her crotch came up, to caress her pubic hair, taking her undershirt with it, to cup the breast, from underneath, holding the nipple between thumb and forefinger and elongating it. She had never experienced that before; neither Hussein nor Ricimer had ever been much interested in her breasts, and Selim had always massaged rather than caressed. The sensation was delightful, and sent rivers of pleasure running into her chest and down to her groin.

At the same time, his tongue seemed to curl around hers, and their lips came together, while his other hand went round her back to sift through her hair. She felt herself falling backwards, slowly, as his hand was acting as a brake. She uncoiled her legs as she pivoted on her bottom, before her shoulders touched the cushions. He doesn't even mean to undress me, she realised with a start of surprise. For now that she was lying down he was kneeling beside her, bending from the waist to hold her mouth with his, but his hands were gone, as they fumbled at his various belts.

She wondered she felt no disgust. Hussein had been almost a husband to her; Ricimer was her husband. This man was an itinerant Italian scoundrel, by his own confession, and she had observed his cruelty. In addition he was clearly gratifying himself, with no interest whatsoever in her feelings. And yet she could feel passion boiling in her belly as it had not done for a very long time.

Because it had been a very long time, surely, she told herself. For he was moving again, and his naked thigh touched hers. She closed her eyes, and wished to pretend it was someone else. Not Ricimer. That was impossible. David, perhaps. My God, she thought, what an adulterous thought.

But was she not committing adultery? The realisation made her tremble, and her arms, hitherto lying spread on the ground, suddenly closed on his back, but he took it as a gesture of passion, which indeed it was. For she could feel his penis caressing her flesh, and found that she had spread her legs, as wide as she could, and knew she trembled upon the brink of an orgasm, her first for over a year, and wanted to cry out but choked it back, and enjoyed the first thrust, a slow, careful entry in case she might be dry, but she was wet and he grew bolder, sliding back and forth, while the passion built and exploded in a long gasp of the uttermost pleasure.

I have had the best moment of my life, at the hands of a scoundrel, she thought.

Her eyes opened, and she gazed at the drooping moustaches.

"*Ya Habibti,*" he said. "Indeed were you well named. Rescuing you, *Ya Habibti,* has given me greater pleasure than anything I have previously experienced in this war." He pushed himself up, rose to his knees. "Our march back to Algiers will be slow. May I hope you will join me for dinner again tomorrow?"

Catherine sat up, slowly straightened her shirts, restored her *haik* to some order. "It may be possible, Major Yusuf," she said, listening to her voice as she might have listened to that of a stranger. "Presuming you honor your part of the bargain."

Yusuf stood up, tucked his shirt into his breeches, pulled them about his thighs. His smile was wider than before. "Bargain, madame?" His eyes were the coldest Catherine had ever seen; they made Hussein bin Hassan appear almost charming. "I never honour bargains. But I will tell you this; should you not do me the honour of your company, tomorrow night, then your artist friend will spend yet another night, and indeed, every night until we regain Algiers, eating sand."

226

Jean-Pierre waited at the entrance to her tent. "And is lady well pleased?" he inquired caustically.

Catherine merely looked at him. Her brain seemed to have been seized in an icy grip of the purest fury. The Ice Maiden, David had called her. Well, then, he would have his Ice Maiden, even if she had to kill for it. In her present mood it seemed quite a natural thing to do.

And yet her thoughts were perfectly clear and precise, her voice was as quiet as ever, and she had no doubt that her face was composed.

"Come inside," she said, and stooped to enter the tent. A candle burned in the centre of the ground, and by its light she saw that Gebhard was fast asleep, rolled in his *yourgan*. Catherine sank to her knees to kiss the boy, then blew out the candle. "We are going to escape this place."

"Lady?"

"And lower your voice," she said. "I will need your help."

"Escape is not possible, lady," Jean-Pierre said, kneeling beside her. "There are guards . . ."

"Four of them," she agreed. "Each posted on a different mound, overlooking at once the desert and the camp. They will not see us."

Jean-Pierre apparently decided not to comment on such optimism. "There is also the desert itself, lady," he said. "How may two people, and carrying a child, walk on the desert without perishing?"

"Three people," she said. "We are taking the legionnaire with us."

"David Mulawer," he said, perhaps to himself. "Need I remind lady that she is married, and to a jealous and violent man?"

Catherine frowned at him. But she supposed Ricimer was, a jealous and violent man, even if he had never been so to her. But then she remembered his anger on their wedding night. And felt her teeth come together as her mouth settled into a hard line.

"We are aiding a fellow human being who is also a friend," she said. "No more than that."

"We will be taken, and punished," Jean-Pierre said sadly. "I will be punished most of all."

"If we are taken, we will suffer together, I promise you," she said. "But we will not be taken, if you will do as you are told." She picked up Gebhard, still wrapped in his *yourgan,* for the night was chill. "Are you ready?"

"Now, lady?"

"Now. Bring that knife."

Jean-Pierre sighed, followed her out of the tent. They stood for a few moments in the silence, disturbed now by a cold breeze sweeping out of the desert, which had the horses and the camels stamping and complaining.

"Now listen carefully," she said. "The camels are tethered to four stakes in the ground. I wish you to go over there and release them."

"But, lady, should I do that, they will wander off."

"That is my intention. They will wander off, and one of the guards will see them, and raise the alarm, and no doubt also fire his musket, which will make the camels *run* off and turn the camp into a great pandemonium."

Jean-Pierre raised his arm, almost as if he would scratch his head. "But how may we then use them, lady?"

"We are not going to use them, Jean-Pierre. You know where David is secured? Once you have released the camels, join me there. Haste now."

He hesitated for a moment, then stole away into the darkness. Catherine hugged Gebhard in her arms and went the other way. Her heart was pounding, but her brain was quite cool and clear. She refused to think of what might happen were she to fail and be caught. Instead she closed her free hand over the knife, and prayed that Gebhard would not wake up.

She left the first circle of tents, and could see the trees and the reeds which grew by the water's edge. Beyond was the cavern. And there, under the shade of trees, and facing the water as Yusuf had promised, lay David. Every so often he moved, or rather twitched, she thought,

228

to show that he was awake, and in agony, as he must be from cramp as much as thirst.

She moved forward, and froze in sheer horror as she saw the man, a legionnaire sergeant, get up from where he had been sitting beneath the next tree. But she could not turn back now. She walked towards him, Gebhard hugged tight, inhaling as slowly as she could to get her breathing under control.

"Good evening," she said as she approached.

The sergeant peered at her. "Baroness," he said. "Come to inspect your friend?" His teeth gleamed at her in the darkness. "I poke him with a stick every now and then, just to wake him up. Can't have him sleeping, eh, supposing he could. That would rob us of sport."

Do I prostitute myself again? she thought, for now he was very close. *And be mocked again? Or do I kill a man, for the first time in my life?* But there was more involved even than the sheer fact of murder. Were she to do so she would be declaring war upon France, as much as any Arab, as much as Ricimer himself had done. Return to Paris would be quite impossible, ever.

But was she not in any event as involved as Ricimer? It suited Yusuf to treat her as a lady. How could she tell to what she would be subjected when she was returned to Algiers? And in any event, why should she hesitate to destroy this man, when she had watched him destroy other men whose sole duty was to protect her, who had fought only in self-defence. The sergeant was guilty of cold-blooded murder, and she would play nothing more than his executioner.

He was very close now, and stretching out his hand to slide the cowl from her head. "The most beautiful woman in Africa, they say of you," he muttered. "And they're lying at that. Why not Europe?"

"Why not the world, sergeant?" she whispered, amazed as usual at the calmness of her voice.

"Aye," he said. "The world. The major will have you in irons, if he discovers you're visiting the prisoner."

"The major need never know, sergeant," she said. Still she could not make herself do what she knew she must, eventually. "Would you not humour me?"

"It will be my pleasure, madame."

"Then release the prisoner. At least empty the sand from his mouth and give him a drink of water and allow his limbs to stretch."

"Now why should I do that?"

"Because if you do I will spend the rest of the night here with you. And just before dawn you can tie him up again, and no one will be any the wiser."

Once again she saw his teeth. "Well, now," he said. "There's an offer. You must be very fond of that fellow."

Catherine licked her lips. She was not going to succeed. "He is an old friend."

"Well, madame, I will tell you this. You will spend the night here with me, or I will kick him in the balls, once every fifteen minutes. You won't hear him scream, because he can't, but you may hear him choking."

Her eyes flickered past him, for she had caught the flutter of Jean-Pierre's *haik* as he returned from his mission. That meant time was running out; they had to be securely in the cavern before the alarm went off.

"Then choke yourself," she whispered, and stepped against him, driving the knife underneath his ribs and upwards. His mouth opened and his eyes turned up, but his knees were already giving way and he was dead before his scream could reach his throat. Catherine stepped away, the knife sliding from her fingers to hit the ground at the same time as the dead man. She threw her other arm round Gebhard. *My God,* she thought. *What has become of me? To kill a man, and with my son in my arms.*

Jean-Pierre hurried up to her. "Lady, they will cut off your head," he said.

She did not reply, dropped to her knees beside David, picked up the knife again, slit the ropes binding his arms and legs together, and then pulled the gag free. He rolled on his face, gasping and spitting. "Take the boy," she snapped to Jean-Pierre, and heard the shout of the guard.

She threw her arms round David's body, got him to

230

his knees. He nearly fell again, and she needed all her strength to keep him upright. "Just a little way," she promised. "Just a little way."

A shot rang out, and then another. She thought she could hear the frenzied squealing of the camels, but the noise would serve its purpose of driving them into the desert, leaving sufficient scattered tracks to interest the legionnaires.

Suppose they gained shelter without being seen.

"Lady," Jean-Pierre gasped, running behind her.

"Be quiet," she said, straining to drag David beside her. Her feet sank into the soft earth of the pit that was still filled with water. Then it was up to her knees and David was throwing himself down to take in some of the precious fluid. Once again she had to drag him up and push him in front of her, to scramble up the far side and scrape the earth away and to roll him into the narrow aperture. Behind her there came more shots and a flurry of shouts. But David was gone, and she was crawling beside him, to be joined a moment later by Jean-Pierre and the by now awake Gebhard, beginning to wail.

"Hush, my darling," she whispered, rocking him to and fro against her breast. "Jean-Pierre, the earth. Hush, my darling."

They lay flat, their bodies against each other. Jean-Pierre reached out to start an avalanche with his fingers that rumbled stone and earth across the opening, but the noise was lost in the utter pandemonium coming from the encampment, as now more shots were fired, more orders shouted, and a bugle joined in the cacophony, sending its message blaring through the early morning.

"Cathy," David whispered. "Oh, Cathy. They will condemn you to death."

"Only if they catch me, David," she said. "Only if they catch me. Lie still now. We must watch, and wait."

The noise continued, but the shouting was assuming some semblance of order. Already it was near dawn, and the first glimmers of grey were shrouding the black of the night. And now there came a more urgent shouting as the sergeant's body was discovered.

"Cathy," David whispered.

"I killed him," she said. "He would not let you go."

She would not look at him, but she could feel his gaze. He was wondering if he knew her at all, if he had ever known her. He was wondering what had happened to the shy girl who had given him her glove as a keepsake.

The men were being marshalled into lines. Now she could hear Yusuf, quite clearly, as the rest were silent.

"They cannot have gone far," he said. "And with the sun, we shall have the camel tracks to follow. Make no mistake, my children, we will soon catch up with them. And then, my friends, we will avenge your sergeant. This woman who I thought to treat as a lady, this baroness, is naught but a murderess. Bring her to me, my children, that I may treat her as such."

She could not resist a shiver, and David found her shoulder to grasp it. Gebhard stirred, restlessly, and she rocked herself to and fro, praying he would go back to sleep.

"So march, soldiers of the legion," Yusuf was saying. "A deserter, a eunuch, a woman, and a babe. Not much to find, my children. March."

They listened to the tramping of boots on the stony ground, and waited for it to dwindle. Catherine wanted to scream for joy. Her plan had worked. She watched the sky lighten as the sun began to rise, and turned to look at him for the first time.

"They have gone," she said. "We are safe."

But she made them stay in the cave until she was quite sure the legionnaires would not be coming back. Gebhard had gone back to sleep, and was breathing quietly; Jean-Pierre stared moodily out of the opening, and Catherine could at last look at David, for the first time, properly, in six years.

"Did you really join the army to find me?"

"Are you angry with me for that?"

"I think you were very foolish. It might have cost you your life. It *would* have cost you your life."

"That would have been a release, had I not found

you, Cathy. I have scarcely lived, these past six years, in any event."

"Tell me," she begged. "I know nothing of what has happened in France."

"Well . . . it was several days before the news of what had happened reached Paris. Presumably your father learned earlier; he had already been down to Brittany when I saw him."

"You saw him?"

"I called at your house, as soon as I heard. I found him distraught, as you may imagine, and unable to tell me anything. Baron Ricimer had disappeared as conclusively as you and your stepmother. But what was worse, there was no Ricimer Château to be found either. He went to call upon Madame Despards, but it turned out that she had only rented her house, and she also had packed up and gone. We traced you to St. Malo, and to a ship owned by the Baron, which had left the port the same day as your disappearance, but no one could say where it had gone. There was nothing to relate the Baron to Algiers, you see. Your father even conceived that you might have been taken to America, and sent messages across the ocean in search of you, but to no avail. He suffered terribly."

"But he is well. Tell me he is well?"

"I think so, as well as can be expected. We became friends, he and I."

She squeezed his hand. "I am glad of that, David. And you?"

He shrugged. "What could I do, save mourn the loss of the most precious object I had ever possessed. Not that I had ever possessed you. I possessed only your memory, and your glove, which shared my pillow every night."

"I am sure you soon forgot me," she said, endeavouring to lighten the conversation.

"Never," he said. "I swear it. With every day my longing grew more intense. I even sketched you, from memory. I hung the picture above my bed, and looked at it every night as I tried to sleep. I never believed you were dead. I was sure we would meet again, one day, and

I was determined to wait for that day. And then, three years ago, Algiers fell, and out of the ruins, who should emerge but your stepmother. Can you imagine the story she had to tell?"

"It would have been quite a tale," Catherine agreed. "Had she related nothing more than the truth."

"No one in France doubted that it was the truth," David said. "Nor do I now. It was a tale of rape and mistreatment on a scale no one suspected to exist. It set all Paris on its ear, was at least partly responsible for France's determination to remain here to insure that such a society could never again flourish. But I . . . whatever she told me, I was overjoyed. You *were* alive, Cathy, and you were well, and you were more beautiful than ever. I was not in Paris when your mother returned. I had found the city too depressing, and I had taken a post in Amsterdam. It was not until I returned to Paris, at the end of 1832, that I learned what had happened. As I say, I was overjoyed, and immediately wished to set off for Algiers to find you again. But how to do that? There was only one way, to join the army. And fortunately, at that very time, this regiment of foreign nationals was being formed for the express purpose of the Algerian campaign."

"I still think you were very foolish," she said. "Very romantic, but very foolish. In all this desert wilderness, you expected to find me before you got yourself killed?"

"I was likely only to die of frustration in the beginning," he said. "For having signed myself in, after which there was no prospect of signing myself back out for five years, I discovered that we must spend month after month in training and learning to be soldiers. We did not land in Algiers until last autumn. But by then everyone had heard of the Baroness Ricimer, the blonde beauty living deep in the desert."

"How?" she asked in wonderment.

"The Arabs spoke of you, in whispers. And it was easy to decide who they were talking about, at least for me. I knew then that I would find you."

234

"And you did and all but lost your life in the process," she said, smiling at him.

"But still . . ." He sat up, holding her hands, head bent to escape the low roof of the cavern. "I have found you, Cathy. Or you have found me. I care not which."

She bit her lip, gently freed her hands. "I think it is safe for us to go outside now." She rose to her knees, lifting Gebhard, parted the bushes, peered at the deserted *ouadi*; the water still bubbled into the hole, the sand was still scuffed with the print of a hundred boots. With a pounding heart she looked for the body of the dead sergeant, but the legionnaires had either buried it or taken it with them. "Jean-Pierre," she said. "Will you climb that hill and look out at the desert. Make sure the French have gone."

Jean-Pierre bowed and slowly made his way across the waterhole and into the trees. Catherine sat to slide down the slope, felt the water caressing her ankles. She set Gebhard on the ground, cupped her hands, held some water to his lips, then drank herself.

"Mama . . ."

"We are safe now, my sweet. Would you like to go with Jean-Pierre?"

"Oh, yes, Mama." He toddled off towards the trees.

David had also been drinking, carefully rinsing his mouth to get rid of the last of the sand.

"Cathy . . ."

"I am married, David."

He sat beside her. "To Ricimer? To the man who abducted you? To a traitor who fights for the Arabs? To the man who . . ."

"Has fathered my child," she said, very quietly. "As for being a traitor, David, he is not a Frenchman, but an Austrian, and is also a Moslem by inclination if not actually by faith."

He gripped her arm tightly. "Do you love him?"

Of course I love him, she thought. *He is my man. I fell in love with him the first time I ever saw him, and my love was sealed in the cabin of his ship.*

Then what of David? She had never loved David,

surely. It was impossible to love, completely, without having known physical intimacy. David was a lover of the mind, not of the body. It was possible that even if she allowed him to love her body she might not love him; that she would then realise she *could* not love him.

His hand fell away. "You love him."

"He is my husband."

"And suppose I said I would take you back to France, love you with every inch of my body, every centimetre of my brain, as indeed I do. Would you come with me?"

"Whether I would or no," she said gently, "it is quite impossible. You must realise that. You are now a deserter from the French army, in time of war—you would be executed. And I have killed a French soldier. I would be guillotined. There is no possibility of either of us ever returning to France."

His face was a study of distress. "What are we to do?"

"I must make my life here," she said. "At least as long as my husband wishes to do so, which will certainly be until there is a settlement of this war. I am sure I can persuade Kurt to find some gainful employment for you as well."

"Then I would certainly be a traitor."

Catherine sighed. "I have just attempted to explain that in the eyes of the French you are already a traitor."

"And do you suppose I could possibly exist, in your company, but knowing you only as the wife of another man?"

She faced him. "Would you have me commit adultery? In a society like that of the Arabs only usury is a greater crime."

"My Ice Maiden," he said. "How magnificent you are when you are angry, Cathy. Just say that you love me, a little, and I care not whether I live or die."

She hesitated, once again sucking her lip beneath her teeth and biting it, and he leaned forward and kissed her, so softly, so chastely indeed, that she was taken quite by surprise. Yet her hands had closed on his arms before she had intended to, holding him against her, and his own hands were between them, gently caressing her

236

breasts, and she knew she was lost, that here was the man she truly loved, the man she would always love, the man she must love now, with all the passion at her command . . .

And was interrupted by Jean-Pierre, running into the trees. "Lady. Lady," he called.

"Not the French?"

"No, lady. Touaregs. They are approaching at speed." .

"Touaregs?" David inquired.

"Men of the desert," Catherine told him.

"We have been told better to die quickly than fall into the hands of a Touareg," he said.

"But you are no longer fighting for the French," she pointed out. "They will be eager to help us, when they discover who we are." She followed Jean-Pierre through the trees, held Gebhard's hand, watched the cloud of dust that was developing into a band of horsemen, perhaps a hundred, she thought, carrying spears and muskets, and with their multicoloured *burnouses* flowing behind them. Her heart still pounded and her mind seemed to soar. She did not mind who the newcomers might be, so long as they were not French. She had found David again, after six years. Nothing else mattered.

"Touaregs are bandits by nature," Jean-Pierre said at her elbow.

"They will not harm us," she said, as confidently as she could. Because she truly believed it? Or because she wanted to believe it?

But of one thing she was certain. Her mistake had only been in trying to act the Arab woman, as Ricimer would have her do. She was not an Arab. She was an American, and they would respect her the more for being what she was. She pulled back the cowl of her *haik* to leave her ash-blonde hair exposed.

"Hold Gebhard for me."

Jean-Pierre obeyed, and she walked away from them, feeling the desert stones crunching beneath her sandals, feeling the heat crashing onto her exposed face and hair, knowing she must be making a striking picture, all that pale skin and white hair against the blue of the *haik* and the brown and green of the *ouadi*.

The horsemen continued to approach at a gallop, but she knew this was the Arab way, and stood her ground. When they were seemingly certain to crush her, and not more than twenty yards away, the entire group drew rein, in a tremendous flurry of hooves and a final cloud of dust.

And Catherine felt her knees go weak with relief, because now they were upon her she discovered they were not, after all, Touaregs; their faces were not covered. But more than that, they rode beneath a red and white banner.

She sucked air into her lungs. "*Buyouroum.*" She spoke the Turkish word for welcome.

One of the horsemen urged his mount forward, and it was a magnificent black. But hardly more magnificent than his master, she realised, for although the man was obviously not much taller than herself, his face was the most strikingly handsome she had ever seen, pale, with a small moustache and a pointed beard, above which a pair of brilliantly blue eyes seemed able to penetrate her flesh and see into her very soul. He wore a red *burnous* over a black *haik,* which increased the dramatic effect of his already striking presence, and she observed that his musket barrel was exquisitely inlaid with mother of pearl.

"You are the Baroness Ricimer," he said, his voice soft.

"I am on my way to join my husband," she gasped. "He is at the camp of the *Emir El Miumenin,* Abd el Kader."

The horseman dismounted. "Baron Ricimer is looking for you, Baroness, as are most of my people. I am Abd el Kader."

Chapter 8

∽∽∽∽∽∽∽∽∽∽ INSTINCTIVELY Catherine sank to her knees, but Abd el Kader immediately gestured her up again. As if he had given a signal, at the same time a Negro rode out of the ranks of men behind him, dismounted, and made a back for his master to step upon.

"There is no need for you to bow to me, Baroness," Abd el Kader said. "Your husband is my strong right arm. It is for such as Ben Fakha, here, to act the slave. Because he is a slave."

Catherine regained her feet, drew her *haik* closer about her. But she left her face exposed. She had made her decision, and she was not going to change it, no matter whom she offended. And Abd el Kader was obviously unused to looking women in the face; he kept his eyes fixed on her feet as he stood before her, at the same time giving commands in a quiet, high-pitched voice to two of his Arabs who had ridden forward. Instantly a dozen men turned their horses and rode into the desert, while the rest entered the *ouadi,* dismounted, and began watering their horses.

"I have sent messengers to locate the Baron," Abd el

Kader said. "He will be pleased to know you are safe." He pointed past her. "That is a French soldier."

For David had never moved from his position by the trees, and was now surrounded by half a dozen Arabs.

"A deserter from the French army, my lord," Catherine explained.

"Ah." And watched David being marched forward. "A deserter," he remarked, thoughtfully. "We shall give him a musket, some powder and ball, and three days ration of food and water. Now, Baroness, I know you will be hungry. My people are preparing food."

"No," she said, and watched his head come up. "You cannot send him into the desert. He does not know this country. He will die."

"Should I return him to the French, Baroness, he will certainly be executed. Peace has not yet been signed." He walked past her, into the trees. She turned and hurried behind, wondering what had happened to Jean-Pierre and Gebhard. "Perhaps," Abd remarked, "you think I should offer him employment among my own army. But Baroness, think this: A man who will desert his own people will always desert strangers. He can never be trusted."

"You do not understand." She caught up with him where a carpet had been spread upon the earth, and cushions were being placed; an enormous red and white parasol had been erected to provide shade. "He is not a soldier at all. He only joined the French army because of me. I am the cause of his desertion."

Abd el Kader sat down, cross-legged on a cushion. He still would not look at her, instead drew a jewelled dagger from his belt and began paring his nails. The Negro, Ben Fakha, who had remained at his shoulder, gestured Catherine also to sit.

She sat opposite Abd, and for just a moment his gaze flickered up to allow his blue eyes to shroud her, before dropping again. "What is the penalty for adultery, in France, Baroness?"

She licked her lips. "The husband has the right of divorce, my lord."

"In my country both the guilty man and the guilty woman are put to death," Abd remarked.

Catherine clasped both hands about her neck, and looked up at David, still surrounded by the six Arabs, who waited some yards away. He could not understand what was being said, but he knew his fate was being decided.

"I have committed no adultery," she said in a low voice. *Not with David*, she thought. *Oh, my God, Yusuf. What of Yusuf?* She could still feel him inside her. She had prostituted herself, to Yusuf. And if an Arab would condemn adultery, what would he make of prostitution?

Food was placed in front of her, and in front of the *marabout;* she saw to her surprise that while hers was a normal diet of dates and vegetables, his consisted of a cup of mare's milk and a handful of beans.

He put away his knife. "Explain it to me, before your husband comes."

Catherine talked as rapidly as she could, describing David as a friend of her father's, which apparently he now was, who had elected to see if any trace could be found of the missing daughter. She made no mention of love.

Abd el Kader listened in silence, finishing his extremely frugal meal. Ben Fakha hesitated at his elbow, ready to hand him a napkin.

Catherine completed her tale, and found herself gasping for breath. She had not touched her food.

"Eat," Abd el Kader commanded. "And bring that fellow here," he said over his shoulder. "Serve him food."

Catherine felt the relief spread through her body like a living force. She sipped some milk. She did not suppose she would be able to digest a morsel.

David found himself sitting between them, staring at the food placed in front of him.

"You are a brave man," Abd el Kader said, surprisingly in perfect French.

"I thank you, my lord," David stammered.

"Although not so brave as the Baroness, who risked

241

more than her life in freeing you from your bonds. Capture would have meant dishonour, at the very least."

"I am forever in the Baroness's debt, my lord," David agreed.

"As she conceived herself to be in yours," Abd said, somewhat drily. "She tells me you are an artist. I will have you ride with me, and paint what you see."

"My lord? My lord, I am grateful, but . . ."

"You have heard that reproductions are not permitted in Islam? We will have no statues, no idols to worship. We worship the one living God, and we obey Mohammed His Prophet, Blessed be His name. We need no aids to our faith. But there is no law against painting what a man may see. And perchance you are also able to draw maps. These will be of value. I seek an end to the war with the French, but I know the war against my Arab rivals is only just beginning."

"My lord," David said, "I am eternally grateful."

"I will expect eternal loyalty," Abd said. And looked past them, into the desert. "Baron Ricimer comes."

Catherine scrambled to her feet, watched the cloud of dust that marked the approaching horsemen. Her heart was starting to pound, and it was more apprehension than pleasure. She had not seen Ricimer for several months. And a great deal had suddenly happened. How she wanted him to sweep her from her feet in a paroxysm of romantic love, to make her forget all about Yusuf, all about David, all about everything.

David also stood up, as did Abd el Kader, walking away from the carpet to be the first to greet his chief of staff.

"Allah has smiled upon us," he said. "Your wife has been delivered safe and sound."

Ricimer flung himself from the saddle, *burnous* flying. He bowed to his commander, then looked at Catherine, frowning.

"Kurt . . ." She hesitated.

"Where is my son?" he demanded.

"Oh . . ." She turned, gazed at the trees. As if

summoned, Jean-Pierre stood there, holding Gebhard by the hand.

Ricimer strode across the sand, ignoring Catherine, took the boy, held him up.

"A proud father," Abd el Kader observed, quietly. "You must consider yourself a fortunate woman, Baroness, to be wed to so much manhood."

Was he warning her? She shot him a glance, then gave David one, and slowly walked towards her husband and her son.

"We were captured by a French patrol."

"So I understand." He returned Gebhard to Jean-Pierre's arms. "What was left of your escort reached our encampment with the news, and we set off immediately. But you escaped."

"We were fortunate."

"Why is your face uncovered?"

She raised her head to gaze into his eyes. "I am not an Arab woman, Kurt. In attempting to become one I have been making a mistake, I think. From now on I will act my true part."

She watched his brows drawing together into a frown.

"One would suppose," she added, "that you are disappointed to have me back in one piece."

His gaze moved over her head. "And who is that fellow?"

"A soldier who assisted us."

"Why?"

She sucked air into her lungs. "He is an old friend, sent by my father to find me. You recall, the artist who'd wanted to paint me. David Mulawer."

His gaze flickered back to her for a moment. The frown had disappeared, but in its place his entire expression had hardened. "And will you now return with him, to your father?"

"I can hardly do that, Kurt," she said. "I secured my escape at the cost of a Frenchman's life. But why should I wish to do so in any event? You are my husband. Gebhard is my son. My place is with you, wherever you choose to be. At least as long as you wish."

Perhaps she should not have added the last sentence. He walked towards Abd el Kader.

"Your wife is a heroine, Baron," Abd remarked. "But I think she has had sufficient adventures for one day. Would you not agree?"

Ricimer bowed.

"The peace is all but signed," Abd said. "I doubt there will be more fighting, at least save where the French, as on this occasion, can discover small bands of my people. Therefore we must be sure to travel in sufficient strength, until the war is definitely at an end. I wish you to take your wife to Mascara, as arranged. A house has been made ready for you, Baroness, and there you may live in peace and contentment, with your son. No doubt your husband will soon enough provide you with more children to care for."

Catherine clasped her hands on her throat. *Oh, my God,* she thought. *He does not believe me. He thinks David and I are lovers. But would they not have been, had his arrival been delayed by no more than an hour?*

Ricimer bowed. "And the Frenchman?"

"Monsieur Mulawer will ride with me. He is an artist, and a cartographer, I would hope. I will put him to good use."

Ricimer hesitated, then bowed again.

"It shall be as you command, my lord."

"Then I shall take my men and leave immediately," Abd decided. "Monsieur Mulawer, you will ride with me. Baron, your force will be sufficient to see you in safety to Mascara. May Allah ride at your shoulder."

"And at yours, my lord."

Catherine watched them, watched David begin to turn in her direction and then change his mind. A horse was being brought forward for him to mount, and when he was seated in the saddle, he did at last raise his hand to her.

She waved back, then bowed to Abd el Kader as he also raised his hand in farewell. The Arabs had eaten and folded away their carpets, save for the men of Ricimer's bodyguard, who were already pitching their *douars,* the black camel-hair tents of the Bedouin.

She watched the cavalcade moving past, standing behind Ricimer, felt the dust raised by their hooves settling on her face. Perhaps there was a more practical reason than modesty for covering the mouth and nose, after all. It was all but noon, and the sun seemed to beat on her head, to reflect great waves of heat from the ground. She was utterly exhausted; she had not slept at all the previous night, and it was a night that had begun with Major Yusuf. She wanted only to lie down and sleep. She felt she could do that upon the ground.

But before she could sleep she must suffer her husband.

"You will walk with me, madame," he said.

She hesitated.

"Unless you are too tired," he remarked.

Catherine licked her lips. "I am tired," she agreed. "But not too tired to walk with my husband."

"Out there." He turned towards the desert.

She drew her *haik* around her and followed, keeping her eyes fixed on the ground.

"It must have been a trying experience for you," Ricimer said.

"I was frightened," she said. "More for Gebhard than for myself."

"The French offered you no violence?"

"They treated me well. They said their war was against the Arabs and against you. Not against me."

"Ah." He continued to walk in front of her. She looked over her shoulder. She could just see the scattered trees lining the *ouadi.*

"Kurt . . ." She stopped.

He also halted and turned to face her.

"I *am* very tired. And there is Gebhard to be seen to. If you have something to say to me, we are out of earshot."

He stared intently at her; the breeze had blown the flap of his *burnous* across his mouth and chin. "And what of a scream? Would they hear you scream?"

Her chin came up. "I doubt even that. Supposing I were to scream."

"But Ice Maidens do not scream," he observed.

She caught her breath, watched him come back towards her. "Do you know the penalty for adultery among the Arabs?"

She decided against telling him that Abd el Kader had just used the very words. "Why should I know?"

"You would be exposed on the back of an ass while being taken to execution. Then you would be placed in a sack and smothered in mud. It could be done in that very waterhole over there."

She refused to lower her eyes. "Supposing I *had* committed adultery, my lord."

His hand whipped out to seize her *haik* before she could avoid him, drew her forward. "Liar," he said. "Bitch. American whore."

He threw her away from him, and she lost her balance as she tripped over a stone. She released the *haik* to use both her hands to break her fall and still struck the earth with sufficient force to knock the wind from her body. Before she could even sit up he was standing over her, his feet on the skirt of her *haik*.

"He came to find you," he said, seeming to spit his words. "He joined the Foreign Legion, to campaign in North Africa, in the hopes of finding you. Oh, *there* is love. You are blessed, *Ya Habibti,* to have known such love."

She controlled her breathing with an effort, endeavouring to sit up; but as she did so the *haik* began to slip from her shoulders, trapped by his feet.

"Then I am blessed," she said, "to be loved. I cannot control those who love me. I am only mistress of my own emotions."

He stooped, and she slipped a little farther away from him. The *haik* lay on the ground, and the breeze ruffled her overshirt. Her legs were exposed from the knees downwards and she cautiously tried to gather them beneath her, to rise to her feet. Was she afraid? Oh, yes, she was afraid. But she was more horrified. This was

246

Ricimer, who had himself risked his life to rescue her. Who had himself loved. Who *did* himself love. She had to believe that, above all else.

But he did not at this moment look as if he loved.

"You expose yourself," he said. "You expose your face. Do you know what the Arabs call European women? *Gaiours.* Do you know what that means?"

She shook her head, and rose to her knees.

"It means the daughter of a race that has no shame."

Catherine reached her feet. "Then I am a *gaiour*, my lord. You knew what I was when you married me."

"I did not know that you would betray me."

"I . . ." Curse the fatal hesitation. Curse Yusuf. *At this moment,* she thought, *I would even curse David.*

Ricimer's hand came out again. She attempted to duck, and he caught her hair, forcing her back to her knees. The pain was intense.

"Confess to me."

"I have nothing to confess," she gasped, while tears started from her eyes and dribbled down her cheeks. Honesty at this moment would seal her own death warrant, as well as David's, no doubt. "I cannot claim never to have known another man. I have known Hussein bin Hassan. You are aware of that."

The fingers tightened in her hair, and were now grinding into her head, adding their pain to that of her tortured scalp. "And how many others? How many men in Ain-Mahdi? How many of those French bastards yesterday? How many made you cry out with pleasure?"

Suddenly she was angry, as much with pain as with the knowledge of her own guilt as with the understanding that only anger would save her now. "If you believe that," she shouted, "why do you not kill me now? I have never yielded to David Mulawer. I swear that. I swear it, I have never yielded to David Mulawer."

The fingers released her hair, and she gasped for breath and tried to control her tears.

"But he loves you," Ricimer said.

"I cannot help that," she whispered.

"And you love him."

God, she thought, *forgive me.* Because she did love him. She had always loved him. She could only ever love him. Her love for Ricimer had been nothing more than a sexual attraction, dissipating itself now in fear and hate.

But to live, for that love, and for her son, she must lie, and lie, and lie.

"I love you, my lord," she whispered.

He did not reply for a moment, and she dared raise her head at last. And wished she had not; his eyes seemed to glitter with an anger she had not supposed possible. Directed at her? Or just there?

"Take off your clothes," he said.

"My lord?" She looked up at the sun.

"It will burn your flesh," he said. "But not so much as I."

If he takes me now, she thought. *Will he not know of Yusuf?*

Slowly she raised her outer shirt over her head, threw it on the ground. She would not look at him. She felt like a stranger again, a young girl, going to her first man. And was she not still a young girl? *Oh, God,* she thought, *I am an old, old woman, whatever my appearance.*

The sun burned her thighs, and she hesitated.

"That also," he said.

Even more slowly she raised her undershirt, felt the sun immediately strike at her back and her breasts which had never known it before. It was so hot she shivered, and raised her head, and saw to her utter horror that he had not undressed himself, but had taken off his leather belt.

She tried to rise to her feet and was seized by the shoulder and thrown down again. Her face went through her hands, and she swallowed dust, and tried to regain her hands and knees, to be forced down again by the searing agony of the slicing leather across her bottom. Her head jerked back, and she stared full at the sun, and felt her eyes begin to flood with tears.

While her breath was still gone the leather strap crashed into her again, swung more horizontally this

248

time, to cut across her thighs, curling round her right leg to attack the soft flesh on the inside. She moaned, and pulled up her legs, folding her arms to protect her belly and her breasts, and received another searing blow, this time across her shoulders, that had her straightening again in sheer agony, and instinctively rolling onto her back, only to realise that she was exposing her far more vulnerable front. She brought up her knees to protect her belly and groin, and stared through a mist of tears at the belt again floating through the air, but this time not directed by any hand.

He had thrown it away, and he was himself coming towards her.

A fusillade of musketry brought Catherine out of a doze, at the same moment as her camels came to a halt, with many jerks and grunts of a different kind to those they practiced when actually moving. Gebhard immediately awoke, and she braced herself for the withdrawal of the curtains surrounding her *aatatiche*.

Ricimer was smiling. "Mascara," he said, pointing.

Carefully she rose to her knees. It was in fact only two days from the *ouadi*, from her ordeal in the desert. Her bottom and thighs and shoulders still ached, and when she had cautiously inspected herself that morning she had discovered that great red weals still marked her flesh.

But there was more to her mood than physical discomfort. Following the beating he had lain on her there in the sand and the earth and the pebbles, and these too had left their marks on her body, as no doubt his penis had left its mark on her womb. And yet, she had been loved before, on enough occasions, without loving herself, with hatred and disgust in her heart. She had merely to recall her life in the Dey's *harem* to remember that. Hussein bin Hassan had known her as intimately as it was possible for a man to know a woman, she supposed, and he had made no mark upon her soul, upon her existence. When she had escaped him, she had known only joy.

But she had never been loved in anger, by Hussein. She had never been loved in anger, by any man. Ricimer had been disinterested, once he possessed her. Yusuf had indeed been interested, and Yusuf had brought her to an orgasm she had never previously experienced, even with Ricimer. Yusuf had made her more aware of herself than she had ever been before. Which, she supposed, in the wisdom of her innermost thoughts, was why the *angry* Ricimer had made such an impact, because it had happened within twenty-four hours of Yusuf, and because it had happened within twenty-four hours of David.

Of all men, she supposed, only David truly loved her. She had known that, when he had kissed her in the Bois de Boulogne, supposing such a romantic memory had any reality at all, and was not merely a girlish dream. But that supposed that Papa had no reality at all, or Madeleine, or Madame St. Amant, or Laurens. That world did not really exist here in North Africa. Yet she had understood then that he had loved her, and two days ago, in the foetid heat of that underground cavern, and in the freshness of the *ouadi* immediately afterwards, she had known true love.

A love sufficient to make a man leave the peaceful comfort of his normal existence and join a regiment composed of murderers and scoundrels, where the daily discipline was horrific in its intensity, just in the hopes of finding the woman who was its fount.

And she had rejected him. Out of a misplaced sense of loyalty, to the man whose name she had taken. The man who could stretch her naked on the sand and first of all whip her and then climb on to her belly and drive them both to orgasm in a frenzy of brutal sexuality.

Her husband.

So then, did she hate him? It had taken her nearly two years to understand that she hated Hussein bin Hassan, and the knowledge, permeating even that native caution which she owed to her Scottish-American ancestors, had very nearly cost her her life. She had been bound to Hussein, literally. Until his unexpected deposition as lord of the Barbary pirates.

But now she was bound to Ricimer, by far more serious bonds than iron bars or armed eunuchs. Whether Christian or Moslem, all the people around her believed in marriage. Ricimer could take another wife, and another and another. She could do nothing, save her lord, having taken three more wives, should choose to divorce her to marry a fifth. Until then she was helpless, and the slightest evidence of misconduct on her part could lead to the sack and the pool of muddy water.

So she smiled, and looked beyond his arm, and was pleasantly interested in what she saw. Mascara was a city. It nestled in the foothills of the Atlas Mountains, walled, as Ain-Mahdi had been, or Algiers, but in size and grandeur somewhere between the two, with half a dozen *minarets* where Ain-Mahdi had had but one and Algiers had had more than ten. With a palace rising behind the town, smaller than the Dey's but more imposing than anything in Ain-Mahdi. With narrow streets, and a corresponding increase in population over the desert *oasis*.

And a corresponding barking of dogs and firing of muskets as the caravan was seen approaching, and a corresponding breath of foetid heat as the wind drifted in from the coast to blow the scents towards them.

"You will be happy here," Ricimer said. He seemed entirely unaware that she might in any way be resentful of her beating, that she could possibly not still love him as she had always loved him.

That she might hate him.

And he was the father of her child. She held Gebhard in her arms, kissed the top of his head.

"Mascara is a city, not just an *oasis*," Ricimer said. "There are more people. You will have company. And I have several surprises for you. You will like it here."

"I am sure I shall, my lord," she agreed.

He glanced at her, then touched his horse with his heels and galloped to the head of the column.

I am sure I shall, she repeated to herself. *As I have no choice, and as Mascara is the Emir's capital city, to which he will certainly return, again and again. And to which, therefore, David Mulawer must also return. Whatever the risks.*

In fact she found Mascara, even at first glance, a delightful change from either the desert or Ain-Mahdi. It made her think more and more of Algiers without the oppressive hand of the Turk lying across every shoulder. There were slaves, to be sure, but these seemed perfectly happy as they went about their daily chores, while the Arab men in the market place through which they rode on entering the city gate were a fascinating mixture of Bedouins, and Touaregs, with veiled faces, and remarkably, unveiled women, and also Kabyles, who strictly speaking were not Arabs at all but possibly descendants of a yet older race, among whom neither men nor women wore the veil, as well as Jews.

And this *was* a city. The walls were as high as those surrounding Algiers, and rising as they did out of the solid stone of the mountains that formed a backdrop to every view, suggested an impregnability Algiers had never provided. The houses were Arabic, huddled close together and reached by a variety of narrow and often darkened streets, where bay windows touched one another over their heads, but some were a considerable size, and despite herself she began to look forward to discovering her own.

And here again she was delighted. The camels had been brought to a halt in the square, as her litter would not pass up the narrow streets, and she got down assisted by Jean-Pierre and led Gebhard by the hand. She left her *haik* cowled over her head, but not covering her face, despite a frown from Ricimer, and knew she was the object of every gaze as she followed her husband up the narrow-stepped streets and between the houses, Jean-Pirre carrying her scanty belongings.

They climbed for some time, until they were almost in the shadow of the *minaret* that dominated this particular hill, and then found themselves in front of a flight of steps leading up from the street, and into a small, narrow doorway. This was disappointing, but typical, and at least it was set in the wall of what was obviously a very large house, at least by North African standards.

Ricimer went in first, stooping to avoid bumping his head. She followed, able to stand upright, and paused in delight as she reached the inner end of the entry hall, for this opened on to a large courtyard floored with flags of white marble, having in the centre a pool of water with a palm tree growing out of it. On each of the four sides of this court there ran two galleries, one on top of the other, fronted with beautifully carved wood and supported on marble columns. It was indeed but a smaller version of the *harem* at Algiers, and it was all hers, while in many ways it was far more attractive, for in contrast to the brilliant white walls of the Dey's palace here the ceilings were made from carved wood gilt, and the walls of the apartment, as she could see through the opened doors, were hung with flags and draperies, and faced with varnished bricks, on several of which were inscriptions in Arabic that she recognised as being from the Koran.

And this was on the ground floor, which was reserved for her slaves, of whom there were six, five women and a eunuch, and among whom, she supposed, Jean-Pierre would have to take up residence. But when she followed Ricimer up the narrow winding staircase to her own apartments on the second floor, she discovered that the floors were covered in cushions and carpets of cloth of gold.

Here Ricimer paused, and waited for her to come up to him. "Was this worth waiting for?"

"Oh, it is heavenly," she exclaimed, almost prepared to forgive him.

"And it is yours," he said.

She glanced at him, aware of the heat in her cheeks. "Are we, then, resident in Mascara for life?"

"It will be to our advantage to insure that we are always welcome here," he said seriously. "And also that there is somewhere for us to retire, however much I would hope we may travel in the future." To her amazement he put his arm round her shoulders and gave her a gentle squeeze. "But I am not yet finished surprising you, I hope. Come along."

"May I leave Gebhard?"

"Of course. He cannot slip through those columns."

She released Gebhard, who immediately waddled towards the balustrades. She watched him for a moment, but Ricimer was right in supposing that he could do no more than hang on to the bars and look down at the courtyard, shouting his pleasure in Arabic. He at least was immediately at home.

Ricimer was waiting. She followed him into an inner chamber, and clapped her hands together at seeing first of all the French clock, standing against the wall, and then the tester bed, smaller to be sure than anything in Papa's house, but amply big enough for two people.

"Imported from Naples," Ricimer said. "At great cost."

She sat on it, and controlled the wince of pain that still ran up her back. "It is delightfully soft."

"I wish you to be comfortable." He stood by the inevitable chest, but when he threw up the lid, she saw to her amazement that the clothes inside were French.

She gave a little shriek of pleasure and rushed across the room. "Oh," she cried. Here were gowns in pastel taffetas and silks, belts and sashes, betsies—although she did not suppose she would ever wear one in this climate—ribbons for her hair, supposing she could ever find a hairdresser, as well as combs and artificial flowers, silk turbans and a gorgeous lavender silk bonnet, a magnificent pelisse in golden brown cloth, with high collar and belt, a variety of scarves and shawls, a feather boa, a dozen pairs of heelless slippers, half a dozen painted silk fans, and a velvet reticule in crimson with designs embroidered on both sides.

"They are magnificent," she cried. "Quite magnificent." She turned to him. "They must have cost a fortune."

He was smiling. "I would not wish you to suppose that your husband, if a fugitive, is also a pauper. You are the Baroness Ricimer. Our line goes back a very long way, and in the person of Gebhard is preparing to continue a very long way into the future. And you are the link, *Ya Habibti.*" He took his hands from his pocket, and she saw the glint of gold. It was a chain very like the one he had torn from her neck when she had been abducted, and suspending a cameo. She waited, her eyes closed, while he moved the *haik* from her hair and placed the chain about her neck, then she could lift the circle of gold which lay between her breasts and look at it; it was a likeness of Ricimer himself, and done recently, she supposed.

"Oh, Kurt," she said, throwing back her head to look at him. "I had thought you hated me."

"Hated you, *Ya Habibti?* No man may hate beauty." He held her shoulders, brought her to him, kissed her on the mouth. And for the first time since he had taught her the art of love in the cabin of his ship, six years before, she felt he was kissing her because he wanted to. His mouth worked on hers, his hands slid across her back and down to caress her, tracing the line of the weals on her flesh. *I do not like this man,* she thought. *I hate this man. I fear this man. But oh, Lord, how I love this man. How I wish he would throw me on that bed this instant and lie with me until we are both incapable of movement. How I wish that he would drive the memory of David Mulawer from my mind forever and ever.*

But already he was releasing her, and still holding her hand, turning her to face the doorway.

"But I am not done surprising you, *Ya Habibti.* This house will be your court. I would not have you lonely."

And in the doorway, as if they had been waiting for their cue, there stood Madame Despards and Cora.

"My dear sister-in-law," Madame Despards cried, hurrying across the floor, arms outstretched.

Catherine hesitated. The last time, indeed the only time, she had met this woman had been when she had been pitched into the moat in Paris. But she was her sister-in-law. And was apparently going to share this house with her.

She allowed herself to be embraced.

"It is so good to see you again," Madame Despards

said, kissing her on both cheeks. She wore a blue walking-out gown and laced boots, and looked and felt extremely hot. "When we heard that you might have been taken by the horrid French, oh, my dear, I nearly fainted."

Catherine disengaged herself. "We *were* taken by the French, madame," she said. "But were rescued by our own exertions and the timely arrival of my husband's friends. Cora." She held out her hand, and the maid-servant kissed it.

"You are looking more beautiful than ever, madame."

"Tush. My complexion is quite ruined, would you not say?" She was determined no one would remain in any doubt that it was *her* house, that she was the Baroness, and the mistress of her surroundings.

"The colour is magnificent, madame," Cora insisted. "Especially when set against the whiteness of your hair."

"Aimée," Madame Despards declared. "You must call me Aimée. And where is the little boy? Kurt has told me so much about him. Why, there he is," she cried, and hurried out onto the gallery to sweep Gebhard from the floor. "What a darling child."

Gebhard looked at his mother. "Friend?" he inquired.

"This lady is your aunt," Catherine explained. "She is going to live here with us."

"And be your companion," Ricimer added. "And now, *Ya Habibti,* ladies, I have business."

"Oh . . ." Catherine bit her lip. "You are not leaving so soon?"

"I shall be back this evening," he promised. "But then I must go again for some time. My place is with the Emir." He held her shoulders, kissed her on the forehead. "Until this evening."

"Such a busy man," Aimée Despards said. "Always working. Never time for anything. Well, now, Catherine my dear, let us assist you to undress, and Cora will prepare some sherbet, and we will see to your bath . . . you must be heartily tired of wearing such rags."

Catherine avoided the hand intended for her *haik.* "My eunuch will undress me," she said. Certainly she

256

had no intention of allowing either of them to see the marks on her body.

"Your eunuch?" Aimée stared at her for a moment, then gave a peal of laughter. "Oh, you are become quite orientalised. How scandalous. Tell me, does he really have no . . ."

"He is a eunuch," Catherine said evenly. "But there are things that you may do, dear Aimée. You may bathe Gebhard, and see that he has a change of clothing. And I am sure he also would like to be fed. Cora, I *will* have a sherbet, thank you, and I would be obliged if you would summon Jean-Pierre to me."

Aimée's face went very red. Then she said, "Really, my dear, I am neither a nursemaid nor a servant."

"You are to be my companion," Catherine pointed out. "You will not forget that as Baroness Ricimer I am now the female head of this family."

The flush deepened. "Well," Aimée said at last. "Really . . ."

"I will fetch your sherbet, madame," Cora said. "And summon Jean-Pierre."

"Well," Aimée said a third time, but she picked up Gebhard once more and hurried from the room, and Catherine could throw herself on the bed and give vent to a great sigh that suddenly turned into a delighted laugh. She was married to a vicious and jealous man. But no one could deny he was a man. And at last he was prepared to give her the things that went with his station. *Why,* she thought, *if I have suddenly realised that I do not love him, that I could never love him, I am no worse off than almost any young woman of any standing, doomed to be married off for the sake of money or family.*

And that being the case, she should certainly enjoy herself.

How? By being a tyrant in her own household? There was no other way. She discovered her laughter gone, and sat up to look at Jean-Pierre.

"Lady? I had expected to find you pleased. Is this not an elegant house?"

"An elegant prison," she said. Jean-Pierre had already seen her stripes. She discarded her *haik* and rolled on her face, careless of her shirts riding up. "Where I shall suffer my master's requirements."

She felt the bed depress as he knelt beside her. "You will triumph, lady, as you have triumphed so often in the past." His hand touched the flesh of her bottom, and then withdrew again. "It is certainly not your fate to die unknown and unsung, or you surely would already have done so."

She waited for the hand to come again, but it did not, and she rolled on her side. Hastily he stood up.

"Sit," she said. "And will you be at my side, always, Jean-Pierre?"

"If lady wishes me here, I shall always be here," he agreed.

She frowned at him. "I had supposed you hated me."

"I did, lady. Until I learned to admire your courage. Until I saw you kill, for the sake of the man you love." A tear trickled down his cheek. "I would have wished to be loved like that, had I been a man."

"Jean-Pierre." She sat up, held his shoulders, hugged him against her. "Oh, Jean-Pierre. Then you possess my every secret."

"I shall not betray you, lady. Ricimer is a scoundrel. Should you ever . . . "

She kissed him on the lips, but like a sister. "Ssssh. I shudder to think what fate is reserved for eunuchs who plan the betrayal of their masters."

"I will risk anything to serve you, lady."

She kissed him again. She felt almost happy. She had, after all, secured a friend. "Then you will risk nothing, until and unless I say so, Jean-Pierre. But now, as I am both tired and tormented, I should like you to close that door and apply your hands to relieving my spirit. Do that for me, Jean-Pierre, and let us seal our bond, and toast our mutual survival, and indeed, prosperity."

So am I finally sunk, she thought, *into a true Arab wife, even as they pretend to give me the perquisites of a*

Frenchwoman. For she wore a satin nightgown, one of the dozen that lay in her chest, and smelt of perfume, and lay in her four-poster bed, beneath her husband.

Who went about his duties with a totally self-centered expertise. She was an object of rare beauty, more rare than usual because for the first time in so long he was beholding her as she was meant to be, neither shrouded in a shapeless *haik* nor naked in the heat of a Saharan *oasis,* but enthroned and assisted by every art Western boredom could devise. Thus her breasts, which had grown since the birth of Gebhard, were almost concealed, but only by the masses of lace that clustered over them. Once his touch, his caress, would have had her squirming with pleasure. Now she thought only of kneeling, naked in the desert, trembling with fear.

And thus her thighs, and that new-grown forest between, were encased in the satin that clung to her hips like a second skin, over which he could run his fingers, or lying against her, allow his penis to grow on its own.

And once such a caress would have had her already on the verge of orgasm. Now she could only wait, for the stroking member to reach the weal on her thigh, and make herself control a shudder.

His greatest pleasure was in slowly easing the skirt of the nightgown upwards, kneeling at her feet and moving with it, uncovering slender ankle and exquisite calf, rounded knee and muscular thigh, and then folding the cloth across her stomach. Then she would close her eyes, because she could not bear to watch him prepare his entry. To watch him reawakened all the memory, all the pain of her beating, drove sexuality from her mind and replaced it with anger. With her eyes closed she could concentrate on the feelings, on the spread of pleasure that accompanied the spread of dampness. She could imagine another face whose lips would slide over hers, just as she could imagine another spirit directing the busy fingers, willing the throbbing penis.

But not sufficiently for orgasm. Her senses remained shrouded in fear and anger, more so than even she had known with Hussein. Because Hussein had always been transient. She had never doubted a moment that he would pass out of her life while she was young enough and strong enough and vigorous enough to make her way once again. But now she was the Baroness Ricimer, and this brutal renegade was hers, for ever and ever.

Unless she did something about it.

But what a terrifying thought, for a twenty-two-year old girl who had never sought anything more than a loving husband and a healthy family. She was deluding herself, of course. That twenty-two-year-old girl no longer existed, supposing she ever had existed. This twenty-two-year-old *woman* had killed, for a lover whose love she had never even known. She had prostituted herself. And now, in the truest Arab fashion, she had sought and found her private salvation, with her domestic slave.

And she was here, forever. She could not doubt that, and even had she been disposed to do so, it was brought home to her with brutal force that autumn when the peace was actually signed between Abd el Kader and the French in Algiers.

"Then we can leave?" she cried, almost happy, as Ricimer told her the news.

"It would be unwise, for the moment," he had said. "This peace is hardly more than a truce, and may end at any moment. And in any event, you and I are still proscribed by the French. We cannot return to Paris. Besides, the Emir has sufficient work still to do, to pacify the tribes of the Sahara, and create an Arab nation. He still needs me at his side." Then he had made a mock frown at her. "Are you not happy? You have a magnificent home, magnificent clothes, you go abroad as you wish, you have a healthy son, devoted slaves, Aimée and Cora with whom to gossip, you bear a title, you lack nothing that can make you comfortable . . . I assure you that you will hardly find such comfort anywhere else in the world."

And I am owned by a husband who will beat me like a dog, whenever he chooses, she thought.

He had not lost his ability to read her thoughts. "You do not still smart over that affair in the desert?" He laughed. "A woman should be beaten, from time to time. It is good for her spirit."

A woman, she thought. *I am the woman, to me. And to you also.*

But already his own mood was changing at the thought of it. "And I will beat you again, should that mountebank so much as look at you. I will beat you, *Ya Habibti,* after I have separated his head from his body."

"Is he still alive?" she asked carelessly, heart pounding.

"Oh, he is alive. And something of a favourite with the Emir. As a king must have his jester, so Abd must have his painter. Sketch me that, he commands, and your artist obediently sketches away. But Abd will tire of such childishness, soon enough, and then I will ask certain questions of your Monsieur Mulawer, at the end of my sword."

And then, she thought, *I will kill you, if I am impaled for it.*

But for the moment life in Mascara, after two years in the *harem* of the Dey followed by four in the desert, was pleasant enough. She was mistress of her own house, and in continuing to establish herself as a European rather than an Arab had the freedom to walk abroad as she chose, accompanied only by Jean-Pierre.

In him, in fact, she had at last discovered an ideal companion, almost a second soul. So possibly their relationship was vaguely incestuous, although there was no blood relationship between them, but that seemed irrelevant in the cool privacy of her own bedchamber. Certainly without his company and the soft caress of his hands she would have gone mad, she supposed.

Even with her other comforts, for there were French books to be read, Chateaubriand, Hugo, Rousseau, Voltaire . . . she looked in vain for a St. Aubin, or even perhaps a Balzac, but the plump young man had apparently not scaled the heights of which he had dreamed.

Only in her inability ever to catch a glimpse of David, for all her expeditions to the market place, was she discontented. But Abd el Kader spent little time in Mascara, as now he was freed of fighting the French he tirelessly worked at creating a nation out of the very disparate Arab peoples, and where Abd el Kader rode, so did his cartographer.

So in the spring of 1835 Ricimer was away again, to join the army in campaigning against those tribes which would not accept the Emir's overlordship. They led fifteen thousand horse against Sidi Larbi, *sheikh* of the Chelif, who had revolted at the mere thought of making peace with the Christians. Here was a more equal match for the desert warriors. Abd and his men stormed the Chelif stronghold of El Bordj, and burned it to the ground.

Next was the turn of Mustapha ben Ismael, *sheikh* of the Douairs and the Smela, who announced publicly that he would never take orders from the son of a shepherd who had often eaten with his servants, a reference to Abd's somewhat democratic way of life. Mustapha was encountered outside Tlemcen, and defeated, and replaced as ruler of the Douairs by his nephew, El Mezari, as Abd now undertook the division of his new country into two *khalifaliks,* one ruled from Mascara and the other from Tlemcen.

The news of these events, filtering into the town, kept Catherine interested. She felt that if she knew where Abd el Kader was, she not only knew where Ricimer was, but where David was as well. She wondered how often they met, what they said to each other, how they looked at each other. Or did Ricimer consider David, a court painter, as beneath his contempt?

By the spring of 1835, Abd's relentless campaigning had conquered the entire hinterland behind Oran, with the exception of the tribe of the Angad, whose chieftain El Ghomari was a personal enemy of the Emir's. But the Angad had been driven far from their homes and into the Sahara, and messengers announced that the war was over and that the army would be returning.

And with the war over, Catherine wondered, *would not Abd take up permanent residence at his palace here in Mascara? Would he not then bring his artist back with him?* There was nowhere else that David could go.

Would they then meet? The possibility filled her

dreams, and occasionally turned into a nightmare, as she supposed Ricimer also there. And then receded again, for the army did not immediately return home. No sooner had Abd made his announcement than he learned of the appearance of a *marabout* from the Sahara, El Hadj Moussa el Derkaoui, who commanded an army of Bedouins to exterminate all Christians and all who aided them, into which category he apparently put the Emir. It seemed only in a matter of weeks that his reputation spread as he marched across the desert at the head of his horde, riding a richly caparisoned donkey, and accompanied by all his women and children, and goats and donkeys and camels and horses and dogs, for this was a nation on the march.

But Moussa went the way of all the others. He opposed his horde to Abd's army of three thousand horse and eight hundred foot, accompanied by four ancient cannon. That such a tiny force should be swallowed up in the Bedouin mass seemed entirely natural, but Moussa made the mistake of claiming the aid of Allah, Who, he said would prevent the cannon going off.

The cannon went off, and the rebels were routed. Moussa lost not only his wives and concubines, but even his donkey, as Ricimer told his family with great glee. "Oh, we returned his women," he said. "But the donkey now, that was a different matter."

Then was the campaigning finished? Surely, even if Abd el Kader and his entourage, which included David, seemed in no hurry to return to Mascara. But Ricimer was home, and his presence soon put even thoughts of David from Catherine's mind. For just after she had celebrated her twenty-fourth birthday, after a second long, hot summer spend amidst the futile luxury of her new home, she discovered herself again to be pregnant.

Ricimer was delighted, although from the moment he learned of her condition he, as before, would no longer touch her or even sleep in the same bed. Not that she regretted that. She looked forward to the coming seven months as a relief from him, and in fact life in Mascara was so much pleasanter than life in Ain-Mahdi that even the business of being pregnant did not depress her. Aimée and Cora went out of their way to see to her comfort, to sit and talk with her, to work at their embroidery with her, and in Ricimer's absence there was always Jean-Pierre. *Now I am really become an Arab wife,* she thought, *for all my French clothes and perfumes and books. I should paint my fingernails and toenails, and my nipples, blue, as they do. Why, I doubt not I could step straight into the harem of the Sultan and be perfectly at home.* Even the restlessness of her spirit, the constant sense of unfulfillment, of knowing she was doing no more than marking time, that the future still held a great deal for her, if she could only sustain the necessary patience to get there, was allayed by the fact of her growing belly. For here at last was something tangible on which to wait. Time enough to think, to plan for the future, to regret the present, when the babe was born. Certainly she had no desire to encounter David until that time.

Supposing she ever would again. For in the spring of 1836 the army was once more on the move. The peace negotiations had been carried on between Abd el Kader and the French in Algiers and Oran; the treaty had been returned to Paris for ratification by the French government. Now there came news that after all the French had decided the terms were too lenient, and required a surrender rather than an accommodation with the Emir. Abd immediately declared war and summoned his tribes to meet him north of Mascara, with the intention once again of marching on Oran, where the principal infidel force of some two thousand five hundred men, commanded by General Trezel, was encamped.

Catherine remained on the flat roof of her house until the very last dust cloud had drifted away. She discovered she was frightened, where never during the previous year had she supposed that the army of the Emir could be defeated, certainly not when commanded by Ricimer. But those wars had been against scattered tribesmen or religious fanatics. Here he was once again opposing the might of France, modern weapons and tactics, of which it had occurred to her he knew precious little. When she at last returned to her bedchamber, it was to weep herself to sleep.

It was Jean-Pierre who woke her, one afternoon towards the end of June, running down the stairs from the roof. "Lady," he shouted. "Lady. The army approaches."

"Whose army?" But she was already out of bed, hurrying for the stairs as quickly as her swollen belly would permit, leaving poor Gebhard to scurry behind her as fast as his little legs would carry him.

Aimée and Cora were already there, together with the house slaves from downstairs, staring out at the hills, at the growing cloud of dust, the steadily increasing clang of the cymbals and the high-pitched wails of the bugles. It was Abd el Kader's army. There could be no doubt of that.

And horsemen were riding ahead of the main force. "Kurt," Aimée cried. "One of them is Kurt."

As indeed there could be no mistaking that commanding figure, or the distinctively Western manner in which he rode. The ladies stayed on the roof to look down at the narrow streets below, watch the hubbub of people pouring out of their doorways to meet the conquering heroes, watch Ricimer making his way up the sloping stones beneath them, greeting and being greeted by the excited townspeople, hurried to the stairs to welcome him as he entered the house.

"You have won," Aimée announced.

"Aye." He hugged her, slapped Cora on the bottom, held out his arms for Catherine. Never had she seen him in such good humour. "It was a massacre. We had taken up a position in what they call the forest of Moulay-Ismael. You will not know it, *Ya Habibti,* but it is a wild place, rocky, uneven ground, with scattered trees, pines, and wild olives. The ideal place for an ambush, and we set one. Their advance guard rode right into it. Do you know who was commanding it? Colonel Oudinot. He went down first. They were routed."

"But what of the main force?" Aimée demanded.

"Ah, well, it is not so simple, to win a battle. Abd gave

orders for a general advance. Against my advice, I may say. And so we were repulsed, with loss."

"But you said there was a victory," Catherine said.

"Be patient, *Ya Habibti*. As I said, we were repulsed. But the French were pinned down, and the news of our destruction of their advance guard spread. Why, within twenty-four hours fourteen thousand men had arrived to follow our banner. That was too much for Trezel. He ordered a retreat. But there was his fatal mistake. He decided against returning over the mountains, direct to Oran, fearing another ambush. Instead he marched for the coast road. But that led through the Macta gorge, where the cliffs overlook the swamps of Macta. As soon as we saw the direction of his march, I knew what we must do. It took some persuading, but it was done. We took a thousand horse, mounted another man behind each rider, and galloped through the night. We arrived at the mountains just before the French, and were able to take up our positions."

"And ambushed them again," Cora shouted.

"Oh, it was tremendous. On they came, a battalion of African light infantry, then the baggage train, with the wounded, then two companies of the Foreign Legion and three squadrons of cavalry, then the sixty-sixth line battalion and the last two squadrons of cavalry. The road was so narrow they were strung out for miles. You cannot visualise the panic when we opened fire. The legionnaires broke and fled immediately. The rest were driven into th swamp. We just fired and fired until our weapons were red hot."

"They were all killed?" Catherine whispered in horror.

"Well, several hundred," Ricimer said. "They *should* all have been killed, to be sure, but of course our people fell to looting the baggage train, and Trezel was able to get most of his men out. We cut the throats of all the wounded, though, and gained all their baggage. Modern muskets. Ammunition. Medical supplies. Oh, it is the greatest victory one can imagine. Why . . . " He checked, his face twisting.

"Kurt?" Catherine had felt his arm stiffen as well, and now his face was unnaturally flushed.

"Kurt?" Aimée demanded.

Ricimer gave a gasp, and dropped to his knees, head bowed, both hands pressed to his stomach.

"Kurt," Catherine shrieked, attempting to kneel beside him, despite her condition.

"Cramps. Oh, my God. Oh . . . " He vomited, falling forward on to his face on the floor, writhing in agony.

Catherine grasped at his shoulders, trying to pull him upright. "He has been poisoned," she cried. "Cora, fetch him water. Soup. Something. Quickly. Aimée . . . "

And discovered that hands were also grasping her shoulders, and drawing her away.

"That is not poison," Aimée whispered, her voice stark with horror.

"Not poison? But . . . "

"I have seen that before." Aimée's nostrils twitched, and already the dreadful stench was spreading across the room as the cramps took control of Ricimer's bowels. *"That is cholera."*

Chapter 9

~~~~~~~~~~ "CHOLERA?" Catherine's brain writhed with horror even as she endeavoured to free herself from Aimée's grasp.

"You cannot touch him," Aimée shouted. "You will contract the disease yourself."

Catherine tore herself loose. "He is your brother," she shouted in turn. *And my husband,* she thought. *Whom I no longer love. My God, that I should have such a thought at this time.*

"Gebhard will die," Aimée shrieked. "Your unborn babe will die."

"Cora," Catherine ordered. "Go down the street and summon the physician. Hurry."

Cora hesitated but a moment, then ran for the door.

"Aimée, take Gebhard to the very top of the house," Catherine decided. "That way you will both be removed from contagion."

Aimée also hesitated, just for a moment, before hurrying up the stairs.

"Jean-Pierre," Catherine commanded. "Fetch the servants from downstairs and carry the Baron to his chamber. Hurry now."

And Catherine discovered that she was panting and her knees were weak. She leaned against the wall, stared at the man on the floor. He retched, and moved his hands, feebly, and his robes were already discolouring, while the ghastly stench spread through the hallway and through the entire house. He would die unless speedily cared for. And with Ricimer dead . . . but to think that, now, would make her a criminal.

"They have run out of the house," Jean-Pierre said, standing helplessly at the top of the staircase. "Listen."

She heard the hubbub all about her.

"There are several cases in the army, lady," Jean-Pierre explained. "They are saying everyone will die."

"Then you and I will have to carry him."

"I cannot lift the Baron, lady," Jean-Pierre said. "And for you to attempt it would be to risk your babe and your life."

"But he cannot just lie there . . ." She sank to her knees, watched his eyes open and his mouth move.

"Catherine," he whispered. "*Ya Habibti.* Oh, the cramps. *Ya Habibti,* I am ashamed. I have no control of myself."

"You are ill," she said. "Can you move, now? We must get you to bed."

"Yes," he said. "Yes, I can move." He endeavoured to push himself up, and his face twisted again as he gave a gasp and fell flat, knees drawn up against his exploding belly.

Catherine raised her head, gazed at Cora. "Where is the physician?"

"He cannot come, lady. He must attend the Emir."

Abd el Kader, dying? Oh, my God, she thought. She scrambled to her feet. "Did he say nothing?"

"Warm liquids, lady. And prayer. He could suggest nothing else."

Warm liquids. "Prepare a broth, then," she said. "Make it nourishing but no fats or rich food. Jean-Pierre, fetch a *yourgan* to cover him."

They both hurried off again. At least they were faithful, Cora to Ricimer, Jean-Pierre to herself. Then what of her? She allowed herself to slide down the wall, sat on the floor, gazed at her husband. He appeared to have fainted. Kurt Ricimer, fainting. She should flee. She should gather Gebhard into her arms and run far away from this horror, to where she could breathe the fresh air of the desert, to where she would be safe.

To where David could perhaps find her.

Cora returned, bearing a cup of steaming broth. Between them they raised Ricimer's head, and he opened his eyes.

"You must drink this, sweetheart," Catherine said. "The physician has said so."

They held the cup to his lips, and he swallowed.

"Ya Habibti," he said. "You are good to me, *Ya Habibti."* He swallowed some more of the liquid, then gave a sort of wailing moan and vomited it back on to the floor, his knees once again rising in agony.

Catherine and Cora stared at each other.

"Will he die?" Catherine asked.

"I do not know, my lady. But you are certainly at risk, and with a babe in your belly. You had best go."

"And you?"

"He is my lord," Cora said. "He has been good to me."

"He is *my* husband," Catherine said. "Go and assist Jean-Pierre to bring some bedding down for me. I will stay here."

Cora stood up. "You will fall ill if you stay."

"I will stay," Catherine insisted. "He is my husband."

She had Cora fetch her a bowl of water, with which she washed Ricimer's face, while the woman and Jean-Pierre rolled him into the *yourgan* and arranged a pillow under his head. She wished she possessed the courage to remove his robes and wash his body as well, but her stomach rebelled at the thought. She fed him broth, and a little milk, and endeavoured to talk with him, and watched him once again convulse into agony.

She thought she slept, but awoke in the middle of the night to hear him groaning, and was suddenly cold with fear, for Gebhard. Cora slept on the floor only a few feet away, and she thought she could leave for a little while. She went upstairs, on to the roof, listened to the gigantic moan which seemed to rise from Mascara, found the little boy fast asleep in the arms of his aunt, and sat down herself, to enjoy the cool and to endeavour to rid her nostrils of the stench with which her brain seemed filled.

She slept again, and was awakened by Jean-Pierre, standing at the top of the stairs.

"Lady," he said. "The Emir comes."

She scrambled to her feet, as did Aimée, gathered her skirts, and hurried down. The hall was filled, with Abd el Kader's guards and aides, with the faithful Ben Fakha, and with the Emir himself, kneeling beside Ricimer.

"My lord," she gasped, curtseying. "We had heard you were also ill."

"Not I," he said, straightening. "Though many near to me."

His companions were all Arabs. *Then what of David?* she thought.

"But none so near, or so dear, as your husband," Abd said, regaining his feet. "My physicians will look after him, Baroness. But you must not remain here."

"My place is surely by the side of my husband, my lord."

"In normal circumstances, yes. But you are pregnant, and you have your lord's son and heir to care for. Besides, he will be well."

"My lord?"

"We have seen cholera before," Abd said. "The Baron is still alive, and there is hope. Believe me, my people will care for him. But you must leave this place, and come to my *harem*, and be safe there. Your time is near."

How she wanted to ask him about David. But she dared not. And she dared not go with him. She no longer loved Ricimer. But for him to die, now, with her removed, would be to make her doubly a murderess.

"I will stay with my husband, my lord," she said. "Although I should be grateful for the assistance of your people."

At last Abd el Kader raised his head to gaze at her. "I had supposed you no more than a *gaiour*," he said. "Now I see that you have courage, and loyalty, and determination. These are rare qualities in a woman, Baroness, and are to be treasured. Be sure I shall remember them." He leaned forward and for the first time she noticed a small tattoo mark exactly between his eyes. But she was too surprised with what was following to appreciate it, for although she held out her hand he ignored it and kissed her on the shoulder. "Until your husband is restored to health," he said, and left the room.

"You are favoured," Cora said, in French. "The kiss on the shoulder is the highest mark of esteem."

Catherine was too bemused to think. Her house was taken over, quietly and courteously, by the Emir's people, who lifted Ricimer from the floor, carried him into one of the bedchambers, and no doubt busied themselves washing him and examining him. She was gently required to go to the top of the house, where Cora saw she was put to bed. She slept deeply, and awoke feeling almost content again. The dreadful stench was gone from her nostrils, and indeed from the house, which appeared to have been drenched in perfume. But better than anything else was the feeling she was being taken care of.

She dressed, with Cora's help, ate some breakfast, and asked to be allowed to see Ricimer, and was told he was doing as well as could be expected. The great problem was thirst, the physician explained, for whenever he could speak he called for water, and yet his intake had to be kept to a minimum as anything that entered his stomach irritated it and made him wish to vomit again.

"But he will be well," he added wisely. "There can be no doubt of that. He has lived for twenty-four hours since the first attack. Those who were seized with him are now dead. He will be well."

She spent the morning on the roof with Gebhard, Aimée, and Cora. Poor Jean-Pierre was being required downstairs to make broth and to burn the filth-impregnated clothes Ricimer had worn when he had returned to the city. As was happening all around her. Mascara seemed

shrouded in clouds of drifting smoke as the Emir's commanders made sure anything that might be contaminated
was burned, while the city was also alive with sound as
the cymbals clashed and the bugles blew mournful dirges,
both to accompany the burial of the dead and to soothe
the spirits of the living.

She played at marbles with Gebhard, and felt her
babe move in her belly. *Poor thing, to be born at such a
time.* But it was far away from its delivery as yet, unless
it came on prematurely. *Let it not be premature,* she
prayed.

Cora prepared some food, and they ate in silence.
There was nothing to talk about. It was a matter of waiting, to see if they in turn became ill, or if Ricimer were
to die. Only Gebhard chattered continuously, wanting to
know more about the battle, and about his father's part
in it, wishing to understand why he could not go to him.

In the heat of the afternoon they retired to their bedchambers, and she slept, uneasily, and dreamed of David.
If only I could know, what has happened to him, she
thought. *But who to ask?* Had she really been a woman
of courage she would have asked Abd el Kader himself.
After all, she had been responsible for introducing them.
But she was haunted by a conviction that the Emir could
see into her very brain, read her every thought, and thus
understand her guilt.

And she was well aware that to lose Abd el Kader's
favour would be disaster.

She sat up restlessly, bathed in sweat, went up to the
roof wearing only her shirts, gazed at the stricken city.
But still Ricimer lived, and apparently with every hour,
every minute, indeed, that he did not die, his chances of
survival grew. She leaned on the parapet, enjoying the
afternoon breeze, because most of the heat had now left
the sun, looking idly down at the street below, empty
now save for a single man, who had just mounted the
steps from the next level, and was leaning against the
wall, rather as she was, and looking up at her house.

And realised, to her total consternation, that it was
David Mulawer.

He had not seen her. All she had to do was step back, away from the parapet, and he would not see her. She knew now he was well, indeed, in his bronzed face and powerful shoulders she could tell that he was healthier than ever before in his life, while her own husband lay ill, perhaps dying, only a floor below her. And while she carried his child in her belly.

Yet she was already leaning over, raising her hand. David's head jerked, and his own hand came up.

How can I see him, with my belly swollen? she thought. *I am at my very ugliest. But how can I not see him, when I do not know if I shall ever see him again?* And never could it be safer than now, both because of her pregnancy *and* Ricimer's illness. She was safe at once from indiscretion and discovery.

She pointed down, and he nodded, glanced right and left, and hurried along the street, to disappear. Catherine went down the stairs, looked into Aimée's bedchamber, but she was still snoring away to herself, as were Cora and Gebhard in the next room. Hastily she wrapped herself in her *mashlah,* a lace *tcharchaf* she often wore over her gown as it was a garment that might have been designed especially for concealing pregnancy, and tiptoed down the next flight of stairs, to listen to the murmur of voices coming from Ricimer's room.

A guard stood in the passageway, and saluted her as she approached. She nodded at him, holding the fold of the *mashlah* across her face, entered the courtyard. He must suppose she was but taking a walk. She stepped into the entry hall, pulled the bolt on the door, peered into the gloom of the archway beyond, which ended so abruptly in the dazzling white of the street at the bottom of the steps that she was for a moment blinded.

He was there, not six inches away, pressed against the wall, and waiting for her.

She stepped outside, closed the door behind her, found herself in his arms.

"Cathy," he whispered. "Oh, my dearest, darling Cathy." He kissed her hair, her forehead, each eye, her

274

nose, her chin, each ear, before finding her mouth. His lips moved across hers with a gentleness she could never remember from Ricimer. *I am damned, for ever and ever,* she thought. *But what can I do? I love this man. I have always loved this man. I shall always love this man.*

"You love me, Cathy," he whispered, holding her against him, his face pressed against her hair. "You love me, and now surely you can allow yourself to love me."

She pushed herself away. "Now? Why now?"

He frowned at her. "The rumour is that Ricimer is dead."

She shook her head. "Very ill, but not dead. Indeed, they suppose he will recover, as he has survived this long."

"My God," he said. "Then what do you risk in meeting me here?"

"Could I do otherwise?" She kissed him on the chin.

"You *do* love me, Cathy." His arms tightened, and then relaxed as he felt her stomach against his.

"Supposing I do," she said. "It matters very little, as I am within two months of my delivery."

"My Ice Maiden. Will you not just say you love me?"

She gazed at him. "And torture us both?"

"The sweetest torture a man might ever know, coming from your lips, my darling."

"Do not call me 'my darling,' " she said, fiercely.

"But, Cathy . . ."

"Anything else, but not 'my darling.' Yes," she said, even more fiercely. 'I love you, David, I love you, I love you, I love you. Are you tortured enough?"

"Are you?"

"It seems to be my lot, to be tortured. I am all but used to it."

"Cathy . . ." Once again he kissed her, slowly and lovingly, sending rivers of desire through her. His hands moved up and down her back, sifting the *mashlah* to find her back-bone, slipping down far enough to stroke the curve of her buttocks, before returning to her shoulder blades. "Oh, Cathy, I cannot live without you. I will not. Listen to me, I know this desert now. I have campaigned on it, seen how the Arabs cope with it. I know I can cross it.

I know how to discover water. I know we can survive until we reach safety."

She kissed him on the mouth. "And where is safety?"

"Somewhere. It must be. We will enter Morocco. They are neutral in this quarrel. We will find a ship for Spain. But it does not matter where we go, my dearest Cathy, we will be together."

She sighed. "I cannot cross the desert pregnant," she said. "You know that, David. This is but a dream."

"You will not be pregnant much longer, Cathy."

"I cannot cross the desert with a babe at my breast, either, David. Not if I wish it to survive."

"Ricimer's child."

"*My* child, David. What, would you have an unnatural mother as well as an adulteress?"

"You are become very Arab," he remarked.

"If you mean the desert has taught me a truer sense of values than one may find in Paris society, then no doubt you are right. Should I leave Ricimer, then I leave with both my children, strong enough to travel."

"You are asking me to wait more than a year," he said.

"I am asking you to love me as you say you do."

"Oh, Cathy, Cathy." Once again she was in his arms. "Forgive me. Holding you, here, knowing you, flesh and blood, I thought I had but to wave my hand and all obstacles would vanish. Of course I wish you to be what you are. Of course I will wait for you, now and always." He forced a smile. "I have already waited some seven years. What is another?"

"Then you have my word," she said. "As soon as my child is weaned. But David . . . you understand what we plan, what we do? You understand the consequences, should we be discovered?"

"I understand them, and fear them, for you," he said. "For myself, my dearest, I would die tomorrow, quite happily, at having held you in my arms."

She smiled at him. "I would prefer you to live, my dearest. I would prefer us both to live. So we must be careful about our plans."

276

"Yet I must see you, from time to time, Cathy. I cannot exist without seeing you."

She hesitated, and heard the sound of Gebhard calling to Cora inside the house. "They are awake. I must go."

"We have arranged nothing. Cathy . . ."

"Not during the day. Tomorrow morning. Three hours after midnight. Everyone will be asleep then. I will be here."

"And I will be here too," he whispered, and took her into his arms for a last time. "I will be here, my dearest Cathy. Oh, I will be here."

She was amazed at her calmness. She locked the door behind her, walked across the courtyard with complete composure, smiled at the guard, mounted the stairs, found Gebhard awake as she had supposed, and took him on to the roof to play at marbles. Suddenly she was happy. The uncertainty was over. So was the resistance, the awareness of guilt. David was here, and David loved her, as she loved him. And with their love, they would manage to escape, as he had suggested. Once gain a Moroccan seaport, and perhaps Spain, and then all America lay beyond the Atlantic. There was a dream. But one she knew now would come true.

Or they would perish together in the attempt.

She smiled and conversed with Aimée and Cora, descended that afternoon and insisted upon seeing Ricimer, discovered that he was much stronger, and was able to sit by his bedside and talk with him for a while. *A wife, deceiving her husband,* she thought. But if he had lost her love, it was surely his own doing. She had been his, utterly and without restraint, and he had driven himself from her, firstly by neglect, and then by ill-treatment. *The fault was his,* she told herself almost angrily, while she smiled at him and told him how well he was looking. She had at least never wished his death. Or had she, in fact, wished his death? Were he to die now, would she not be the happiest woman in the world? All her difficulties disappeared, all her fears dissipated, all her rights returned to her, all her life ahead of her.

But he was clearly not going to die. His constitution was too strong for that. And so she must wait, until she was able to put *her* constitution to work.

After an hour the physician suggested that the Baron should rest.

"Until tomorrow, my sweet," she said, and stooped to kiss him on the forehead. To her surprise his hand closed on hers, tighter than she would have supposed possible with a man so very ill, and with a passion she had not come to expect from Ricimer.

"Until tomorrow," he whispered.

Had his illness then made him aware of where his true happiness might lie? Almost she hesitated, wished to kneel beside him again and tell him how much she could love him if only he would love her in return.

Because David was an unknown quantity in the business of love. They had kissed each other, and he had caressed her. Nothing more. His kiss, his touch, had been sufficient to arouse passion, but her passion was easily aroused. Two years in the Dey's *harem*, her every waking moment devoted to nothing but love, had seen to that. It was the satisfying of it that was the difficult art, and she knew nothing of David's ability in that direction. Nor could she, for months and months. To go off into the desert with a man, leaving all behind her, and then discover that her companion could not make her happy would be the most catastrophic event of her life.

Whereas Ricimer she knew could bring her to orgasm without even trying. Perhaps she knew there was something beyond what even he could accomplish, but if there was, then it was a rapid climb to paradise, and perhaps never to be attained. Save that she had felt just a surge of something over and above any previous experience when lying beneath Yusuf. Would that haunt her for the rest of her life?

Anyway, she reflected as she smiled at him and squeezed his hand in return, there could be no going back. To consider that was to delude herself, and dangerously. He might wish her love now, when he had just scrambled out of the pit of hell, and he might even wish

278

to love her at this moment, but it would not last. With the return of his health would come the return of his old self-centred arrogance, and only a fool would ever forget that.

"I leave him in your good hands for the night," she told the physician, and went upstairs to join Gebhard for their evening meal, to listen to the *muezzin* calling the faithful to their prayers, and then to retire early, because they were all exhausted, herself most of all.

She was almost afraid to sleep, in case she did not wake in time, and instead fell into a deep sleep from which she awoke with a start. The moon was bright outside, and by its light she saw the time on the clock was quarter to three.

She got out of bed, dropped her shirt over her head, settled it on her shoulders. She needed nothing else, in the silence of the night.

She fluffed out her hair, tiptoed down the stairs, waited while she made sure the guard was asleep and snoring peacefully. She walked past him, her bare feet silent on the cold marble, reached the courtyard, walked round it rather than cross the brilliant moonlight—for fear of heaven, surely, rather than of any human watcher—and reached the door and slipped the bolt, slowly and carefully.

"Cathy?" His voice was a wisp in the darkness.

She stepped outside, leaving the door just ajar, waited in the utter darkness of the archway and felt him beside her. His arms went round her and his lips were exploring her face.

"Oh, Cathy, my dearest. Is this really true? Can we be together again, after all this time?"

She held him as tightly as she could, and slipped her hands down his clothes, to find the front of his *jibba* and the hardness that lay beneath, still tormented by her fears of the afternoon.

"Cathy," he whispered, his voice a mixture of delight and alarm.

"You knew and loved a girl," she said. "Have you the courage to love a woman, David?"

"If I loved a girl, it was only because I saw the woman who was coming, Cathy."

"Then enter me," she said.

"But . . . you are pregnant."

"Does that matter? So I cannot take your weight. But I can still know your love. I *must* know your love, David. I must want that above all else, for you know not the temptations to which I am exposed."

"But . . ." Still he hesitated. "Here? On the ground?"

"There is nowhere else," she pointed out, sitting down on the earth, her back against the wall of the arch. He sat beside her, kissed her again, and while he did so, slid his hand so gently over her breasts, and shuddered as he did so, that she feared he had spilled his seed in passion.

A hasty investigation reassured her, and she raised herself so that he could get beneath her shirt, to raise it and take a nipple between his lips, very gently, and kiss it and suck it at the same time, so that she wanted to shout for joy, and then lowered his head to kiss her stomach, and nuzzle the soft curl of her pubic hair.

"Oh, my sweet," she whispered, holding his head against her. "Oh, my dearest, dearest, boy. Now, David. There is no cause to wait. There . . ."

She raised her head as the door swung open, gazed in the utmost horror at Ricimer, standing there, *tulwar* in his hand.

David had also looked up. Now he released her and scrambled to his feet, dragging his own sword from his belt.

Catherine found herself on her knees. "No," she whispered. "You are ill."

"As you supposed," Ricimer said, each word seeming to drip from his lips like molten lead. "Adulteress."

"Widow," David said and lunged. But Ricimer's blade came up and the steel clashed, the sound reverberating in the narrow alleyway. Catherine pressed herself against the wall, hands to her throat. How could an artist like David hope to face an experienced swordsman like Ricimer? But David had been a soldier, and she had seen the fury with which he could fight.

Ricimer's flickering blade was knocked from side to side before the force of the sweeps it encountered, and the Baron was forced up the steps until his back touched the wall by the gate. Catherine could hear him pant as he called on all his skill to defend himself, but still David's blows showered on him until on a sudden he gave a groan, and slipped to a sitting position, his *tulwar* resting on the step beside him.

David's blade was still swinging, and Ricimer threw his head back, almost as if to anticipate the blow that would end his life.

"No," Catherine cried, and gasped with horror. She had not intended to speak.

But the blade had been checked, and now dropped.

David was also panting. "If he lives," he said, "we both die, Cathy. You must understand that."

Oh, my God, she thought. *Oh, my God.* But she was speaking again, still without meaning to. "He is my husband," she said. "He is the father of the child in my belly."

"He is the man who abducted you, who prostituted you, who will now execute you as an adulteress."

"No," she said. "Not now. Say you will not, Kurt."

Ricimer stared coldly at them in the semi-darkness. He was slowly regaining his breath.

Catherine stood up. "I am begging for your life, Kurt," she said. "Say you will seek vengeance against neither David nor me."

"You'd trust *his* word?" David demanded.

"Yes," she said. "If he swears." *Only let him refuse to swear,* she thought. *Let him die as he has lived, arrogant and contemptuous. Then will my conscience be assuaged.*

"And what of us?" David asked, his sword point still inches from Ricimer's chest.

"He will divorce me," she said. "Let him swear that also." *He will never agree,* she thought. *He can never agree.* "Swear," she said, going closer, "that you will seek no vengeance, and that you will divorce me. Swear it."

Ricimer gazed at her; he did not seem interested in the blade so close to his breast.

"Swear," she hissed at him, bending forward. *Now,* she thought, *now, it has to be now.*

"I will seek no vengeance against either of you," Ricimer said in a low voice. "I swear this, by Almighty God."

Catherine's knees gave way again, and she knelt. He had sworn. Kurt Ricimer had sworn, to forgive and forget.

David was lowering his sword point. "Are you satisfied?"

Catherine's head jerked as she peered into the darkness. Was Ricimer smiling? Certainly his mouth had widened for a moment.

"No," she said. "He is not a Christian. You must swear by . . . by the Beard of the Prophet."

Ricimer gazed at her, his smile gone.

"Swear," she said again. "I will not ask it again."

"I will seek no vengeance on either of you," he said, still speaking very softly. "I swear this by the Beard of the Prophet Mohammed, Blessed be His name."

"And you will divorce your wife, the Lady Catherine," David said.

Ricimer hesitated once again. "I will divorce my wife," he said at last. "Catherine, Baroness Ricimer."

"Swear this also," David said. "By the Beard of the Prophet."

Ricimer shrugged. "This also I swear, by the Beard of the Prophet Mohammed, Blessed be His name."

David glanced at Catherine, then slowly lowered his sword, stepped back. "He is capable of regaining his own bed," he said. "We must leave."

"If you go with him now," Ricimer said, "before I have divorced you, you will be condemned in the eyes of the law, and my oath will not suffice to save you."

"Then divorce her now," David said. "It is a simple declaration, is it not, in Moslem law."

"Not that simple." Ricimer held onto the door to pull

himself to his feet. He did not bother to regain his sword. "The declaration must be done before a *marabout,* and in the presence of witnesses. In our circumstances, Monsieur Mulawer, the *marabout* before whom we should appear must be the Emir, as he is the employer of us both."

David hesitated. His sword moved, restlessly.

"He is right," Catherine said. "It will be done tomorrow. We would be foolish to break the law now." Her knees felt weak again. Her whole body felt weak. He had sworn, by the most sacred oath a Moslem can utter. She was free of him. Just like that. It had happened so suddenly, and so decisively she could not believe it.

"You expect me to leave you here, with him?" David asked.

"He will not harm me," she said. "He has sworn."

Still David hesitated. Then with sudden decision he reversed his sword and thrust it through his belt.

"I will expect you, at the palace, in six hours' time," he said. He lifted Catherine's hand, kissed it. "And so help me God, if a hair of her head is harmed, I will kill you, Ricimer."

He stepped into the moonlight, hurried up the street.

"Will you assist me?" Ricimer asked. "I doubt I have the strength to stand, and it would embarrass me to call the guard. I have never been bested in swordplay before."

She took his hand, passed his arm round her shoulder, and helped him get to his feet. "It was foolish of you to attempt a duel while you are ill with cholera."

"Foolish of me," he agreed. She half-pushed him through the gate, closed it behind them, reached for his arm again, and had her own gripped, so tightly she made an involuntary exclamation of pain. "Foolish of me," he whispered.

"You are hurting me," she gasped.

"I have not yet begun to hurt you, *Ya Habibti.*"

"You . . . you swore an oath."

"Which I shall keep. Musa," he shouted.

"You . . ." Desperately she pulled at her hand, but could not free it, and now his other hand drove into her hair, seizing it and tearing it away from her scalp, so that she fell to her knees while stars spun before her eyes.

The guard arrived, and also the physician.

"Take my wife," Ricimer said. "Take her to her bedchamber. Musa, you will stand guard over her until the carpenters arrive in the morning."

"The . . . the carpenters?" she gasped, afraid to move less he tear her scalp from her head. And she had thought him too weak to walk.

"We need bars, and locks, and solid doors, for you, *Ya Habibti*. You have tried your wings once too often."

"You swore," she gasped. "You swore . . ."

"That I would seek no vengeance against either you or that Jew. Vengeance means death or mutilation. I shall not mutilate you, *Ya Habibti,* and I shall not kill you. You may be sure of that."

"You . . ."

"I also swore to divorce you, according to Moslem law. This I shall do, tomorrow morning. But we underwent a Christian ceremony as well, *Ya Habibti,* and were I a Christian, I would most certainly be a Roman Catholic, a religion that does not recognise divorce at all. You would not have me go against my religious principles, *Ya Habibti?* However, as you will no longer be my wife according to the laws of the land in which we are living, it will be necessary to conceal you from the public gaze." His hand tightened so that she thought she would faint with the pain. "From any gaze, save mine." The fingers slowly relaxed. "As I am sworn to keep you alive, and as you are but twenty-four years old, *Ya Habibti* you will be in that room for a very long time. We must make sure that you are comfortable."

She thought the sound of the hammers driving the nails through the wood of the bars would remain inside her head forever. But that sound was only a symptom of the crashing despair that had descended upon her like a shroud.

She had trusted Ricimer. After knowing him for eight years, after understanding that his ideas of honour would not measure up to those of a snake, she had still trusted him, blinded by her love for David, by her surge of joy at the prospect of escape.

Now she could not even see the sun. The bars over her window had been placed so close together only the thinnest slivers of light filtered through; the door had been strengthened and itself barred, and now sported a massive brass lock. She had been walled up alive, she thought, staring around her, attempting to control the surging terror. Except that Ricimer had no intention of allowing her to die. That would be too easy. As for not harming her, his forbearance had been entirely because of the child she carried. His child. What would happen when it was born? She was in fact a condemned felon of a century before, surviving in prison only by virtue of her pregnancy.

But the delivery, two months in the future, was hardly to be considered. She was too concerned with the present. The true horror of her situation only infiltrated her mind slowly and uncertainly. She had been dragged in here, placed on the bed, and left to herself, save for the guard, Musa, who had remained just within the doorway, watching her. Then it had still been dark. It had been with the dawn, and the arrival of the carpenters and Ricimer himself, that she had understood her situation.

"I would like to see my son," she had said.

And Ricimer had stared at her with those flintlike eyes. "You have no son," he had said.

While the carpenters rapped, bang, bang, bang.

She had fought against the panic then. "Then let me see my eunuch," she had said.

"You have no eunuch," Ricimer had said.

Bang, bang, bang hammered the carpenters.

Now the fear had been clawing at her consciousness. "You are condemning me to life imprisonment," she had said.

He had bowed in her direction. "You are alive, madame, which is more than you deserve. You should learn to count your blessings."

"Then why do you not strangle me now?" she had shouted. "If you pay so little heed to your oaths."

"I am obeying my oaths precisely," he had said. "And as for strangling you, *Ya Habibti*, that is something I shall save and look forward to, for when, perhaps, you cease to interest me. Certainly until after your child is born."

Bang, bang, bang thundered the carpenters, and the last of her light had disappeared.

And she had wanted to scream, and scream, and scream. *David. What plans did he have for David?* But she dared not ask.

"I wish to see the Emir," she had said. "I wish to place my case before the Emir."

Ricimer had smiled. "The Emir will learn of your case, and this morning, you may be sure. And do you know what he will say? That you should be executed. It will require all my eloquence to save you. And to save the life of your lover, should I choose to do so. Do you know the punishment decreed by law for a Jew who has intercourse with an Arab woman? It is impalement, while still alive. The most horrible of all deaths, *Ya Habibti*. Why, I doubt not that you will hear his screams from here, as the stake slowly penetrates his bowels."

"Oh, my God," she had whispered. "I am not an Arab woman. I am not an Arab woman."

"The Emir will certainly think of you as one." The door was in place. Ricimer bowed once again. "I will leave you to your own company, *Ya Habibti*. Be sure you enjoy it. It is all you will have, for the rest of your life."

The door had closed, and she had left the bed to lean against it and sob. She was entirely in his power. And no doubt he was right. Abd el Kader had described her as a courageous woman, a woman to be admired, but he had also described her as a faithful wife. And to a Moslem, an adulteress was the lowest of all living creatures.

She had not committed adultery. Thus she lived. And thus David might be permitted to live. Oh God, David, impaled.

She had lain on the bed and wept. She had wanted to weep and weep and weep, until all the strength flowed from her body, all the horror from her mind. And all the regret. Had she escaped the *harem* and joined the French army. If only she had done that . . . but the choice had never been hers. It had been to go with Ricimer or be smothered, there in the courtyard, while the women had laughed. It seemed to her that the last eight years had all been lived on the edge of a precipice. And yet she had contrived, from time to time, to be happy.

The door had opened, and it had been Cora. She had leapt to her feet, to ask questions, about Gebhard, about David, about what Ricimer had said to the Emir, and what the Emir had said to Ricimer. And Cora had placed the tray of food on the table, bowed coldly, and left without a word. She was Ricimer's creature, and would always be Ricimer's creature.

So, then, suicide? But the tray lacked any utensils whatsoever. She must eat with her fingers. *Then do not eat*, she thought, *and starve to death. Or beat your head against the bars.*

But that would destroy her child. And why not, as it would be taken from her the moment it was born? But it was her child as well. She must live, for the child, if only to raise it in hate against its father.

She was delivered in September, 1836, after the longest and hottest and most miserable summer she had ever known. Cora was her only visitor; even Ricimer never came near her. And when she lost her patience and attacked the *khalfa*, there was always a guard standing at the door to manhandle her back on to the bed.

She possessed no books, no needlework. Her only exercise was to perambulate her room. Even her clothes were taken from her, no doubt on the off chance she might try to strangle herself with a chemise. She was allowed her two shirts, and nothing more. And soon enough she discarded even these, partly because of the heat, but partly because of the embarrassment it posed both Cora and the guard.

Not that it put them off their duty.

She went through periods of utter despair, when she could do no more than lie on her bed and weep, and periods of vicious anger, when she would overturn her divan and tear her *yourgan,* and curse at Cora when she came in to tidy up.

"He wishes the child," she would shout. "What sort of child will he have delivered from such a tortured womb?"

But as the time approached, she became calmer. Perhaps he wished to drive her mad. Well, then, he would fail. For as she lay awake during the midnight hours, she began to form a plan of escape. She had escaped the French at the *ouadi,* by using her brains and her strength and her courage, and above all, her determination. Surely she could escape this house. Because she needed no more than that. She reasoned to herself at great length. Ricimer had told the Emir very little. Had he accused David, and had him executed, he would certainly have come to tell her, blow by blow, what had happened.

Oh, David, she would think. He had held her in his arms only four times. But she could remember every second of each of them. He had never made her his, but he had been about to when they had been interrupted, and she could use her imagination to feel what must have been hers only a moment later.

But what did he think of her disappearance? Had he called at the house to find her? That would have been highly dangerous, but he would have done it. Or had he accepted that she had changed her mind, once more bewitched by the manhood of the Baron?

Either way, she was sure, could she but reach the Emir, and throw herself on his mercy, all would be well. She had *not* committed adultery. No one need ever know about Yusuf. Therefore she was being cruelly and quite unjustly confined. Abd el Kader was famous for his justice. And if her plea failed, why then, she would kill herself. There it was. But she would kill Ricimer first. On that she had resolved.

But all that dreadful prospect waited upon her child, and she could hardly believe the months of restriction were over. As before, it was an easy birth; she had eaten little during the previous six months and the child was not large. It was a girl, and was immediately removed by Cora.

"But who will feed it?" she cried.

"There is a *taya* waiting," Cora said. "Arab milk. The best."

"And what of mine?"

Cora's lip curled. "Shall I send a slave to lick it from your teats, lady?"

A slave. She had almost forgotten Jean-Pierre. Her most faithful slave, who had helped her before, would help her again. But he was not allowed to see her. She did not even know if he was still alive.

Sometimes she thought Ricimer would succeed, and she would go mad.

But now she could begin her task. She waited, for two weeks, milking her own breasts, in the interim spending much of her time walking her room, to build up the strength in her legs, restore her health as rapidly as possible. Then she commenced. Time had no meaning, which was as well, as she possessed no tools save her wedding ring, her silver anklets, and various pieces of bone she secreted from her occasional dish of *couscous*. She worked at the corner bar, sawing away, slowly and deliberately, determined not to exhaust herself and collapse in despair, determined also not to make any noise.

For a month she made no impression at all upon the stout cedar, but after a month there was the faintest depression in the wood, and she wanted to shriek in her joy.

And realised she had not been making the most of her surroundings. Her divan was stuffed with camel hair. She used her nails as a knife, lying on the floor and nearly suffocating as she worked on the underside of the mattress, and finally opened an aperture through which she could draw some of the stout threads. She twined several into a narrow cord, and used it as a saw, and watched her depression become a cut, even as her fingers became raw and aching.

And while she worked, she thought, and planned. She remembered her days at Madame St. Amant's, she remembered Seraphine and Laurens, she remembered that insecure young man, Honoré Balzac, and the sights and sounds of Paris. She remembered Papa and she remembered Madeleine.

And she remembered David.

She thought of her own children, wondered what Gebhard thought at never being allowed to see his mother, what the daughter she had seen for only one hour was like, what indeed was her name, because she had not even been given that priceless piece of information. It was all part of Ricimer's plan to drive her mad. Well, she was not going to be driven mad. She called the child Henrietta, after her own mother.

She worked her way into November, hardly able to conceal her excitement as she watched the wood thinning. Several times she thought she might be able to pull it away, because her hands and arms had grown extremely strong with the constant labour, and she was afraid that Cora might notice her suddenly bulging biceps. But the wood remained too strong for her. Yet her progress was a constant spur. She would be free by the end of the year, of that she was sure.

But three days before her birthday, she was alerted in the morning by the stealthy whisper of a thousand marching feet. A sound she had heard before, in Algiers, the day the world of the Deys had come crashing down. But here the stealth was dissipated by the blowing of flutes and the clashing of cymbals. She could hardly wait for Cora to come with her meal, and for once even Cora was willing to talk.

"The French have taken the field, all over again," she said. "They would avenge their disaster at Macta, and march on Mascara itself with eleven thousand men. But they will never get here. The Emir goes out to meet them, at the head of *his* men." She smiled at her victim. "Baron Ricimer goes as well. He plans to destroy the French at the tombs of Sidi Embarek."

The door slammed and she was once again alone, staring at the wall. Eleven thousand men. The French had never before put such a force into the field. The victory at Macta had been gained over two thousand five hundred. That the Arabs were confident was because they had no experience of encountering a real European army.

And David would be with them, if he still lived. While she was trapped here. She could hardly wait for the night, so that she could again saw away at her bar, again try her strength on the unyielding wood. To no avail.

The following day she was asleep when Cora came, but awoke instantly. "There is news?"

Cora shrugged, and closed the door. Catherine listened at the window. But the hubbub in the city was as usual. Until near evening. Then it began to grow, and this time there were no cymbals and no bugle calls. She hammered on the door. She wanted to know if the Emir had been defeated, if the French were coming. If she was going to be taken and guillotined for the murder of the legionnaire sergeant. But no one answered her call.

She turned away from the door and worked at the window again, while the noise in the city grew. Now there were screams of terror, punctuated with musketry. It was Algiers all over again, and the cannon had not yet even started to play upon the walls.

But it was not Algiers all over again. These Frenchmen were not coming to rescue her. They were coming to destroy all who fought against them, and she was included in that number.

Her knees gave way and she slipped against the wall, crouching there in sheer exhaustion, and suddenly jerking into full wakefulness as the house around her came to life, and she heard a voice shouting orders.

Ricimer. Instantly she was back on her feet, once again banging on the door. Ricimer was here, come to take her away again, as he had before. Ricimer. "Ricimer," she shouted. "Come to me, Ricimer." She wanted only to escape the coming holocaust.

But no one came. *Perhaps no one could hear her,* she thought, they were all making so much noise. She could heard Gebhard shouting, and a thin crying which had to be her daughter, and Aimée wailing, and Cora snapping, and above all Ricimer, exhorting them to greater haste, to fetch this and to leave that. They were abandoning Mascara, evacuating the city in the face of the French advance.

And leaving her behind. She hammered on the door until her fists ached, shouted until her voice cracked. And she listened to the house slowly empty itself of sound, until the dull thuds of her own fists were all that could be heard.

Once again she sank to the floor, leaning against the door, the tears flowing down her cheeks. He had gone, and left her. He had taken the children, and left her behind. "No," she sobbed. "He cannot have taken my children, and not me. He cannot." She clasped her hands about her throat as if she would strangle herself rather than exist in such misery, and started again at the sound of hands on the outside of her door.

She leapt to her feet, backed away from it, eyes wide. Ricimer, come back? But these were stealthy hands. The French? There was no musketry. Arab marauders? They would have made sufficient noise. They were making sufficient noise all about her, in the city.

The lock turned, slowly, carefully. Catherine found her knees against the divan, watched the door swing in.

"My lady?" Jean-Pierre whispered. "My lady? I have come to set you free."

292

Chapter 10

FOR a moment she gaped at him in amazement. Then her gaze drifted over the gallery behind him, the house so strangely silent against the background of noise.

"Free?" she whispered. "Ricimer was here."

"And gone, lady. He came for his family and his servants, and left again. I hid, lady, or he might have taken me with him, or killed me. I hid until he had gone. He was in a hurry, and did not waste time in searching."

Catherine stepped past him. "And left me behind," she muttered.

"I heard him speak," Jean-Pierre said. "Let the French have her, he said. They will take her to the guillotine. He laughed, lady. He said, perhaps we shall be there to see it. She will make such a pretty corpse. He laughed, lady."

She glanced at him, stood at the balustrade, looked down into the courtyard. The marble slabs were discoloured with sand and earth, the pool had been trampled in. "If I could understand."

"The Emir has been defeated, lady." Jean-Pierre stood at her elbow. "They say he attempted once again to ambush the French, but his plans were betrayed, lady, and the Arabs were driven back. Then the French counterattacked, lady, and the Arabs were scattered into the desert. The French are marching here now, lady. We must get away, into the desert, while we can."

"My children." The terrible fear that had gnawed at her mind for the past few minutes suddenly burst into the open. "Where are my children?"

"The Baron took them with him, lady."

She turned to face him. "He took my children?"

"He said they were his children, lady." Jean-Pierre licked his lips. "Lady, we must leave this place. The Baron was right in saying they will send you to execution. Lady, we must hurry. I will find you a *haik*. Do not move, lady. I will not be long."

He went down the stairs. Catherine watched him go, then she hurried along the gallery and into the room where Gebhard had slept. Every evidence of a hasty departure. But he was gone. And Henrietta was gone too. He had taken her children, and abandoned her here to die. She felt her fingers curling into fists, her nails biting into her flesh. *Ricimer. A man she had never liked, had only loved.*

A man she now knew how to hate, with an anger that made her hatred of Hussein bin Hassan seem childish. *Ricimer.*

She heard a crash from outside, and returned to the gallery. The door to the courtyard was bursting open before the impact of several shoulders. Frenchmen? Her hands clasped on her throat even as her reason told her that was impossible; the French had not got here yet. But she was suddenly aware, at the prospect of meeting *any* man, that she had not been allowed a bath for three months.

Jean-Pierre dashed up the stairs, carrying a white *haik*. "Quickly, lady," he gasped, wrapping her in it, but she moved the fold from across her face and watched the men, Arabs, pause in the centre of the courtyard, look around them, then give a shout as they saw her. "Oh, my God," Jean-Pierre moaned.

"They seek only plunder," she said, amazed at her calmness. Or was it her deadness? She suddenly seemed to have lost all fear, lost all emotion, save only hate. No man could harm her now. Ricimer had done all that any man could do to her, and more.

She went down the stairs, and after a moment Jean-Pierre followed.

The men watched her coming towards them. "The French are near," one said, staring at her face. "You must flee, Highness."

"The house is yours," Catherine said. "Be sure you leave nothing for the infidels."

She walked past them, through the shattered gate, under the gloomy archway where she had held David in her arms. *David*. But she did not wish to think of David now. He had had to learn to love her all over again after watching her kill a man, for him. Could he ever learn to love this hate-filled creature?

And did this hate-filled creature ever wish to learn to love again herself?

Jean-Pierre caught up with her, panting. "Lady, I thought . . ."

"That they would wish to rape me? Men rape from an excess of excitement, of relief and exhilaration at having won a victory perhaps. They seldom rape from fear, Jean-Pierre."

They paused where the alleyway joined the street, for the street was filled, with men, and women, and children, and donkeys, and dogs, and carts with household goods. *Yashmaks* had been forgotten, *haiks* trailed awkwardly in strong contrast to their normal neat envelopment. The people of Mascara were fleeing, to the desert.

"We must go with them," Jean-Pierre shouted in her ear. "We cannot remain here."

"Do you think they will survive, in the desert?" she asked him. *And I must survive*, she thought. *No matter what happens, I must survive, to find Ricimer*.

"It is our only hope," he insisted, and pushed her out of the alleyway. She stumbled, but before she could fall she was picked up in the rush of people and hurried along, down the sloping street towards the marketplace. She found herself running with them, gasping with them, perhaps even shouting with them, she could not be sure, and checking, with them, as there was a sudden whine and a roar, and a shell burst in front of them; the French had arrived.

Catherine found herself on the ground; there was a pain in her back, but she had been running towards the blast, and she reasoned that she could not have been hit except by a human hand. For a moment there was what seemed complete silence, although she realised it was merely the singing in her ears, then the day once more erupted into sound, screams, wails of pain, shrieks of terror, the whole overlaid by another thundering crash that sent dust and shattered pieces of baked clay whirling through the air.

She sat up, looked at Jean-Pierre crouching by her side. He was shouting at her, but she could not hear him. She looked at a woman, lying on her back not six feet away; her *haik* had been blasted away and the shirts underneath were red with blood—she no longer appeared to have a face.

Strangely, she felt no horror, no disgust, no pity, even. She had seen too much, since the day she had been kidnapped. She had known too much. Now she could only hate.

People, those who still could move, were scattering in every direction, howling their fear. Muskets exploded and shells continued to burst. And Jean-Pierre was dragging her to her feet.

"We must go," he said. "We will be safe, in the desert."

She stared at him as if he were a creature from another world. Safe, in the desert? With the scorpions and the adders and the vultures? Were the French worse than that?

But she allowed herself to be dragged down the last of the hill to the market place, debouching into the open space, now suddenly littered with dead bodies and with several craters in the soil, in the midst of a screaming horde, but becoming aware that the singing in her ears was dying; no shell had burst for several seconds. Yet the noise of the mob was once again overlaid, with the galloping of hooves.

She found herself against the wall of one of the houses that surrounded the square, gazing at the gates leading out of the city. But the gates no longer existed. One of the shells had landed on the wall and torn a great breach in it, and through the breach she saw the cavalry approaching, a splendid sight, for their blue uniforms were enlivened by flowing red capes, and the sun glittered from their swords.

The others saw them too, and scattered with a great wail of fear. Jean-Pierre tugged at her arm, but she could not move. Her destiny was rushing at her, unstoppable and unchallengeable. No man, or no woman, could oppose *Kismet*. Thus Ricimer, how many centuries ago.

The first horseman soared over the rubbled stone of the breach, and was followed by his comrades. Catherine stared at them with a sense of detached horror, because she had recognised the officer at their head, the thin moustache, the cruel face. Yusuf had been promoted, as he had wished, into the cavalry. And Yusuf was here to bring her life to an end.

Women screamed, and threw up their hands; the horsemen leaned from their saddles and swept their sabres through the air. Blood flew, and with it a head, cut cleanly from its neck, long black hair flying, features frozen, in shock, at once at being so suddenly exposed to the world and at being so abruptly taken from life. Another woman ran towards Catherine, where she stood against the wall, carrying a child in her arms. A horseman galloped behind her, sword arm extended, and the blade took her in the small of the back. She fell to her knees, pitching the child into the air.

Jean-Pierre ran forward, and caught the wailing infant. Catherine discovered she was clasping her throat so hard she could scarcely breathe. The horseman had brought his horse to a halt, and the beast was rearing, high above the eunuch and his precious burden. Jean-Pierre turned away, and the hooves came down, catching him on the shoulder and sending him sprawling. The child was in the air again and striking the earth heavily. Catherine pushed herself away from the wall. The horseman swung at her with his sabre, and she fell to her hands and knees, waiting for the sudden surge of pain. But there was none, and she saw him some feet away, where he had been carried by his rush. But now there were other horsemen, surrounding her.

She reached the child, she had no idea whether it was a boy or a girl, cuddled it in her arms, and heard a shout from behind her. She turned on her knees, saw Jean-Pierre, who had picked up a sword dropped by one of the dead Arabs, and was lunging at the first horseman. The soldier was taken unawares and could not bring up his own weapon in time. Jean-Pierre's thrust took him under the ribs and he tumbled backwards from his horse, dead before he hit the ground.

"Run," Jean-Pierre shrieked.

Catherine hurled herself at the nearest alleyway, gasping for breath, hugging the child against her. Behind her she heard shouts and the clash of steel. She reached the wall and staggered into semi-darkness after the brilliance of the sunlight, turned, watched Jean-Pierre. He was on his knees, a sword protruding from his chest. *All gone,* she thought. *All gone. Save me.*

She saw the *spahis* peering into the gloom, eager to find her, and turned away from them. She stumbled forward, through the opened doorway of a house, half-shattered by a shell burst that had destroyed one wall and half of the roof, and left gaping holes in the floor. She ran for the back of the house, and suddenly there was nothing beneath her. She fell no more than six feet although it seemed forever, struck the earth heavily, and lost all her breath. But she still held the child in her arms, and she had broken its fall.

She lay still, and listened, to her own breathing, to the throbbing of her own heart, it seemed, to the turbulent despair of her own mind. Then her private sounds were overlaid by the crashing of boots above her head.

"Yellow hair, you say?" demanded a voice in French, and her heart rose to her throat as she recognised it as Yusuf's. "Pale yellow hair?"

"White hair, my colonel," someone else said. "But on a young woman. I swear it."

"White hair," Yusuf said. "Then find her. She came through here. She must have got out the back. Find her, sergeant. I want that woman. I want to hear her scream."

Desperately she tried to hold her breath, prayed the child would not cry. Desperately she wanted to pull down more debris on top of her, but her commonsense told her she was best off not moving at all, not while the soldiers were up there. Boots thudded, and she wondered if they would come down into the shell craters. But then the sound of the feet began to recede, and she could breathe again.

Yet she would not move. Her body ached, she was exhausted, and she had nowhere to go. She had no one to go to. *David?* He was in the desert, with Abd el Kader. Supposing he had not died in the disaster at Sidi Embarek. She would never find him. She would only lie here, until she fell asleep, and perhaps never wake again.

But the child. Her head reared back, and she pulled the *haik* from the tiny, frozen features. Its skull was split, and it had been dead for some time. It must have happened when it had been tossed away from Jean-Pierre.

Jean-Pierre. She began to weep, still holding the babe in her arms, rocking her body gently as if she would put it to sleep. She lost track of time, had no idea how long she lay in the darkness, crying her misery. But suddenly she was alerted by the nostril-tingling smell of burning wood.

She raised her head, inhaled, cautiously. There was still a lot of dust floating in the air. But she was undoubtedly close to flames; she almost thought she could hear them roar.

She rose to her knees, left the dead child lying on the ground. If the house was indeed on fire, it could have no better grave. She dusted her hands, scraped dust from her cheeks and eyes, looked up at the floor of the house, sagging towards her, and some six feet above the level of her hole. She supposed she could just reach it with her fingertips. But what then?

She listened. And could hear nothing but the sound of the flames. *I am not to stay here and burn to death, surely?* she thought. *Why not,* she wondered? *All else is destroyed. The Arab cause is destroyed. My family is destroyed. Jean-Pierre is destroyed. And now Mascara is being destroyed. Why should Catherine, Baroness Ricimer, be spared?*

Because she was Catherine, Baroness Ricimer, who had a husband, who had absconded with her children, who had left her to die, and on whom she would be avenged. She sucked air into her lungs, jumped as high as she could, caught the wood with her fingers, and felt them slipping. She landed on the rubbled earth with a jar.

The roaring of the flames came closer, while the night, because she realised that it was night, seemed to grow warmer by the moment.

I shall not die here, she thought. I shall not, and leapt again. This time she gripped so tightly her hands hurt, but her weeks of sawing away at the bar in the prison had given her tremendous strength in her arms, and she was able to draw herself upwards, with a surge of power, until she got one elbow over. Then she wanted to stop, and pant, but immediately she began to slip again, and it was necessary to make another tremendous effort, get her breasts over the sill and then her other elbow, legs kicking wildly, and suck herself forward, inch by inch until she felt her knees touching, and then throw herself clear of the hole, to lie on the shattered floor and gasp for breath, and feel sweat trickling out of her hair.

She rolled on her back, gazed through the broken roof at the night sky, and felt the heat coming ever closer. And now it was punctuated by a crash or an explosion from close at hand. She sat up, rising to her feet in the same instant, careless of the rivers of exhausted agony that seemed to be flowing through her muscles.

She could not afford to fall into another hole. She

wrapped her *haik* round her and made her way across the floor on her hands and knees, prodding the boards in front of her, and reached the doorway. She inhaled, slowly, the chill night air drifting in from the desert, but inhaled, too, the smell of dead bodies. She had lain in her pit for several hours.

She stood up, stepped outside, looked back at the city. Mascara burned, and the fires had been set. The flames leapt from several places, already encompassed the *minarets* and the house on the hill, but they were also following the streets, seeping from house to house, cracking the baked clay walls and seizing on the embroidered *yourgans* and divans within.

And consuming the dead bodies. In time, she supposed, the flames would even consume these dead bodies. She stepped away from the doorway, looked at the mounds of white cloth, each a man, or a woman, or a child. The *spahi* slain by Jean-Pierre had been removed, but Jean-Pierre still lay on the ground, recognisable by his blue *haik,* by the sword that lay beside his hand.

She knelt. After all, he had turned out to be a hero. Poor, poor Jean-Pierre. His life had been one long catalogue of disaster, almost from the moment his mother had decided to marry again, and through no fault of his own. Simply because his stepsister had been a beauty. There was an undeserved fate.

She rolled him over, hastily rose to her feet. The French might have left in a hurry, but they had not forgotten to collect their tally of ears.

Had he been happy, towards the end? When he had finally succumbed to her charms, to sharing her loneliness? She hoped so. He had made her happy, from time to time.

Once again the heat, striking over even the cool of the mountain wind. She ran across the marketplace, tripping over a body and landing on her hands and knees, regaining her feet with an effort. She reached the breach, peered through, her heart constricting with terror. Out there were the French. She knew it, although she could not discern their banners or their uniforms in the dark-

301

ness. But she could see the glint of their swords, reflecting from the thrusting flames of the city, and she could hear the shouted commands. They were preparing to return to the coast, their mission accomplished. They had destroyed Abd el Kader, and they had destroyed his city. They had even destroyed his palace, for now she could see that that too was well alight.

She crouched by the stones, warmed by the immense heat behind her, waiting. She dared not be taken by the French. But they would move off, eventually. And what would happen then? Where should she go? Where was Ricimer? Where could Ricimer go to be safe? Only with Abd el Kader. There was the encampment she must find, somewhere out there, in the mountains, or even in the desert beyond. There was where she must go.

She crawled out of the breach, once again crouched by the tumbled stone, listened to the noise of the army retreating. She was aware of an empty belly, of a tremendous thirst, but these things seemed irrelevant. She must decide where Abd el Kader would have gone. Surely he would not be far. Surely he would hang upon the flanks of the French, waiting his opportunity to harass them, and perhaps even defeat them in another ambush. The last had failed because his plans had been betrayed. Surely he would not despair, because of an act of treachery.

The heat increased. It was necessary to leave the breach, and run across the stony ground towards the shadow of the nearest hill. Her feet caught in soft earth, and she fell to her hands and knees in the stream which watered the *oasis*. She lowered her head and drank and drank until she felt she would burst. Then she lay down in the flowing liquid, rolled over and over, felt it stroking three months of dirt and sweat from her body, felt it rinsing through her hair.

She crawled out, reached the first hill, did not take off her *haik* but wrapped the sodden garment round her, shivering in the night air. She watched the city burn. And in time she lay down and slept, the sleep of utter exhaustion. And awoke, to find it daylight, and herself and her clothes dry, and the morning air heavy with the scent of smouldering wood and decaying flesh, and closer at hand, of men and horses.

She sat up, reaching for her *haik,* looking at the people around her, every one hidden behind a blue *burnous* wrapped around his mouth and chin. Touaregs, the veiled terrors of the desert.

She rose to her knees, and one of the men dismounted. His *burnous* and his *haik* were no more distinguished than any of his companions' but he carried a musket in which the inlay was in gold. He stood above her, and she found herself panting. She was too tired to think, too tired to do anything, save kneel.

The man stretched out his hand, touched her hair. "You are the Baroness Ricimer," he said, in Arabic. "I have heard much of you."

She raised her head, gazed at the black eyes. They seemed to fill his forehead, to shroud the morning, to take her into their own keeping.

"You are a woman among women," the Touareg chieftain said. "You will be my woman among women." He gestured to her to rise. "I am El Ghomari."

The name penetrated even her dulled brain, and her head jerked. Perhaps the chieftain smiled; his eyes flickered.

"You have heard of me," he said.

Catherine stood up, straightening her clothes. "You are the enemy of Abd el Kader."

Now she was sure he smiled. "And you are the wife of Abd el Kader's general, who has lost his last battle. It is fitting that you should be mine."

Oh, Lord, she thought. But nothing could happen, here, and now. Nothing could happen until after she had been able to rest. She thought she could face anything, if she could just be allowed to sleep, for twelve hours.

El Ghomari was pointing. "You were in Mascara?"

Catherine nodded.

"A place of vultures," he said. "And who knows,

the *marabout* may return to look at the ruins of his city. We will leave." He held out his hand, and after a moment's hesitation she took it. There was nothing else she could do.

El Ghomari led her to his horse, then released her fingers, slid his hand along her arm and over her breast in a movement that was half exploration and half caress, but done with an incredible lightness that sent a shiver down her spine and right through her legs to her toes. From the age of sixteen she had been groomed and conditioned for nothing but the touch of a man's hand, and in the past year, save for those brief, stolen and entirely unsatisfactory moments with David, she had been touched by no man. For the past three months, she had not even been touched by her eunuch.

Oh, Lord, she thought, *help me.*

But El Ghomari had now used his left hand for a similar exploration, at the end of which his fingers settled on her waist, and he swung her from the ground as lightly as if she had been a feather, and placed her in front of his saddle. Before she could decide whether or not she was about to fall off from sheer exhaustion, he had joined her there, and raised his musket above his head. His men obediently wheeled and rode behind him, without a sound save the thudding of their horses' hooves, in the strongest contrast to the normal Arab excitability.

Catherine turned her head, for a last look at the smouldering city, and seemed to impale herself on his eyes.

"*Ya Habibti,*" he said. "That is your name, Baroness. *Ya Habibti.* You will be my *Ya Habibti.*"

She looked to the front again, at the mountains towards which she rode. Her heart was throbbing so hard it was almost painful, just as the heat of the sun on her legs told her that they were exposed as the *haik* fluttered in the breeze.

"*Ya Habibti,*" El Ghomari said, perhaps to himself. His arms were round her body as his rein was in front of her. Now one of them left the rein, as he first of all slung his musket across his shoulders, then suddenly closed his fingers on her waist. She started, but once again the touch was so gentle as to be almost dreamlike, and the quality of existing in an unknown world only grew as he moved upwards, over the woollen material of her *haik,* to hold her breasts. He did not finger, he did not squeeze, he did not caress; he just allowed them to fill his hands, so that he could feel them swelling into his palm as she breathed, so that she was almost unaware of being held, but only of being captured, mind and body and soul, as the slow stream of pleasure flowed away from each nipple, while the movement of the horse coursed up between her legs to fill her groin, and suddenly she went quite dizzy, because she had expected nothing like this, because she had not wanted an orgasm, had not supposed she could have one, sitting astride a horse in total exhaustion.

She felt his breath rush against her hair, and realised she had fallen back against his chest. And also that he knew what had happened; his hands had left her breasts. He had *known* what would happen. *Oh, Lord,* she thought. It was too late to ask for help, now.

"Ya Habibti," he said, and picked up his reins again.

They rode for perhaps three hours, threading their way in and out of the mountain passes while the sun rose ever higher, and Catherine waited for him to touch her again. She dared not think, dared not reason. She was Catherine, Baroness Ricimer. She was dedicated to revenge, and she was in love with David Mulawer. Those were the only important facts of her life.

But she had never known a touch like that of El Ghomari, and her body cried out for it again, through all of her exhaustion, all the hunger and thirst that was rapidly growing. So now she was damned. Here was a Touareg chieftain. Even the Turks had regarded the Touaregs as monsters of cruelty, desert ghosts who considered life less important than the food they ate. And she was their captive. She was *his* captive. El Ghomari. And he had just given her an orgasm merely by holding her.

There was no hell for her to descend to, after this. Or was there no heaven into which she could rise? Had her ability to reason, her sense of values, her awareness of herself as a Christian and a lady, become so distorted?

Or was she somewhere near attaining the truth of life and death and humanity at last?

They rode down a valley, between two high hills, and debouched into a small plateau. Catherine saw the black tents of the nomad encampment, watched the outriders who had guarded and overseen their march come down the hillsides towards them.

"*Ya Habibti,*" El Ghomari said into her ear. "Here is the encampment of El Ghomari. Here you will be safe. From the French."

His hand was back on her waist.

He walked his horse into the circle of low black-hair tents, was immediately surrounded by his people. Dogs barked, children wailed, questions were asked. Catherine gazed at the women in amazement, for none of *them* was veiled, and they seemed to wear nothing more than a single robe, mostly in blue, and belted at their waists, which allowed tantalising glimpses of shoulders and breasts and legs as they moved. And they were a handsome people, tall and straight, with aquiline features and masses of black hair, rendered the more striking by silver rings caught in the dark strands, while the majority also wore silver bracelets.

The prevailing air of confidence, of health, made her once again feel filthy, in her two worn shirts.

But El Ghomari had already swung from his saddle and was now reaching up for her, to set her lightly on the ground beside him.

"You have done well, El Ghomari." The woman was old, but still strongly built and well featured.

The chieftain bowed. "I thank you, my mother. She is the Baroness Ricimer. You have heard of her."

The woman peered at Catherine. "I have heard of the white-haired woman who rides with Abd el Kader," she said. "She is an enemy of our people. You should feed her to the dogs."

306

Of which several were at that moment clustering around Catherine's legs, sniffing her toes.

"I will take her as my woman," El Ghomari said. "That is better than feeding her to the dogs. Abd el Kader will know of this, and envy me for it."

Once again the old woman gave Catherine a long stare. "And what of the city?"

"It is destroyed," El Ghomari said. "And the French retreat. They have taken with them the Jews, and such plunder as they could secure. The Arabs are killed or scattered into the hills. Abd el Kader is no more. He is a desert chieftain. When next we meet, it shall be as equals, and then I will destroy *him*."

It was the woman's turn to bow, before she turned and walked away.

"I am so very hungry," Catherine ventured. "And thirsty."

"Then you will eat." El Ghomari walked in front of her, and after a moment's hesitation she followed him, to the largest of the tents, inside which she discovered a good twenty people gathered, as well as a similar number of dogs, already growling at one another over scraps left from the last meal. But Catherine was once again amazed to discover that half the assembly were women, who obviously intended to sit down with their men, in strong contrast to any previous Arabs she had known.

"Sit here," El Ghomari commanded, himself sitting cross-legged on the ground. Catherine obeyed, tucking her outer shirt round her legs, watched the bowl of beans brought closer. Saliva filled her mouth, but when it arrived she took a dainty handful, licked her fingers free of the gravy to soothe her parched throat. But soon there were mugs of mare's milk, and she began to feel almost human again, and to listen to the conversation about her that consisted mainly of a description of the rout at Sidi Embarek that had apparently been overseen by some of the Touaregs, and of the sack and destruction of Mascara.

"They will come again, the French," someone said.

"They will not come again," El Ghomari objected. "Their war is with Abd el Kader. They do not seek to destroy the tribes of the desert. They have no interest in the desert."

"And will we now return to the desert?" asked a woman.

"Soon," the chieftain agreed.

Catherine observed that he did not even uncover his mouth to eat, but rather passed the food under the fold of material that concealed him.

"This evening," said one of the men.

"Tomorrow," El Ghomari said, and without warning rose to his feet. "My men are tired. Those who rode with me these last days. And I have this one, *Ya Habibti,* to see to."

"She is beautiful," observed one of the women. "But she is French."

"I am not French," Catherine objected.

The women gazed at her.

"You ride with Abd el Kader," said another. "You are his woman."

"I have never ridden with Abd el Kader," she said. "I am not his woman. I am the Baroness Ricimer. My husband rides with the Emir."

"Not anymore," El Ghomari said. "As of this moment, you have no husband, *Ya Habibti,* you have only me. Rise."

She stood up, her heart beginning to pound. "Where is my husband?" she asked. Was he trying to tell her that Ricimer was dead?

"You have no husband," he said, and turned and left the tent. Catherine looked after him for a moment, then glanced at the people around her, who all watched her—the women with hostility, the men, so far as she could tell from their eyes, with some admiration. *What is going to happen to me?* she wondered. But her instincts told her that without El Ghomari these women would quickly tear her to pieces.

She ducked through the entrance to the tent, ran behind him.

The chieftain waited before the flap of a smaller tent, and this was even lower than the previous one. She

308

doubted they would be able to sit upright. But they were not entering it to sit upright. Her knees knocked together. And yet she was not afraid. She did not suppose she would ever be afraid of sexual relations with any man, ever again. But she was apprehensive, of the man himself. The Touareg.

He held the flap for her, and after a moment's hesitation she dropped to her hands and knees and crawled inside, settled on her haunches to peer in the sudden gloom at the camel-hair mattress, inhale the faint scent of the man, and felt the flap close behind her, as his fingers once again touched her hair. She let her *haik* fall to the ground.

"Such hair," he said, "has never been seen in Africa before. Is your body hair of a similar colour?"

"No," she said, and found that she was panting.

"Why not?" he asked, still kneeling behind her.

"I . . . I do not know. It never is."

"With us, all hair is the same colour," El Ghomari said, and crawled round to sit in front of her, cross-legged on the mattress. "Show me."

She licked her lips, then once again rose to her knees; her head just brushed the roof of the tent. She raised her two shirts together, held them just above her navel.

"It is lovely hair," El Ghomari said, and leaned forward, to touch it, again with that almost terrifying gentleness that sent a shiver running through her muscles.

The fingers withdrew. "Are you afraid of me?"

She raised her head. "Do I have cause to fear you, El Ghomari?"

"No," he said. "No, *you* do not have cause to fear me, *Ya Habibti.*" He took off his *burnous.*

Once again she was having difficulty with her breathing: she had no idea what to expect. Save a masculine version of the women she had seen outside.

And was thus quite unprepared for the beauty that revealed itself. Unlike the Bedouin, he wore no beard, and his face was quite perfect in feature, high, pale forehead, long, thin nose, wide mouth, firm chin, deep black eyes that continued to glow at her.

She felt heat in her cheeks and knew she had betrayed her pleasure. His mouth widened into a smile.

"Now you are less afraid of me."

"I am not afraid of you," she insisted, but now she wondered if she was indeed telling the truth. "I but was considering why a handsome man should conceal his features."

"It is the law of my people," he said, simply. "And now you have looked upon my face, *Ya Habibti,* you belong to me, and should you ever look upon another man's face, I have the right to cut off your head."

She would not lower her gaze. "Upon any other man of the Touareg nation," she said.

His features tightened, but did not lose any of their attraction; rather it increased the obvious power of his personality. "Any man of any race, *Ya Habibti.* Now, I would look upon your body."

She had sunk back on to her haunches. Now she lifted first one shirt and then another over her head, laid them on the ground beside the mattress, raised her hands to fluff out her hair, almost felt his gaze burning her skin, like the sun. "You see me at a disadvantage, El Ghomari. Were I bathed, and perfumed . . ."

"You would be like a doll," he said. "I prefer a woman." He discarded his own robe, and she caught her breath. Not so broad shouldered, so big chested as Ricimer. Yet the slenderness of his form was even more attractive, and his legs were long and muscular. But to her alarm she saw that he was soft.

"I do not please you," she said.

"You please me, *Ya Habibti.* You pleased me even before I saw you, when I had only heard of you. You please me. But is not the pleasure of lovemaking as much in the approach to the breach as the breach itself? Come."

She hesitated, licked her lips. *My God,* she thought, *what has come over me? I should be shrinking away from this man, preparing to fight him. I am married. To a man I hate and am sworn to destroy. Well, then, I am in love. With a man I have never known, have never even seen naked. Who I do not even know will please me. Oh,*

310

God, that Ricimer had left his interruption of them for just a few minutes longer.

But now I am bewitched. Now I know I will receive pleasure. I would receive pleasure from just looking at so much beauty, much less knowing it against me, inside me.

El Ghomari smiled. "You *do* fear me, *Ya Habibti*. I will not harm you. You are beautiful. I am beautiful. It surely is our destiny to be beautiful together."

Catherine pushed herself forward, onto her hands and knees, crawled towards him. She was terribly aware of how undignified she must look, and she had been determined to maintain her dignity above all else. But where was dignity, when she was alone with El Ghomari?

His hand came out, to touch her forehead, and she paused, still on her hands and knees. His fingers stroked down the line of the cheek and then her jaw, and she knew where they were going, but still with that so wondrously light touch, moving down her neck and on to her shoulder. She wanted to close her eyes, but she kept them open, gazing at his face, watching it come closer as his body came closer, wondering if he would kiss her.

And was taken quite by surprise when he did so. His face followed his fingers, which were now moving down the front of her chest to seek her breast, and hold it, as he had done on the horse, so that she felt her entire body seem to come alive, every drop of blood in every vein suddenly turn molten to set her flesh into flame, and then his lips closed on hers, and she realised that never in her life before had she really been taken possession of. But it was happening now. He did not move his mouth, as Ricimer had done, had taught her to do. Rather he seemed to absorb her into his own mouth, lips and tongue and saliva and even teeth, she supposed, sucking her throat dry, while his hand left her breast and began its wandering journey down her ribs towards her belly.

Passion exploded in her chest, and her thighs touched as they clamped together, while her hands left the ground and found his member, felt it come hard beneath her fingers; she was supported entirely on her knees and by

311

his mouth as she leaned forward, for now his hand had reached her groin and was softly sifting through her hair before reaching on to find its way between her tightened thighs.

She sighed, and felt herself falling, because he too was falling, and carrying her with him. But she might have been falling through all eternity, a fall she did not ever wish to stop. And yet his hand was gone, up her back to hold her shoulders, as she lay on his chest and felt his penis move against her belly. *Now,* she thought. *Let him come in now.*

But he was far from ready, and instead at last released her mouth, leaving her with a feeling of total desolation, while he gently rolled her off him and on to her back, and she discovered to her surprise that she was actually being guided on to the mattress. El Ghomari himself rose on his elbow, and began to kiss her body, beginning with her eyes, then her chin, then moving down to her neck, then to each breast in turn, taking the nipples into his mouth with the utmost gentleness, as always, holding the aureole in his teeth without in any way hurting her while he sucked the teat, drawing it into his mouth by the sheer force of his suction.

She exploded in another orgasm before he moved away, but still lingered at her breasts, kissing them from underneath, not sucking now but rather caressing with his mouth as he pushed them up, and then moving down her stomach and ribs. She was being explored, by his mouth, as she had been explored by his fingers. And she knew she wanted the ultimate exploration, as she had wanted it from the moment his lips had touched hers, and she had known the power that lay within them.

And there it was. She seemed to be flying through the air. Her heart pounded so hard she had no doubt it was about to burst its way out of her chest. She knew she was talking—or was she screaming—her pleasure. The roof of the tent seemed to descend to touch her and then receded away again until it almost made a part of the sky beyond, she discovered that she was reaching for him with her fingers, with her nails, seeking to hurt him where he was giving her only pleasure, but being unable to reach him, and suddenly lying back in utter exhaustion as the passion ebbed and his lips also moved away.

She lay on her back, staring at him; his face was serious, and suffused with blood, because he had not climaxed. And suddenly she was at once disappointed and afraid, because how could she hope to feel more than she had just felt, ever in her life? And therefore how could she not be a disappointment to him? Especially now, when she was so drained of all emotion, all feeling.

He was rolling her onto her face. Slivers of alarm drifted through her mind, called upon her to resist. But her exhaustion as much as her suddenly returning passion had her acquiescent. If this was what El Ghomari wished, then who was she to oppose that wish? She thought he could wrap his fingers around her throat and commence to strangle her, and she would not resist him but rather have another orgasm while her life slipped away.

For he was stroking her again, gathering her thighs together to raise them from the mattress, and then he was inside, and she discovered with a combination of inexpressible relief and soaring pleasure that he had not sodomised her after all, but had merely entered from this to her unknown angle, and was now pressing her thighs together, and summoning her legs as well, so that his were outside hers, and she could feel, and feel, and feel, as she had never done before. She squeezed her legs together, and enjoyed the triumph of trapping him inside her as she could never have done on her back, while his penis seemed to have grown until it filled her from her groin to her neck, and she thought she would burst with the excitement of it. Then his breath was searing on her shoulders as he drooped forward, and she felt him explode, even as she exploded herself, her face falling to the mattress, her opened mouth sucking the rough material, all consciousness seeming to stream away from her for several seconds.

She knew she need never fear Ricimer again.

His weight left her, but she did not wish to move. Save to touch him again. He lay down beside her, and she rolled on her side, to rest her head on his shoulder, her back to him. She did not wish to look at him, or anyone. Twenty-four hours ago she had crouched in the shell crater while Yusuf and his men had searched for her. For three months before that she had been imprisoned. But had she not been imprisoned all of her life, quite without realising it? As a child, at Madame St. Amant's, during her brief spell as a young lady in Paris, always imprisoned, behind a wall of rule and convention. Ricimer had freed her body, but only to imprison her mind and her physical being, in the Dey's *harem* and then behind the wall of his own personality. There was no freedom for women in North Africa, save in a Touareg encampment, where they met their men as equals, and where sex took on a new concept of freedom.

So, then, was she supposing she was falling in love with El Ghomari? How could she? Love had to be more than a sexual partnership, and El Ghomari knew nothing about her, save the texture of her skin, the feel of her body. To love El Ghomari she would have to attend to his education. There was a remarkable and entrancing thought.

But what, then, of David, who loved her? There was the vital point. Because she could not suppose that El Ghomari did that. He desired her, he desired her body and the fact that she was associated with Abd el Kader, however vaguely. But he was an Arab, of the desert, and therefore unlikely to love her with the romantic fervour of a European, especially a European from the most romantic of all nationalities, the Poles.

But this was supposing David was still alive, or that she would ever see him again. This was looking to the future, as she had spent her entire life doing. But she was twenty-five years old. *My God,* she realised, *yesterday, the day I lay hidden in the rubble of burning Mascara, was my twenty-fifth birthday. Time to stop looking forward. But not yet time to look back. Time to exist, in the present.*

Time to forget? Gebhard and Henrietta? Jean-Pierre, dying with a sword in his hand? Time to forget Ricimer, and her so recent oath of his destruction?

Time to forget everything, saving only El Ghomari. For his fingers were back, sliding over her breast and belly, and she felt him rise against her buttocks. This time he took her in a more normal manner, and with less foreplay. But even this was different, as he seemed to move his body from side to side, so that she felt more of him, so that her nipples scraped across his chest, so that she started moving herself, rocking on her hair. She reached orgasm before him, had not achieved another when he came. But he was pleased, and kissed her gently on the nose.

"It is time for prayer," he said.

"I am a Christian."

"So it is said. Do you then never pray?"

She opened her mouth, and closed it again. Because she seldom did, except when in dire need. "I am a very bad Christian."

"And you live and are beautiful," he said. "Yours is a forgiving God. Allah is not so." He pulled on his robe, went outside, left her to a contemplation of her own feelings, once again.

But thought really was irrelevant, in a Touareg tent. For the first time in her life she felt like doing nothing save lying here, and waiting. She thought she could wait forever, for his return, for him once again to take her in his arms.

Nor was it long delayed. Ten minutes. Once she had thought, ten minutes, only ten minutes, while she had waited for Hussein bin Hassan to come to her. But this ten minutes passed in a flash of heavenly anticipation, and he was with her again, while the dogs barked and the women talked with their men and the evening breeze drifted down from the mountains, and the camp of the Touaregs waited, for their leader to wish to resume his march, where, she neither knew nor cared, and neither

315

did his people, she supposed. Here was the perfect existence, each day much like the next, each march much like the next, driving their dogs and their herd of goats and their horses with them, pitching their camps as they chose, living, from day to day, as surely humanity had always been intended to live, and loving their nights away, as surely humanity had been intended to love.

And fighting, murdering, looting, whenever the opportunity presented itself. The Touaregs were on the move the next morning at dawn, the moment they had completed their prayers. The tents were folded and stowed on the backs of their donkeys, the dogs and goats were herded in a group, and surrounded by the women and children, also mostly mounted on donkeys, although many remained on foot. Catherine was given a horse, as one of the elite, but this day she wore a blue gown belted at the waist, and nothing else. She was El Ghomari's woman.

Her mood had not changed. This had happened to her, and there was no way in which she could oppose such a manifestation of *Kismet,* even supposing she wished to. She was El Ghomari's woman, and she must remain El Ghomari's woman, for as long as the situation remained. She did not suppose it would remain unchanged forever. Her immediate passivity had passed with her exhaustion. This morning she was again filled with memory—and with hatred of Ricimer. El Ghomari could remain no more than an interlude, until she knew whether Ricimer lived or died, and if he lived, where, and what he had done with her children. She conceived herself entirely an Arab in the fierce determination of her vengeance.

But only for a few hours. To her surprise, instead of making south, into the vastnesses of the desert, the Touaregs headed north, led by El Ghomari and his warriors, while the inevitable flankers rode the hills to either side, watching, but also seeking, and in the middle of the morning two of them came galloping back to the main party, proceeding placidly in the valley below.

There was no firing of muskets, as they had done on

316

their approach yesterday. This was done in silence, save for the drumming of their horses' hooves, and they drew rein in a lather of sweat, next to El Ghomari, who listened, and then made his dispositions, quietly and expertly.

"Stragglers," he said. "A French platoon which has turned back to round up those who fell by the wayside during the night. They will be easy."

Catherine gazed around her at a scene of ordered chaos. Stakes were driven into the ground, and the goats and spare donkeys were tethered. The old women, the old men, and the children, dismounted and prepared a camp, posting their own guards from amongst the teenage boys and girls. The fighting men, and, to her surprise, all the young women, remained mounted.

"You will stay here," El Ghomari said.

"Am I not a woman?" she asked.

"These are infidels, like yourself," he said. "Will you see them killed?"

"I have no love for the French," she said. "They are my enemies."

"Yet must you kill, should you come with us," he said.

"I have killed," she said.

He frowned at her for a moment, then took a long, sharp-bladed knife from his belt, and handed it to her. "Remember," he said. "I will be unable to assist you."

"I do not expect you to," she said.

"But I will hold you in my arms, when we have gained the day," he said, and wheeled his horse to lead his men before she could ask him, why take the risk of action at all? Because she knew the answer. To fight, anyone at any time, was these people's sole rule of life.

The men cantered off, following the rising ground, behind the two scouts who had informed them of the presence of their prey. The women walked their horses and donkeys more slowly.

"Why do we not make haste?" Catherine asked.

"Our time will come," said one of the women, and

smiled at her. "Your time will come, *Ya Habibti*. Be sure you use it well."

Catherine gazed at the rim of the hill, below which the Touaregs were mustering, reining their horses, priming their muskets, unsheathing their *tulwars*. Why am I here, she asked herself? Why am I doing this? I am Catherine Scott, from Boston, Massachusetts. I have no part in killing, and dying.

But then I am Baroness Ricimer, wife of a soldier of fortune. And even more I am the woman of El Ghomari. The desert has entered my brain, my veins are filled with sand, hot and savage.

She realised with a start of real surprise that she knew no other way of life now. Kill or be killed. Hate or be hated. The heated passion of El Ghomari's tent had no existence without those two rules to govern it. It too would not obtain in Boston, Massachusetts.

El Ghomari raised his arm, and his men moved forward in a long line. Catherine's heart began to pound. She could not see, but she could imagine the tiny column below, marching over the uneven ground, wiping sweat and taking surreptitious swigs from their water bottles, gazing fearfully at the surrounding hills, praying that those rims remained empty, about to discover that their prayers were not to be answered this day. About to wonder why, with their very last thoughts of all.

The Arabs lined the rim, and she could hear a distant shouting punctuated by a few scattered shots. El Ghomari raised his arm again, and his men moved forward, still slowly, saving their mounts for the final charge. They disappeared, and the women increased their pace. Catherine found herself panting, listened to another fusillade, but still distant; the Touaregs had not yet opened fire.

She gained the hilltop, looked down on the next valley. The blue-coated soldiers, hardly larger than toys, and numbering about forty, she estimated, had formed two ranks, one kneeling and the other standing, facing the Arab horsemen. Behind them was a miscellaneous collection of civilians, women and children as well as men; she could see the flutter of their skirts. And between them and the women on the hill the warriors had again formed line, just beyond musket range, perhaps two hundred yards from their enemies.

But now they were moving forward again. The French opened fire, little puffs of black smoke rising above the shakoes, forming balls of grey in the morning air. One of the Touaregs threw up his arms and tumbled back from his horse, and Catherine glanced at the women beside her. That man must have had a wife. But no face changed expression. Their eyes gleamed, their mouths worked, and each right hand held a knife as long and as sharp bladed as her own. These were not women, she realised. They were beings, as consumed with hate and blood lust as ever she had wished to be. And she was one of them.

Another Touareg had fallen, but the line of horsemen held, and now checked, and fired in turn. Several of the Frenchmen collapsed over their muskets like puppets whose strings had suddenly been severed, and she heard a thin wail of fear from the doomed civilians. For El Ghomari had dropped his musket and drawn his *tulwar*, and from his throat there uttered a most terrifying roar, '*Ul-ul-ul-Akbar*,' as he led the charge, his hundred-odd warriors behind him.

The kneeling Frenchmen rose, and bayonets flashed in the sun. But the horses were upon them in a moment, and they were engulfed beneath the flood of flowing blue and white.

"Come," said the woman who had first spoken, touching her mount with her heels. The others followed, cantering down the hill towards the frenzied dust cloud that marked the battle. But the battle was already over. It was time for the slaughter to begin.

The dust was clearing. The Touaregs were rearranging themselves, with the utmost military precision. Half formed a circle around the dead, the dying, and the prisoners. Of the other half, part attended to those of their comrades who had fallen, dragging or carrying them clear of the French, laying the dead to one side, the living to another; the remainder began a systematic looting for everything they could find. They picked up cartridge belts and bandoliers, muskets and bayonets, swords and daggers; they tore reticules and bundles away from the women and children, emptied their contents on the ground, and sifted through them to select anything of value, to a Touareg. They collected haversacks and water bottles, spilled wine upon the sand.

Of the French, those who were dead lay in their blood. The living, including those only wounded, huddled together, staring in terror at the mounted horsemen who surrounded them, and in even greater terror at the women, who rode their horses past their menfolk and dismounted, talking among themselves in Arabic, their savage tones no doubt sending even greater terror into the hearts of their victims.

But Catherine could understand what they were saying, and knew immediately that this scene was not for her. She pulled at the reins of her horse, brought it to a standstill, and heard the first scream, high and shrill. This was still of terror. It came from the throat of a young soldier, only slightly wounded, and who had been seized by three of the Touareg women. He endeavoured to fight them, but they were too strong for him. Catherine heard the sound of ripping cloth, watched his feet kicking, and heard him scream again, and this time the sound was pure agony.

And was taken up by his comrades, and by the women and the children, for the Arab women were busy. A man burst from the group, running blindly towards the nearest hummock, and was brought back by two of the mounted warriors, riding their horses beside him and forcing him to go where they wished.

Catherine's stomach turned, and she wheeled her horse to walk it away, discovered El Ghomari beside her.

"Your heart bleeds for the infidels," he said. "After all your brave words, they are still your people."

"No," she said. "No. But they are men, who fought bravely. If you hate them that much, why do you not shoot them? But to cut them to pieces . . ."

320

The entire valley had turned into a cacophony of wailing agony, wailing humiliation, wailing bestiality. She felt sick.

"And if they were to defeat us," El Ghomari said, "do you think they would treat us with more mercy? They would rape our women, debauch our children, and they would chop off our heads, while we still lived. I have seen these things. I know they are true. Besides . . ." His eyes bore into her. "Our women are not as yours. We do not leave them behind, in safety, when we go to war. We are always at war, and our women are at war with us. We expect them to march at our side, to die at our side. We expect them, when our *douar* is attacked, to fight beside us and die beside us. It is necessary that they share in our conquests, that they share a taste for the blood of our enemies, that like our blue veils, their knives strike terror into the hearts of our enemies. You will have heard this: Better to die than to be taken by the Touareg women. Those men down there will not die for some time. They will be stripped of their manhood, they will be stripped of their toes and fingers, they will be stripped of their eyelids . . ."

"Stop it," she cried. "Stop it."

He gazed at her for some seconds. "But if you would be one of us, *Ya Habibti,* if you would truly be El Ghomari's woman, then you must play the part. Now."

She returned his stare. Only a few hours previously this man had taught her a new dimension in the meaning of physical love. Were he to dismount and tell her to stretch herself upon the ground at his feet she knew she would be unable to hesitate for a moment. She wanted to be his woman, again and again and again, until the madness left her and she became once again Catherine, Baroness Ricimer.

But if she did as he now asked she would never again become Catherine, Baroness Ricimer. Then she would truly have become a Touareg, and every last vestige of Western veneer would have been lost, never to be regained. David would have been lost. Her children would have been lost even if she ever managed to find them.

"It must be," El Ghomari said, "or I must leave you with those other *gaiours,* to the mercy of the vultures."

Her heart gave a great lurch, and then blood pounded through her veins and she knew she flushed. *God, give me strength,* she thought.

"It cannot be," she shouted, and kicked her horse. El Ghomari reached for her bridle, brought the horse to a standstill before she could make it move, and then suddenly released it again, his head jerking backwards, his eyes for just a moment losing their intensity in a look of bewildered dismay.

Catherine turned her own head, to follow the direction of his gaze, and caught her own breath in amazement. The hill down which they had ridden was lined with horsemen, as was the hill facing it. And these were not a few score, but hundreds, perhaps more than a thousand. And in front of the men who immediately overlooked them there sat a diminutive figure on a white horse, wearing a black *haik* beneath a red *burnous.*

Chapter 11

CATHERINE became aware that El Ghomari had released her bridle. Her horse was already moving forward, while the Touareg chieftain raised his musket and fired, not at her, but into the air, to alert his people.

She was fifty yards away before she regained control of her mount, then she turned it to look back. The Touaregs had formed a group in front of their late victims, women and men together as the women regained their horses. But how small they looked, compared to the Bedouin host, just as they had themselves appeared a host compared to the French patrol.

And the Bedouins were moving forward, slowly, down both hills, forming a gigantic ring around their enemies, every horseman armed with a musket as well as a lance.

And in front of them remained Abd el Kader, keeping his distance before his people, gradually approaching her. Her heart began to pound, her body broke out in a sweat. The Emir's face was hard, his blue eyes glinted.

"Baroness Ricimer," he said, as he approached. "Where is your husband?"

She frowned at him. "I had supposed him with you, my lord."

He glanced at her, for hitherto his gaze had been fixed upon El Ghomari, who awaited his arrival behind her.

"Do not lie to me, *gaiour*," Abd said in a low voice. "There is no power on earth save my will can prevent your execution, and within the hour. Tell me the truth and at least protect your soul."

Her heart slowed; she had not supposed his voice could be so filled with anger. But suddenly her mind, her voice, was also angry. It was the only emotion left her, the only emotion she ever wished to feel again.

"I do not lie, my lord," she said. "My husband has kept me imprisoned in a single room these last three months; two nights ago he returned to Mascara and removed the rest of his family, including my children. He left me in my prison, from which I was rescued by a favourite slave. Where he has gone I do not know, but he has my children with him, and I will find him, or I will perish in the attempt."

Now the Emir's head did turn, to look straight at her for some seconds.

"I believe you do not lie," he said at last. "We will talk of this later. Perhaps we will seek your husband together. I also wish his head. It was he who betrayed my cause at Sidi Embarek, conveyed to the French the disposition of my men."

Catherine felt her jaw drop, and hastily closed it again. "Ricimer?" she gasped. "But . . . the French have placed a price on his head."

"And on yours," Abd pointed out. "Perhaps Ricimer has discovered a way to avoid his."

"Why?" she asked. "Why should he do so?"

"Because more and more French soldiers land in North Africa every day. Because even my own people have no longer any faith in ultimate victory. Because Ricimer is consumed with ambition, which causes him to trample his honour in the dust. His action is not surprising to me—save perhaps in abandoning so precious a pearl as yourself." His gaze moved again. His men had all reached their allotted positions, surrounding the Touaregs at a distance of perhaps a hundred yards. And still El Ghomari waited; he had not troubled either to reload his musket or to draw his sword.

"People of the Ben-Angad," Abd el Kader shouted. "My quarrel is not with you. My quarrel is with your *sheikh,* who has defied me, and insulted me, and challenged me to mortal combat. People of the Ben-Angad, I demand only your allegiance."

The warriors stared at him, waiting on a cue from El Ghomari. But El Ghomari said nothing, seemed content to wait.

"You are defeated, *marabout,*" said a voice from the crowd. "Your armies have melted away. These we see before us are all you have left. Where are your cannon, *marabout*? Where are your infidel advisers, *marabout*? Where are your tens of thousands, *marabout*?"

"Where is your parasol, *marabout*?" shouted another voice.

"And your women? The French have them all."

Catherine glanced at him in horror. His face had grown even more pale than usual, and he was biting his lip.

"Answer them, my lord," she whispered. "For God's sake, answer them."

"How may a man answer the truth save with the truth?"

"They talk of the past, my lord," she said. "Can you not draw a truthful picture of the future?"

His turn to glance at her. "Without men? Without arms? Without a general?" His face broke into a bitter smile. "Without my parasol, without even a city? Oh, I have my women. They are wrong about that."

"You are defeated, *marabout,*" came the voice. "Leave us to go our way in peace. You can demand no allegiance from us."

It suddenly burst upon Catherine's brain that her waiting was over. That everything that had happened to her throughout her life had but been preparing her for this moment. That even losing her children had been but an act of God or of the devil, she knew not which, to free her for this supreme task, just as her twenty-four hours with El Ghomari had been necessary to free her mind from the very last of its civilising restraint.

"You will have arms, and men," she said. "I swear it. And a European adviser."

He frowned. "Are you then a witch, who can give me these things with a wave of her broomstick?"

Catherine sucked air into her lungs, tossed her hair back on to her shoulders. "I can give you these things, my lord. If you will but trust me."

She felt a wild excitement flooding her chest. Fate, *Kismet,* had given her this role to play, had selected her for this role many, many years ago. Perhaps from the very first day her father had asked her to take down some copy for him.

"I swear it, my lord," she said. "Or you may cut off my head. I swear it."

Abd el Kader looked at her for the last time, then he turned to face the Angad.

"My armies will rise again," he shouted. "I will have cannon, and I will lead my people to victory. But I must fight the French. They are our enemies. They stand in front of us. I can have no enemies to stand at my shoulder, waiting to strike me down from behind. Any True Believer who does not march at my side will be destroyed. People of the Ben-Angad, the choice is yours."

A hush fell on the valley, broken only by a wailing cry from one of the dying soldiers.

Then El Ghomari spoke. "And what of me, Abd el Kader?"

"You have sworn to kill me," Abd replied. "Therefore you must die."

Catherine caught her breath.

"You will meet me, now, on an open field," El Ghomari said.

Abd el Kader hesitated, glanced at the woman, and then shook his head.

"You fear me," El Ghomari said.

"I fear no man," Abd el Kader said. "I would kill you, El Ghomari, supposing Allah wills it. But Allah

326

has given me a greater task than the settlement of a personal feud. Allah has called upon me to free Algeria from the rule of Franks and Turks alike, and to risk my life in a duel would be to go against His will." His hand moved, away from his body, but horizontal to the ground.

El Ghomari realised he had just been condemned to death. He gave a shout, stood in his stirrups, and urged his horse forward. It leapt into action, a tremendous sight, a flowing picture of man and beast in coordinated action, a moment in time, to be captured by her memory for all time, Catherine supposed. For even as he shouted, a hundred muskets had spoken. Black air and black sound reverberated in the valley, and the chieftain of the Angad fell, with his horse, the picture distorted into a kicking leg and a flow of blood across the brown of the desert sand.

"It is done," Abd el Kader said. "The quarrel of my people with the Angad is over." He glanced at one of his aides who had ridden to his side. "Cut off his head, and show it to his people, that they may understand the Will of Allah."

An interlude, but the most important twenty-four hours of her life, during which she had changed from a civilised woman into a valkyrie—when she had seized her own destiny—and in doing that, made it into her own weapon, instead of remaining, as she had for so long, as so many people, perhaps, remained throughout their lives, nothing more than its plaything.

She had gazed on those handsome features, frozen forever in death. Not twelve hours before, those lips had touched hers, while that body had taken her through the doorway of life into a paradise of love. For perhaps two hours time had stood still, while she had communed with her own soul, had finally learned to understand the magic of her own body.

Then it had been over for El Ghomari. He had lived, violently, ruthlessly, cruelly, dramatically, and he had died, violently, ruthlessly, cruelly, dramatically. There had been no regrets on those features, no fear, no apprehension of what might be going to happen next. And he remained, in her, certainly, forever more, as he doubtless remained in the heart and the mind of every woman he had ever loved. He would affect her every thought, her every ambition, for the rest of her life. There could be no doubt of that. But for the day with El Ghomari, she would never have spoken to Abd el Kader as she had, never have risen to a sudden pinnacle of importance in the eyes of the Emir.

Yet El Ghomari, whatever his influence, had not been able to make her join the band of harpies torturing the French prisoners. Some part of Catherine Scott remained, beneath the mystical magic of *Ya Habibti*. But that was for her secret hours, when she was alone with herself. It was not for public display. She had taken upon herself a role to play, and she must play it for all its worth.

Thus she rode her horse into the *smala* of Abd el Kader, keeping her station at the Emir's elbow. And was distressed in her new role of seeing all life through the eyes of the authors of her girlhood, at the indiscipline, of men as much as animals, as much as organisation, with which she was immediately surrounded.

Douars were everywhere, women and children and donkeys were everywhere, goats and camels wandered through the mob, the noise was incessant and loud, laughter, chatter, the screams of some unfortunate who had angered the Emir suffering beneath the bastinado. Then in the very centre of the chaotic mess there waited the thirty-foot tent of the Emir himself. Here Abd drew his mount to a halt, and Ben Fakha was immediately there to assist his master to dismount. Another slave made a back for Catherine.

Abd entered first, and she followed, surprised by the height of the canvas chamber, for it was roughly twice that of a man, and gave an impression of air and even light. About two-thirds of the way down the tent there was a woollen curtain, obviously shutting off the Emir's sleeping chamber, while the canvas walls of the main room were lined with arabesques and crescents, in a variety of colours, red, blue, green, and yellow. The only furniture

328

was a divan, covered in an exquisitely worked carpet, and situated between two large chests, very like the one that had contained her clothes, both in Mascara and in Algiers.

"My home," Abd remarked, somewhat acidly, and clapped his hands. Catherine discovered that even Ben Fakha had left, and they were alone. She wondered she was not apprehensive or at the least anticipatory. He was a handsome and attractive man. But her instincts told her he was also a totally dedicated man—wed to the business of creating his nation and defeating the French. *Well then*, she thought, *had you not best become totally dedicated as well?*

The Emir sat on his divan, motioned her beside him. Ben Fakha reappeared, carrying a tray on which there were cups of coffee, hot and delicious.

Abd el Kader sipped. "You were inspiring, out there in the desert," he said. "Was it inspiration, or have you something real to offer me, Baroness? You will understand that my people, and I am one of them, find it difficult to believe that a woman can be more than a mother and a mistress. But you are a Frank, and perforce I have had to make a study of the Franks, during these past few years. Your friend David Mulawer has told me much of them as well, and I am aware there are women in your history who have proved as formidable in war as their menfolk."

How her heart pounded at the mention of that name. "I do not see Monsieur Mulawer in your camp, my lord."

"Because he is not here, Baroness. Oh, he is not dead. But when your husband explained the circumstances under which he was divorcing you, I was forced to take action against the culprit." Abd commenced to play with the rosary which hung around his neck, fingering each black bead in turn.

"And so you punished David," she said, softly.

"Not as perhaps he deserved, Baroness. He swore there had been no intercourse between you, and I believed him. But when Ricimer told him that he had sent you to the French—for this is what he claimed, saying

329

his oath had been to divorce you and not to harm you personally, but not necessarily to yield you to another —David attempted to assault him, and had to be restrained. And so I sent him away, to the city of Tlemcen, where he will be well taken care of. I intended to bring him back, when his grief has run its course, when he has been married to some well-born Arab girl, who will rid his mind of criminal thoughts regarding you."

She would not lower her gaze, although she could feel the hectic spots on her cheeks. But to live as anything less than she wished now was folly.

"I will have him brought back here now," she said. "I will not have him marry."

Abd el Kader's eyes hardened. "You would presume to command me, Baroness? You would attempt to change the law?"

"I ask you to listen to me, my lord," she said. "I have been betrayed, as you are betrayed, by my husband. You know now that he only divorced me as a Moslem, not a Christian. That he kept me confined for three months, and treated me as you might treat a condemned criminal. And then, not only did he leave me to die, but he has stolen away my children. I own him as no husband of mine, now or ever, and the next time I see him I will kill him. I am not an Arab, and neither is David. We are acting here in accordance with Western law, or with the law of the animal, for we are both animals. You seek vengeance against Ricimer, and so do I. You seek to re-establish your authority. For that you need guns and ammunition. I can give you those things. You need a victory. It would be foolish to attempt to gain one over the French, until your army is rebuilt and rearmed. But I know how to give you a victory that will resound through all of Algeria. In return I ask only two things: The head of my husband, and the company of David Mulawer. Were you to turn away from your destiny on account of such a refusal, history would never forgive you."

He sipped his coffee, thoughtfully. "You have just explained that you are still married to Ricimer, in the eyes of the Christian law. You would live, in adultery,

330

within the confines of my camp? For such a request I should have you strangled now."

"Then do so now," she said. "I know how I will live, or I will die."

He gazed at her for some seconds, and then his face broke into a smile. "I have observed, in my meetings with them, that all the Frankish men are as if haunted, seldom sure of themselves. And I have wondered why this should be, as they have proved so successful in the field of war, of science, of politics. Now I believe I know the reason, if their women are all like you, Baroness."

"Could it not be said that it is because a majority of their women are like me, my lord, that they have proved so successful? And will continue to do so."

He stared at her intently. Then he shrugged. "You are not an Arab. If you choose to direct your soul, and that of your lover, to eternal hell, then it is your choice. I will send for Monsieur Mulawer." He raised his finger. "But there will be no intercourse between you until your husband is dead. And should you fail to deliver what you have promised, I will have you executed within sight of each other."

Her chin came up. "Should I fail, my lord, I would have no interest in living, in any event."

Abd nodded. "Well, then, where are these guns, these munitions, this victory, of which you speak?"

"Where is the *oasis* which has consistently resisted your every effort to unite your people, my lord?"

His brows drew together. "Ain-Mahdi, by the Beard of the Prophet. Ain-Mahdi." He glanced at her. "It is a fortress. It has the guns and the munitions we lack. How may a desert army do more than flow around its walls like the sea around a rock?"

"I will show you how, my lord."

He stared at her. "You lived there, for some years, when you were first married. Those people gave you shelter. Why do you seek to lead me against them?"

"Because in Ain-Mahdi, my lord, I will find my husband."

*   *   *

The noise was tremendous. Catherine had only ever before heard the Arab army from a distance; now it was all around her, oboes, big drums, little drums, donkeys braying, horses neighing, camels snarling, the whole overlaid by a constant veil of dust that settled on everything, got inside her *haik* and her shirts, seemed to discover every orifice and indeed every pore, made her itch and wriggle uncomfortably in her saddle—the days of the *aatatiche* were long behind her—convinced her that she was crawling with lice, which indeed was more than likely. But her horse was a splendid grey stallion, which she had named Monroe, after her favourite President. And she was free. More free than she had ever supposed possible, because it began in her mind.

But it was a freedom, like all such immense gifts, that carried great responsibility.

Above even the noise of the army, there rose the chatter of the men, the bleating of the sheep, the barking of the dogs. She would not have supposed it possible for there to be such an absence of discipline in a fighting force on its way to a battle. She frowned at Abd as he rode his black horse alongside hers, smiled at her.

"My men are happy. They believe in our victory."

"And you do not, my lord?" She licked dust from her lips.

"I am waiting to be shown, Baroness."

"But did you lack confidence, my lord, you would be entirely justified. Suppose you were to suffer a sudden attack?"

"We could not. I have outriders."

"And suppose one came in at this instant, my lord, and informed you a French force was even five miles away. Would you have time to organise this rabble into defence?"

His turn to frown. "We of the desert are not defensive fighters."

"An army, my lord, which is to win, regularly, must be able to defend as much as it can attack. Without discipline, without some organisation, it is like the unharnessed wind, sometimes blowing with such strength that it is irresistible, more often dissipated into a gentle, useless zephyr, or able to be harnessed by those who would use it for their own ends."

"And you would change all this?"

"*You* must change all this, my lord, if you are to be successful. I can but tell you how."

He stroked his chin with thumb and forefinger. "How?"

She smiled at him. "In good time, my lord. Let us first of all take Ain-Mahdi."

"Then begin. I came to tell you it is beyond that hill."

Her heart gave a sudden great leap. It had been simple to promise, because she had not doubted she could fulfill her promise. But now the moment was upon her, she remembered too well that these people had given her shelter, that her orders would result in their death and destruction.

But they had given her shelter as Ricimer's woman, not for herself. And if he had gone anywhere to escape the wrath of the Emir, it would be here. She kicked her horse and rode it forward, Abd el Kader at her side. They emerged from the front of the noise and the dust, stood on the rim of the hill and looked down on the city. *What fear must they inspire in those hearts down there,* she thought. But Tedjini would have known of the advance of this horde days ago.

"Well, Baroness?"

"You have not yet fulfilled your part of the bargain, my lord. Where is David?"

Abd el Kader allowed himself a smile. "He came yesterday, Baroness."

She turned in her saddle, mouth open, angry pink springing into her cheeks. "Yesterday?"

"He does not yet know you are riding with me. It is a big *smala*. I have sent for him now. But Baroness, you have not yet fulfilled *your* obligation."

She gazed past him at the horsemen approaching. Their leader was unmistakable. Her heart seemed to be leaping about between her belly and her throat.

He drew rein, saluted. "The place is as strong as is

reputed, my lord. I do not see . . ." He looked at Catherine, and his jaw dropped.

"David." She urged her horse forward, and Abd el Kader moved at her side.

"Cathy? But . . ."

"There will be time for explanations, at a more suitable moment," Abd el Kader pointed out. "The Baroness Ricimer seeks her husband and her children, David. And she believes they are within the walls of that city. She also believes she knows how we may take it. We are waiting, Baroness."

Catherine licked her lips, stared at David. And he stared back. *I love you,* she wanted to say with her eyes. *I love you and I have come to you. I want only proof that you love me, that you can love me, my dearest. Without that, I am no more than a savage.*

"Baroness?" Abd el Kader's tone was sharp.

"You will send an embassy, my lord," she said, hardly recognising her own voice. "This embassy must be commanded by a man of observation, who will use his eyes and his ears and his nose, if need be. He will summon Tedjini to surrender, in the name of the Emir. And should Tedjini surrender, then I have fulfilled my promise."

"Oh, indeed you will have done so, Baroness. But it is unlikely that he will surrender, is it not?"

"Then the leader of your embassy, when he returns, must answer me certain questions, my lord, and I will show you how to take the city."

"And suppose my embassy does not return? Suppose Tedjini fires their heads at me from his cannon?"

"Tedjini is a man of honour, my lord. He will recognise an embassy. But should he not, then I weep for such brave men, but the city will still be ours. I merely wish to be sure we capture as much as possible of the munitions we seek, intact."

Abd el Kader gazed at her for some moments, then he nodded. "It shall be as you wish, Baroness. David, you are observant and quick of wit. The task is yours."

334

The chant of the litany seeped through the *smala*:

The Sultan is great, but Mohammed is still greater.
The Sultan is very great; he is generous, holy and brave.
The *marabouts* of Mecca are very great and holy.
The Sultan has fine horses; the Sultan has many horses, and they are all excellent.
The Sultan has immense treasures and much powder.
The Arabs have fruitful plains; they have mountains covered with trees, and many rivers flow from them.
We have beautiful women.
Our horses are swift; no other horse can keep up with them.
Our camels are very strong; we have great herds of cattle and sheep.
Our guns are very good.
We have plenty of powder—plenty of powder.
Let us pray that all Christian dogs may perish.

"With the possible exception of yourself, Baroness," Abd remarked with a twinkle in his eye. He sat on her right, as his elder brother, Sidi Mohammed Said, sat on her left. The only other person in the tent was Ben Fakha.

Catherine sipped coffee. These last four days she had lived on coffee. David had been gone too long.

"Supposing we gain the victory here, Baroness," Sidi Mohammed said, conversationally, "what will happen next?" He was taller than his brother, and had the same handsome features. But unlike Abd he enjoyed the trappings of authority; his *haik* was decorated with gold thread, and there were rings on his fingers.

"I would hope that the desert tribes, and the hill tribes, would return to my banner," Abd said.

"And you must keep them under your banner, my lord," Catherine said.

"That will be easy enough, providing we suffer no

more defeats. Have you not claimed that as *your* province, Baroness?"

"I can but teach you how to improve your chances, my lord. I am no sorceress."

"Then explain to us the reason for this vast amount of timber you have had our people accumulate," Sidi Mohammed said. "They must have destroyed every tree in every *ouadi* over fifty miles. Will you have us make wooden cannon, and bewitch Tedjini and his people into supposing they are real?"

"No, my lord. My plan is simple enough. It requires only time, and we have sufficient of that."

"Time?" Abd demanded. "Where is this time, with the French overrunning my country, and my people no longer believing in me?"

"Thus you have time, my lord. More than you will ever have again," Catherine insisted. "The French, as you say, have defeated you, seen your armies dispersed, yourself vanished. Oh, they will soon know that you are here, before Ain-Mahdi, and they will clap their hands for joy and say, the Arabs are gone back to squabbling among themselves far into the desert. They will not trouble us again. While your rivals among the *kaids*, why, they will say the same. They will say that Abd el Kader is losing his senses, in assaulting an *oasis* as strong as Ain-Mahdi. They will say, soon the sands of the desert will swallow him up, and we shall hear no more of him."

"And will they not be speaking the truth?"

"I hope not, my lord. When you re-emerge you will be greater and stronger than ever before. Men will flock to your standard, and you will lead them to victory. But, my lord, it will be necessary to make them loyal to you, and you alone. And that cannot be done by victory alone. Many of the *kaids*, as you well know, my lord, are jealous of your power, regard themselves as your equals, and resent having you place yourself in authority over them."

Abd was frowning. "What would you have me do, bow to a perpetual council of war?"

336

"No, my lord. I would have you take a new title. *Emir el Miumenin* is too vague, too indeterminate. I would have you call yourself, *Khalifa* of the Sultan."

There was a moment's silence.

"I hold no command from the Sultan," Abd said at last.

"The men of the desert will not know that, my lord. But let them suppose you hold your command by authority of the Porte, and they will support you without jealousy, with common endeavour. But more than that, my lord; I would have you send messengers to Constantinople, and *request* the Sultan's authority for what you are doing."

"The woman is mad," Sidi Mohammed remarked. "We fight to *free* ourselves from the Turks, not beg for their rule to return."

"How can their rule return, my lord?" Catherine asked. "The rulers of Algiers, from this moment forth, are either the French or yourselves. No Turk will ever return here. They no longer have the power of Suleiman the Magnificent. But at this time, my lord, you are considered by the world no more than bandit chieftains. To win this war, and even more important, to hold the fruits of victory, you need the sympathy and the support of other nations.

"You need international recognition. And once you have that, my lords, will you care if you pay lip service to a weakening Sultan, a thousand miles away?"

Abd el Kader stroked his beard, and glanced at his brother, and then at Ben Fakha, who had approached and was bowing.

"The Jew returns."

"David." Catherine made to rise, and felt Abd's hand on her arm. She sat down again, watched David enter the tent. He looked well enough.

"My lords." He bowed. "Baroness. The *Kaid* Tedjini rejects your demands for surrender, my lord. He says there are not sufficient men in all the Sahara to force the surrender of Ain-Mahdi. He says he has guns and ammunition, and food and water, to withstand a siege of a

337

hundred years. He bids you go back into the mountains, where you belong, and fight the French."

Abd glanced at Catherine. "And did you secure the information required by the Baroness, as to the disposition of the cannon, and the powder?"

"Indeed, my lord. I have drawn a map." He took it from his pouch.

"Then you have done well, David. Baroness?"

Catherine at last raised her head. "And my other charge?" she asked. "Are my husband and my children hidden behind those walls?"

David sighed. "Alas, Baroness. They are not. Tedjini says that the Baron has sought service with the French."

"The French?" Catherine cried. "But they have put a price on his head."

"Which he has clearly negotiated away," Abd pointed out, "by his betrayal of me at Sidi Embarek. Well, Baroness, this will make our task the more difficult, as he knows our every method of fighting, as he designed it himself."

Catherine's fingers rolled into fists. He was gone, beyond her reach, and with him Gebhard and Henrietta. And the French certainly still had a price on *her* head that would have been increased as Abd had allowed the survivors of the Touareg attack to make their best way back to the French army, and they had all stared at her ash-blonde hair before they had left.

So then, was she to admit to herself that she had lost her children, forever? Or could she regain them by forcing the French to make peace, make them allow her to return to Europe in her quest?

"But for the time being," Abd el Kader said, gently, "it is necessary for us to continue with our present plans. You may have lost your reason for forcing the surrender of Ain-Mahdi, but such a victory is even more necessary to our cause. Baroness?"

She raised her head, looked at David for a moment, and sighed. "Let me see your map."

He held it out, and for a moment their fingers touched;

she could feel the thrill all the way up her arm. She studied the rough drawing, the half dozen gates which breached the walls. "There," she said. "That is our point of entry."

Abd el Kader looked over her shoulder. "You propose to use the Biblical method, Baroness, and blow a trumpet in the expectation that the wall will crumble?"

"I propose that we should make the wall crumble, my lord, by digging a mine beneath it."

The two Arabs stared at her.

"Our people will start digging now, my lord," Catherine said. "With David's help, I will work out their proper approach, and their proper depths, and I will show them where to dig their air passages."

"You mean . . . dig below the ground?" Sidi Mohammed asked.

"Yes, my lord."

"And will not the earth cave in on those doing the work?"

"Not if it is shored up with timber, my lord. And we have accumulated sufficient timber, have we not?"

The brothers looked at each other.

"It will take a very long time to dig a tunnel from our camp to that gate," Abd remarked.

"A matter of about two months, I would estimate, my lord. As I said just now, you have the time, and it is the victory we require, by whatever method. Our only problem is water. But your people know enough about survival in the desert to overcome that. Indeed, we can withdraw the *smala* to the nearest *ouadi,* leaving only a sufficient force here to protect our mine. And in the meantime you will carry out the regular envelopment of a siege that will but the more convince Tedjini, and any others who may learn of it, that defeat has robbed you of your senses, as everyone will know Ain-Mahdi can withstand a siege far longer than you may camp in the desert outside it."

Once again the brothers exchanged glances. "It may work," Abd said at last.

Catherine stood up. "It will work, my lord. Have I

339

not staked my head upon it? And now, if you will excuse me, I will retire."

"I will give my orders to have the digging commence immediately," Abd agreed. "But Baroness, you will no doubt bear in mind that your husband still lives, and will continue to do so for some time."

Catherine bowed to them both, walked past David without a word, sought the shelter of her own tent, dismissed Yasmin, the Arab woman who had been given to her as a slave. She knelt upon her *yourgan*, chin slumped on her breast, and gave herself up to despair. They were lost, beyond her reach, and she was lost, committed to take part in a desert war she could not see ending. She had thought deeply about Abd's problems, had endeavoured to remember everything she had ever read in her father's library, and was confident her ideas would give the Arabs a much better chance of not again being defeated by the French, supposing they would agree to do as she intended to propose. But not being defeated, carrying on a hit-and-run kind of warfare, was a very long way from defeating a great warrior nation if it was truly bent on conquest. She could sustain Abd's cause forever, she supposed; but she could not see them ever driving the French into the sea, without international support. And that would be a long time in coming. And she was twenty-five, and Gebhard was five, and Henrietta would soon be a year old.

Her head jerked, as she heard fingers moving across the outside of the tent.

Instantly she crawled towards the sound. "Who is it?" she whispered.

"David. I have but to free this spike from the ground. I dare not enter by the flap."

"David." How her heart suddenly leapt into life. But into apprehension as well. Not only on account of the risk they were taking with their lives, but of what they were risking with their emotions, their love.

She sank on to her haunches, listened to the sounds of the *smala* all around her, listened to the gentle scrabbling as he dug out the tent spike with his fingers, and saw his hand, pale in the darkness. A moment later he was inside, only inches away from her, his face half-hidden, as no doubt was hers.

"Oh, my sweetheart," she whispered. "If you are caught . . ."

"We will both be executed," he pointed out. "If you would like me to go . . ."

She held his hands, kissed them. "I would not have you go, even supposing Abd el Kader came in the tent this moment. Oh, David, David . . ." She slipped her hand up his arms to bring him close, to kiss his mouth, and renew that pleasure at the least. But if only her fear of the coming moments would dwindle.

"If I could understand, my dearest. Ricimer said he had sent you to Algiers. I had supposed you executed, or at least imprisoned."

"Instead he locked me up in a barred room in his house," she said. "For several months. Until indeed, but a short time ago, he deserted Abd el Kader's cause and left me to die."

"But you did not die," he said. "You are here, and in favour, at last, and . . ."

"Waiting only for you, my sweet," she said.

His hands slid across her shoulders, on to her back, gently, but hesitantly. She had no knowledge of his experience of women, of his success with them. She only knew that unless this most treasured of meetings would turn into a disaster, she must take control, must guide him, must remove his fears and make him confident.

She held his hand, guided it back across her shoulder, and on to the softness of her breast. His breath rushed at her, and she felt the desire she always knew when she was so touched streaming down to her belly. She held him back, for a moment, lifted first one shirt and then the other over her head and threw them on the floor, came against him once again, naked, felt his hands return to her breasts, holding them from underneath as she liked best, and wanted to scream for joy.

Then she was lying down, and he was beside her, his

hands hesitating on her belly. Once again she took one, guided it down to the curl of her hair, waited for his fingers to find their way further, and was not disappointed, felt the passion rising in her belly, and exploding away, endeavoured to forget Ricimer and Yusuf and El Ghomari, to think of no one but this man who loved her as none of those had done, and whose hesitancy was caused entirely by that love.

"Cathy?" he whispered. "My dearest . . ."

"It is nothing," she said. "No, it is something. You have made me happy, David."

"With my fingers? But . . ."

Silently she cursed the inhibitions of his upbringing. "With anything you choose, my dearest," she said. "Anything at all. Our business here is happiness, my sweet. Just happiness."

"But . . ."

She found his penis, hard enough, and fondled it harder still. She wished she had light, to look at it, to kiss it and caress it too to orgasm. But that would also require the time, and that too she lacked. Perhaps later.

"Cathy," he whispered.

"I am all of an Arab woman, David. Have you never loved an Arab woman?"

"I . . ." He bit his lip. "I would not lie to you."

"Nor I to you. I have been taught to love as an Arab woman, David. There is nothing you need be afraid to do to me, so long as it brings us both pleasure. But come inside a moment, my sweet. Let me feel you."

He lay on her belly, but too heavily. She scarce felt the entry beneath his weight, and wanted to cry out in disappointment. He worked himself, up and down, and she still felt nothing, and remembered El Ghomari.

"Wait," she whispered into his ear. "Wait. Rise up."

He pushed downwards, rose to his knees. "I have hurt you."

"No," she said fiercely. "I but seek the ultimate pleasure." She rolled on her face.

"Cathy . . ."

"Do it," she commanded. "Love me, David. I ask

nothing unnatural. I ask the ultimate sensation, and for both of us."

She rose half onto her knees, holding herself from the ground with her left elbow, reached behind herself to find him again and guide him as she wished. He gave a long gasp, and now she felt him, as she had felt El Ghomari. She had not been able to look, but here surely was something as large, something as questing, something which would fill her womb to the uttermost limits of pleasure. Because there it was, a pulsating series of thrusts that renewed her passion and had it bursting like a star, to send streaks of the purest delight rocketing through her brain. And still she felt him, and now she felt his chest on her back, and one of his hands had come round in front to hold her breast as he thrust. His fingers were tight, and they seized her nipple harder than she had ever known, and yet in this moment and this ecstasy she loved even that, wanted to feel him and feel him and feel him as she had never felt before, and felt the surge of his ejaculation which seemed to overtake her from her toes to her head, and allowed herself to sink flat on the ground, to taste the earth with her mouth, and to know that after nearly ten years she could look forward to the future with complete confidence. David Mulawer had made her his.

"It goes well." David Mulawer's face was streaked with dirt, as were his clothes. His fingernails were thick with dirt. But he was full of good humour and confidence.

While Catherine, sitting her horse beside Abd el Kader, dared not meet his eye. She had given him that humour and that confidence, at a cost, perhaps of every rule and convention that would have been instilled in his brain from boyhood. Her body was his, some twice a week, and they had been digging the mine now for six weeks. In that time he had learned to explore, with lips as much as with fingers, to hold her in his arms and know she would collapse from sheer passion, time and again. He had counted them both damned, and she had been able to reassure him that what they shared between their bodies was as irrelevant as what she had shared with the bodies of so many other men. All that counted was what the body sharing could do towards the mind sharing, and in this they were as one, religions and social differences forgotten, even as the different paths they had been forced to follow in the desert were forgotten. She was his and he was hers, and only the knowledge that Ricimer still lived, and lurked, cast a cloud across their lives.

That and their enforced secrecy, the enforced campaign upon which they were embarked. And to which she must now give her mind.

"That is good," Abd el Kader said, and wheeled his horse.

Was he suspicious of them? He never seemed to overlook anything among his people. His eye could pick out a movement on the desert a half a mile. Could she honestly believe, then, that he had not noticed the uplift in her spirits, in David's spirits?

He reined before his encampment. "Are you pleased, Baroness?"

She surveyed the concentric circles of *douars*. For her first suggestion had been that order be established in the *smala*. It had taken time, but at last it was completed. The outer circle was reserved for the infantrymen; fifteen to a tent. Then there was a space, and the inner circle was reserved for the cavalrymen. Again there were fifteen men to a tent, but these were pitched farther apart, as each platoon tethered its own horses immediately outside its own flap. Thus the cavalry was never more than ten seconds away from being mounted and able to take the field.

Abd el Kader's *douar* remained in the centre, with the tents of his brothers and his commanders to either side, and behind these, the kitchens, the herds of goats and camels, the source of the army's food.

"I am pleased with this, my lord."

"But you are still not satisfied."

"We have but begun, my lord. An army requires more than an orderly camp to be an army. It requires uniforms, that it may recognise itself, that it may take pride in its appearance."

344

"Uniforms?" demanded Sidi Mohammed. "Like the infidels, you mean?"

"Or the janissaries, my lord."

"Our ancestors needed no uniforms to conquer half the world," Abd objected.

"Your ancestors opposed a Europe more backward than themselves, my lord. Now the Europeans are the masters of the art of war. Believe me, my lord. A man in uniform is less likely to desert. And he is less likely to succeed in desertion."

"And where do we get these uniforms?" Sidi Mohammed inquired.

"We use what we have at hand, my lord. What we have most of. I have observed that nearly all your people wear the *tarboosh*, although they disguise it beneath their *burnouses*, or wrap it around with a turban. My lord, this *tarboosh* is invariably red. Why not make this your insignia. Every man in Abd el Kader's army must wear a red *tarboosh*, and be seen to do so."

Abd frowned at her. "You would discard the *burnous*?"

"I would retain the *burnous*, for when the wind blows the sand, or when the sun is at its hottest. But for drill and for battle, the *tarboosh* should be worn. Just as your officers should wear epaulettes and badges of office. These will be easy to make."

"Drill?"

"This is to be my next recommendation, my lord. An army needs to drill. Our strategy must be to hit and to run again. To ambush, as you have tried before."

"And failed. I had hoped for something better, Baroness."

She refused to lower her eyes. "Your ambush failed, first because you were betrayed, and second because you had no set plan upon which to fall back, when your first went astray. We must drill, and we must practice, not only set manoeuvres, but easily understood words of command and signals, so that when we have to improvise a tactic in a hurry, your people will yet understand, and obey."

345

"By Allah," Sidi Mohammed remarked. "You think these men will drill? They follow us to fight, not to play at fighting."

"They will drill, my lords, if you force them to it." Catherine said.

"They call you *Ya Habibti*," Abd said. "I suspect there is more of iron than softness in your soul."

"You wish to win this war, my lord," she said. "I am but endeavouring to show you how. But the harshness of your discipline must be tempered with an improvement in their conditions. The uniforms will help, but your men must receive two meals a day, and they must be more nourishing than beans and milk. I know such a scanty diet satisfies yourself, my lord. But all men are not as you. They must have meat, *couscous*, at least once a day, and they must have biscuits as well as beans."

The two emirs stared at her for some seconds.

"She would have us become more French than the French," Sidi Mohammed remarked at last.

"In order to beat the French, my lord."

Abd el Kader turned his horse to gaze at the distant walls of Ain-Mahdi. "Then it shall be as you wish, Baroness. Once those walls crumble before your trumpet."

Catherine had never been in a tunnel before. She picked her way along the narrow, dampened corridor, skirt of her *haik* held from trailing in the ground, shoulder every now and then brushing one of the wooden uprights, looking above her head at the cross timbers that sagged beneath the weight of sand and dust and rock above them, taking comfort only from the presence of David immediately in front of her.

"We must be quiet now," he whispered, and pointed at the pile of gunpowder barrels stacked against the wall.

"Where are we?" she asked, clutching his arm.

"Immediately beneath the gateway you designated, and some twelve feet down."

"It is horrible," she said, and watched desert ants crawling out of the fresh turned sand. "I had not known how horrible. It is too easy to make war out of books."

"You'll not weaken now, Cathy. I had never supposed it possible for you to weaken at all."

How little you know, she thought. *How little you know of the hundred and one incidents in my past when I shivered with fear, and abased myself in the hope of survival.*

"I shall not weaken," she said. "I was but thinking, I have no quarrel with these people. My quarrel was with Ricimer, and with them only if they sheltered him. As they do not . . ."

"If you and I would prosper, Cathy, we must win the day for the Emir."

She did not reply, released his arm and went forward to look more closely at the barrels and timbers. He had followed her instructions to the letter. No gate could stand this charge, and it was more than likely that some of the wall would collapse as well.

"Then let us make haste," she decided, and hurried back along the passageway, pausing when they were a hundred feet from the powder barrels, a place carefully marked and where the slow fuse began. David glanced at her, and she nodded, and he scraped his tinder and lit the fuse. They watched it burn for a few seconds, then continued on their way as quickly as they could, Catherine's brain a storm of conflicting thoughts, conflicting emotions. This was her doing, her creation, born of her anger and her hate. There was no holding back, as she had done with the Touaregs, to let others do the killing. This slaughter was hers, and hers alone. Pray God that there was no great amount of it.

She stumbled into the open air, fell to her knees. Instantly Abd el Kader took her arm to raise her to her feet. "Is it done?"

"It is done, my lord."

He could see the tears in her eyes. "And now you regret your part in it, Baroness. After all, you are no more than a woman. Even if an exceptional one." He turned, still holding her arm. "How long?"

David had taken his watch from the folds of his

gandoura, was peering at it. "A matter of seconds, my lord. You may count . . ."

The explosion took them by surprise. They turned together, stared at the distant town, at the cloud of smoke and dust and debris that rose into the air. Abd el Kader released Catherine and ran for his horse. His men were already mounted and leaving the encampment, the infantry running behind, the paean of victory echoing already from their throats.

A slave waited with horses for Catherine and for David, but she shook her head. "We have played our part," she said. She allowed herself to lean against him, felt his arms go round her, hugging her close. He could do this, in their moment of triumph. Because it was a triumph. She continued to look at the city, her heart surging as she saw the white flag being hoisted above the walls. If Abd could hold his men, there need be no slaughter.

"We will go," she decided, and swung into the saddle. David rode beside her and they cantered down the hillside, acknowledging the cheers of the soldiers on either side who had also seen the surrender. She drew rein at the breach, gazed at the collapsed earth, the remnants of the men who had stood upon the wall, then urged her horse forward and into the square, where she could see the red and white standard of the Emir.

"Baroness Ricimer," he cried. "You have met the *Kaid* Tedjini."

"We have met," Catherine said, once again halting her horse and gazing at the old man.

"Is this how you repay our hospitality?" Tedjini asked. "The Emir says it is your magic that destroyed my gate."

Catherine bit her lip, looked for and found Lalla, standing behind her lord, and then a host of other men, and women whose *yashmaks* undoubtedly hid faces which would be equally familiar. She could think of nothing to say.

"The Baroness fights for the cause of all Arabs, Tedjini," Abd said. "Not just one. You have surrendered, and will be treated leniently. I wish only your guns and

348

your ammunition, your cannon and a levy of food. And the best of your young men."

"And who will defend Ain-Mahdi?" Tedjini inquired. "With what weapons?"

"You will need no weapons," Abd promised him. "The defence of the desert peoples will be my charge." He turned his horse, rode alongside Catherine. "You have kept your word, Baroness. You will find that I can keep mine."

"Then give me a safe conduct, and an escort, to the Moroccan border."

He frowned at her. "You think to find your children in Morocco?"

"No, my lord. I shall not find them anywhere in North Africa. But I find no pleasure in taking life. I have given you your victory, my lord. I desire to be allowed to leave."

"With your artist admirer."

She would not lower her gaze. "That was our bargain, my lord."

He smiled, and shook his head. "Your husband still lives, Baroness. Besides, your task is not yet finished. Word reached me yesterday that the French have taken Tlemcen."

"Tlemcen?" she cried.

"The very last of my cities. And this they have not burned and evacuated as they did Mascara. This they have garrisoned and mean to hold. We must throw them out, Baroness. You must show us how, *Ya Habibti.*"

Chapter 12

"WE have cannon," declared Sidi Mohammed Said. "We have ten thousand men, and more joining every day. Why do we not boldly assault the city?"

He sat his horse, beside his brother, and Catherine and David, and two other *kaids*, with Ben Fakha waiting patiently behind them, on a spur overlooking the valley and the road which wound slowly across and through the hills by Rachgoun, the vital link between Tlemcen and Oran.

"Because it *is* a city," Catherine explained. She flicked flies from her eyes, pulled her *burnous* closer about her face. It was all but noon, and the sun was at its hottest. Normally the Arabs would be in camp, huddled beneath their *douars*. Only madmen and Europeans went abroad in the midday sun. But Europeans did, and it was Europeans they must combat. "And our cannon are old, my lord. They are more valuable for morale than for knocking down city gates."

"Then what of another mine?" Sidi demanded.

"Because the garrison of Tlemcen is French, my lord. They know all about mining. They would hear the noise

350

of our workmen, and they would drive a countermine, and defeat us under the earth."

"So we are reduced once again to waging war like bandits."

"We are waging the best war that is available to us, my lord. It has worked very well, for the Spaniards against the French, not twenty-five years ago, for my own people against the British, sixty years ago. We are like the fishes in the sea. They are forced to travel together, we come together and strike, and then we disappear into the desert. Do you not believe this, my lord?"

She addressed Abd el Kader, who had taken little part in the endless discussions forced upon her by his more impatient brother. Now he watched the distant peaks.

"I believe this, Baroness." He pointed. "There is the signal."

They watched the road, where it debouched from amid the nearest of the hills, and saw the glitter of steel. Catherine found her throat dry, and not merely from the heat. Once again it was her plan, her decision, that people should be killed. Frenchmen. Men she might have passed on the street in Paris. But that had been Catherine Scott, not the Baroness Ricimer. And those men down there, however they might have bowed and smiled and raised their hats to Catherine Scott, would stretch Baroness Ricimer on a board and cut off her head. She told herself she must remember this, now and always.

But she was grateful for the quick touch of David's hand, the squeeze of his fingers, as they turned their horses and rode back down the hill, to dismount.

"You will accompany me, Baroness," Abd said.

"Your enemy is in sight, my lord," she said. "I have played my part."

"It is your battle, Baroness. I would have you give the signal. Be ready, my brother."

He went forward, and she followed, pebbles crunching beneath her sandals, heat striking the hard earth and seeming to bounce back at her legs. She felt exhausted, ready only for sleep. They had travelled fifty miles a day to get here from Ain-Mahdi, up and down the hills,

351

through the valleys, all the while being joined by more and more men, who had brought with them their women and their children and their goats and their camels and their donkeys and their dogs. The *smala,* not twenty miles away from where they now stood, covered an area of several square miles. It was situated close to a *ouadi,* but by this evening the river would have been drunk dry. It was an immense millstone hanging about their necks. She could remember nothing like it, in her reading of the Peninsular War, or of Washington's campaigns. She thought she would have to go back to Tacitus, and his descriptions of the moving nations of the Gauls and the Germans, for a comparative situation. And Caesar had slaughtered *them.*

Abd el Kader stood against a boulder that hid him from the road below. "You are pensive, Baroness. You should be pleased. You gave me Ain-Mahdi. Now you are going to give me this supply train. I understand and agree with your strategy. If we prevent the French from ever reinforcing or victualling Tlemcen, then they must eventually evacuate it. Why do you frown?"

"We still have problems, my lord," she said. "Some I do not find an answer for."

He smiled. "We will talk of your problems, Baroness, after this day is completed. See."

She stood beside him, moved the *burnous* from her head, looked down on the valley, on the column proceeding slowly along the road. Some four thousand men, she estimated, mostly infantry, marching in front and to either side of the ponderous wagons that carried the food and munitions for Tlemcen. They counted the Arabs defeated, scattered into the mountains; they could not yet have heard of the fall of Ain-Mahdi. Thus they had no cavalry, no scouts far out on either side to sacrifice themselves and warn the main body of the proximity of an enemy. They did not even have any skirmishers.

"They will be an easy victory, this time," Abd el Kader said, echoing her thoughts. "Will you not give the signal, *Ya Habibti?*"

With a great roar, "Ul-ul-ul-Akbar," the Arab horsemen swept down from the hills, converging from both flanks as they had against the Touaregs, many of whom were riding in this attack. Catherine felt her heart constrict as she watched the bursts of black smoke rising above the charging horsemen, as she watched the French hastily form square and begin to return fire.

David moved his horse alongside hers. He had out his sketch book and was making a hasty drawing. "It is magnificent."

"Men are being killed."

"It is how men were meant to die," he pointed out. "It is far superior than dwindling away of an illness in a stinking bed."

She glanced at him, and then looked down again. Having fired their muskets, the Arabs were now closing on the square to use their pistols. Several of the blue-coated Frenchmen were already lying on the brown earth of the roadway, and there were a few crumpled heaps of white or blue scattered across the hillside. Her battle. Therefore her victims.

The horsemen were withdrawing, regrouping to deliver their second, and hopefully decisive charge with lance and sword. She watched the frantic activity of the French, the muskets being desperately reloaded, the wounded being dragged back to the wagons, and had her eye caught by a flash of light from the distant hilltop, where Abd had posted a patrol. She fumbled at her saddlebag, found the telescope the Emir had given her as a present, levelled it and focussed on the signalling darts of brilliance.

"What do you see?" David was still drawing.

"Another column." She bit her lip, looked down the hill as the roar once again swelled from several thousand throats, and the dust flew as the cavalry commenced their charge.

"You'll not stop them now." But he restored his sketch book to his haversack.

"I must," she muttered, and kicked her horse forward.

"Cathy," he shouted. "You'll be hit."

She heard him behind her, and urged her mount into a gallop. Beneath her all was pandemonium, because the fury of the Arab charge had indeed broken the square. Muskets and pistols exploded, powder and dust clouded the still midday air, steel clashed and men and horses screamed. And her own horse's hooves drummed as she gained more level ground and raced forward, her *burnous* slipping from her head to allow her hair to stream behind her in the wind.

"Cathy," David bellowed, riding as hard as he could. "Cathy."

Horsemen debouched away from the conflict, and surrounded her. She recognised Sidi Mohammed Said, his normal elegance disappeared in black powder stains and brown dust while sweat poured down his cheeks; his sword blade was dull with blood. "Hold there, Baroness," he shouted. "This is no place for you."

Ben Fakha caught her bridle and brought her to a stop. "The Emir would be grieved were you to be hurt, lady."

"The Emir," she panted. "I must speak with the Emir."

The noise was dying. The remnants of the French force had accumulated into a tiny knot, empty muskets still grasped in firm hands, bayonets pointing outwards, surrounded by the Bedouins as a wounded traveller might be surrounded by a horde of wolves.

Catherine shrugged herself free of Ben Fakha's hand and rode forward.

"Surrender," Abd el Kader was calling in French. "Surrender, or die."

The commanding officer, from his epaulettes Catherine estimated him to be a major, stepped away from his men. "We will die with weapons in our hands. Not at the hands of your women."

Catherine forced her way through the Arabs; they parted willingly enough for *Ya Habibti*.

"Surrender," she cried. "I beg of you. Your lives will be spared. You have my word."

The major took off his hat. "I am honoured to make your acquaintance, Baroness Ricimer, having heard enough of you. Your word, madame? Do you not ride with the Touareg women?"

"I ride with Abd el Kader," she said. "And we will injure no man who surrenders."

The major looked at her for some seconds longer, then at the circle of Arab horsemen, at the red and white banner fluttering in the faint breeze. Then he sighed, reversed his sword, and held it out. "I surrender to you, Baroness."

She took the blade, slowly, reluctantly. She had not held a sword since she had played with her father's, as a girl. "You will make sure of my promise, my lord," she said in a low voice, and reversed it herself to hand to him.

"Keep your trophy, Baroness," Abd said. "And you may be sure, as it is my promise to you, that it will be kept. Let us get those wagons moving."

"And quickly, my lord," she said. "There is another French force approaching."

He frowned at her. "A great many?"

"From the number of flashes, a large number, my lord."

"Well, let us defeat them also," Sidi Mohammed declared. "Our men are ready for it."

"Indeed, Baroness, we shall never have more spirit at our backs."

"My lord, I promise nothing if you attempt to meet an equal French force in the open field. You may win. You may not. Surely our task is to eliminate the risk of a defeat? You have achieved your task. These wagons are yours, should we get them moving quickly enough. Tlemcen must do without victuals for another season. Why jeopardise it all in the hazard of an equal battle?"

"Because we are warriors," Sidi Mohammed insisted. "Because it is the honourable thing to do."

"Honour?" she cried. "How can there be honour in battle? It is a brutal, bloody thing. If you wish honour, challenge them, and lose, and see your people melt away back into the desert. And think too of your women and your children waiting in the *smala*."

"You are right, of course," Abd el Kader said. "This

war must be fought with our heads, not our hearts. Disarm those men, and then turn them free. Major," he called, riding away from the conference. "You will remain here."

"Without arms?" the officer demanded.

"You have five thousand arms, just beyond that hill," the Emir said. "They will be with you in three hours." He wheeled his horse. "Ride with me, *Ya Habibti*. This is your day."

She turned her horse, David at her heels, rode through the ranks of the warriors. Their paean swelled around her. "*Ya Habibti, Ya Habibti, Ya Habibti.*"

She raised the captured sword above her head as she passed them. Her battle, her trophy, her day. Her victory.

But my God, Catherine Scott, she thought, *where do you go from here?*

"Peace. They seek peace." Abd el Kader reined his horse beside Catherine's, where she sat, watching the infantry go through their drill, marching and countermarching, wheeling and forming square at the word of command. Her commands, not issued from her mouth, certainly, but devised by her brain and her memory, as best she could.

But what an occupation for a young lady from Boston? And even more, what an occupation for a mother-to-be. Because she was sure of it now, although she had not yet even confided in David.

Her problem was how to confide in the Emir. Yet today he looked pleased enough.

"They have asked for peace before, my lord."

"Oh, indeed they have, Baroness. This time Clausel has merely declared that the war is at an end, without consulting me, and has apparently taken himself off to Paris for a holiday. But this new man, Buguead, he seems to be of more practical stuff. It was he commanded the relieving force at Rachgoun, you know. Thus he will have seen the evidence of what we can accomplish with his own eyes. So he has begged a parley."

"And you have seen him?" He had been absent from the *smala* for the past week.

"Aye. He has offered to recognise me as Bey of Tittery if I will cease harassing their columns."

"And you have agreed, my lord?"

"It is a start, is it not?"

"It can be no more than a truce, my lord. You must understand that. They offer you the hinterland while they prepare to conquer the coast. Is there not a rumour they are assembling an army to march on Constantine?"

"I suspect that may be true. But there are two points to be considered, Baroness. In the first place, Constantine is probably the most difficult city in all Africa to take by assault. They will not find that so easy to accomplish. And in the second, have you not said that if you could but have six months of peace you could turn this rabble of mine into an army?"

"Never one capable of meeting the French in the open field, my lord. Forget that for a moment and you are lost."

Abd nodded. "Nevertheless, one which the French may never defeat, so long as we continue our present tactics. Oh, I shall not forget that, Baroness. But come. Buguead wishes me to meet his officers. What he has in mind, to be sure, is to impress us with his strength and his discipline. But I suspect we may be able to surprise him, just a little. We must make haste."

"You do not need me for that, my lord."

Abd smiled at her. "You most of all, Baroness. The general wishes to see this famous and fabulous woman who rides at my side, and is my right arm."

"They make a handsome show. Would you not agree?" Abd el Kader handed her his glass. They sat their horses, together with David and Abd's staff, on a hill looking down at the valley below, at the French regiments, six of them, drawn up in perfect precision, but already wilting in the midday heat; the barrels of their cannon seemed to be glowing rods of red-hot metal. It was so hot, indeed, that there were even clouds gathering, rare enough in the desert.

"Indeed, my lord." She prayed they would complete the meeting and be done. She wanted only to lie down, and she had a mortal fear of injuring the child. David's child. She glanced at him, handed him the glass; still he did not know.

"Perhaps you could sketch them for me, David," Abd suggested. "Shall we dismount?"

Catherine raised her eyebrows. "Are they not expecting us down there?"

Abd smiled. "Indeed they are, Baroness. But should we always be where they expect us to be?" He dismounted, and Ben Fakha was there to assist her to the ground. The parasol had already been raised—a new parasol this—and the carpets and the slaves were preparing tea. "We will let them wilt a while longer."

She sat down, watched David, who had also dismounted, but had not joined them, and remained leaning against the rocks, beginning his picture.

"So, we buy time," Abd mused. "Nothing more than that, perhaps. But time is always valuable. And I am negotiating for more than that. I have asked for information regarding your children."

Catherine raised her head. "My lord?"

"You wish to be reunited with them, do you not?"

"Indeed I do, my lord. But, supposing we do make a lasting peace, may I not be permitted to go in search of them myself?"

Abd sipped coffee, watching her over the rim of his cup. "I doubt it will be so simple, Baroness. Your name was mentioned, and explicitly excluded from any pardons that might be given French traitors in my ranks."

Her heart lurched. "But I am not French. How may I be considered a deserter? Or a traitor?"

"Ah, you see, your husband now works and fights for them. Those were the terms of his desertion of me. His knowledge of the desert is invaluable to them. And he has spent his time poisoning their minds against you. Why, do you not know that in Paris you are represented as a Gorgon, with all that magnificent hair no more than a nest of vipers? And worse, as a prostitute who shares her couch with every man in the Arab army."

Catherine inadvertently took a gulp of coffee, and burned her throat.

"Insults," Abd remarked, "which I shall be pleased to avenge, once the opportunity arises. But it may take some time. I pointed out to this General Buguead that Ricimer was now a traitor to *my* cause, and asked for him to be returned to me. And he refused. But my people are looking for him. They will find him, soon enough."

Catherine's heart was pounding, and her stomach had curled itself into so tight a ball she thought she might be going to have a miscarriage on the spot.

"They will find your children as well, hopefully," Abd said. "Although I suspect they may have been returned to France. But one hardly supposes it is your fate to be a mother, limited to the confines of a *harem*. At least, not until we have won this war. Have you given thought to the problems of our *smala*, of our necessity to travel with such encumbrance? To move from *oasis* to *oasis,* in search of food and fodder?"

She had to shake her head to restore her thoughts. "Indeed I have, my lord, but it *is* a problem. *Oases,* cities, are too easily assaulted and held, by the enemy. If we could find some means of establishing hidden granaries, hidden depots of food and fodder and munitions . . ."

To her amazement, Abd rested his hand on top of hers. "Do not fret about it, Baroness. The solution will come to you. But apart from your value to me as an adviser, I have another reason for not regretting the French decision to outlaw you. Another reason, perhaps, for wishing Ricimer dead."

She raised her head, gazed into those clear blue eyes, that pointed chestnut beard, that magnificent forehead, for he had allowed his *burnous* to slide to the back of his head. *Oh, my God,* she thought. For the first time in years she was totally surprised.

"I have three wives, as you know," Abd said. "My cousin, Lalla Kheria, Aicha, and Embarka. I love them all dearly, and they have each given me a son, as well as

359

my dear Yahmina. I do not talk of the other." He paused, and Catherine bowed her head. Abd's second daughter had been born with a feeble brain. "But it is written that a man is not fulfilled until he has taken his fourth wife," he said softly.

He had stopped. She raised her head again, licked her lips.

"You are not pleased," Abd said, and smiled. "It is a strange business, to approach a prospective wife about being a wife. I have no experience of it. But I have studied to understand your Western ways."

"My lord, I am not a Moslem."

"And I am a *marabout,* with responsibilities to the law and to the religion of my people. You will not change your religion?"

Sweat was standing out on her shoulders, streaming down her back. "My lord, I . . ."

"I honour you for that decision. And yet, I wonder what the law would say? You are an infidel who has devoted her life to our cause. There is time, *Ya Habibti.* The Baron still lives and plots. He must be dealt with first. This will give me time to consult with my *muftis* who interpret the law for us. Believe me, I am sure a dispensation can be found to enable us to discover our happiness. I but wish you to say that what I propose is in accordance with your wishes."

She licked her lips again, gazed at him in stark horror.

"Do I then fill you with disgust?" he asked, his voice still soft.

"My lord, I . . . of all men, I honour you the most. Of all men, I have no doubt that to be your wife would be the most splendid thing that could happen to any woman."

"But not to this woman?"

"My lord . . ." She glanced at David, before she could stop herself.

"Ah," Abd said. "Still the Jew. You would favour a slave, for he is little more, over an Emir?"

"My lord . . ." She sucked air into her lungs. "I bear his child."

360

Abd's brows slowly drew together, while his eyes seemed to harden even as she looked into them.

"You understood the terms under which I spared your life?" His voice was still soft, but it had a cutting edge.

"For over a year, my lord? I am a young woman. I am a passionate woman. I was taught to be so in the *harem* of the Dey. I cannot live without love. Especially in close proximity to the man I love."

"You are a whore."

Her chin came up. "Then you but agree with French opinion, my lord. I see myself as a woman in love. I would remind you that I met and knew and loved David Mulawer before I met either my husband, or the Dey of Algiers, or yourself. *There* is my misfortune. Had I encountered you, my lord, I would no doubt have loved you, with as much constancy as I have loved David. For the constancy is there, my lord. It has now survived nine years."

Still he stared at her, his normally pale cheeks flushed with anger, to be interrupted by Ben Fakha, bending low beside his cushion. "The infidel comes."

He rose immediately, not glancing at Catherine, walked away from their carpet. Catherine also stood up, watched the Bedouin cavalry hastily mounting their horses and forming line, watched the tricolour appearing above the rocks as the French party rode forward. She gazed at the general, dismounting to greet Abd el Kader. He was one of the biggest men she had ever seen, at once tall and powerfully built, with a plump, but strong face, and a florid complexion. His eyes were light grey, and seemed able to take in everything at a glance. His mouth was large, and suggested that in private he might not be so hard as he seemed. But she did not doubt that at last the French had sent to Algeria a man who would, if circumstances required it, destroy the Arabs forever.

A man Abd el Kader expected her to oppose. Supposing he had not already decided to order her execution.

The Emir had turned in her direction. "Baroness."

She moved forward slowly, and shrugged her *mashlah* from her head to reveal her hair.

"General Buguead wishes to meet his arch-enemy," Abd said, smiling. But his eyes remained cold.

"Baroness." Buguead raised his cocked hat. He was wearing full dress uniform, although even the gold braid seemed to be tarnished by the heat. His head was almost bald, save for a few silver hairs which stood straight from his scalp. "I will be the envy of Paris."

"Yet you will still chop off my head, should you be able to arrange it, general," she said.

"The fortunes of war, madame. You cause those gentlemen at the War Office endless sleepless nights." His eyes twinkled. "For what reason I cannot say. And I, I am but their servant. And now I must take my leave." His gaze roamed over the Arab encampment, the cavalry, their weapons, their uniforms. "I have dismissed my own men, as the sun is too hot. And I have explained to the Emir that there is a saying in my country that when Mohammed will not go to the mountain, then the mountain must go to Mohammed. Madame, I salute you. My lord." He bowed to the Emir.

They watched him mount, and turn his escort, ride back down the hill.

"He is angry," Abd el Kader said, stroking his beard. "At being kept waiting. But he respects us."

"He respects you, my lord."

He glanced at her. "And you also, Baroness. Did you form an opinion of him?"

"He will be the most severe of your enemies, my lord."

Abd nodded. "I have the same conclusion. We must return to the *smala*."

She stood her ground. "I must know my fate, my lord."

"No man, and no woman, can understand *Kismet*."

"*My* fate, my lord. And that of my lover, who is to be the father of my child."

At last he looked directly into her eyes. "You would have me break the law, for you? I would not even break the law, for myself."

She controlled her breathing with an effort. But it was

as if her peril had made her brain ice cold, so that she could not only gamble with her life, she could understand the problem that had been troubling her for the last four months. It came to her like a flash of lightning, as indeed there had just been a flash of lightning, from the lowering clouds.

"Then execute me now, my lord. But before you have me dragged away, I have one last piece of advice for you."

He frowned at her.

"We have talked of this, many times, of the vulnerability of your cities to attack, of your *oases* to capture. We have thought, if we could find a secret *oasis*, or several of them, where we could store our munitions and our food, where we could retire upon, to the confusion of our enemies, then could we *never* be defeated."

"And we have found no answer. There is no answer."

"There is an answer, my lord, and I have it. Is it not true that wherever there is a *ouadi*, there is a chance of finding an underground cavern, eaten out by the long dry waters?"

His frown deepened. "That is true. I have seen them often enough."

"I escaped from the French by hiding in one, my lord. Supposing you turned each of these caves into an underground granary? Only you and your generals would know their location. So when the French columns pursue you, encumbered as they are with their baggage and their supply trains, instead of retreating upon known *oases* or cities you would melt away into the desert, intent upon discovering only a lonely *ouadi* where you might find all the necessities of war."

His hand had returned to his beard. "By the beard of the Prophet," he said. "You are a woman of rare ability, Baroness."

She bowed. "Now you may strangle me with a clear conscience, my lord. I doubt I have anything more to offer our cause."

He stared at her, while the thunder suddenly rumbled out of the afternoon, building to a climax immediately above their heads, and set the horses neighing and the cavalry shouting.

Abd looked at the sky. "An omen? A reminder, that we have still work to do." He clapped his hands. "Ben Fakha, prepare a litter for the Baroness. It is not fitting that a prospective mother should ride."

Here was happiness, and she had supposed she would never know it again. She was forced to conclude that Gebhard and Henrietta were gone forever, just as Ricimer was undoubtedly gone forever; he might be giving the French the benefit of his knowledge of the desert and the Arabs, but he took care never to venture back into the desert himself, and risk capture by those who hated him so much.

So that part of her life was closed, just as it seemed that all of European, or American, existence was also closed to her. She fought against it, for a while. Obviously to escape and ride for Morocco was impossible while she was pregnant—in many ways she felt she had retreated through the years and was back carrying Henrietta and waiting for the burden to pass. But by the time Omar was born Mascara had been rebuilt, and she had been installed in her old house, with David and a new household of slaves. She had supposed she would be too afflicted by memories, of her children, of poor Jean-Pierre, of her imprisonment, of those few stolen moments in the archway with David, ever to be happy here again.

But she had reckoned without Omar. As with all her children, he proved an easy birth. She supposed her active life, her many hours in the saddle, the total health with which she was endowed no less than the muscles that gave her almost the strength of a man, were to be thanked for this. And then the child himself. Almost from the moment of his birth he greeted the world with a smile, gurgled in Abd el Kader's ear as his godfather held him up to the cheering army, and mingled his belches with happy smiles as he chewed on her breast. He was a child in a million, and he was David's. No more reason was needed. Now at last was she settled in total domestic bliss. They walked together and they rode together and they talked together and they played together. And they loved together. For him, she was a wonderland of uninhibited passion, unrestrained desire. She shocked him, continually, broke down the barriers of his religiously controlled upbringing, penetrated the deep recesses of his heart and his mind to discover and enjoy every hastily repressed sexual urge he had ever known. For her, he was a joy, because he loved, simply and with total commitment. Perhaps, she sometimes thought, the years of waiting, unfulfilled, had made her more precious in his eyes. Or perhaps she was as beautiful as men claimed. But it was most, she decided, because he had never known that woman could, or would dare provide such variety, such delight in the mere act of making love, such eagerness to hold him in her arms, to respond.

So then, should she thank Ricimer? Hussein bin Hassan? El Ghomari? But these were shadows, and there were enough of those to haunt her midnight hours, when David slept deeply at her side.

El Ghomari was dead. Hussein bin Hassan was dead. But Ricimer lived. As did Yusuf. And Ricimer had her children. Those were indeed in France, as Abd el Kader had supposed, no doubt being looked after by Aimée Despards, and by Cora as well. Being taught that their mother was a whore and a renegade, who rode at the head of the Bedouin horsemen, clad in a cloak of flowing red (thus the Paris newspapers) eager to be the first to assault the wounded, to maim and to torture, to gallop across the savage sands with her ash-blonde hair streaming behind her head. What child would wish to know such a mother? Especially in the case of a girl who would not even recall her face.

So all happiness was necessarily allayed by some sadness. She should count her blessings, in David, in Omar, in the pleasant surroundings in which she lived, in her conversations with Abd el Kader, who saw that she was at his side whenever they rode abroad to inspect his arms factory at Tagdempt, to supervise the creation of the vast network of underground storehouses which had been her brainchild, to watch his men drilling, to visit the *kaids* and bring them to his way of thinking.

For he was busy now in organising his kingdom on a scale never previously seen in an Arab country. He divided his territory into eight *khalifaliks*: The main ones were Tlemcen, ruled by Bou Hamidi, Mascara, ruled by his brother-in-law Ben Thami, Miliana, ruled by Ben Alla, and Medea, ruled by El Berkani. Each *khalifalik* was subdivided into *aghaliks,* ruled by *aghas,* and the *aghaliks* were further subdivided into the tribes, ruled by their own *kaids*. Thus a continuous chain of almost feudal command was created, and thus each *kaid,* each *agha* and each *khalifa* knew exactly what forces he was required to bring into the field, should war ever return.

He supervised the training of his army, now developed into eight thousand infantry, two thousand cavalry, two hundred and forty gunners, divided equally between the eight *khalifaliks*. He took Catherine's advice, and created badges, crescents worn on the chest or stripes on the sleeves to indicate regiments and ranks; his officers, known as *rais,* wore gold epaulettes inscribed with the motto "With those in authority, patience is the key to divine aid." The wearing of uniform was made compulsory, with severe punishment for disobedience.

It occurred to Catherine, indeed, that but for the severity of the criminal laws with which she was surrounded, she could consider herself taking part in the creation of a unique society, dominated by the religious ethics of Moslem law, to be sure, but even more dominated by the humanity and wisdom of the Emir. And yet even he was given to bursts of rage when he sought only to strike, when the lowered hand which indicated the bastinado, or the horizontal hand that indicated death, was too much in evidence, and the camps echoed with the screams of those unfortunates who had incurred his displeasure. At such moments it was only the gentle chiding of the faithful Ben Fakha could calm him.

Yet to her he was always kindness itself. It was as if, having overcome his initial revulsion at her adultery, he now found himself able to regard her entirely as a

Western woman with whom he was fortunate enough to be associated. Certainly he encouraged her to be as different to his own people as possible, and secured for her Western clothes, especially a splendid pale green riding habit, worn over a white bodice and underskirt, with white lace at her wrists and her neck, and with a black tall hat, which she was commanded to wear whenever they went abroad. This was not entirely to enhance her beauty, she realised; the other Arab chieftains, to whom she was only a rather remote figure, found it easier to listen to the advice of a woman if she was so obviously not of their own.

Was he jealous of her relations with David? Did he lie awake at night, one of his wives in his arms, and dream of her? She doubted either, but mainly because of the almost ascetic self-discipline he imposed upon himself. But had he truly loved her, or had he regarded her as a symbol, like the falcon he invariably carried on his wrists, or indeed the bird droppings that stained his clothes and of which he was proud—like any Arab chieftain, to have stains on his *haik* was a mark of his proficiency in this oldest of sports.

Only occasionally did she discover him watching her with an expression of almost longing, immediately to be turned into a jest when he realised his discovery, or into a serious discussion on other matters, for he loved above all else conversation, on politics, on military history, on law, on the social structure of society. Only on religion was he disinclined to listen. "Christianity," he said, "is based upon falsehood. Consider only this, *Ya Habibti*: If God can have a Son, then He must necessarily have had a Father. When you, or any priest of yours, can answer me that riddle, I will believe in your Faith. Allah accepts no such connection with earthly aspirations. He is One, eternal and indivisible, and as such He is the truth."

Then it was time to escape back to the comfort of David's arms—they never discussed *their* religious differences—to dream of their future together, when the peace treaty would be ratified, when even Abd would agree she had done all she could towards the security of his people, when they would be free, to find a ship to take them and Omar to the United States, there to begin a new life.

And there to be married? But this was something else they dared not discuss. Ricimer remained the great shadow across their happiness. Until the day, in the autumn of 1839, that news came that the French government had finally rejected the treaty as it stood, and that an officer was on his way to Mascara to place further proposals before the Emir, proposals that would leave no doubt in anyone's mind that the Arabs were a conquered people, subject to the ultimate will of Paris.

Abd el Kader faced his *kaids*. The city of Taza had never seen an assembly like this. It seemed every man of note in all the Regency was gathered in their square, to listen to the words of the Emir. And the townspeople were gathered too, for here was an opportunity to peer at the *gaiour, Ya Habibti,* who stood at the Emir's side, wearing her green riding habit, her long pale hair floating in the gentle breeze, her face equally pale, equally determined.

"They say our agent, Miloud Ben Arach, has signed a revised treaty, when he visited Paris," Abd said. "I will tell you this, Miloud Ben Arach signed no new treaty. If his signature is attached to any piece of paper, it is a subterfuge. How could he sign a treaty, when he has no authority?"

He paused, and the *kaids* exchanged glances and nods, and murmured agreement among themselves.

"I have written letters," Abd el Kader said. "I have written to Monsieur Thiers, and I have written to Monsieur Gerard. Not one of my letters has been answered. Must I submit to these insults, which are insults to us all, to our people?"

This time the heads were shaken.

"Now I have received news that more and more French soldiers are landed every day, in Oran and in Algiers. They say there will soon be fifty thousand French soldiers in Africa. This is not a garrison. This is an army of conquest. Will we wait, until they have a hundred thousand? Until the entire French army is ready to fight us, here in our country?"

The murmurs of no were clearly audible now.

"Then hearken to me," Abd el Kader said. He turned away from them. Ben Fakha was waiting with the red and white striped *kaftan* denoting the rank of *Khalifa* of the Sultan. Abd thrust his arms through the sleeves, turned once again to face his people. "Then I declare a *jihad* against the infidels. Let every man who is able take up arms, and never lay them down until the last Frenchman is killed or re-embarked upon his ship. Let every *kaid* assemble his people, and join my army outside Mascara. But listen well. We go to war, against an experienced and powerful enemy. I wish no women and children, I wish no goats and donkeys. I wish only men, and arms."

"How will we live?" a voice called from the crowd.

"That will be my responsibility," Abd el Kader said. "No man will starve. No man will go short of powder. But hear me, and obey."

The *kaids* rose to their feet, coagulated into little groups, began sidling for their horses. Abd watched them, fingering his prayer beads. Catherine stood up. "It is done, then. Once more to war."

"*Kismet.* It must be *Kismet.* I have not wanted this war. You know that, *Ya Habibti.*"

"Yet as it is here, my lord, you may as well undertake it with all your heart."

"And you, *Ya Habibti?*"

"You have no further use for me, my lord. You have your disciplined army. It is small, but it is as good as most regiments in the French army. It will be a core around which these others, the desert tribesmen, may operate. You have your hidden granaries that will confound and dismay the French. You have your tactics, strike and withdraw, before they can muster sufficient force to overwhelm you. I can teach you nothing now, my lord. My son is two years old. I have lost two children already. I would like to devote my time to his education, rather than to warfare. That is man's work, and I am a woman."

"A woman among men," Abd el Kader said. "Besides, *Ya Habibti,* are you not a symbol, meaning success to our arms?"

"Superstition, my lord."

"That may be. But symbols, superstitions, are necessary to make men believe in themselves. We have already suffered a grave defeat in this war."

"My lord? No shot has yet been fired."

"Indeed not. But the new French commander in chief, Vallée, has just completed a march from Constantine to Algiers, with five thousand men."

Catherine frowned at him. "Then that is to our advantage, my lord. If he intends to concentrate upon Algiers, the rest of the country is the more exposed to our assault."

"Perhaps. But it is how he got to Algiers that is important. Have you heard of the Iron Gates?"

"Yes, my lord. It is a mountain pass."

Abd nodded. "So narrow, so precipitous, that it is written in legend that any army passing between those walls will be crushed out of existence, as the walls move inwards."

"Again, superstition, my lord."

"Perhaps, *Ya Habibti.* But a superstition that has been believed for two thousand years. Even the Romans preferred to take the longer route round than risk themselves within the Iron Gates. But Vallée has taken five thousand men through there. My spies tell me his musicians have already composed a tune, called *La Marche des Portes du Fer,* to celebrate his triumph. When the news of this reaches the tribes, they will be afraid."

"My lord . . ." She licked her lips.

"And do you know who guided Vallée, *Ya Habibti*?"

She stared at him in horror. "No, my lord," she lied. "How can I know?"

"It was your husband, Baroness. While he fights for the French, I need you at my side."

Chapter 13

〰〰〰〰〰〰〰〰 SMOKE, rising slowly into the desert air, mushrooming as it reached the high altitudes, drifting downwind, a pall for all to see, for all to shudder at.

Were I a Catholic I could cross myself, Catherine thought. *Were I a Moslem, I could get down from my saddle and kneel to the east, and pray to Allah for guidance. But I am a godless woman, a creature of destruction, a legend of death. So I sit my saddle, and watch the smoke, knowing what it must mean.*

She glanced at David. There was her only comfort. And stretched out her hand to touch his, to watch the tight muscles at his jaw slowly relax as he looked at her, and then turn away again to watch the horseman galloping towards the red and white banner.

"Tagdempt is no more, oh lord. It is destroyed. Every building. Every stone. Every dog."

"And my people?"

"There are dead men, my lord. But no women, and no children."

"May Allah be praised. They have escaped to the hills." Abd touched his horse with his heel, rode forward. His entourage followed, as they had followed him for a year,

371

up and down the desert, through a dozen desperate skirmishes in which French columns had been cut to pieces, away from every superior French concentration. Catherine's strategy had filled its purpose. The French could claim no victories. But neither could the Arabs, and meanwhile Buguead's men burned and slaughtered. Even the dogs.

They looked down on the rubble that had been the Emir's last city. Tagdempt was where she had come, often enough at his side, to oversee the munitions factory. She would not come here again.

But the city was not smoking. The spiralling black came from the hills immediately behind the town. Abd turned his horse and rode towards them, towards his skirmishers, who had suddenly set up a great wailing. And Catherine's heart constricted with horror as she understood what they were saying. The women and children had not escaped to the hills; they had taken refuge in the caves at the foot. And the French had assembled rubbish and brushwood, and set it alight, allowing the breeze to take the suffocating smoke into the confined passageways. It was a mass grave, of fifteen hundred women and children. It was warfare on a new and unsuspected level of depravity.

"The prisoners," Abd said. "How many have we?"

"There are thirty-two," said Sidi Mohammed.

"Cut off their heads," Abd commanded. "Stick them on stakes, around the entrance."

"My lord," Catherine protested. "You cannot."

"Will you enter that cavern, Baroness?"

"No, my lord. But to fight barbarism with barbarism is surely wrong. You are honoured for your humanity. My lord . . ."

"This is honour, Baroness? They will fight me with terror. I will reply with terror. Cut off their heads." He wheeled his horse and rode away from Tagdempt.

"The infidels approach, lord." The Bedouin sweated, as did his horse. The obvious excitement of the animal set all the others, even Monroe, to prancing.

"Are they many?"

"Yes, lord. Four, five thousand of them, with cannon. But, my lord . . ." the man hesitated.

"Well?" asked Sidi Mohammed.

"I saw no baggage train, lord. No wagons."

"Are you sure? They are three days from Mascara."

"I watched for some time, lord."

Abd looked at Catherine. "Can you explain this?"

"I would have to see for myself, my lord."

"Five thousand," Abd mused. "You would not have us attack so large a force?"

"No, my lord."

"But suppose they have lost their baggage train?" Sidi Mohammed asked. "Suppose there was a storm, or some other mishap, and they are staggering through the desert, weak with hunger and thirst? It would be an opportunity for a great victory."

"Indeed, my lord," Catherine agreed.

"But you do not think they have lost their baggage train," Abd said, half to himself. "Yet how may an army advance across the desert, without food, without munitions?"

"Let me see them," she said again.

He nodded, gave his orders. The Bedouins prepared to pitch camp, in the valley behind them. The *smala* was five miles away, secure in another valley, for how could they leave their women and children in their homes, in safety, when there was no longer any safety in their homes? No longer any homes. When Abd went forward he was accompanied only by his brother, Catherine and David, Ben Fakha, and half a dozen outriders, together with the scout to guide them. They rode across the desert, winding their way between the dunes. It was still early in the morning, and quite cool. But soon it would be very hot indeed. And supposing the French had, mysteriously, managed to lose their baggage train . . . as Sidi Mohammed had suggested, it could be a massacre. Another massacre. *My God,* she thought. *Where will it end? Where can it end? What do they want?*

All of North Africa, to be sure.

The scout had come to a halt, and they reined their horses. Abd el Kader beckoned Catherine, and they rode forward together, topped the next rise, looked down on the desert below, and on a *ouadi,* winding its way through the sand, fringed in the near distance by bushes and stunted trees.

"That is one of our granaries," Catherine said.

"Aye." Abd el Kader was peering through his glass. Now he handed it to her without a word.

She took it, heart thumping, levelled it at the desert beyond the *ouadi.* The French force was marked by the dust pall, but it was moving slowly, and it was possible to make out the men themselves. Foot soldiers, only fringed with cavalry, plodding across the sand. No baggage train, but each man carried a heavy pack, and the caissons for the artillery were also larger than usual. And even the uniforms were different from those she was used to. Gone were the high shakoes and the stiff collars that kept a man's neck swimming in sweat. These men wore light caps, with cloth kerchiefs, it seemed, attached and hanging down behind to protect their necks from the sun, while the collars were soft and unfastened. Buguead had been thinking about campaigning in the desert.

Catherine lowered the glass. "They are carrying the necessary food and ammunition on their backs."

Abd nodded. "They seek to match our mobility. But that is not important. Look in front of the main body."

Catherine focussed again, frowning; and made out the long line of soldiers, spread out in front of the column as they approached the *ouadi.* There must have been several hundred of them, she estimated, walking across the desert at ten-foot intervals, like the most extended order of all marches, and armed not with rifles but with long poles, which they drove deep into the sand at every step. It was a tedious, and no doubt exhausting process, and accounted for the slowness with which the entire column moved.

She lowered the glass. "I do not understand. Do they seek water?"

374

"They can see the *ouadi, Ya Habibti;* they know there will be water, there. They seek our granary."

"Oh, my God," Catherine said, raising her glass again.

"And they will find it," Abd said. "There is a brain at French headquarters who knows the desert, who has thought about it, who has reasoned with your mind, *Ya Habibti.*"

She gazed at him. "Ricimer?"

"It has to be." He turned his horse. "We must march. I had planned to reprovision from that granary. Now our people will go hungry. But there is another forty miles from here. We will make for that."

"My lord," she said, and stopped, biting her lip.

He twisted in the saddle to look at her.

"The French will find that one also, my lord," she said. "Once they know that any *ouadi* may conceal our stores, they will explore every one. My lord, you have no cities. Your entire nation is concentrated in the *smala.* There must be sixty, seventy thousand souls there. Would you have them starve?"

"What would you have me do, *Ya Habibti?* I cannot conjure manna from heaven, like Moses."

"My lord . . . " She sucked air into her lungs. "We are defeated, my lord. This war is lost. My lord, I am guilty of deception. I thought I could teach you to wage war forever, as my people would have done against the British. But North America is a land of flowing streams, deep forests filled with abundant game, where ten thousand men may lie concealed. And the British were themselves divided as to whether or not they would pursue their conquest. Even with all our advantages, it is improbable we would have won our war had they pressed home with all the power, and all the determination they used against the French a few years later. And even more, my lord, would we have secured our independence had not the French and the Dutch and the Spanish come to our aid? My lord, I had supposed, I had hoped, that the French were but embarking upon an adventure, for political stature, perhaps, to enable their people to regain some of the glories they had enjoyed under Napoleon. My lord, I now see they are intent on conquest. Whereas we have no friends, our people are being whittled away, our civilisation is dying . . ."

"You would have me surrender." He spoke softly.

"Even Bonaparte surrendered in the end, my lord. When it was clear he could go no longer."

He pulled his beard, walked his horse away from her, checked again. "When that moment comes, *Ya Habibti,* I will surrender. But it is not yet here. You have made a good point. We have no friends, but that is careless on the part of our friends. For if the French do indeed mean to conquer all of North Africa, then we are merely the first to be destroyed. Morocco will be next."

"You have appealed to Abd er Rahman before, my lord."

"I have written him letters, sent him ambassadors. This time I shall visit him in person."

"You, my lord? But . . ."

"I risk nothing. He may be reluctant to support me, but he hates the French. He will not betray me."

"Then let me come with you, my lord."

His turn to hesitate. Then he smiled at her. "You are sure this advice, to surrender, is not given because you are weary of this life?"

Her chin came up. "I am weary of this life, my lord. I have now spent ten years in this desert. That is a long time, for one who was not born to it. I grieve for the children I have lost, I fear for the child I still possess. But I shall not desert your cause, until you ask me to leave."

He nodded. "A jest, *Ya Habibti.* But it will be a long and difficult journey. Stay with your son. And your lover. Stay with the *smala* and give them hope. Bou Hamidi will command in my absence. He is the best of my generals. But I will return soon enough."

"A toast." David raised his mug of mare's milk. "To us."

"There is a dismal prospect." But she drank, anyway.

"Why is that? We have each other. We have Omar. We have the sun and the moon, the sky above and the

376

earth below. And we have sufficient to eat, for the present, at least. And we have our health."

"And your optimism." She smiled as she said it, and he put down his mug to clap his hands.

"There is something you should practice more often, my sweet. Your smile is unlike any others. A thing of utter joy. And recently you have kept it too well concealed. But you will smile again. This is a special occasion. The sixth of March, 1841."

"Why is it special?"

"It is the anniversary of our first meeting. Do you not remember? In Chantilly? You came crashing down the slope on your toboggan, and I was hiding behind the fence, watching you. And falling in love with you."

"My God," she said. "Thirteen years. On my next birthday I shall be thirty. My God."

"A good age, thirty. You are more beautiful now than then."

"And considerably more haunted." She got up, walked away from the fire, arms folded across her chest. It was late in the evening; Omar had been asleep for several hours. As were most of the inhabitants of the *smala*. And yet it *seethed,* with noise, murmured voices, snores, cries in the night; with the barking of the dogs. And it stank; there was no sanitation, no water for washing. The *ouadi* they had chosen for this encampment had been drunk dry on the first night, and tomorrow they must resume their weary trek. *They were no longer an army,* she thought bitterly. *They were a moving nation, a refugee nation, in their own homeland.*

She stood on the edge of the last circle of tents, the infantry tents—for they clung to her plans, even if they no longer meant anything—and gazed into the night. There was no moon, and the desert was black and silent. But out here the air was clean. And she could hear David behind her.

"You take too much responsibility upon your shoulders," he said, linking his arm with hers.

"And do I not have responsibility?"

"No longer. These people came to you, and said, *Give*

377

us the benefit of your knowledge. You have done that. Without your advice they would have been defeated long ago. But if the French are too strong for you, then they *are* too strong for you. Believe me, we Poles have a long experience of what it is like to live next to an overwhelming power."

She found a rock and sat on it. "And us?"

"We are alive, my dearest girl. Nothing else matters. So long as we love each other."

She took him into her arms, slipped from the rock to the ground, kissed his nose and his eyes and his cheeks and his lips, reached down to roll up his *haik* even as he did the same for her, held his penis and enjoyed his hands between her legs, then coming up to caress her breasts. *Perhaps he was right,* she thought, as he came inside. *Could a woman ask for any more happiness than to lie in the arms of her lover? Did it matter whether it was on the sand of the desert or between the satin sheets of a four-poster bed? Did it matter if she had no perfume, if her hair was undressed, if her clothes were unwashed? Did the future matter? So long as the present came along, day after day after day?*

The orgasms came quickly, and within seconds of each other. They made love like children, discovering each other for the first time, for all that they had lived together as man and wife for more than four years. He adored her body, every inch of it, just as he adored his new found freedom to command that body, to caress it and to kiss it and to explore it as he chose. He never tired of it.

And she enjoyed his explorations, as she had taught him most of them herself. *Perhaps,* she thought, as his weight slipped from her chest and his head rested on her shoulder, *perhaps every woman should be placed in a harem for a year, at sixteen, should be given over to eunuchs and whoremasters like Ricimer, should be taught to extract the utmost from her physical feelings.* Because then she had been given the opportunity to be happy, providing her mind could be similarly educated and released. To be happy no matter what happened, where she was. To be happy even if she was alone, but to know ecstasy could she discover herself with a loving man. And at the end of it all, what more was there to be sought in life? Could chests of gold, strings of pearls, diamond rings, equal the touch of a man's hand? Could crates of wine, tables laden with succulent food, mansions filled with exquisite furniture, equal the pleasure at holding a child in your arms, and knowing that its father sat beside you?

Then what of the women and children lying suffocated in the cave outside Tagdempt? The French prisoners whose heads adorned the ground beyond? *They* had not been guilty, at least of *that* crime. But they had suffered, because the crime had been committed. The whole desert was burning, with a desperate hatred, a cruelty it had never known before. Because it had been at war too long.

Which only made moments of happiness like these the more to be treasured.

She slept, on the floor of the desert with David in her arms, and awoke, still in darkness, to a sudden drumming of hooves, a sudden shrieking of voices, a sudden explosion of pistols and muskets. A sudden awareness of disaster.

The French had discovered the *smala*.

The thundering of hooves overlaid the night, obliterating all the other tumultuous sounds in the menace of their echoing power. And now there came the blast of a bugle call, well calculated to send terror through the minds of the sleepy Bedouins.

David rolled over, taking Catherine with him, seeking the shelter of the rocks beneath which they had lain. The charging cavalry were very close, sabres drawn, horses foaming. And now they crashed into the tents, scattering camel hair and animals and men and poles and stakes, screaming their triumph, making the night groan with calamity.

"Omar." Catherine rose to her knees.

"You'll be killed." David grasped her arm.

"Would I live, with him dead?" She pulled herself away, reached her feet, then sank back to her knees as she recognised Yusuf, riding in the moonlight at the head of his men, lean face glowing with the urge to destroy, looking from left to right, but fortunately not seeing her.

She closed her eyes, heart seeming to slow as that night in the *ouadi,* so many years ago, came back to her. The night she had killed, the night she had been taken by a savage who sought her still. She opened her eyes, and he was gone, but still the horsemen flooded by. There must be several hundred of them, she supposed. Yet her brain still worked, still assured her this could be no more than a raid. Even several hundred horsemen could not destroy a *smala* of seventy thousand people.

And now they were also gone, into the tents, cutting and thrusting and firing their pistols, shrieking their vengeance into the darkness, yet being swallowed by the gigantic wail of terror that arose from the shocked Arabs. Catherine ran into the tents, tripped over a fallen pole and landed beside a dead man, staring sightlessly up at the invisible heaven. One of her hands had landed in his blood. She gave a gasp of horror and regained her feet, gathering her *haik* almost around her waist to free her legs, raced through the tents, tripping again, scrambling back to her feet, jostling with other women, with terrified children, with desperate men firing their muskets without any target at which to aim, with roaring camels and squealing goats, with neighing horses and barking dogs, with all the endless racket of the *smala* doubled and redoubled in their seething fear.

And reached the inner circle of tents in a long gasp. Dust eddied, men lay dead, her own tent had collapsed around its pole. Desperately she dropped to her hands and knees, burrowed inside, panting for breath, oblivious to the cacophony around her, listening only for the one sound she wished to hear above all others, and giving her own shriek of joy as she heard the disturbed whimpering of her son.

"Omar." She pulled him clear of the camel hair, hugged him in her arms. "Omar."

"Mama? Mama?" He blinked at her. "Mama, the French."

"Have gone." David stood at her shoulder. He must have run behind her through the camp.

"Destroyed," wailed Bou Hamidi, tearing at his beard. "We are destroyed."

"They have gone," Catherine said, rising to her feet, Omar still clutched in her arms. "It was only a raid."

"But their army will be close," Bou Hamidi said. "Cavalry do not march by themselves."

"Then are we fortunate that they charged on their own," David pointed out. "Had we been surprised by the French army, we *would* have been destroyed."

"But what are we to do?" Bou Hamidi wailed, still plucking at his beard. He looked around the circle of *kaids*. "What are we to do?"

His morale was too shattered for reason. Perhaps the French charge had not thrown away a decisive victory, after all, Catherine realised. A demoralised *smala* was no enemy at all. In that brief few moments Abd el Kader's army had been done irreparable harm. She could hear their defeat wailing through the night.

"They will desert," Sidi Mohammed said. "Our people will melt away, just as soon as they can collect their senses. My brother told them the *smala* was safe."

They were looking at her. In Abd el Kader's absence there was nowhere else for them to look. She sighed, and hugged Omar against her chest. "We cannot stay here, and be slaughtered," she said. "We cannot fight, at this moment. And if the French army is out there we cannot fight in any event. We must find shelter wherever we can." She pointed. "It is fifty miles to the Moroccan border. We must anticipate our lord's success in his negotiations."

Like Abd el Kader, Abd er Rahman was a small man, with a pointed beard. But he lacked the Emir's obvious integrity, obvious nobility. His gaze seemed to strip Catherine, and although this day she wore her green riding habit, with a white scarf, and her black beaver, yet those brittle eyes took her all the way back to her first day in

Algiers, when Selim the eunuch and then Hussein bin Hassan had inspected her.

"The Baroness Ricimer." The Sultan's voice was soft. "I have heard much of you, lady. Your name circulates around every campfire."

She curtsied, head bent low.

"And this, my lord Emir, is your army?" Abd er Rahman surveyed the *smala,* scattered over several miles, disorganised, noisy, odorous. His general, El Guenaoui, smiled.

"My people met with catastrophe, but two weeks gone, Highness," Abd said.

"Tragic," remarked the Sultan. "I have heard naught but ill news of your people, my lord Emir. Is it not true the French have taken Tenes, your very last seaport?"

"That is true, Highness."

"And is it not true that the Ben-Angad have surrendered to Buguead, and many others?"

"That is true, Highness."

"And now it is said that Buguead has proclaimed the war to be at an end. Well, no doubt that is also true, as his war is with Abd el Kader, and Abd el Kader is now in Morocco."

"The war will never end, Highness," Abd said. "We will fight the French as long as there is one of us with red blood in our veins. We but ask the assistance I have already requested. Arms and ammunition, and a place of refuge while we regroup our people."

"And will the French not follow you into Morocco?" the Sultan inquired, gently enough.

"Highness, they will follow us into Morocco whether you shelter us or not. Their aim is the conquest of all North Africa."

"Should one Frenchman cross that river Islay," declared El Guenaoui, "we shall crush him into the sand. We are men."

Certainly, Catherine thought, *they made a splendid enough sight.* The Moroccan *spahis* carried lances as well as muskets, and wore red jackets embroidered with gold lace, and scarlet fezzes.

"Of course we shall destroy them," Abd er Rahman agreed.

"And it is your duty to do so, Highness," Abd ventured, "as they are infidels who would desecrate our country and our people."

Oh, dear, Catherine thought. *That was tactless.* Abd er Rahman was frowning.

"I am no *marabout,* my lord Emir. My father was Sultan, as was his father before him, and his before that, back into the shades of antiquity. But I know my duty. You will learn of my decision. For the time, this valley is yours to command." He stepped forward, and Catherine began another curtsey, but instead had her hand seized, and kissed in a perfectly European fashion. "Baroness, I am your slave." He looked past her, and she knew he inspected David. Then he turned away and walked to his horse, where a slave waited to assist him into the saddle.

El Guenaoui bowed, and followed his master. Abd el Kader watched him go. "To this we are reduced," he said softly. "Begging air to breathe from dogs."

"My lord . . ."

He turned abruptly. "I would speak with you, *Ya Habibti.* Alone."

Catherine glanced at David, who nodded. She followed the Emir. Ben Fakha held open the flap of his *douar.* Abd sat on his divan, motioned her beside him. She took off her hat, laid it on the ground, released her scarf to allow her neck to sweat.

"Was it terrible?" He took coffee from Ben Fakha's tray.

"Because it happened, my lord. The fact, not the event."

He nodded. "Can you not find a name for me, *Ya Habibti?* You are not my slave, that you should lick my feet."

"My lord, I . . ." She smiled. "Forgive me. Were I to call you anything, it would have to be *Ya Aslanam,* with your permission."

His turn to smile. "My lion. I like that. *Ya Habibti, Ya Aslanam.* I am honoured. Do you know, *Ya Habibti,* that had you consented to marry me, that day, I would have surrendered by now. I would have allowed myself to be imprisoned forever in some tiny cell, supposing only I could have you at my side."

"My lord . . ."

"*Ya Aslanam*," he corrected, gently. "Thus I am grateful to you for refusing me. For reminding me of my duty. And yet, *Ya Habibti,* whatever a man may feel for a woman whom he can never possess, that I feel for you. I have only realised it these last months, when we have been separated."

She felt tears gathering in her eyes. He was undoubtedly the greatest man she had ever known, or would ever know, she supposed. And he would know how to love. When he looked at her like that she was almost ready to surrender, to say, *Well, possess me anyway.*

He continued to smile at her. "But we have a duty, you and I, *Ya Habibti*. We work in harness, and that is our reward. Such as it is. I will not pretend I am happy to be in Morocco. I do not trust Abd er Rahman. In my despair I have written to the Queen of England, asking her assistance. I pointed out that the French were intent on conquering all North Africa, that it could not be in British interests to have the Mediterranean, where Nelson fought, become a French lake. And I have received no reply. So then I even wrote the Sultan in Constantinople, offering to acknowledge him once more as our lord in the Regency, in return for some military assistance. And have received no reply. The entire world has turned its back on us."

"Save for Abd er Rahman," she pointed out.

"For the time being, to be sure. We must hope that Buguead is impetuous, and sends his *spahis* across the border to seek us out. Then, who knows?" He looked up as the flap to the *douar* was lifted; it was not Ben Fakha, but another of the many Negro slaves who haunted the *smala*. "I did not send for you, fellow."

"But I have been sent to you, Abd el Kader," the slave said, and his right arm, which had been hidden behind his back, now came round the front to reveal that he held a pistol. Catherine gave a shriek and hurtled herself forward, in front of the Emir, and received a most tremendous jolt that seemed to knock her sideways. She was aware of lying on the ground, of smelling gunpowder, of hearing an army of voices and of being assailed by an army of hands. Yet for the moment, to her surprise, she felt no pain.

And then she saw Abd el Kader, kneeling beside her. "*Ya Habibti*," he said. "*Ya Habibti*. Would you have given your life for mine?"

"*Ya Aslanam*," she whispered. "Are you safe?"

"Oh, I am safe enough. You took the bullet. But you also will be safe, once we extract the lead. It is lodged in your shoulder. You will be safe, *Ya Habibti*. I swear it. And your assailant is dead. I killed him myself."

"But . . ." She licked her lips. How thirsty she was.

Abd el Kader's face was solemn. "Aye," he said. "We will never know who sent him: The French, or Abd er Rahman."

I will be well. Abd el Kader had promised her, and he would keep his word. Thus she must be equally determined. For during the long months she lay in her divan, or in her litter as the *smala* travelled, she sometimes thought she would never recover her health.

The bullet was extracted without too much difficulty, though with an enormous amount of pain that had her weeping through clenched teeth and tight closed eyes, while she squeezed David's hand for all it was worth. But then a fever set in, and there was increasing risk of an infection that might well develop into gangrene. In her weak state of health movement was purgatory, it was necessary, as the *smala* drank *ouadi* after *ouadi* dry. Abd had to create a special police force to patrol the water holes and endeavour to insure that everyone obtained his or her fair share of the precious liquid. But even so there were daily reports of men, or women, or children, found dead of thirst.

Perhaps, she thought, *it was her knowledge of the destitution to which the Emir and his people had been*

*reduced that robbed her of the mental strength to fight
against her illness.* All around her were the usual noises
of the *smala,* but they were seldom happy noises. And
every day more and more of the Bedouins packed up
their tents and stole away with their women and their
goats and their camels and their mares, seeking the
freedom of the desert life from which they had been
taken.

David did his best to be cheerful. He sketched away
and brought his work to show her, while Omar played on
the ground by the divan. She supposed they were as
completely married as it was possible to be. But if the
Bedouins considered themselves to be exiled, merely by
having crossed the Islay River, what must she consider
them, she wondered?

"We are soldiers of fortune," David insisted. "Is that not
a romantic consideration?"

"But where will it end?" she said, half to herself. "I
am afraid we shall lay our bones to rest in this ghastly
place."

"Not yet, sweetheart. There is news. The French have
demanded the surrender of Abd el Kader, and the Sultan
has refused. So there will be conflict. Indeed, I believe a
French squadron has bombarded Tangier."

"Then I must get well," she said, attempting to raise
herself on her elbow.

He kissed her on the forehead and gently forced her
back on to the divan. "You will get well, if you will but be
patient," he promised her.

Abd el Kader confirmed the news a few days later,
when he returned from a visit to the Moroccan army,
which was encamped not fifty miles away. "War has been
declared," he said, "and Buguead is on the march. Sixteen thousand men, I believe, including four thousand
cavalry."

"My God," she said. "With what can we oppose them?"

He shrugged. "The Sultan is as confident as ever. He
commands forty-five thousand men. Or at least, his son
Moulay Mohammed commands them, with El Guenaoui
at his side. It will be quite a battle."

386

"They will oppose the French on an open field?" She was aghast.

"At odds of three to one, surely that is the right thing to do. And the field will not be so open, as they are entrenching themselves along the banks of the river itself, and the French will have to attack them across the water. I would say there is every chance of a Moorish victory, and think what that could mean to us, *Ya Habibti*. We know there is considerable opposition to this war in France, not only on moral grounds but because of the sheer expense of it. Now that it has spread to Morocco as well, the outcry will grow. It is controlled only by the determination of Buguead himself, by his victories, by the fact that he has chased me out of the Regency. But should he be defeated . . ." Abd el Kader sighed. "It goes against my instinct to have others fight my battles for me."

"You will not be there?"

"Oh, I will be there, *Ya Habibti*. But as an observer. Moulay Mohammed does not require Bedouin assistance. He says."

"Then I must be there too." She made herself sit up.

"You are still too weak, *Ya Habibti*. I forbid it."

"I can travel in a litter, if I must," she said. "My lord, *Ya Aslanam,* I have fought at your side for too long not to be present at what may prove the saving battle of our cause. You will not forbid me that."

He smiled, and took her hand to kiss the fingers. "So thin," he said. "You look like a young girl, all over again, *Ya Habibti*. No, I could not refuse you. I would feel uneasy were you not at my side. We will ride together. It may be for the last time."

Forty-five thousand men. Certainly Abd el Kader had never commanded such an army. There were foot soldiers and horsemen and even a camel corps. And they were well positioned. The Islay could be forded only in this one place, where the river bed had eaten its way down between high bluffs on the Moroccan side, and here the infantry were lying in wait, some twenty thousand of them, to destroy the French as they sought to cross. While when the infidels had broken, the twenty thousand horse waited to chase them from the field, lances poised, swords loosed in their scabbards, *fezzes* gleaming with gold lace.

"A handsome sight," Abd confessed.

Moulay Mohammed smiled at the small band of Bedouins, with their threadbare *haiks* and *burnouses,* their lustreless weapons. "It is the finest army in all Africa," he declared. "Perhaps in all the world. This day, my lord Emir, you will see the end of French ambitions. Baroness, I have heard you have military knowledge. Can you fault my dispositions?"

He was a handsome, cocksure youth. Far too young, indeed, to have had any previous experience of warfare. The position must have been chosen by El Guenaoui.

"No, my lord prince," she agreed. "Today will be famous in the annals of Moroccan history."

"Indeed," he agreed. "My lord Emir, I should be obliged if you and the Baroness would ride with my staff. And your servant, also, Baroness. He is a draughtsman, is he not? He can draw me a picture of this victory."

Catherine glanced at David, who merely smiled and inclined his head. She touched Monroe with her heels and moved forward beside Abd el Kader and Sidi Mohammed and Bou Hamidi, to the hill on which the green and gold Moroccan standard fluttered, and where El Guenaoui waited with his staff.

"Look there," said the general, and Catherine gazed across the river at the column of men. Abd gave her a glass, and she could make out the blue jackets with the white cross belts over the deep red pantaloons of the line infantry; their shakoes had red pompoms that nodded in unison as they marched. No desert undress here; these men had come prepared for battle. The infantry formed the centre, with the artillery lumbering behind, but to either side there was a mass of cavalry, somewhat in advance of the infantry, and these were curassiers, breast-plates reflecting the rays of the sun, burnished helmets gleaming.

388

"A pretty sight," Moulay Mohammed remarked. "Sixteen thousand men. Bah. But is that not an unusual formation for an army on the march, El Guenaoui?"

"It is, my lord prince."

"It is his order of battle," Abd el Kader said, quietly. "It makes me think of . . . of the head of a boar. Those cavalry brigades are the tusks."

"Ha ha," shouted Moulay Mohammed, flushed with excitement. "Then we shall hunt the boar. Oh, it will be sport." He clapped his hands in joy, while Catherine caught her breath in a mixture of admiration and dismay. Those men were her enemies. They would cut off her head could they catch her. But they were the people among whom she had spent her youth, and they were magnificent. They came on without a pause, and now the watchers on the hill could even hear the distant beat of the drum, marking the time. And they were indeed marching in order of battle, for as they reached the water the whole army plunged in without hesitation, the cavalry forging ahead of the infantry, swimming their horses towards the farther bank.

"Shoot them down," Moulay Mohammed screamed, rising in his stirrups. "Shoot them down."

El Guenaoui gave the signal and the bugle blasted forth. Black smoke rose from the bluffs, and was followed by the reverberations of the musketry. The river seemed to come to seething life, and she watched blue-coated infantry slumping into the water, to drift away from their companions like the petals of a flower, shaken by the wind and dropping into a garden pool. She found herself clutching her throat in horror.

And then releasing herself with a gasp. For still in the middle of the stream, the French infantry had formed line, and returned fire. The crash was perfectly timed, perfectly delivered. Catherine could not see the Moroccan forces on the bank, but she could hear the sudden wail of consternation. Moulay Mohammed settled back into his saddle. "Get down there," he snapped. "See what has happened."

El Guenaoui saluted, and galloped down the hill, followed by his staff.

"Look there," Abd said, and they turned their glasses to watch the left wing of the French cavalry forming rank on the Moroccan side of the river.

"They at the least will be destroyed," Moulay said, and nodded to his bugler. The notes rang out, and the Moroccan cavalry began to move forward. Twenty thousand men. Catherine caught her breath in anticipated horror; the French brigade could hardly number more than two thousand. But they were already trotting, their officers out in front, the brilliant sunlight flashing from their swords.

David was sketching away with his pencil. Abd and his brother and his general watched in rapt delight. Catherine could hardly breathe. The curassiers were now at full gallop, hooves scarce seeming to touch the ground, dust powdering away behind them to form a pall over the river. The Moroccans were still at the canter, but they too were almost lost to sight beneath the enormous dust cloud. The clash was clearly audible, a gigantic explosion of metal upon metal, of human voices screaming at once defiance and fear and agony, of squealing, neighing horses, of obliterating dust, and suddenly of fleeing Moors, urging their horses in every possible direction, intent only on escaping the slashing sabres of the French. Catherine looked at Moulay Mohammed. He scarce seemed to be breathing, and his face had turned a deep red as he stared at his stricken cavalry. But there was a drumming of hooves closer at hand. El Guenaoui came to a halt beside his prince in a flurry of dust and sweat and foam.

"They have broken, my lord prince," he said.

"I can see that," Moulay said.

"I mean the infantry, my lord prince. Following their volley, which killed many of our people, the French charged behind the bayonet, and our men have fled. My lord prince, you must withdraw. The battle is lost."

Moulay stared at him for some moments, then he turned to Abd el Kader.

"My lord prince . . ." Abd said, and paused as Moulay's hand came up, the finger pointing.

"We are lost," Moulay said. "And it is your doing. By the Beard of the Prophet, Abd el Kader, if your *smala* remains on Moroccan soil at this time tomorrow, my army will march upon *you*."

Now there could no longer be any denial of the simple fact that they were outlaws. The smoke rising from beyond the hill came from a pro-French *oasis,* and they had been killing their own people, less in retaliation for having sided with their enemies than simply in search of food and water. Yet Abd el Kader looked pleased enough as he led his Bedouins down the hillside towards them, shouting and firing their muskets.

"A column approaches," he said, wiping sweat from his forehead. "One of Buguead's flying columns. He grows overconfident, this Duke of Islay."

"You have not the men to risk a battle," Catherine protested. She had regained her strength, and felt indeed as strong as ever in her life. But she was so tired. It was her brain rather than her body which had suffered all of which it was capable. She had been part of a fighting army for nearly nine years. Her son was due for his circumcision ceremony on his next birthday, and he had never known anything save the unruly pandemonium of the *smala*. And he was no more than typical of a thousand other sons. It was too late, she thought, even for victory. How could these people ever again learn the arts of peace, having known nothing but war for so long?

"Not on open ground," Abd agreed. "But it may be possible to trap them, if they move sufficiently far from the reach of their comrades." He frowned at her. "You do not approve?"

"What will it serve, *Ya Aslanam*?" She asked. "Had we not better make our way into the desert, and try to make a kingdom there? What will it serve?"

"And I had supposed you well again, *Ya Habibti*. Whereas I now see you are still sick at heart. A victory, over Buguead, may still turn the French away from continuing this war. They have forgotten Abd el Kader. They think I am dead, or gone into hiding. They have forgotten *Ya Habibti*, who rides at my side with her white hair flowing in the breeze. Well, we shall remind them. There are five hundred men in that column. It is too small to defeat us, if we are careful, but it is big enough to make France rue the day she interfered with our lives, can it be destroyed. Is not the ravine of Sidi Brahim only ten miles away? It could be Macta Gorge over again. These French commanders, they envy Yusuf, who destroyed the *smala*. They would wish to do so again. Well, suppose they came upon the *smala* encamped in the ravine."

Catherine sighed, and then shrugged, and nodded. "It could be a victory, *Ya Aslanam*. Providing they will fall into your trap."

"They found the *smala* once before. It is likely they will do so again. Whether they will risk an attack on it . . ." He shrugged. "We will have to wait, and hope. But you wish no part in it."

"I am a woman, *Ya Aslanam*. I wish no more part in bloodshed. I gave you what I could, of my knowledge. Because I dreamed, with you, of victory. Now you have fought the French for fourteen years, and I have been at your side for nine. Now I wish only to be a wife and mother."

He frowned at her for a moment, and then smiled. "You shall be those things, *Ya Habibti*, in an Algiers which is at peace. And this victory will bring us to that happy day. But I will not have you take part, if it is against your wish."

"I will remain with the *smala*."

He shook his head. "No. There is danger. I would not risk a hair of your head, *Ya Habibti*. Bou Hamidi."

The *kaid* rode out to join them.

"You will select twelve men, good men, Bou Hamidi, to escort the Baroness Ricimer and her son. Take them over the hills, to the tomb of Sidi Brahim. They will be safe there, and when this victory is won, we will send for her."

Bou Hamidi saluted.

"But . . ." Catherine bit her lip. She did *not* wish to see this battle. She did *not* wish to travel with the *smala*, as a bait for a trap. She remembered Yusuf's charge too vividly. But how could she desert them now?

"It is best," David agreed. "The Emir is right. You are not yet fully restored to health, however much you think you are. It will only be for a little while."

"And you?"

He leaned from his saddle to kiss her on the nose. "I will be with him. It would make a change to sketch an Arab victory."

Still she hesitated, watched Omar riding out from the tents on his donkey, escorted by a Bedouin warrior.

"It is best," Abd el Kader said. "Besides . . ." He smiled. "It is an order, *Ya Habibti*." He wheeled his horse and cantered off, followed by his brother and David and his staff, and immediately all was confusion as the tents were struck and the *smala* prepared to move.

"We must make haste, lady," said the captain of her escort.

She nodded, turned her own horse, waited for Omar to come beside her.

"Where are we going, Mama?"

"To a place where we may rest for a day or two," she said.

"But Mama, I have heard there is going to be a battle, that the French are going to be beat. I should like to see that, Mama. Could I not stay with Papa?"

She shook her head. "Time to be with Papa when you are older, at least in battle." Because there would always be battles, endless battles, taking their toll of the Bedouin young. And Omar? No doubt he would grow up to be a *kaid*, and a commander of horse, and in time be as famous as his mother.

The little party rode out of the valley and into the next. The tomb of Sidi Brahim was not far, and they would make it by dusk. And tomorrow, if they listened carefully, they would hear the sounds of the French being massacred in the ravine that bore the name of the saint, supposing the French fell into the trap.

They topped a hill, rode down into the next valley, turned into the next, and found themselves face to face with a squadron of *spahis,* riding under the tricolour of France. Catherine drew rein and felt her heart crashing down to the very pit of her belly. For even at a distance she recognised both of the officers who walked their horses in front of their men: One was Yusuf, and the other was Kurt Ricimer.

Chapter 14

CATHERINE sucked air into her lungs. "Ride," she shouted. "Ride," she screamed, her voice seeming to crack. She wrenched her horse's head round, watched the Arabs scattering for the hills. Omar hesitated, and she struck her crop across the rump of his animal, sending it too careering for shelter, while behind her there came the cracks of several muskets, and she saw one of her escort tumble from the saddle.

But instantly Yusuf shouted, "Cease firing. I wish that woman alive."

"Oh, God," she whispered, bending low over her horse's neck, urging him to greater speed, aware she was not going to escape. Only she, because only she did they wish to capture.

She rode Monroe up the slope, looked down on the next valley, on the Arab horsemen speeding away from their unpleasant surprise, glanced over her shoulder, panting for breath, and felt her blood seem to coagulate as she saw three of the *spahis* within thirty feet of her. She turned Monroe again, away from them, kicked him in the ribs, and lurched with him as he lost his footing and went down on his forelegs. Before she could stop herself she had slid over his head to land on her own hands and knees with a jolt that knocked all the breath from her body, had her hat falling off and rolling across the sand.

Slowly she regained her feet, as did Monroe, looking apologetically at her. But there would be no point in attempting to remount. She was entirely surrounded by *spahis*. And at least Omar was certain to escape. And tell Abd el Kader what had happened.

She panted, and watched her captors part, to allow Yusuf through. He dismounted, his face breaking into that ghastly smile she remembered so well, even from ten years past. "The Baroness Ricimer," he said, and walked slowly towards her. "By all that is holy. How I have dreamed of you, Baroness. How I have dreamed of listening to your screams. And do you know, I thought to myself, ah, bah, even if I ever do capture her, she will be an old woman, wrinkled and haglike. The girl I knew will no longer exist. But you are more beautiful than ever, *Ya Habibti*. Truly is this my lucky day."

He stood immediately in front of her, and she licked her lips while she felt her knees touch and sweat trickled down her shoulders. Yusuf stretched out his hand, held her chin between his fingers. "There are so many things I wish to do to you, Baroness, I hardly know where to begin. But it had better be where we left off, I think. Sergeant . . ." He never took his gaze from her face. "We will pitch camp."

"She is my wife, Colonel."

Catherine's head jerked. She had not noticed her husband's approach, so taken up had she been with the man facing her.

"She is a murderess and a wanted rebel," Yusuf said, still gazing at her. "She will be treated as such."

"She is still my wife." Ricimer dismounted. "And I retain all the privileges of a husband, until she is condemned by a court."

Catherine turned her head to look at him. But why look at him, when she could look at Yusuf? There was no difference, save that Ricimer's expression was even more terrible. Both looked older than she remembered them.

There were traces of grey in Ricimer's hair, and she realised he must be over fifty. Both men had driven her to ecstasy, in the past. But she knew better than to suppose any ecstasy was going to be *hers,* on this occasion. So then, should she lie down and weep before them? Go to her fate, whether it be rape or execution, in fear and trembling? She was *Ya Habibti.* She was a legend. No matter what was about to happen to her, it must happen to the legend, not the woman.

She inhaled. "And how are my children, Kurt?"

A first victory. He was taken by surprise, glanced at Yusuf, and had the grace to flush.

"Ah, she does not lack courage," Yusuf said. "Nor, I suspect, venom. Hell hath no fury, eh? But more from a woman who has lost her children, than from one merely scorned. We shall have sport, Ricimer. Together. Come now, is that not a fair offer?"

"And after?"

Yusuf smiled, and once again Catherine's knees touched. "You are wondering what she might say to Colonel Montagnac? I am wondering if so famous a woman as the Baroness Ricimer, so fearless a desert warrior, might not fight us to the last ounce of blood in her body, might not in fact, effect her escape, during interrogation, you understand, and be shot by an overzealous sentry. Then we can cut off her head, and take it to the Colonel, and earn ourselves a great reward. Tell me true, Ricimer, have you never wished to *hurt* your wife?"

Ricimer gazed at the major for a moment, then his head turned back to look at Catherine, and she could feel the blood draining from her face.

"Aye," Ricimer said. "I have always wished to hurt her, Yusuf. But now . . ." He licked his lips.

"Then why let us waste time? Our tents are pitched." He gave a mock bow. "Baroness, will you not accompany us, to your death?"

Oh, God, she thought. *What am I to do?* But what could she do? She looked left and right. The *spahis* were going about the business of pitching camp, but they were watching her, surreptitiously and salaciously. There was no help there. There was no help anywhere. Save from her own brain. But her brain seemed paralysed.

"Or would you rather be dragged," Ricimer said. He flicked the scarf at her neck. "That would spoil your habit."

She made herself move, walked between them towards the tent.

"You should have died, in Mascara," Ricimer said. "All those years ago, you should have died. Why did you not die?"

She controlled her breathing with an effort. His voice was perfectly matter of fact. She must match him at that, at the least. Was she not the Ice Maiden?

"You forgot Jean-Pierre," she said. "He released me."

"Jean-Pierre," he said, half to himself. "Indeed, I had forgotten Jean-Pierre."

"We killed *him,* at least," Yusuf remarked, and held the flap of the tent for her, almost like a gentleman. "After you, Baroness."

She hesitated, then ducked her head, put up her hand to hold her hat in place and remembered it had fallen from her head. But there might be weapons in the tent. She might be able to seize a sword and turn on them, and at least force them to kill her, quickly.

There were no weapons in the tent. She sank to her knees, resting her bottom on the heels of her boots, and waited. She listened to them enter, watched the sunlight dim as the flap was returned to place.

"A gag, you think?" Ricimer asked.

"Why should she not scream?" Yusuf asked. "I have always wanted to hear her scream."

Why should I not scream, she thought? *Why should I not scream now, instead of waiting for them to hurt me?* She wanted to scream now.

But in any event, she would not have to wait very long. Ricimer was stroking her hair, scooping it away from her neck, gathering it into a ball, and releasing it again. Like a child with a toy. *Let me think,* she thought. *But do not let me think, or I will know too well what is happening to me.*

"We should like you to undress, Baroness," Yusuf said. "Take your time."

He sat before her, cross-legged, as he had that day in the *ouadi*.

"You'll not forget she is *my* wife," Ricimer said.

Was that a hope, a chance?

Yusuf shrugged. "You may enter first, if you wish. We will not kill her until we are both satisfied."

That was no chance.

"We are waiting, Baroness," Yusuf said.

At least she could die, as she would suffer, with dignity. She stood up, and her head brushed the roof of the tent. Ricimer was also kneeling now, at her feet. She reached behind her, unfastened her habit, shrugged it forward from her shoulders, allowed it to settle around her ankles. Her heart was pounding so hard it seemed to obliterate everything else in the tent. The blood pounding through her brain made thought impossible.

Ricimer leaned forward to touch the scar on her shoulder. "You have been wounded."

"Some years ago," she said. "By an assassin's bullet."

She stepped out of her shift—she wore no other underclothes in the heat of the desert—sat down to pull off her boots.

"We will do that for you," Ricimer said, and seized her right ankle.

Yusuf gave a laugh and took her left ankle. *They mean to tear me in two,* she thought desperately. Her legs were extended, so hard that she fell over and bumped her head on the ground, and realised she still wore her scarf. She reached up to release it, and discovered her feet were free. But she was not free. Ricimer lay on his stomach beside her, kissing her mouth and her eyes and her chin, *knowing* her as he loved to do, while his hands moved down to find her belly, and there to encounter Yusuf, who was kissing her pubes. Her knees started to come up and she forced them flat again. That would only make them hurt her. If only she could think.

Ricimer lay on her belly, sucking at her lips as he entered her, careless now of whether or not she was ready, sending rivers of pain away from her groin, only to meet rivers of desire flowing down from her breasts, because there Yusuf was, chewing and sucking on a nipple. *Like an animal*, she thought. *They are animals. I am taken by animals, who when they are done will cut off my head.*

And it was coming closer. They did not speak, but rather grunted like the savages they were. And now Yusuf, having observed Ricimer's ejaculation—she had not noticed it, had merely felt his body bumping on hers—was pushing him to one side and making his own entry. *Oh, God Almighty*, she thought, gazing at the roof of the tent. *I could be pregnant.* And she was feeling passion. The sucking of her breasts always gave her passion. She was wet, at once from Ricimer and herself, and Yusuf had given her an orgasm last time they had lain on the floor of a tent.

Yusuf was there, and Yusuf was climaxing, and he was giving her an orgasm. Even as she resisted the very thought of it, as her mind cried out in horror, she felt it building, knew it was irresistible, knew that it had to happen, felt her arms wrapping themselves about Ricimer's neck . . . Ricimer's neck? She dug her fingernails into his shoulders and allowed herself a wail of mingled pain and pleasure, and could hear again, the absolute quiet of the tent.

And could think again. How clear her brain was suddenly become. The Ice Maiden. She needed only the catalyst of a sexual explosion to turn her into the valkyrie she wished to be.

Yusuf rose to his knees, looked down at her. "There is a woman," he said, to no one in particular. "I think we should cut off her head, slowly. She gives too much pleasure. I must see her die, horribly, or I will be haunted by her."

"Do as you wish," Ricimer said, rolling away from her. "I do not wish to see her again."

Quickly, she thought. *Be quick.* She sat up, scooped sweat-stuck hair from her forehead. "Are you not interested in why I should be riding, alone with an escort of twelve men, in the desert?"

Ricimer's turn to sit up, and Yusuf's to frown.

"I would bargain for my life," she said.

"You?" Yusuf said. "Aye, you would, if you could."

"I ride at Abd el Kader's side," she said. "This is well known. Where I am, Abd el Kader is never far distant. Would you forego the chance of capturing the Emir?"

They peered at her, and began reaching for their clothes. "Well, then," Ricimer said. "Tell us where he may be found."

She tossed her head. "It would do you no good. What, eighty *spahis*?"

"There are sufficient of us, within reach," Yusuf said. "I think you are prevaricating."

"Take me to those others," she said. "I will tell what I have to say to your commander."

The two men exchanged glances.

"She is a devil from hell," Yusuf said. "She merely wishes to accuse us of rape. And Montagnac is a confoundedly honourable fellow."

Ricimer chewed his lip. "To capture Abd el Kader . . ."

"He has Sidi Mohammed and Bou Hamidi with him," Catherine said.

Yusuf's turn to chew his lip.

"I will say nothing of this . . . this affair," she said. "I swear it. I am condemned to death. I cannot escape you. I wish only to save my life. Imprison me, lock me up for the rest of my life. I do not wish to die. I will give you Abd el Kader."

Yusuf smiled. "They said she was of great courage, great stature. This *Ya Habibti* of yours is naught but a frightened woman."

Catherine licked her lips, stared at Ricimer. His was the decision.

"Should your information be false," he said, "even Montagnac will give you to us, again."

"I will show you the *smala* of Abd el Kader," she said. "I swear this upon my mother's grave."

* * *

They watched her dress, like tigers overseeing their meal being prepared. She allowed them what they wanted, being careful about settling her shift, sitting down to roll on her stockings and lace her boots, fastening her habit with great care, fluffing out her hair, and combing it with her fingers. They were hers now. Even if she died for it, and she did not suppose there was much doubt of that, she would see them perish with her. Her brain was an ice-cold fury of anger and revenge. And she would not have had it any other way; their rape of her had been necessary, to reawaken the hatred that had almost dissipated itself over ten years of campaigning.

Yusuf held the tent flap for her, and she inclined her head to him as she stepped outside, to blink in the sudden glare. Monroe waited for her, and the rest of the troop also stood to their horses. She mounted, Yusuf to one side and Ricimer to the other, and Yusuf gave the order. She wondered if Omar and the guard had yet regained the *smala,* what Abd's reaction would be. She prayed he would not lose his head, would proceed with his plan. But he would know she had been taken. David would know she had been taken. And yet, surely they would suppose they knew enough about French character to be sure she would not be harmed until after a formal trial.

The troop rode down a narrow ravine and came upon a picket of four soldiers and a sergeant. Beyond lay the French camp, and Catherine's practiced eye found it a simple matter to approximate the number, perhaps three hundred, she estimated, to which must be added the eighty cavalry of Yusuf's patrol. Four hundred men. She could not believe it. They had to have disobeyed Buguead's express commands that small flying columns were too vulnerable to attack. Or the French had entirely dismissed Abd el Kader from their minds as a possible threat.

A group of officers waited for them under the tricolour. "Any news, Colonel?" The commanding colonel was grey-haired and dignified in appearance, and had a kindly face. And she must send him to his death, along with her enemies. But he was also her enemy. He would cut off her head.

"The best, Colonel." Yusuf dismounted. "A prisoner. And what a prisoner."

A lieutenant assisted Catherine from the saddle, and the colonel saluted.

"Madame?" He seemed to notice the colour of her hair, the pale green of her habit, for the first time, glanced at Ricimer. "But it cannot be."

"My wife, Colonel," Ricimer said. "After all these years."

The colonel flushed. "Madame," he said. "Colonel Montagnac, of the Chasseurs d'Orléans, at your service. But you understand that there is a warrant out for your arrest."

Catherine licked her lips. "I understand, Colonel."

The colonel sighed. "And you understand the charges, madame?"

Catherine allowed herself to glance at Yusuf. "I understand them, Colonel. But this gentleman gave me to understand . . ."

Yusuf smiled. "She wishes to bargain her friends for her life."

The colonel frowned. "You will lead us to Abd el Kader?"

"If you will save my head, Colonel." How distant seemed her voice over the drumming in her ears. But it was a calm voice, as ever.

The colonel glanced at his officers. "Well . . ." He hesitated. "I will confess, madame, that you are not entirely the heroine I had been led to expect. But I am engaged upon a war, not a sentimental symposium. Where is your lord?"

"Do you have a map?"

One was hastily spread on the ground, and Catherine knelt. Montagnac knelt also. His shoulder brushed hers, and he moved as if stung. Catherine prodded the stiff paper. "The *smala* is encamped in the ravine of Sidi Brahim. There. You will see it has but a single entrance. Once you occupy that, you have them at your mercy. They know nothing of your presence in this district, and those of my escort who escaped will report only the squadron of *spahis*. But of course there will be sentries posted. You will need care."

Montagnac studied the map for some moments, then raised his head. "It will be dark in two hours. We will march then, and fall upon them at dawn. Dutertre, alert the men. Major Coste, you and Captain Gereaux will remain here with a hundred men. Major Cognord, you will command the infantry, Colonel Yusuf, you will command the cavalry." He stood up. "This is a great opportunity vouchsafed to us, gentlemen. Let us not waste it."

Catherine remained kneeling. "And I, Colonel?"

"Will remain here, under guard, madame. Should your people not be in that ravine, I will have you condemned at a drumhead court-martial and executed on my return."

"And if they are where I say they are?"

"Then I will intercede with the Duke for clemency on your behalf, madame. And leave you to your own conscience." He turned to Ricimer. "Will you ride with me, Baron?"

Ricimer shook his head. "I have brought you this far, Colonel, and delivered your enemies into your hands, as I always said I would. Now I would like permission to remain with my wife." He smiled at Catherine. "Ten years is such a long time."

"There will be a tent for you, madame," Major Coste said. "With a sentry outside."

"Thank you, sir." She glanced at Ricimer. "I would prefer to sleep alone."

"My dearest Catherine," Ricimer pointed out. "I am your husband."

She continued to address the major. "It will be rape, Major Coste," she said. "My husband deserted me ten years ago. He can have no rights."

Coste nodded. She had already formed an opinion that he did not exactly care for Ricimer. "I think madame is entirely correct, monsieur," he said. "In the circumstances."

Ricimer gazed at him for a moment, then shrugged and walked away.

"A detestable fellow," Coste observed. "I will protect you from him, madame, but you understand that you are an enemy of France, one over whose head a death sentence hangs."

"And one who has betrayed those who trusted her," she said, softly. "To preserve her own life." She smiled at him. "Do you not condemn me for that also, Major?"

Coste's turn to shrug. "I am not in possession of all the necessary facts, madame. Not even the certain knowledge of how I would act in similar circumstances. But I also find it difficult to admire you as I should. Will you dine with Captain Gereaux and myself? I am afraid Baron Ricimer will also be present."

Catherine shook her head. "In the circumstances, Major, I would prefer to act the prisoner I am, and dine alone."

He clicked his heels, inclined his head. "As madame wishes."

The flap of the tent dropped into place, and she was alone, and could kneel, and bow her head, and remember, and anticipate. But she did not wish to think at all. She had gambled, and lost. No matter what happened at Sidi Brahim, she was firmly in French hands and it was unlikely they would let her go.

An orderly brought her food and wine, and she ate slowly, drank deeply. Once again she had not tasted wine for a very long time, and how she wanted to become drunk. But there was not sufficient for that.

She lay down without undressing, felt the tears running down her face. *I will not even have the satisfaction of seeing Ricimer die,* she thought. *No doubt he will visit me in my prison cell, to taunt me. No doubt he shall bring my children, to add their condemnation to that of the world.*

Then what of Omar? Oh my God, what of Omar? She did not even know if he had regained the *smala*, and if he had regained the *smala* whether he would survive the French attack. Yusuf had destroyed it once before, and with fewer men than he now possessed.

She sat up, realised that she must have slept, that the first fingers of dawn were creeping under the skirts of the tent, and that there was the sound of gunfire in the distance. Rolling volleys, one after the other, seeping through the dawn. And bustle in the camp.

She got up, opened the flap, gazed at the back of her sentry. "What is happening?"

"We are engaged, madame, listen."

She looked past him, at men falling in, still rubbing sleep from their eyes. And at others, being placed in defensive positions among the boulders which littered the ravine. And at Major Coste, mounting his horse.

"Let me out, please," she begged. "I can hardly run away."

The sentry hesitated, and then presented arms. She hurried towards the flag.

"Ah, madame," Coste said, saluting. He was already mounted. "You hear the sounds of battle, no doubt. I go to their support. With half my force. Captain Gereaux will command here."

Catherine glanced at the captain, a somewhat small, swarthy man with a dark moustache. Ricimer stood beside him.

"I have given Captain Gereaux the necessary instructions for your safety, madame. Now you will excuse me." He rose in his stirrups. "Chasseurs d'Orléans, forward."

The infantry marched at the trot, rifles carried in their right hands. They jogged along the ravine and disappeared from sight. The sound of firing had momentarily died.

Captain Gereaux took his cap and wiped his head with his kerchief. "We can do no more than wait," he said. "Madame, I must ask you to return to your tent. We have enough to consider without you."

She walked away from them. Had there been a messenger, or had Coste acted on his own initiative? If he had, it must have been because he had concluded, from the sounds of the firing, that the battle was not going well. But in that case he had made a considerable mistake. There were only fifty men left in this camp. And Abd would know where to find them.

The flap dropped into place behind her, and she discovered that her heart was pounding and that she was sweating; and the morning was still cool. There was nothing to do but wait, as Gereaux had said.

The flap raised, and she gazed at Ricimer. She rose to her knees, found her back against the canvas.

He smiled, came inside. "There is no need to look so terrified, *Ya Habibti,* or so vituperative." He sat down, cross-legged.

"I was promised immunity from you," she said.

"Oh, I shall not touch you, much as I would like to. But Gereaux is more a man after my own heart. He hardly sees the beautiful woman. He sees only the renegade who has caused the death of so many gallant Frenchmen. Why, were I to assault you I doubt he would raise a finger to help you."

"And you think I would not tell the colonel, this time?"

Ricimer continued to smile. "I doubt he would believe you. But as I say, I am not here to assault you. I merely wish to be with you, to look at you, to talk to you, to act the husband. I have missed you, you know. I have often thought, how much better it would have been to have taken you along, if only that I might have been able to whip you every day. I would have enjoyed that."

Her muscles were tight. She had to relax them with an effort. "And I would surely have found a way to kill you," she said.

He nodded. "I am sure you would have tried, from time to time, which would have allowed me to beat you the more. But . . ." He cocked his head. The firing had almost entirely ceased, but now there came the drumming of hooves. "A messenger."

He stepped outside, and Catherine crawled to the doorway of the tent to look out, and to clasp her hands round her throat with horror. A single horseman had galloped into the camp, and brought his exhausted mount to a standstill. The animal was streaked with dust and foam and blood, but it was in far better shape than its rider. He had lost his cap, and received a sabre cut across the head, a flap of skin hung over one eye and blood poured down the lefthand side of his face. His collar was opened and there was blood on his jacket as well. He had lost his lance and his musket, but still carried a bloodstained sword, drooping from his right hand.

The men, and almost the entire force left in the camp had abandoned their posts to surround him, stared at him in horror. "What has happened?" shouted Captain Gereaux. "In the name of God, man, what has happened?"

The trooper attempted to straighten himself in the saddle, to regain some measure of military bearing. "All gone," he said. "All gone."

"What?" Ricimer shouted, hurrying towards him. "What do you say?"

"They are gone," the man shouted. "Destroyed. Colonel Yusuf would charge the *smala,* at the head of his *spahis.* At our head, monsieur. And as he did so a force formed in front of him. Eight hundred Arabs, monsieur. There could not have been a man less. Ten to one. They cut us to pieces. I alone survived, and returned to Colonel Montagnac with the news. He formed square, sent me to warn you."

"Then he is still fighting," Gereaux said.

"No, Captain. I drew rein at the top of a rise and saw him surrounded and overrun. There were Arabs everywhere."

"My God. Major Coste?"

"Was pinned down in the next valley. I heard the firing and rode over there too. They are lost, Captain. We are lost. All lost." He suddenly kicked his horse hard with his spurred boots. The animal gave a snort and a whinny, and rushed forward. Men scattered in every direction and the terrified horse with its distraught rider hurtled out of the camp and into the desert. His voice drifted slowly back to them. "All gone. All gone."

Lieutenant Chapdelaine saluted. "You wish me to ride after him, Captain?"

Gereaux stared at him as if he were a stranger, then turned to Ricimer. "What's to be done? They will be here, next."

"Cut off her head, for a start," Ricimer said, pointing.

They cannot, Catherine thought. *Not now. Not when it is possible for me to live again.*

"Sir, you disgust me," Gereaux said. "Chapdelaine, the map."

The lieutenant spread it on the ground. The Chasseurs leaned on their rifles, looking faithfully along the path, hopefully at their officers. And at their captive? Because they were doing that too, although with what emotion Catherine did not care to imagine. She felt weak, and her heart pounded as she listened for the clash of cymbals which would mark the advance of Abd's victorious army.

"Sixteen miles to the fortress of Djemaa-Ghazouet," Gereaux muttered. "We cannot make that before tomorrow morning."

"They will be upon us by then," Ricimer pointed out.

"Yet it is a hope," Gereaux said. "Fall the men in, Chapdelaine. No bugles. Madame, you will march with my men. Chapdelaine, we also will march. Take two men, mount them and yourself on my horse and the Baroness's horse and the Baron's horse, and ride to that high ground. You will see the Bedouins before they may close with us. Haste now."

The lieutenant saluted, mounted his scouts, and rode off. The remainder of the chasseurs had already fallen in.

"Leave the tents where they are," Gereaux commanded. "We will not need them, and cannot be encumbered with their weight. Besides, they might lead the Arabs into supposing we are still here. Chasseurs d'Orléans, *en avant*."

The infantry sloped their arms and tramped down the valley. Catherine walked between Gereaux and Ricimer, her boots crunching on the desert stones. The sun was climbing high, by now, and the heat was intense. Rivers of sweat ran down her shoulders and gathered between her breasts; she could feel her toes swimming inside her boots. And what would the heat be doing to the nearly four hundred Frenchmen who lay scattered about the ravines behind them, watched by the circling vultures? What had Yusuf thought as a lance or a bullet had brought an end to that so ambitious career? Had his last thought been of her, of lying on her belly only hours before? Had he known how she would sing with joy at the news of his death?

When next she was in a position to sing for joy.

She glanced at her companions. Gereaux's entire face was tight, teeth and jaw clenched, little bobbles of muscle forming and dissolving at the side of his lips. Whatever his pretensions, he knew he was doomed, and his men were doomed. And Ricimer? He smiled at her.

"Do not worry, *Ya Habibti,* you will die, before they cut off my head."

"You they will give to the women," she said, and had the pleasure of watching his smile die. But then it returned readily enough.

"In which case I must be sure you suffer commensurately before they take me, sweet Catherine."

She sighed, and gazed at the stones before her. What an insane conversation, in an insane place, at an insane time. But the greatest insanity of all was that it was in deadly earnest. He *did* mean to kill her, as brutally as possible. And Abd *would* give him to the Touareg women in his camp, when he learned what had happened.

"Captain Gereaux." It was the sergeant, hurrying forward, to attract his commander's attention, and point at the hills. The column halted, and Catherine watched the horsemen galloping towards her.

"The Arabs," Chapdelaine shouted as he came within earshot. "They are beyond the next rise."

"Form square," Ricimer snapped. "It is our only hope."

"Fifty men?" Gereaux demanded. "Surrounded by two thousand? We may as well blow our brains out."

"Captain." Chapdelaine panted as he drew rein immediately before them. "There is a chance. From the hilltop I saw a tomb. What the Bedouins sometimes call a *marabout,* one of those big stone buildings."

"Sidi Brahim," Catherine said, and wondered why.

"It is defensible?"

"It is better than an open desert."

410

"Then haste, haste," the captain shouted. "Chasseurs d'Orléans, at the double. Haste."

"Mount behind me, madame," Chapdelaine offered, reaching down from the saddle. Catherine glanced at Gereaux, and received a nod. She held Chapdelaine's arm and was swung on to the back of the horse. The infantry were already a hundred yards away, trotting along, rifles at the sling. Chapdelaine used his spur and sent the animal bounding forward, the other scouts at his heels. They galloped up the slope, and looked down upon a much wider valley than before, indeed it was hardly a valley at all, but a long stretch of level country. And below them at the foot of the hill was the glowing white marble of the tomb.

"We could hold that forever, would you not say, madame?" Chapdelaine inquired.

"With determination, monsieur," she agreed. "And sufficient water."

He urged his horse forward once again, rode down the slope, and was arrested by a shot. He dragged on his rein and the weary animal sank to its haunches, with the result that Catherine, equally surprised, slid over his rump and found herself standing.

Chapdelaine regained his balance, waved his scouts to halt. There was another shot from the tomb, and then another.

"Bedouins," said one of the scouts.

"How many?"

"I saw three flashes. But not together."

"We must rush them," Chapdelaine decided. "Madame, if you attempt to run off I will shoot you down. Chasseurs, follow me."

They galloped down the slope. Catherine's knees gave way and she found herself kneeling, but instantly she dragged herself back to her feet, looked left and right . . . if she could find somewhere to hide . . . she knew the Arabs could not be far off. If . . . she heard shouts behind her, and looked back to see the main body of the chasseurs topping the hill, some pointing at the tomb, others at her. She sighed, and sat down on a rock. While she lived, there was yet hope. She would accomplish nothing with a bullet in her back.

There were shots in front of her now, a sudden flurry of them, while Gereaux barked a series of orders, and the infantry formed line and fixed their bayonets. Ricimer hurried down to her.

"Trying to escape?" he inquired.

"I was left here by Lieutenant Chapdelaine," she said.

"Well, come on then. The tomb is ours."

He seized her wrist and pulled her to her feet. She tripped over a stone and nearly fell, staggered behind him down the slope towards the building. Chapdelaine stood in the doorway.

"Three Arabs, Captain. They are dead."

"Then get them outside. Corporal Lavayssiere, take a detail and locate water. Haste now. Madame, you'll accompany me." Gereaux went inside. The place smelt of age, and dust, and fear, and blood. Chapdelaine's men dragged the three dead Arabs past her. She preferred not to look at them, stared at the circular chamber; the vault was in the centre, and reached by a flight of steps leading down. There were windows, hardly more than loopholes really. And the walls were more than a foot thick. The ideal place to withstand a siege, providing there was water. But for fifty men, and one woman?

"Captain." Chapelaine spoke from the doorway, quietly enough, but with a good deal of emotion. Catherine followed the captain and Ricimer, watched the top of the hill. Several horsemen stood there looking down on the tomb. The Arabs had arrived.

Chapter 15

〰〰〰〰〰〰〰 "EVERYONE inside," Gereaux
snapped. "Lieutenant, recall those scavengers."

Chapdelaine gave a series of orders. Ricimer seized
Catherine's arm and jerked her back into the doorway of
the tomb. But she had time to see that the entire hilltop
was by now clouded with Bedouins.

"You have no chance," she said. "Your only hope is to
surrender."

"And trust you to intercede for us?"

"I will do so," she said. "If you will agree to return my
children."

He gazed at her for a moment, then glanced at
Gereaux, who had re-entered the chamber, while the door
was closed and barred. His men were already taking their
places at the loopholed windows; the room was suddenly
filled with the smell of leather and of sweat, and of fear.

"There is no water," Gereaux said in a low voice. "Save
what we have in our canteens."

"And very little food," Chapdelaine said.

"Well?" Gereaux looked at Ricimer.

"You cannot surrender," Ricimer said. "You know how
the Arabs treat their prisoners."

"That is not true," Catherine protested. "At least where the Emir commands. He is an honourable man."

"If you will believe her, you *deserve* to be cut up by the Arab women," Ricimer declared. "She is one of them. Don't you know that? She will take a knife herself."

Gereaux chewed his lip. "There must be two thousand of them," he muttered. "The situation is hopeless."

"Listen," Ricimer said, "Barral. Was not Colonel Barral due to reach Djemaa-Ghazouet today? Was not the very fact that he was coming with a relief of a thousand men the reason for Montagnac embarking on this absurd adventure? He suspected *he* was about to be relieved as well."

"You supported his plan, Baron," Chapdelaine protested.

"I agreed to guide him," Ricimer insisted. "I told him I knew it was against the Duke's express orders. And does that matter, now? Barral. He will be at the fort by now. He will know we have left in pursuit of the *smala*. He will surely come to our support."

Gereaux pulled his nose.

"Captain." Corporal Lavayssiere stood to attention. "There is a flag of truce."

"A trick," Ricimer said.

"Perhaps not. Open the door, Corporal." He glanced around him. "Lieutenant, you had best take the Baroness down into the tomb itself."

"And make sure she is bound hand and foot," Ricimer said.

"Oh, come now," Gereaux protested. "If madame will give us her word . . ."

"You'd be a fool to accept it," Ricimer said.

Gereaux looked at Catherine.

"I will escape if I can, Captain," she said.

Gereaux hesitated, then shrugged and turned away.

"If madame will accompany me," Lieutenant Chapdelaine said. His cheeks were pink and he covered his embarrassment by tugging on his moustache.

Catherine went down the marble stairs into the chamber of the tomb; the coffin itself occupied the centre of the floor, standing like a sarcophagus on a raised plinth. She reached the floor beside it, and waited, discovered that Chapdelaine was accompanied by one of the chasseurs, who carried two belts.

"If madame will sit down," Chapdelaine invited, clearly embarrassed even more.

Catherine obeyed, sitting on the floor, which was surprisingly cool, with her back against the plinth.

"You understand that I regret this necessity, madame," the lieutenant explained.

"Of course." Her heart seemed to have slowed. Abd had come for her. It was only a matter of surviving until he reached her. She could hear the shouted words from above her.

"I speak for the Emir." The voice belonged to Bou Hamidi. "He wishes to know if you possess the Baroness Ricimer."

Chapdelaine, nervously folding back her skirt to expose her boots, raised his head also to listen.

"We do," Gereaux called.

"And she is alive and well?"

"She is."

Chapdelaine bit his lip, and then commenced unlacing her boots.

"Then the Emir calls upon you to surrender," Bou Hamidi said, "and save your lives. Your comrades are all dead, or prisoners. There are more French prisoners in our camp than you have soldiers in that tomb. Surrender. Deliver the Baroness to us safe and well, and the Emir promises you your lives. Should you defy us, then your comrades will die, and you will die. Where is the value of this?"

There was a brief silence, so far as Catherine could make out; no doubt Gereaux was conferring with Ricimer. Chapdelaine eased her boot from her foot, gazed reflectively at her toes.

"I apologise, monsieur," she said. "They have spent too long in these boots."

"They are still beautiful, madame," he said, and turned his attention to the other.

415

"Tell your master," Captain Gereaux called, "that the Chasseurs d'Orléans die, but they do not surrender. If he would have the Baroness Ricimer returned to him, then let him set his prisoners free and withdraw his people. Once we have regained the fortress of Djemaa-Ghazouet, then she will be released."

Chapdelaine drew off the second boot.

"The Emir will never trust you to do that," Catherine said. "Especially as he will have been told my husband is with you. For that matter, I would not trust you myself. You have signed your own death warrants."

Chapdelaine sighed. "And yours, madame."

She listened, while the strap was placed about her ankles and drawn tight. There was another short silence from above her, no doubt while Gereaux's reply was relayed to the Emir. Chapdelaine gently pulled her arms behind her back, and secured her wrists; she heard a voice speaking in good French.

"You are right, Gereaux. Do not surrender. Do not . . ."

It ended in a gasp.

"Oh, my God," she whispered.

Chapdelaine got to his feet, gazed up the steps. The men at the windows were muttering to each other, shifting and stamping their feet. Then she heard the clang of the door being closed, and watched Gereaux come to the top of the steps. His face was harder than she would have thought possible.

"That voice you no doubt heard, madame, belongs to Adjutant Dutertre. Your Emir sent him out to tell us to surrender, and when he encouraged us to resist, the Arabs killed him, and cut off his head. Now tell me, madame, why I should not throw out your head, to them?"

Catherine felt her muscles tense, and her stomach seemed to turn over, but she refused to allow them the pleasure of seeing her fear. Ricimer stood behind Gereaux.

"No doubt the Emir supposes you have already done that," she said. "As you would not use my life to save yours."

"Ha," Gereaux said.

"Surely we must preserve some difference between ourselves and the savages, Captain," Chapdelaine said.

"If they are savages," Catherine said, "then you have made them so."

Gereaux gazed at her for some seconds, then jerked his head at the sound of a shot. "To your posts," he snapped, and a moment later the firing had become general, although the French, anxious to conserve their ammunition, replied only when they actually saw a target.

The noise was tremendous, the explosion of the muskets within the tomb echoing like cannon shots, while the clumps of the bullets biting into the stone made it seem that a giant was standing outside armed with an axe. Then the interior of the building slowly filled with black smoke, and inevitably one of the Frenchmen was eventually hit and lay on the floor, close to the steps, Catherine estimated, gasping and groaning.

Her own situation was very little better. The stone on which she sat seemed to grow harder every moment, while her hands and feet slowly lost all feeling, no matter how she wriggled her toes and fingers. Her throat was dry and her belly was beginning to rumble, but it was not until dusk that Chapdelaine brought her a piece of biscuit and a half cup of water.

By then the firing had died down, and the wounded had been attended to, but the tomb remained a place of restless sound and seeping odours.

And Ricimer. He sat at the top of the steps and looked down at her. "I wonder you waste the food and water, Chapdelaine," he remarked. "Whatever eventually happens to us, she dies."

Chapdelaine ignored him. Catherine licked her lips. "He will not be allowed to visit me during the night?" she begged.

The lieutenant shook his head. "I will see to it personally, madame." He got up, climbed the steps. "Should you descend into that vault, Baron, I will have you placed under arrest."

Ricimer merely grinned at him, and continued staring

at Catherine. She closed her eyes, and tried to compose her mind. Supposing the Arabs rushed the tomb, would the French kill her before being overrun? Chapdelaine certainly would not permit that. Ricimer just as certainly would try to do it himself. But the decision would be Gereaux's, and he she could not estimate at all.

So, then, she was close to death. But she had been close to death before. And fought against it with all the strength at her command, and survived.

She moved her numbed hands against the strap, futilely. But how she wanted to survive. Just out there were David and Omar, and Abd and Ben Fakha, and Bou Hamidi and Sidi Mohammed. The friends with whom she had lived most of her life. Her people.

But she was in here, with her enemies. With the greatest of all her enemies. Her husband.

Amazingly, she slept, but then she was exhausted. She awoke at the first chill suggestion of dawn, and discovered she had fallen over on her side; her muscles were knotted masses of cramp. And one of the lookouts was shouting.

"There. Look there."

The garrison stirred, feet clumped on the stone above her. Catherine pushed herself into a sitting position, listened to the eager talk.

"Barral. It must be Barral."

"Those are certainly horsemen."

"More than a thousand. See the dust?"

"Will the Arabs attack them?"

"Or withdraw?"

Outside the fort there was not a sound.

Chapdelaine's voice. "That body of men is not approaching, Captain."

"They *must* be able to see the tomb," Ricimer said.

"Then surely they can see the Arabs," Gereaux complained.

"Unless the Arabs have withdrawn," Ricimer suggested. "They have no stomach for fighting except at overwhelming odds."

"Withdrawn?" There was a moment's silence, and

Catherine could imagine him chewing his lip. Then he spoke with sudden decision. "We must communicate with them. I need a volunteer."

"I will go." Chapdelaine's voice was eager.

"No. You are my deputy, and who knows what will happen?" There was another brief silence, and Catherine could picture them both looking at Ricimer.

"I volunteer, my Captain." A voice she did not recognise.

"You are a hero, Private Blain. And will be recognised as one, I promise you. Now, take one of the horses, and ride like the wind for that column. Like the wind, now."

"I will fetch them, Captain."

She listened to the stamping of hooves as the horse was made ready, wondered if it was Monroe, heard the clang of the door being opened. A welcome breath of fresh air even reached her in the vault.

"Like the wind," Gereaux shouted, and the hooves suddenly thundered on the desert.

To be followed a moment later by a burst of firing. The sounds of the shots echoed in the morning, and slowly died. Inside the tomb there was utter silence.

"They will have heard the shots," Chapdelaine said at last. "He did not die in vain."

"Then why are they not turning this way?" Gereaux demanded. "This was your idea, Baron. You supposed the Arabs had withdrawn."

"It had to be tried," Ricimer protested. "Would you have sat here and watched Barral march by?"

"Is he not doing that?" Gereaux demanded. "And I have sent a man to his death."

"We are all going to our deaths," Ricimer said. "Perhaps Blain was the lucky one."

The morning descended once again into silence. The chasseurs changed guard, or sat around the upper level of the tomb, smoking and gossiping. Chapdelaine and Gereaux appeared to spend some time together conferring—Catherine could hear their voices murmuring, close above where she sat. But she did not hear Ricimer's voice, so it seemed they were not taking him into their confidence.

And even the muttered conversations died as the morning drew on, and became increasingly hot, and the defenders of the tomb became increasingly thirsty. There was little shooting. If the Arabs had *not* withdrawn, they seemed content to wait. And Barral had marched on, if the dust cloud had been Barral, into the desert, looking for men who to all intents and purposes were already dead.

She was left to herself, save for two visits from Chapdelaine, with biscuits and half-cups of water. He smiled at her, and she attempted to smile back. Her discomfort was intense, the soreness of her back, the cramp in her hands and feet, the misery in her brain, the physical agony from thirst and growing hunger all coming together in a cloud of despair that was increased by the sweat that seemed to form a separate layer between her gown and her flesh.

And throughout the day there was hardly a sound from without the tomb. Roughly every hour a shot was fired, to go crunching into the ancient marble. Abd was letting hunger and thirst gain his victory for him, without sacrificing lives. With reason. By dusk several of the chasseurs were clearly close to collapse.

The end was coming. By tomorrow morning, Catherine reckoned. And for her? She began to feel almost confident again as the heat began to leave the air. Clearly the main reason he was not launching an assault was his fear the French would promptly kill her. But if they were forced to surrender, common sense suggested they would attempt to use her to bargain for their lives. And Abd would accept that, she was sure. Tomorrow. Despite her discomfort she managed to fall asleep again, to awake with a start, in utter darkness, at the feel of a man beside her. Her eyes flopped open, and she stared at Ricimer, dimly visible in the gloom.

She opened her mouth to scream, and his fingers closed on her throat. She endeavoured to shut her mouth

420

again, and he drove his other fist into her belly, sending a balloon of pain bursting away from her stomach, emptying all the breath from her lungs in an explosion that forced her mouth open again; instantly Ricimer's fingers were pushing a folded piece of cloth inside, her own scarf, trapping her tongue, leaving her able to do nothing more than gurgle.

She felt exhausted, and slumped back against the side of the tomb. She felt Ricimer's breath on her cheek. "We are going to die," he whispered. "But you will not be there to see it. You are going to die first. You are going to die so horribly that your Emir and that artist scoundrel will go mad at the thought of it."

She sucked air through her nostrils, carefully. She was afraid of choking on the scarf in her mouth. She tried to lift her heels to drum them on the floor, but her bare feet would make no sound, and now he was kneeling across her, reaching behind her to release the neck of her habit.

She attempted to roll, and he closed his knees on her thighs, holding her steady while he pulled the habit free and over her shoulders, using his fingers to burst the straps of her shift and pulling that down as well to expose her breasts.

She gasped and moved her head, to and fro, desperately trying to expel the scarf, but without success, and now he was caressing her right breast, holding it from underneath, as he had always known she liked, stroking the aureole and the nipple to bring it hard, and sending, despite her frantic disgust, trickles of passion through her chest and down to her groin.

He smiled at her. "That was always your favourite sport, eh *Ya Habibti*. But now I'm going to cut it off."

Her eyes widened in sheer horror, and she felt as if he had hit her again. For the fingers were gone, and a moment later she saw the faint gleam of a knife.

He tested it with his thumb. "Will it be sharp enough, do you think? There's a lot of flesh." He held the breast again, lifting it away from her chest. She felt herself choking with terror, with anticipated pain, with an unutterable despair that she should have survived so much throughout her life, to die in the end in such a ghastly fashion. And heard the crunch of boots above her.

"Baron? What are you doing?" It was Captain Gereaux.

The knife had disappeared. "Ten years, Captain. It is too long for a man to be separated from his wife."

"Hm," said the captain. *He cannot mean to abandon me,* Catherine thought. "You will have to contain yourself, Baron. It would be a poor example to the men. Besides, Chapdelaine has conceived a plan."

The feet started down the stairs, and Ricimer hastily pulled the scarf from her mouth. She licked her lips, slowly, wondered if she should endeavour to accuse him. But the two French officers were clearly too preoccupied even to notice her torn clothing.

"If we remain here we are lost," Chapdelaine whispered. "Agreed?"

"The last of the food is gone," Gereaux whispered.

"I understand the situation," Ricimer said. "But what would you do? Die in some futile charge? Those of us who were not killed outright would have an unhappy time."

"We have been observing the enemy," Chapdelaine explained. "All yesterday, and during tonight. Their shots have come from four separate positions, evenly spaced about us. And now their campfires appear to be in those same positions." He paused, expectantly.

"So?"

"Lieutenant Chapdelaine is of the opinion that the main Arab force has been withdrawn," Gereaux said. "After all, if there is no water to be found here, there can be none in the desert either."

"I think we are contained by four outposts, no more," Chapdelaine said.

"That is quite possible," Ricimer agreed. "But each outpost no doubt includes more men than our entire command."

"Surprise," Gereaux said. "It is a chance. A slender chance, but our only one."

"If we could break through one of the outposts," Chapdelaine explained. "As quietly as possible, we could then march on Djemaa-Ghazouet. It is only twelve miles from this tomb, according to our map."

"Do you not suppose, even if you manage to overrun one outpost, the main body of the Arabs will not soon catch up with you?"

"Of course. In which case we must endeavour to hold them off until we at the least come within earshot of the fort."

"I think you are mad," Ricimer declared. "If you plan to march on Djemaa-Ghazouet, holding off the Arabs over twelve miles, then we should have done so two days ago, while our people were still fresh, instead of taking shelter in this hole."

Gereaux sighed. "You are right, of course. Then we trusted in Barral. But in our present circumstances, to stay here and die is less acceptable than at least to make a grasp at freedom."

Ricimer appeared to consider. "And the woman? My wife?"

"She will accompany us. When the Bedouins see her in our midst they will be less anxious to overrun us and risk her life. I see her as our trump card."

"Then she should be gagged," Ricimer said, "or she will certainly cry out and warn the outpost you choose to attack."

"There is a good point," Chapdelaine agreed. "You will excuse us, madame, but you understand our necessity."

"Wait," she said. "Wait. He . . ." But her jaw was already gripped by Ricimer's fingers, and Chapdelaine was himself thrusting the scarf inside.

"The moment we are out in the desert you will be released, madame," Gereaux said. "You have my word as a gentleman. Now, let us be at it."

"Now?" Ricimer asked.

"The hour before dawn. There cannot be a better. Baron, I leave your wife in your care."

"Mmmmmmm," Catherine screamed, shaking her head to and fro. But the noise was hardly audible, and Ricimer was releasing the strap holding her ankle.

"You will survive a while longer, *Ya Habibti*," he whispered. "But you wish to bear in mind that I will kill you before I die myself. I have sworn this."

She gazed at him, eyes wide, attempting to control the racing of her brain, as he dragged her boots over her feet, laced them. They had not noticed her disarranged clothing. Surely they would notice it when it became light. She allowed herself to be helped to her feet, found she could not stand as there was no feeling in her ankles, and sank to her knees. Ricimer gave a grunt of annoyance and heaved her up again, pulling her up the steps.

Where the chasseurs were being marshalled by their officers.

"The moon has set," Gereaux said. "It will never be darker than this. Leave the two horses. They will only give us away."

"And remember, no firing," Chapdelaine insisted.

"Cold steel will settle this day. And was not cold steel always the French soldiers' best weapon? Victory or death, my children."

"Victory, or death," said Corporal Lavayssiere.

Oh, my God, Catherine thought. *Oh, my God.* Always in the past she had been an observer, a planner, never an actual participant. Now she was being forced to take part in a suicidal assault against a determined enemy. Her confidence of a few hours before had quite disappeared. Whatever happened, she seemed certain to be killed. And she could not make a sound, could not even move a muscle save for her aching feet, so tightly was Ricimer holding her.

The door was opened, and the chasseurs filed out, each man with his bayonet already fixed, while Chapdelaine and Gereaux had drawn their swords, and Ricimer had unsheathed his sword stick.

"There," Gereaux pointed due north, and the little band stole across the darkened desert. Catherine found herself creeping at Ricimer's side, heart pounding, breath clouding against the scarf round her mouth. She could only attempt to feel, attempt to think through the coming

424

minutes, at the end of which she would either be alive or be dead.

Except that it was the coming hours, not the coming minutes.

There was a startled exclamation from immediately in front of them; the advance party had stumbled upon a sleepy sentry. The man's grunt became a shout that ended in a wail as a bayonet was driven into his belly. The chasseurs charged forward as Gereaux waved his sword, and although they were her enemies Catherine could not help but admire at once their elan and their faultless discipline, for not a man uttered a sound.

In contrast to the Arabs, who reached for their firearms and discharged them without any attempt at taking aim, who leapt to their feet with screams of mingled fear and anger, and of pain as the chasseurs crashed into their midst.

"Down," Ricimer snapped, pressing on her shoulders. Her knees gave way, and she knelt in the shelter of a rock, Ricimer at her side, while around her the darkness became a bedlam of snarling men, crashing steel, and groaning agony. But it was over surprisingly quickly, and she discovered Chapdelaine standing beside her.

"You may get up again, Baron," he said with thinly disguised contempt. "They have fled. The way to Djemaa-Ghazouet is open."

Chapdelaine himself released Catherine's wrists and took the scarf from her mouth, seemed to notice for the first time that her habit was undone and gave one of his scarlet flushes. "If you will attend to your toilette, madame. We have a long way to go."

She reached behind herself to fasten the buttons, fell into the rhythm of the march. For the moment the chasseurs were elated. The Bedouins had been taken entirely by surprise and had fled in every direction. The sun was only just peeping above the horizon to bathe the desert in its enormous red glow, and the morning remained cool. And Djemaa-Ghazouet was only twelve miles away.

Only twelve miles. Walking at first was agony to her, because her feet had not yet recovered from their cramping bonds, but gradually they seemed to settle down, and allow her to observe more of what was going on around her, and to know what it must be like to belong to one of these desert columns. The heat grew rapidly, and she had no hat. She walked with her eyes squinted, felt the sweat trickling down her back, watched it darken even the blue jackets of the men in front of her. As they, she stumbled over stones and had to be helped back to her feet by Chapdelaine—the chasseurs used their muskets. Ricimer marched at the back of the party.

And like them, she stared at the brown stones, the brown rocks, the brown hills to either side. Often she had stood on those hills, looking down on the French, waiting the right moment to attack, wondering what it felt like to know that every hummock might conceal an enemy. Today she knew. And yet, for most of the morning, the hills remained empty. *Abd cannot have withdrawn altogether,* she thought.

And yet, she reasoned, *why should he not?* He had gained the victory of which he had dreamed ever since the Macta Gorge. An entire French force had been destroyed save only these fifty men. Why should he waste more lives and ammunition in seeking to annihilate them? Would it not be sounder military strategy to *let* these shattered ghosts return, to spread the news of the disaster? Especially if he supposed her dead, and how could he suppose otherwise, as the French had refused to use her to negotiate their own safety?

Gereaux held up his hand, and the weary column came to a halt. Many of the men immediately sank to their knees, to rest leaned on their muskets. Catherine found herself leaning against Chapdelaine.

"Two miles, in my estimation," Gereaux said. "There is a sixth of the distance, and it is only mid-morning. We shall sleep safe in our own beds this night, my children. Now rest, for ten minutes." His sweat-stained face broke into a smile. "And do not waste your water."

The men sat or lay on the burning sand. Catherine

released Chapdelaine and sat down herself. *And where shall I sleep tonight,* she wondered? Or shall I sleep at all? Shall I . . . The sound of the shot sounded dull in the desert, but there was nothing dull about the scream from the man sitting not six feet away. He half rose to his feet, clutching at his back, and then fell forward on to his face. Blood seeped out from beneath the blue coat.

"To arms." Gereaux was already on his feet, gazing at the mass of Arabs who rode down from the surrounding hills. Hundreds of them, thousands of them. Catherine scrambled up, identified Abd, on his black horse, identified Ben Fakha, and identified David, riding at the Emir's side. Her heart wanted to leap clear out of her throat for joy.

"We are finished," Ricimer shouted. "There is no hope. The woman must die."

The knife was already drawn from his belt, and Catherine shrank against Chapdelaine.

"No," the lieutenant shouted. "She *is* our only hope." He ripped the knife from Ricimer's hand, held Catherine's arm, pushed her forward, stood there, gazing at the approaching horde. Catherine wanted to fall. But he was determined to save the lives of his men, if possible. She could only stand there, and wait, knowing that her habit was fluttering in the breeze, that it was clearly visible.

And watching Abd wave his men to a halt. "Now march, Captain," Chapdelaine said in a low voice. "With the Baroness out in front. They'll not rush us."

Gereaux assembled his men, and Catherine was pushed to the front, to march between the two officers. Ricimer discreetly took his place in the centre. She wanted to turn her head, to look at Abd and at David once more, but she dared not; Chapdelaine's fingers ate into her arm as he urged her forward, into the desert, into the sun.

Which grew higher and hotter. She supposed if some omnipotent Force was looking down on this scene, even He would find it strange. The tiny band of blue-coated, white-trousered Frenchmen, proceeding across the brown desert, the horde of white and blue and brown and black *burnoused* horsemen who rode to either side, almost like an escort. But still riding, still waiting. For what, she wondered? Abd was faced with an impossible decision. Let the French escape? In which case she went in any event to her death. Or charge them and cut them down, as he could so easily do, and watch her be cut to pieces before his eyes. But yet he waited. For something.

A shot rang out, and one of the column gave a shriek and threw up his hands. The rest came to a halt, clutching their weapons, looking around them. Chapdelaine's fingers tightened on Catherine's arm, and he glanced at his commander. His face was pale beneath the red of his sunburn and the layer of sweat.

Gereaux attempted to lick his lips, without success. "I wondered when they would think of that," he said. "Kill her now, and they will overrun us."

"That marksman can pick us off, one by one," Chapdelaine said.

"We are wasting time," Ricimer said from behind them. "Let us die like men. But let us have the pleasure of killing her first."

Gereaux looked at the Arabs. "Two can play at that game," he decided. "Chasseurs, present, aim. Fire."

The orders were given so rapidly the Bedouins were taken by surprise. Some of them had approached to within a hundred yards of the column. Now the musketry burst upon them, and as the black smoke cleared Catherine could see at least a dozen crumpled figures on the ground, while their horses charged to and fro.

"Chasseurs, march," Gereaux commanded, and the muskets were slung as the men turned away once again. There could be no questioning their courage or their discipline. They were magnificent soldiers. But did they never question the hand Fate had given them to play, that they should be left to march across a desert, dropping with fatigue and thirst, surrounded by their enemies?

Yet for the moment they had won. The Arabs would not approach within musket range, either to shoot or to be killed. There was nothing to do but march, until, after the longest and hardest and most incredible day she had ever spent, they topped a rise and could see in the distance the palm trees of the *oasis* of Djemaa-Ghazouet. And before it, the trickling stream breaking the surface of the desert.

* * *

"Water." The whisper spread through the ranks, and suddenly became a shout. "Water." The men surged forward, forgotten energy suddenly flooding their muscles.

"Wait," Gereaux bawled, pushing the leaders back with his hands, turning to face them. "It is over a mile away. You cannot run that. And once we break ranks the Arabs will be upon us. Besides, there is the fort. Do you not suppose they can see us, as we can see them? There will be a column out to help us, soon enough. And the water will not run away. March, my children. March in step. March as French soldiers march. Keep your discipline. There will be water for all, soon enough."

The men fell back into column, muttering, but their grumbles were overlaid with optimism. They had fought their way across the desert, and safety was in sight.

Catherine glanced to right and left. She was so exhausted it was an effort even to breathe; rivers of pain ran down her legs and concentrated in her toes; her head was a mass of throbbing pain; she could feel the flesh on her cheeks burning. And still Abd waited. And David with him.

But they had waited on the water. Because now she watched a body of Arabs debouch from the main force, and ride for the *oasis,* for the stream. To cut the French off? Certainly the chasseurs thought so. They stared at the Arabs, and the muttering grew. Then one man gave a shriek, threw away his rifle, and ran for the water. Instantly another followed, and then another.

"Halt," Gereaux screamed. "Halt." He looked from right to left, desperately, realised he would not hold them, that the Arabs were poised for the kill. The first man had already plunged to the ground, shot through the head.

"Form square," Gereaux bawled, taking his position by a larger than usual boulder. "Form square. The men from the fort will soon be here. Form square."

Chapdelaine released Catherine to add his voice to his captain's. "Form square," he bawled, waving his sword. "Form . . ." The words were whipped out of his throat by the bullet that tore through his face, spinning him round and sending him crashing to the ground at Catherine's feet. For a moment she stared at him in utter incomprehension, for blood had scattered across the bodice of her habit. Then she knelt beside him. In only two days she felt she had come to know him as well as any man in her life. And to like him as much.

Someone knelt beside her; it was Corporal Lavayssiere. "He was a brave man," he said. "The bravest of the brave." He drew a knife from his pocket.

"What are you doing?" she gasped in horror.

"I wish to remember the lieutenant," he said simply, held the end of Chapdelaine's moustache, and cut it off, stuffed it into his pocket. "Supposing I survive myself."

She raised her head. The desert had suddenly turned into a seething dust cloud, a kaleidoscope of men and horses and screams and groans and yells, of sweat and blood, and of anger and of fear. Lavayssiere regained his feet, dragging her up, looked at Gereaux, lying on his back beside his lieutenant, sightless eyes staring at the sky.

"Brave men," he said again, and looked at Catherine.

She licked her lips, would not beg for her life.

The corporal smiled, and shrugged. "As you are a brave woman, Baroness. I salute you." He touched his cap, and dashed into the dust. Catherine's knees gave way, and she sank into the shelter of the rock once again, staring at Chapdelaine, for a moment unconscious of the mayhem around her, until she raised her head and saw Ricimer.

"Bitch," he snarled, crawling towards her. "But you are not going to survive, *Ya Habibti*. When they find me, they are going to find you beneath me."

Chapdelaine had fallen across his sword. There was no hope of drawing it out. But there was a pistol in his belt. She pulled it clear, levelled it, holding it in both hands, watched an almost comical expression of dismay pass over Ricimer's face, and wondered, irrelevantly, what her own face looked like as the hammer descended with a useless click; the lieutenant had never reloaded.

Ricimer smiled. "So now, *Ya Habibti* . . ." He reached for her, and was arrested by a kick on the shoulder, which sent him tumbling sideways.

"Run," David snapped. "Find Ben Fakha."

Catherine stayed on her knees, staring at him. He had pushed the *burnous* back from his face, and his hair fluttered in the breeze. He held a bloodstained *tulwar*.

Ricimer also regained his knees, his face twisted. "You'd commit murder at the end, Jew? I would have expected nothing better."

Using his foot, David pushed Chapdelaine's body over on to its side, exposing the sword. Then he stepped back.

Catherine dragged herself to her feet, found herself against the boulder. Most of the fighting had ceased, at least in their immediate vicinity. The Arabs were clustering around, and she saw Abd el Kader. But he would not interfere. He knew how important was this particular feud.

Ricimer reached for the sword, slowly, carefully. His fingers wrapped themselves around the hilt, and he drew the blade toward him, then suddenly, without giving any warning, he lunged. Catherine clasped both hands to her throat, but David had never taken his eyes from his enemy, and he parried the thrust easily enough, returning with a cut which sent Ricimer in turn scrambling backwards.

Then they were on their feet, facing each other, circling. Catherine felt a hand on her arm, and discovered that Abd el Kader had dismounted, and was now gently pulling her to the safe side of the boulder. The swords clanged as both men advanced, slithered along their lengths, and struck air. Ricimer paused for a moment, breathing deeply, then lunged again. David turned the blade but Ricimer was expecting this, and hurled his whole body forward, his left hand suddenly emerging from behind his back to show that he still held the knife. David gave a cry, and fell to one knee, blood dribbling down his side, and the Arabs gave a yell of anger.

But Abd el Kader raised his hand and they fell silent again. For David had regained his feet, and was turning to meet the next thrust. This time Ricimer was too confident of victory. He launched his entire body forward, and the blade once again seemed to be slicing through David's flesh. But he was swinging in turn, and the blade of the *tulwar* was biting into the side of Ricimer's neck, where it joined the scalp, sending him hurtling to one side, to go rolling over twice, to come to a rest by the boulder, staring upwards, while blood cascaded.

Catherine found she was again clasping her throat while she stared at him. His face twisted, almost into a smile.

"*Ya Habibti,*" he whispered, and died.

"Now, now we can plan," Abd el Kader declared. He stood in the centre of his *douar,* looked from one to the other of his *kaids,* looked at his brother, Sidi Mohammed, looked at David Mulawer, looked at the Baroness Ricimer.

The Baroness Ricimer no longer, she supposed, with a start of surprise. The dowager Baroness Ricimer; the title was now held by Gebhard, wherever he might be. So much had happened so quickly she and David had not even been able to give thought to their marriage. It had been enough to be reunited, after they had counted each other lost forever.

"More people came in every day," Abd said. "The news of Sidi Brahim has spread across all of North Africa. My agents inform me it is the talk of the moment in Paris. Four hundred and twenty men, and but sixteen regained their fortress. And of the sixteen, only the corporal, what was his name, retained a rifle."

"His name was Lavayssiere," Catherine said. "And he was a brave man."

"Yet a defeated one. No disaster on such a scale has overtaken the French army since Waterloo. Now is the moment to strike and strike again, and drive the *infidels* forever out of Algiers."

He paused, and looked from face to face, a frown slowly gathering between his eyes.

"Are these the men with whom I have fought these last fifteen years?"

Sidi Mohammed bowed his head, and glanced at Catherine.

"Well?" Abd demanded. "Will no one speak to me?"

"My lord Emir," Catherine said. *"Ya Aslanam.* As you say, we have fought for fifteen years. How different it was, then. How generous and chivalrous we all were, fifteen years ago. What are we now become? Wolves, eager to savage our enemies. When you and I were away from camp last week, twelve of the French prisoners were massacred, in cold blood. How could this happen, *Ya Aslanam?"*

"I have condemned the act," Abd protested. "I have punished the murderers."

"Yet it happened, *Ya Aslanam.* Fifteen years ago it could not have happened. And it will happen again. Your warriors are brave men, *Ya Aslanam,* but I tell you this, the French warriors are equally brave. They are disciplined, they have the resources of a great nation behind them."

"And they have been defeated," Abd said. "You would have me surrender, in the hour of victory?"

"I would have you negotiate a surrender, *Ya Aslanam,* because of that victory. The French had supposed you beaten, lost in the desert. You have proved them wrong. So you are in a position to resume the struggle, and they will surely now bring all their forces to bear upon you, to avenge Sidi Brahim. You may well fight for another fifteen years, and at the end of that time, if you are not dead, if all your people are not dead, you may well gain another such victory. But will you have served your people, *Ya Aslanam?* The French will never give up this war. There is too much at stake now, their entire reputation as a power rests on the outcome of this conflict. Yet would they be happy enough to bring it to an end, to conserve the lives of their own people, to save themselves the vast expense of maintaining a huge army so far from their homeland. Approach them now, *Ya Aslanam*, and say to them, enough is enough. You have proved that you can strike, and strike hard. Now prove that you are man enough, prince enough, to call a halt to a fight which otherwise will never end, will drain your people of all their strength."

She paused, panting, gazing at the Emir, whose frown had deepened.

"And who knows, my lord," David said, "what the future will hold? There have been empires before, and they have passed away. This same France was once overrun by the Roman legions, and the Gallic chieftains were forced to make peace. Yet in time the Romans went again, leaving behind them a civilisation upon which the Gauls could build. And which now is the greater, the strength of France, or the weakness of the disunited city states of Italy?"

"A thousand years," Abd muttered.

"But a second in the history of man, *Ya Aslanam*. And it may not be a thousand years. Who can say that at the end of a *hundred* years Algiers will not be free, independent, and strong? But of one thing you may be sure, *Ya Aslanam*, the name of Abd el Kader will be preserved forever, will be honoured even at the end of a thousand years."

Abd stared at her, then looked at his brother, and even at Ben Fakha.

And sighed. "And who will enter the French lines as my emissary? Did they not capture Bou Hamidi and force him to drink poison? Who will take such a risk, on the behalf of this wounded lion?"

Catherine's turn to sigh. But somehow she had known, from the moment she had first ridden at his side, how many centuries ago, that this would be her lot at the end.

"I will carry your proposals, *Ya Aslanam*."

"You? They will cut off your head."

"If they do, you will have a cause to fight for the next hundred years, will you not?"

434

She felt David's fingers taking hers. "We will ride together, *Ya Habibti.*"

There was no wind, and the rain fell in almost solid sheets, limiting visibility to a few yards, crashing on heads and soaking *burnouses* and *mashlahs* in seconds, disturbed only by the occasional rumble of thunder and the pale gleam of a distant lightning flash. The whole of North Africa might have been weeping for Abd el Kader.

And for his emissaries. For this last occasion she had resumed Arab dress, wore her two shirts beneath a white *haik,* and over all a blue woollen *tcharchaf,* with a *bashurti* on her hair, but because of the rain she was soon glad enough to use the cowl of the *tcharchaf* as well. Not that it made a great deal of difference.

David, riding at her side, was also wrapped in a *haik.* They had not spoken for some time. Apart from the rain, there was nothing to say. They had lived together long enough to know what the other was thinking, and on such a day, and such a mission, those thoughts could only be sombre.

But now the end was in sight, even if sight was not practical. They had followed the route given them, and the French outposts could not be far away.

"Halt." A man wearing a blue greatcoat, rain dripping from the peak of his kepi. He carried a rifle, with a fixed bayonet.

Catherine drew rein. "I come from the *Khalifa* of the Sultan," she said. "The Emir Abd el Kader."

The sentry peered into the rain. Now she could make out the faint loom of tents beyond.

"From Abd el Kader?" The sentry snorted. "You don't look like emissaries to me. And what does he want, anyway?"

"That I will tell your commander," Catherine said. "As for myself . . . " She drew a long breath, threw back the *bashurti* and the *tcharchaf,* allowed the rain to beat on her hair. "I am Catherine, Baroness Ricimer. You will have heard of me."

The sentry stared at her as if he had seen a ghost,

slowly backing into the morning. "Sergeant," he bawled. "Sergeant."

The tent flap was raised, and a head pushed out. "What is it now, soldier?"

"The woman," the soldier cried. "The woman with white hair. She's here, Sergeant. Here."

The tent exploded men. The sergeant had forgotten his cap, and his tunic was unbuttoned. The rest of the guard stood behind him like frightened puppets.

Catherine dismounted. "I am the Baroness Ricimer," she said.

"You've come to surrender?" The sergeant was incredulous.

"I have come to speak with your commander," she said, as always throughout her life amazed at the evenness of her voice. "Who is he?"

"Major . . . Major Lamoriciere," the sergeant stammered.

"Take me to him."

The sergeant wiped pouring water from his brow, looked to left and right at his equally alarmed men, and then saluted. "If you will follow me, Baroness."

They walked behind him, feet splashing in the mud. "So far so good," David said at her elbow.

She let her hand drift back to squeeze his fingers. She had to maintain and preserve the aura and the name that he had given her, nearly twenty years before. The Ice Maiden. Only that would suffice.

Another tent, drooping beneath the rain. Another sentry, presenting arms as he recognised the sergeant. Another flap, to be opened.

Catherine stepped into the comparative shelter of the canvas, although water was flowing down the tent pole and dripping from the several patches which composed the walls. But it was also dripping from her hair and clinging to her forehead and cheeks. She had to blink to be able to see.

The major got to his feet, slowly. She had heard enough of him, as one of the most daring of French field commanders. He was surprisingly young, with thin moustaches to match his thin features. He looked eager, hungry. But he also looked as upright as Chapdelaine. They might have been brothers.

"Madame Baroness," he said. "I did not believe my ears." He looked at David.

"My . . . my fiancé," she said. "Mr. David Mulawer."

He inclined his head. "I have heard of Monsieur Mulawer," he said. "A deserter from the Foreign Legion."

"Sir?"

"As you are a wanted criminal, madame, with a price on your head and a death sentence waiting to be executed."

She would not lower her gaze.

"I am here as an emissary of Abd el Kader, Major, and you would do well to listen to me. The Emir is of a mind to end this senseless war. He feels that at this moment he is in a position to demand terms with honour, in view of his great victory at Sidi Brahim. But should I and Monsieur Mulawer not return to him, then be sure that he will carry fire and sword the length and breadth of Algeria for another fifteen years."

Lamoriciere gazed at her for a moment, and then snapped his fingers. "A stool for the Baroness," he said. "And for Monsieur Mulawer." He sat down himself. "I have no power to negotiate with the Emir. Our terms are surrender. Nothing less."

"The Emir is prepared to discuss a surrender, Major." She settled herself on the stool, the damp folds of her skirts wrapping themselves about her legs. "What he requires is a safe conduct, to meet with your general, the Duke of Islay."

"The Duke of Islay has been recalled," Lamoriciere said. "We are now commanded by the Duc d'Aumale. A royal duke, madame."

Her heart began to pound again. "He served here some years ago."

"Indeed he did, madame."

"Then it is a good omen. The Emir would meet with the Duke, if you guarantee him safety."

Lamoriciere once again gazed at her for some seconds.

Then once again he snapped his fingers. "Bring me a pen and paper."

An orderly immediately stood at his elbow. But the paper was sodden, and dripped on to the ground. Lamoriciere smiled. "It seems even the heavens do not wish an end to this war." He stood up. "But we will end it if we can, Baroness." He unbuckled his sword, held it out. "It is sufficiently well known, as it has never before left my side. Give it to the Emir, and tell him that if he brings this with him, no Frenchman will fire upon him. You have my word."

She took the weapon, slowly; how cold it felt. "I thank you, Major. May we go now?"

"In this rain? Will you not stay for a cup of coffee at the least?"

"The Emir awaits us." She got up. "I thank you, for receiving us."

"And yourself, Baroness. You ask no safe conduct, no pardon even?"

She met his gaze. "My fate is that of the Emir's, Major. I shall return, at his side."

The weather had brightened, although it remained January cool. The wind drifted down from the mountains and ruffled the *haiks* and *burnouses,* played with the horses' manes and tails. The Arabs rode in silence.

They were a small body, not more than fifty in all. The main part of the *smala* had disappeared during the night, following Abd's speech when he had advised them of the hopelessness of their cause. Now they sought the safety and concealment of the desert, from which they had come to follow this man. And his wives and children waited at a safe distance from the French camp. So there was only Abd himself, and Sidi Mohammed, with Ben Fakha as ever at their heels, and then his immediate bodyguard, people of his own tribe, who knew no other leader, and no other way of life.

And there were Catherine and David, and Omar. The boy was old enough to sit a horse as well as a man, now.

And if they were going to be parted forever, she wished him there to say goodbye.

Was it wrong of her to expose him to the risk of so much grief? She did not know. Having thought, and planned, and exhorted, and advised, for so long, she no longer wished to think at all. She wanted to do nothing more than feel, and *know*. The only course left to her was patience.

The tricolour fluttered in the breeze before a forest of tents. It seemed the entire French Algerian army had turned out to welcome the Emir. And half a mile from the camp there was a group of horsemen, commanded by Lamoriciere himself.

"Your Excellency." The major saluted.

"Your sword, Major." Abd handed over the weapon.

"It has gained in honour, sir. You'll inspect the guard?"

Abd inclined his head, rode down the line of waiting *spahis,* each man rigidly at attention, lance poised, ponton waving in the breeze. Lamoriciere rode at his side. He had not spared a glance for her, or for any in the Emir's entourage. So they rode behind, gazing into the weather-beaten, moustachioed faces. These were the men who had actually won the war, Yusuf's *spahis.* One or two of them allowed their eyes to wander behind her as she passed, and she smiled at them. She had seen both sides of this conflict. She could respect both sides.

They came to the end of the line. "Splendid, Major," Abd said. "They are splendid. Had I commanded men like these, I should not be here now."

"Had you commanded men like these, Your Excellency, *we* would not be here now, either." Lamoriciere dismounted, waved away the orderly, himself held the Emir's horse. David assisted Catherine from the saddle. A table waited before the tricolour, and in front of it, standing away from his magnificently accoutred staff, was the Duke of Aumale. He was tall, and broad, but not so big or so menacing as Buguead, as he was many years younger, with light auburn sideburns bushing to either side of his mouth, although his lips were clean shaven.

"My lord Emir." He extended his hand, and Abd shook it. "I have read your letter, my lord," the Duke said. "You ask for honourable exile in either Acre or Alexandria. It shall be so. You have my word."

Abd gazed at him for some seconds. "I thank you, your Grace," he said at last. "And my people?"

"Your family and a suitable entourage will be permitted to accompany you, my lord Emir. Your *kaids* will receive a free pardon, providing they swear never again to take up arms against the French."

"And my military advisor?" Abd turned, his hand held out, and Catherine went forward. "You have not met the Baroness Ricimer, my lord Duke."

Catherine extended her hand, and the Duke took it to kiss her knuckles, then straightened. His face was grave but his eyes were twinkling. "It is a great pleasure, madame. I have heard sufficient about you."

Catherine licked her lips. "You flatter me, your Grace."

"And this is her husband, David Mulawer," Abd said, gesturing David forward.

"Your name also is familiar to me, Monsieur Mulawer. This is a famous day."

"I will require free pardons for Monsieur and Madame Mulawer as well, your Grace," Abd said.

"I think that can be arranged," the Duke said. "But . . . " He held up his hand. "She cannot be permitted to remain here in Algeria, where she is already too much of a legend. Nor may she accompany you, my lord Emir. It is feared that she is far too much of a warlike influence upon you."

"Then where would you have her go?" the Emir inquired, speaking softly but with a hint of iron in his voice.

"I doubt she would be very well received in France, either," the Duke said. "But I believe she has a father still living in Boston. A lonely man, as he has been deserted by his wife, who prefers to maintain a dubious existence in the demi-monde of Paris. A passage has been arranged, for Monsieur and Madame Mulawer, and their children. The boat leaves tomorrow from Algiers for Gibraltar, where they will join their ship. I would advise you to make haste, madame."

Catherine stared at him, her heart pounding so hard she could not for a moment speak. "Children, your Grace?"

"That is your son, is he not? But you have two other children, the orphans of the late Baron Ricimer. I had them brought to Algiers the moment we learned of the Emir's intended surrender."

"But . . . " She bit her lip. "Do they not hate me? They will have been taught to hate me."

"I doubt they will hate you, madame. For the past ten years they have been confined in an orphanage. It seems that neither Baron Ricimer nor his sister had any more interest in them than to separate them from you. They need, and they will be grateful for, a mother's love."

He turned to the tent behind him, and the sentry opened the flap. First out was a tall young man, well shouldered and handsome, with a glint of steel in his eyes. A glimpse, she realised, of what Ricimer might have been as a young man. Because he was sixteen years old.

She gazed at him, and he gazed at her. Then he ran forward and took her hands. "Mama."

"Gebhard." She kissed him on the cheek, looked past him at the twelve-year-old girl with the light-blonde hair and the composed features who waited behind, little pink spots in her cheeks. "Henrietta?"

The girl frowned at her, and Gebhard stepped back. "Henrietta, Mama? Her name is Catherine."

"Catherine?" She took her daughter's hands. So, even as he had left her to die, he had wanted to perpetuate her memory. She smiled through her tears. "We cannot have two Catherines in the family, my dear. We shall rename you Henrietta. Now I would have you meet your step-father, and your brother."

She turned with them, and faced Abd el Kader.

"We must say goodbye, *Ya Habibti,* and I would have our farewell be brief. Throughout all the misfortunes of our desert adventure together, no man has ever seen me weep. It would be unseemly to end on such a note." He held out his hands, pressed a heavy leather satchel into hers. "You will need money."

"But my lord, what of yourself?"

His smile was bitter. "I am going to spend the rest of my life as a guest of the French, *Ya Habibti,* however fine the words spoken here. I shall not need money." His fingers squeezed hers. "I have been privileged as no other man, to have you at my side for ten years. I shall not forget."

"I came to Algiers a slave," she said, "wishing only to die. Now I would not change a moment of the last nineteen years, if to do so would mean I should forego one moment of your company, *Ya Aslanam.* God go with you. You shall ever walk my dreams."

The guard was waiting for her, and David. She hesitated for a moment, gazing down the line of *spahis.* She had indeed, come to his land as a slave, nineteen years before. And what a nineteen years they had been. She closed her eyes, and seemed able to see them all, Hussein bin Hassan, Selim the eunuch, Yusuf the *spahi,* El Ghomari the Touareg, Jean-Pierre, Chapdelaine and Gereaux, and looming above them all, Ricimer, smiling his sardonic smile.

But before any of them had existed, there had been David. And now they were all gone, there was still David. She opened her eyes, and took his hand.

And smiled at him. "Boston has been a long time coming."

He returned her smile. "It will be the better for that. And you will be going home."

"And you?"

"Me?" His fingers tightened on hers. "My home is wherever you happen to be standing, *Ya Habibti.*"

NORAH LOFTS

W01104

Norah Lofts weaves a rich tapestry of love, war and passion. Here are her most entertaining novels of romance and intrigue. You may order any or all direct by mail.

☐ BRIDE OF MOAT HOUSE	22527-5	$1.50
☐ THE BRITTLE GLASS	23037-6	$1.75
☐ CHECKMATE	23488-6	$1.75
☐ THE CONCUBINE	Q2405	$1.50
☐ CROWN OF ALOES	23030-9	$1.75
☐ ELEANOR THE QUEEN	Q2848	$1.50
☐ THE GOLDEN FLEECE	23132-1	$1.75
☐ HAUNTINGS	23393-6	$1.75
☐ HEAVEN IN YOUR HAND	23382-0	$1.75
☐ THE HOMECOMING	23166-6	$1.95
☐ HOW FAR TO BETHLEHEM?	23277-8	$1.95
☐ JASSY	Q2711	$1.50
☐ THE KING'S PLEASURE	23139-9	$1.75
☐ KNIGHT'S ACRE	X2685	$1.75
☐ THE LUTE PLAYER	22948-3	$1.95
☐ THE LITTLE WAX DOLL	P2270	$1.25
☐ LOVERS ALL UNTRUE	Q2792	$1.50
☐ NETHERGATE	23095-3	$1.75
☐ OUT OF THE DARK	23479-7	$1.75
☐ A ROSE FOR VIRTUE	23435-5	$1.95
☐ SCENT OF CLOVES	22977-7	$1.75
☐ TO SEE A FINE LADY	22890-8	$1.75
☐ THE TOWN HOUSE	X2793	$1.75

Buy them at your local bookstores or use this handy coupon for ordering:

Dorothy Eden

One of today's outstanding novelists writes tales about love, intrigue, wealth, power—and, of course, romance. Here are romantic novels of suspense at their best.

Mary Stewart

"Mary Stewart is magic" is the way Anthony Boucher
puts it. Each and every one of her novels is a kind of
enchantment, a spellbinding experience that has won
acclaim from the critics, millions of fans, and a permanent
place at the top.

☐	AIRS ABOVE THE GROUND	23868-7	$1.95
☐	THE CRYSTAL CAVE	23315-4	$1.95
☐	THE GABRIEL HOUNDS	23946-2	$1.95
☐	THE HOLLOW HILLS	23316-2	$1.95
☐	THE IVY TREE	23251-4	$1.75
☐	MADAM, WILL YOU TALK	23250-6	$1.75
☐	THE MOON-SPINNERS	23073-2	$1.75
☐	MY BROTHER MICHAEL	22974-2	$1.75
☐	NINE COACHES WAITING	23121-6	$1.75
☐	THIS ROUGH MAGIC	22846-0	$1.75
☐	THUNDER ON THE RIGHT	23100-3	$1.75
☐	TOUCH NOT THE CAT	23201-8	$1.95

Buy them at your local bookstores or use this handy coupon for ordering:

FAWCETT BOOKS GROUP
P.O. Box C730, 524 Myrtle Ave., Pratt Station, Brooklyn, N.Y. 11205

Please send me the books I have checked above. Orders for less than 5
books must include 75¢ for the first book and 25¢ for each additional
book to cover mailing and handling. I enclose $_____ in check or
money order.

Name_____

Address_____

City_____State/Zip_____

Please allow 4 to 5 weeks for delivery.